THIRTY-SEVEN HOUSES

Every heart finds a home

Anna Vandenbroucke

a novel

Park Place Publications
www.parkplacepublications.com

Thirty-Seven Houses
Every heart finds a home

Anna Vandenbroucke

ISBN 978-1-935530-48-0

Printed in U.S.A.

First U.S. Edition: October 2011

Author photo by Jane Morba Photography
Cover and text design by Patricia Hamilton

For my children,
my constant reminders of what true love is.

Acknowledgements

I give thanks to the following people for their contributions to this book:

To my first readers, Annabelle Vandenbroucke, Mary Cunove, Elizabeth Sorenson, Tina Adams, Amber Lindhout, and Kent Carlson for their honesty and unwavering support.

To my editors, Marnie Speery and Laurie Gibson, for their perseverance and belief in the project.

To Patricia Hamilton, of Park Place Publications, for her guidance and expertise.

To my dear friend, Cindy Anderson, who taught me when everything falls apart, have a good laugh before trying to put it back together again.

To my husband, Jerome, for his gentle strength and glowing patience.

To Cole Kauai, Logan Lanai, and Annabelle Abby for their love and inspiration.

And finally, to the real Steve Henry, for graciously loaning his name.

THIRTY–SEVEN HOUSES

Every heart finds a home

chapter one

October House
1961

An oyster-colored sky hovered above the Oregon coastline and across Clackamas County. As Thanksgiving approached, carloads of holiday travelers drove slowly over the crowded Columbia River Bridge and into the outer regions of Portland.

In a litter-ridden neighborhood of Oregon City, three small boys had been kicked out of the Henry house while their uncles slurped Miller High Life and watched the fuzzy, crackling television. With dirty boots and meaty fists, they tried to slam the football game into focus while their women toiled in the kitchen.

Victor and Ross Henry were nine-year-old identical twins and now ably in charge of showing their little cousin Stevie the ropes of their street. Five-year-old Stevie Henry had come with his parents the seventy-two miles from Salem, which was a yearly tradition.

Once the rambunctious boys were tossed outside, they found a dented Campbell's soup can and three bare sticks, and headed down the street like soldiers off to war. The wind began to pick up; high and brisk enough to shake up the power lines, agitate animals, and rip off the last of the maple leaves.

"Let's go over to Shaw Street and poke at Rasmus!" said Victor.

"No, Victor, he's scary," said Stevie. He had heard all about the monster Rasmus, who was said to have the body of a Rottweiler, the jaws of a pit bull, and the temper of a tortured grizzly bear. His owner was known as a ruffian who kept the dog chained in his backyard and used him for betting and fighting.

"Oh don't be a pussy!" said Victor. "The guy feeds him chickens and cats— *live* ones," he snickered.

They kicked the can along the street, under trucks and into gutters filled with car oil and black leaves. When they stopped before a dirty white house on Shaw Street, it was Ross who seized the can and flung it over the chain-link fence covered with overgrown bushes. They heard the tin can clank and roll around. When the clatter stopped they gawked breathlessly at each other. Overhead, the telephone lines swung.

"Come on," said Victor. "You can see him through this hole." The boys nudged their way, poking their sticks and stepping on each other's feet to get a peek through the fist-sized hole in the fence. They saw only a concrete slab.

"I'm gonna get the can," said Victor.

"No, Victor," said Stevie.

Victor slid over to the metal gate, reached up, and yanked on a rusty bolt the size of a crowbar, then dragged the gate open. They peered around the backyard and filed in. The wind slammed the gate behind them.

There in the corner sat Rasmus, a muscled, black, mangy dog with a sawed-off tail and a gnarled, scarred face. A heavy chain a yard long weighed down his 150 pound body. It was attached to a solid metal pole set in cement. Hardened piles of poop lay around a heap of mangled hubcaps, a broken toilet tank, and the skeleton of an old Christmas tree. Rasmus lay still. He stared at the boys with sharp, black eyes. In front of him was the soup can.

"Please don't get the can," Stevie begged.

Rasmus' ears, which looked like they'd been whacked off with hedge clippers, pitched forward then back, but he stayed on his haunches next to the can—until Victor came at him with the stick.

Rasmus shot through the air, baring brutal teeth and huge paws that knocked Victor face-first to the ground. The boys screamed as the dog pounced and pressed his powerful legs into Victor's shoulders and began stripping the flesh off the boy's neck and back. Victor shrieked and tried to roll himself into a ball. When he kicked both legs, the dog lunged hard enough to flip him over and jump on his torso, cracking the boy's ribcage. Ross tried to grab a piece of his brother's shredded flannel shirt and pull him away, but the dog had enough chain length and fury to haul Victor back like a raw steak.

Stevie stood frozen.

With his razor claws and killer instinct, the dog slashed the silken skin from the failing twin's hands. Then he went for his face. He locked his crushing jaws into a boneless hunk of flesh and shook his jowls as he ripped.

Blood flew in all directions. When Stevie felt a splat of his cousin's blood on his face, he fled for the gate and tried to escape first. The jutting bolt impaled his shoulder and tore through Stevie's arm down to the elbow, but he kept running, leaving a Ked stuck in the fence. Ross followed, screaming for help.

By the time the owner of Rasmus made it to the backyard, the dog had torn away and swallowed half of Victor's face, leaving the boy unconscious, lying in a pool of carnage. When the man saw what remained of the boy, he turned to the snarling dog.

As reported in the *Oregonian*, I was launched into this world on my parent's fourth wedding anniversary, the very same day as the tragedy with the Henry boys. It was all there on the front page: a November storm that knocked the power out of three counties, a horribly maimed boy, a murdered dog, and a new baby girl, Eve Elizabeth, born to Ted and Gloria Chanteau of Oregon City.

My birth certificate stated that my father was a twenty-three-year-old musician and my mother, also twenty-three, was a housewife. At the time of my birth I had two brothers. Tim was three years old, and Toby was one.

Dad was made of pure sensitivity, compassion, and musical talent. He had been recruited to play the piano in a jazz band at the age of fifteen. Dad was tall and lean, had piercing blue eyes, and dark hair that he combed straight back to reveal his distinctively handsome face. He could sing like a dream and spoke in a soft, soothing tone. Like most little girls,

I believed my dad was the man I would marry.

Mom had a powerful presence in a scary sort of way. A pretty woman who liked pretty things, she was a ticking time bomb of repressed passion and entrapped creativity, often unleashing a force that was powerful enough to change the weather.

Dad brought home a small paycheck from playing in the band. For weeks at a time he was gone to unknown places, leaving Mom to handle things. Sometimes we would have to move to a new house while he was gone, but he always found his way back to us when he returned from a job.

Shortly after I was born, I was brought to the doorstep of my grandparents. Dad explained to his mother that he and Mom needed to leave baby Eve while they went away to seek fortune and freedom. He said Gloria was down in the dumps and he feared I wasn't getting enough to eat, and was very sick.

Grandma took me in her arms and assured her son that she would take care of his infant until their return. She said that some women get hit real hard with the baby blues.

In the days that followed, Grandma took me to the doctor, who said I was sick and needed some fattening up. Following the good doctor's orders, Grandma fed me on muslin sugar teats and nursed me back to health.

My parents did return a few weeks later, after I had some meat on my bones and color in my cheeks. I was handed back to Mom and Dad, restored to my little world where I was both a beautiful and a bothersome baby.

Our family's lifestyle was built on survival, struggle, and perpetual motion. Dad claimed we were waiting for a lucky break. In the meantime we moved from house to house. We were like a family of ungainly nomads roaming the Oregon countryside in a Chevrolet station wagon. Throughout our childhood years we inhabited a total of fourteen different rentals. My parents were on a permanent house search, a never-ending venture for satisfaction never found. What percentage of those homes we were evicted from I knew not, but I did know what it was like to uproot and attempt a new rooting. All the years of our gypsy impermanence instilled in me a troubling conviction that *nothing* is forever.

Among our fourteen houses were a few places where the real memories were made. We often named our houses, not as people name their idyllic second-home cottages, but more as a way of remembering them all.

When I was almost three years old it became apparent that I had a special gift for causing trouble. Toby was four and Tim was six when our parents rented a house that we called the "October House." We gave it that name because for eleven hours one day we hunkered down in order to survive a great October tempest that became known in local history as "The Columbus Day Storm." The October House stood firmly intact as the storm devastated the Oregon countryside, leaving in its wake splintered trees and mangled remains of farmland property.

The October House belonged to Mr. Zander, who lived a few miles down the road but didn't come around very often. It stood on a knoll, looming amid the grand black oaks. These trees surrounded the mammoth house, dangling long strands of oak moss and holding large balls of mistletoe in their branches. The house was not only big, but also very old and had a large front porch too rotten to be stepped on.

The house was cold and creaky and never seemed to brighten up under the grayness of the Oregon sky or the dim haze of the afternoon sunlight. We lived mostly in the kitchen and bedrooms, for the wind howled more loudly through the living room than it did in the meadow below. When it got too cold in the house, Tim, Toby, and I went outside seeking warmer, more promising places to play.

There were old shops and sheds around the October House, full of interesting stuff left by whoever had lived there before. There were dusty John Deere tractors and plows, a rusting combine, and an unbroken windshield. The property was a virtual graveyard for old car parts, bumpers, and abandoned truck grilles. Temporary inhabitants of Mr. Zander's property, we had little use or need for many of those ancient October items. But we kids spent hours out there in our salvage yard playground.

Being good brothers, Tim and Toby felt it was vital that they teach me all about engine parts, gas tanks, and transmissions. We used old car mufflers for secret communication devices, and stacks of blown-out tires for hideouts from the enemy. We spent hours battling in wars and making barriers and forts out of scrap metal. Tim rigged up an abandoned station wagon hood that we called Fort Ford.

Toby was one year, one month, and one day older than me, and already knew he was going to be a car fixer guy when he grew up. He was sweet, sensitive, and temperamental as all get-out. Toby had a beautiful mane of dark hair like Dad, little round features, and a tiny pug nose. He was a follower and Tim was a leader. Tim and I were daring, Toby hesitant. When I wasn't constantly coaxing Toby to do something out of his comfort zone, Tim was telling me to do something out of mine. I was a little nervous about our junkyard games, because Mom had specifically told *me* to stay away from Mr. Zander's stuff.

In one of Mr. Zander's decrepit outbuildings was a dark, greasy storage shop cluttered with rusted tools of days gone by, including a scythe and a loose vice grip that rested against a moldy wall. This shed housed my parent's stash of belongings, a collection of boxes sealed and ready for the next quick move.

One February day, Dad kissed me goodbye and told me he would be back before the Easter Bunny came. He said because I was such a good little girl he would bring back some carrots in hopes we would get to see the Easter Bunny and feed him ourselves.

As I gave him a long hug, he leaned down and said in his gentle voice, "I love my girl. You be careful while I'm gone, okay?"

"Okay, Daddy. I love you too!"

"Why don't you go play now?" He blew me a kiss and was gone.

I decided I would play like I was a bunny and went outside to hop around. Toby saw me hopping and said, "Playing like a bunny is stupid."

"Is not," I said.

"Is too! You don't even look like a real bunny—plus a super hero is way better than a stupid rabbit."

"Whatsa super hero?" I asked.

"Come on, stupid, everybody knows a hero saves your life!"

I consented to play his special version of hide-and-seek-super-hero-spy-man.

We set up a series of empty cardboard boxes in the musty storage shop. We were just the right size to fit into any one of the twelve fruit boxes. Toby ordered me to go outside and count to twenty, which I couldn't do yet. I covered my eyes and screamed, "One two three eleven twenty! Ready or not, here I come!"

I tiptoed into the dark, still room. Filtered sunlight pierced the wallboards and I used that as my searchlight. I walked cautiously among the rows of boxes, peeking in anticipation of finding him crouched inside a Bartlett pear box, and sure enough, there he was. I yelled, "Found ya!"

He popped up and screamed, "You cheater!"

"I did not cheat," I said.

"Did too!" he yelled.

"Did not!"

"Now you hide and I'll count," he demanded.

He couldn't count any better than I could, and came running back into the shop after "One two six, here I come!" I quickly squeezed into a Gravenstein apple box. I didn't have enough time to adjust myself so I was actually sitting in the upended box with my head tucked tightly into my chest. I closed my eyes to make myself invisible. My heart pounded as I heard Toby bounding into the shed. Much to my surprise, he began kicking each cardboard box with all his might. As the boxes exploded across the room he shouted, "Not in that one!" Pow! "Not in this one!"

Before I knew what hit me, my apple box hideout was slammed against the wall and into the iron vice grip. It sliced through the side of my head and flayed open my scalp. I lay there screaming and grasping my head, blood squirting over my hands, my face, and the vice grip.

Toby was terrified and began screaming, "I killed you! Did I kill you? I did! I did!"

I unfolded my limbs, staggered out of the shed, and began running toward the house, dripping a trail of warm blood.

Suddenly Tim was running beside me, yelling for Mom. She appeared in the doorway and screamed at me, "What the hell did you do? Were you messing with something that wasn't yours? I told you not to touch those things out there!"

Tim shouted, "Mom, she needs a doctor!"

"She doesn't need a doctor. Tim, get a towel."

Toby's hysteria escalated as my vision narrowed into blackness and I disappeared into it.

When I came to, it was dark and I was lying in my bed in a warm pool of fleshy-smelling blood. My head felt as if it were split in half. I gently felt around in the darkness and touched the soggy strip of ripped bed sheet that someone had tied around my head. I slipped back into unconsciousness with a faraway voice saying, "I told you not to mess with Mr. Zanders' stuff."

My head continued to bleed for three days and nights. Tim and Toby came into my room and brought me water. I heard Tim say I should have a whole bunch of stitches but Mom said no. I tried to retrace the accident in my fuzzy mind, but I had no reserve, no mental capacity for figuring out how much trouble I was in.

After nine days of changing the sheet strips and being careful, the gaping split was well on its way to being healed, and I eagerly thought of seeing the Easter Bunny. When Mom removed the bandages for the last time, she said, "Doctors. They don't know their ass from a hole in the ground. You'll be alright."

Mom was my hero.

chapter two

Vortex

Dad came back with the carrots as promised, but we had no luck finding the Easter Bunny, let alone feeding him.

"I'm sorry, girlie. I was sure we would get to feed him this time. I know last year you were so close," he said.

"I was?" I asked, surprised.

"Oh yeah! Don't you remember? The Easter Bunny had a thousand baskets to deliver to all those other kids, but he spent his time just coming to see you because he knows who the most special children are."

"Wow," I said.

"I'm sorry we missed him," he said.

"It's okay, Daddy. I'm just glad you came back in time."

"You know what I'm most sorry about?" he said.

"What, Daddy?"

"That I have to go away again."

"Well, are you coming right back this time?"

"Right back as fast as my fingers can bring me."

"How can your fingers bring you back?" I asked.

"As soon as I play exactly twenty-four love songs in your honor, the job will be done and I'll be on my way home," he said. "Meantime, you can find something fun to do while I'm gone."

"I will, Daddy. I love you."

"I love you too, my girl." He kissed me on the forehead and got into the car.

I watched him drive away and then looked around the yard for the boys. I found Tim and Toby digging a hole to China toward the back of the property.

I decided I would also occupy my time until Dad's return. I found an old paint can full of nails and got Toby's blanket and nailed it to the grassy ground with a big rock. I wanted to do something special for Toby to make him realize that it wasn't his fault that my head got hurt a while back in the shed.

I lined up each nail and pounded until it wedged securely into the wet dirt. I worked diligently until every nail was flush to the ground and so close together they framed the edge of the blanket in a solid line of little rusty metal circles. Then I ran out back and yelled, "Toby! Come here. I've got something for you!"

Caked with mud, he crawled out from his Chinese tunnel and followed me to the site of his surprise.

"Look!" I pointed proudly at the masterpiece. As only Toby could do, he completely fell apart. He threw himself down on the blanket and howled like a muddy coyote with his leg in a trap. I tried to comfort him but he kept screaming, "My blankie! My blankie!"

Mom came rushing out of the house and grabbed me by the arm. Tim ran over to see what was happening just as she dragged me up the steps and into the bathroom. She bent me over and plunged my head into the toilet bowl. Holding me down, she pushed the flusher handle with her foot. Cold water sucked at my eardrums in a piercing roar. With my head upside down, I crushed my eyes closed and tried to pull air through my nose but I was held under. The vortex dragged at my hair, the force of the chokehold around my neck pushed my head further into the flushing bowl. A "head flushing," as Tim called it, was what Mom did when she was super mad.

It took exactly forty-seven seconds for the toilet to complete a flush, which was just how long I could hold my breath. I learned to inhale deeply and squeeze my lips tightly together to keep out whatever was in the toilet bowl at the time.

Mom jerked my head out, grabbed my shoulders, and fell to her knees. Her shirt was wet and so were her eyes. "Why do you have to constantly cause trouble?" she said. "Now you get out there and fix Toby's blanket and keep your hands off things that don't belong to you! You have to learn everything the hard way."

It took me the rest of the day of digging with a teaspoon to pull those nails out of Toby's shredded blanket. But it only took a minute to plan what rotten thing I could do next to make myself feel better.

The craving had begun.

chapter three

Lightbug

I awoke one summer morning to Dad's face lit by rays of sunshine and his voice serenading me with *Glow little glow worm, glimmer glimmer.* He was sitting on the edge of my bed and I sat straight up to hug him.

"Daddy! You're back!"

He finished the song and said, "Of course I am. I always come back to my girl. You're looking bright and shiny this morning."

"That's cuz I have a glow worm inside me!"

"Well now, that's special. What color is your glow worm, and what does he eat?"

"He's yellow, just like the one in the song—and he eats only love."

"Wow, that's a great thing to eat. How do you feed him?"

"I just feel real happy like now when you're here and then he lights up and puffs up and makes my tummy tickle!"

"He lives in your tummy?"

"Uh huh, somewhere in there so he can be safe."

"How big is he?"

"About like this," I said and made my pinkie inch over his palm.

"Does your glow worm have a name?"

"I call him Lightbug."

"That's a good name, given that he qualifies as a highly specialized insect."

"Yeah."

"I mean, just think how important his job is. Being with *you,* the best girl around!"

"Yeah. He's my very best friend."

"Does he ever sleep?"

"Uh huh, he sleeps when I do and he only stops glowing real bright when I get a owie."

"Did you have an owie while I was gone?"

"Yeah, when Mommy is mad I get a owie and it makes him sad so he doesn't shine."

"Does Mommy get mad at you a lot?"

"Not so much, just so *mad*."

"Well, you know that your Lightbug's inside you to keep you safe."

"I know cuz that's what Gramma says too."

"Well then, we *know* it's true."

"Yeah."

"I love you so much, baby, and I don't want you to ever get an owie."

"I love you too, Daddy."

"You listen to Lightbug and keep him shining, okay?"

"'kay, Daddy."

He cupped my chin in his hand and gave me a wink.

"I have to go now, so why don't you hop up and get dressed? You and the boys get to go see Gramma and Grampa today."

"Yay!" I said. By the time I had crawled under the bed to get my shoes, he was gone.

When I ran into Gramma's house the screen door hit me in the butt.

"Hi, Gramma!"

"Hiya, honey! How's my girl?"

"Really good. Guess what?"

"What?"

"Daddy knows about Lightbug."

"He does, does he? Well, that's nice."

"I told him all about how Lightbug eats love and everything, and Daddy says he's a special friend that will protect me, just like you say."

"*This little light of mine, I'm gonna let him shine.*" Gramma sang.

"Hey, I smell chocolate cake!"

"Yes, you do. That's Timmy's birthday cake," she said.

"Is Tim gonna be this many?" I asked, holding up five fingers.

Gramma held up seven fingers and said, "He's going to be seven, and do you know how many that makes you?"

I held up four fingers. "This many?"

"That's right, sweetheart. You're such a big girl."

"When do we get to eat the cake?" I said.

"Pretty soon. Run out and get your brothers so we can have a birthday party."

"Can I help blow out the candles?" I asked.

"Well, Timmy gets to blow them out, but you can make a secret wish when he does, even though it's not your birthday."

"Yay!" I said. I ran out the door and made it almost all the way to the tree swing before I heard the screen door slam shut.

Although Gramma couldn't protect me completely, she could always soothe me with gentle hugs and words of hope. She had raised Dad to be just like her, sensitive and loving. From my earliest memory I found heaven in Gramma's arms and on her lap, in her kitchen and in her garden. She had the voice of an angel, the laugh of a forest fairy, and a heart full of love.

Gramma's people came from Norway, and she had the natural beauty of a true Nordsky. She had thick, shining white hair and the prettiest blue eyes with little flecks of gold in them. She was soft, always warm to touch, especially when she let me sit on her lap in the rocking chair.

Gramma and Grampa lived in an A-frame house on a sprawling Oregon ranch, which was our personal 240 acre playground whenever we got to visit. The land was used for raising cattle and growing hay; we used it for playing games. A rippling creek ran through it, providing water for the grazing stock and hours of fun for us. The lower pastures were shadowed by what we called "Grampa's Mountain." Many trails led over the wooded mountain and to an underground spring that was nestled off the beaten track. The main trail which led all the way to the top of Grampa's

Mountain was steep and well trodden by cows and kids alike.

In the summer, Tim, Toby and I would spend all day up on Grampa's Mountain. When we got to the very top and looked down, we could see for miles, all the way to the highest peaks of the Cascade Mountain Range. The ranchland below spread for thousands of acres, divided down the middle by a long stretch of paved but bumpy road, the Richardson Gap. When Grampa drove us over it real fast, we would scream with terror and delight. Grampa called the Gap the Gut Ripper Road.

The nearest town was six miles away. It was an obscure little place that provided humble housing for all of its ninety townsfolk. For many years the town was not on a road map, and Grampa said that was what he liked about it.

Grampa was a man of the land and always had been. He claimed that two or three hundred acres wasn't enough to do much with and a fellow needed at least 800 acres to make a decent profit. Grampa could work that land, and he could play the saxophone too. Because he had been a musician in his youth, he'd allowed my dad to join a band when he was only fifteen. Grampa could whistle through the little slant in his front teeth, which were worn from so many years of blowing the saxophone.

It was from Grampa that I learned how to saddle up and bridle a horse. He taught me how to ride bareback, catch and boil crawdads from the creek, drive a hay truck, and buck a fifty-pound bale of hay.

Our other grandparents, Grammy and Grampy Koff, were so different that I never did figure them out. I was only five when the Koffs died, but I remembered them as being mean. They didn't like Dad at all, and Grammy fought with Mom over the stupidest things. The few times we did visit them, we were afraid because Grampy Koff stared at us while he overfilled his coffee cup and then slurped loudly from the saucer. When he caught one of us eyeing him he would point his finger and say, "You best mind your manners or I'll beat yer ass." But he never did touch any of us.

chapter four

TLC House

On a fragrant spring day, Tim said Mom had swallowed something and had to go get it taken out because it was stuck inside her. We all
went to Gramma and Grampa's house and waited until she got fixed up.

When Mom and Dad came back, they had a new baby girl named
Angie. She was all wrinkled and just the cutest little thing I had ever seen.
She had long eyelashes and lots of soft, dark hair even though she was
only a few days old. Mom held Angie close and carried her around even
when she was asleep. Mom said the baby's real name was Angela because
she was an angel. Angela stayed wrapped up an awful lot, Gramma said,
so she wouldn't catch a chill.

Mom said she was glad she finally had a good baby girl.

"Well, I'm a girl," I said to Tim.

"No you're not. You were born with a weenie, but they took you to
the sawmill and sawed it off," he said.

"Did not!" I cried.

"Did too!" said Tim.

"It's not true!"

"Yes, it's twoo," said Toby.

Angie had only been our little angel for a few months when she
was loaded into the car with a bunch of other things—and I figured out
that we were relocating once again. It was a timely move, because if we
stayed there any longer, the October House would surely give the new
little baby a great big chill.

We moved from the October House to the "TLC" house after Mr.
Zander asked us to leave because we didn't pay the rent.

Dad explained that the TLC House had true country charm compared to that oversized October House. He said that by providing our next house with just a little Tender Loving Care, we were going to be real happy there. In fact, he added, we would all share one bedroom, which would keep us all nice and cozy through the winter.

The TLC House was a little box made of weathered wood, with tiny windows that Dad said were special because they were Plexiglas instead of ordinary glass. The outside of the house was dirty, the color of Grampy Koff's coffee with too much cream in it. Tim and Toby thought the TLC house was neat because it was like a boys' fort, small and smelly.

As always, Dad was right and when we moved in we were definitely warmer all wrapped around each other at night. Mom and Dad stayed in one bed by the bassinette and we three snuggled up for security, because when darkness and slumber enveloped us, the insides of the walls came alive in vermin frenzy.

Toby and I were the first to hear it. There was a tiny squeaking noise from somewhere inside the house, but then the squeak became more of an *eek*. The *eek* multiplied and became a series of high-pitched frequencies that got shriller and louder as the darkness deepened. Communications between the mice were combined with intensified busywork that lasted all night. It was a miniature construction site with rodents working the night shift in full force.

We could hear them shredding paper, chewing wires, and snapping small pieces of wood. They squeaked and crunched, scratched and scurried so loudly it was like lying in the middle of an amphitheater with surround sound. We covered our ears with pillows and hummed to each other to drown out the noise. The nights were the longest at the TLC House, not only because of the noise but because we were all afraid to get up to go to the bathroom.

Small piles of sawdust began to accumulate around the baseboards and up high around the doorjambs. When we found a new quarter-sized hole in a wall, we plugged it with a sock. When the socks began to shred or most often, disappear, we used tinfoil for plugs. We changed from playing hide and seek to plug the squeak.

Then one day we had to surrender the TLC House. Dad discovered they weren't mice after all, but rats. The TLC House was renamed The Rat Shack.

When the County Health Department got wind of the rodent infestation, they condemned the property. Dad told us the boards had been nailed over the windows of the Rat Shack to make it dark inside and to protect the rats. He said the red plastic ribbon had been tied around the perimeter of the property to let others know that the place was special. He said a study would be conducted there and the results of the study would be an important factor to the future of others.

Dad said important people in high-up institutions evaluated things like the length of a rat versus the length of a mouse. He explained a common house mouse wasn't nearly as special as what we had, therefore ours was regarded as a unique situation and we would be rewarded with a new blue house.

It didn't take long to move out of the Rat Shack because we had to leave some things behind. Dad said that anything that had been chewed on qualified as damaged goods, therefore was to be donated to the *Rodent Investigational Project*.

As we drove away, leaving the Rat Shack behind, I looked out the back window for a last glance. Although I couldn't read, I was sure that the words spray-painted on the outside of the house said something like IMPORTANT STUDY IN PROGRESS, which made me puff up with pride.

chapter five

Shoot Out

We moved right into The Blue House, which was blue inside and out. Although it was tiny, it was rather cheery, especially after some of the houses we'd lived in. The Blue House had three bedrooms, one for the girls, one for the boys, and one for Mom and Dad.

The small kitchen had blue gingham curtains hanging over the window above the sink. There were blue curtains in every room of The Blue House. The most bizarre thing about the house was that, instead of a backyard, there was a concrete slab the size of a church parking lot. Someone who truly loved the color blue had painted the entire slab and the surrounding walls to match the wood siding of the house.

One night I had a nightmare when the breeze was gently blowing the bedroom curtain and I mistook it for an upside-down genie floating toward me. I was half asleep and half awake and wholly terrified when I sat up and screamed.

Dad came running in with a .22 shotgun and snapped on the light. My evil genie disappeared.

"I had a bad dream," I said.

"It's all right, girlie," he whispered. "Just try to go back to sleep," he said as he kissed my cheek. I kissed him back, shivered off the nightmare and nestled under my covers. He turned out the light and left the room. I could hear him using the bathroom, and over the running water, Mom's voice, "Eve! You're gonna get it in the morning!"

"Oh rats," I groaned.

I heard Angie roll over. "What's the matter?" she said.

"Nothin'," I said. "This house is sure blue, isn't it?"

Within three months we had to leave the Blue House. We moved to the "Mollala House," which had a television in it, as well as a few other meager furnishings. The Mollala House was in a real neighborhood, amid little houses just like it all along the street. The yard was dirt and a cement step led from the street to the living room. We kids all stayed in one bedroom, which was connected to the bathroom by a hole rather than an actual doorway. It looked like someone had tried to make a door with a sledgehammer. The boys thought it was great that we had to crawl through the ragged opening to get to the bathroom, but I didn't like it much because I got splinters in my knees and bumped my head. The tiny kitchen had a picnic table attached to the wall. When we all crammed around the table to eat, Dad said that the beauty of a nook was that it encouraged families to be close and it was when you felt especially close that it made you want to eat all your oatmeal.

We were learning what it meant to have neighbors. Mom and Dad had survived a terrible fight a few weeks before, complete with furniture lying broken in the driveway, shattered glass, and a police report from the neighbors. Dad disappeared after that and Tim said he was off working, playing a gig somewhere, but we didn't know where.

We were all awake late one night because Mom said we could watch *The Wizard of Oz* on TV. Somewhere between the wicked witch and the freaky flying monkeys, I saw Mom slip out the front door. She was wearing a big black coat and a fur hat. She also had Dad's shotgun. I continued watching the monkeys pull the hay out of the poor scarecrow and I knew I was going to have bad dreams.

We were all asleep, sprawled about the floor, the TV showing black and white snow, when Gramma and Grampa came into our house. They got us up and into our beds.

We woke up to find Gramma and Grampa still there, fixing us breakfast and looking mad and sad at the same time. We learned that Mom was in jail. She had gone to a house where Dad's band was practicing and, in a fit of jealousy and rage, blasted out the windows of the place in a one-sided shoot-out. Fortunately, no one had been hit and the band members all managed to avoid the flying glass. The police found Mom standing outside the house and arrested her.

Three days later Gramma said, "Your daddy moved away to a place called Alaska."

On that same day Mom came home. She walked in without a word, and without her coat or the gun. We all looked at her, but she went straight to her bedroom and shut the door.

"Give it back!" yelled Toby.

"No, you butt face," Tim said.

"Gimme my blankie!"

"Sucky baby blankie boy! Baby blankie girlie boy!"

Toby began to cry and Tim threw the blanket in Toby's direction.

Mom came crawling out of the hole in the bathroom wall with her hair piled high in a beehive. Her lips glistened with a shade of lipstick made of several Avon samples. Her earrings dangled happily, and as she stood up she smoothed the front of her purple polka dot smock. She wore white pedal pushers and her nails were painted pink with purple dots to match her top.

"Who's fighting out here?" she asked, narrowing her eyes.

"Nobody," the boys said in unison.

I was rooting for Toby and was glad when he got his blankie back so he wouldn't be sad and cry. I always felt sorry for him when his big, blue eyes filled with tears and he looked so helpless. Mom dismissed their fighting then caught an eyeshot of me standing there doing nothing in particular.

"Eve! You get in there and pick up those clothes. That bathroom looks like a pigsty. You better get it together right now and don't make me have to come in there and make sure you did your job. I don't need to tell you what's gonna happen if I find any more of your crap laying around!"

"'Kay," I said and crawled through the hole to pick up everyone else's stuff. As I was wiping a blob of boy slobber mixed with toothpaste off the sink, Mom's scream pierced the walls.

"Get out here right now!"

I fumbled and tripped over the pile of clothes and crawled through the hole back into the kitchen. Mom was sitting at the picnic table with Angie on her lap. She slammed her fist on the table and Angie began to cry.

"What did I tell you?" She glared at me.

"Um . . ." I looked at the floor.

"WHAT did I TELL you?" She hit the table again.

I began to bite my lip and wring my hands. The boys came into the kitchen to find out what she had told me. Toby was clutching his blanket and Tim leaned against the doorjamb.

Mom suddenly began to laugh, which made Angie stop crying. Then Mom sounded like she stopped laughing and began crying. We didn't know what to do. We stood there confused and waited several minutes until she finished the waves of joyous sorrow. When she was done she stood up and bounced Angie lightly in her arms. She looked at us and her face began to beam as if she had swallowed a hunk of sunshine. I started laughing. I clamped my teeth down on my tongue, but couldn't stop myself. Tim and Toby busted up too and then we were all hysterical, even Mom. It was as if we were drowning in happiness and we didn't know why.

Then the room went quiet and we looked at Mom. We were all red and panting.

"He's coming home today," she smiled. "Your dad is coming home from Alaska and he's going to stay."

I got busy and rearranged our bedroom. I refolded all the clothes in my dresser drawer and moved the bed into a different position, which took most of the day.

When he finally walked through the front door, my heart melted. First he went to Mom and they kissed. Then one by one he greeted us kids and hugged us all. When he got to me I asked him if he wanted to come and see how I had rearranged our room. He thought that was a great idea and the two of us held hands and went to look at the bedroom. Dad said I was the best room rearranger in the whole world. He said I looked like I had grown so much while he was away.

"Why did you have to go away for so long, Daddy?" I asked.

"Well, Eve, I didn't plan to be gone for so long, but it turned out that our band had to work way up north, almost at the top of the world."

"The top of the world?" I said, very impressed.

"Yes, ma'am," he said. "It's so far up there that there are polar bears and Eskimos who live in igloos, which are houses made of ice," he said.

"Wow! That sounds cold."

"Oh, it was cold all right, but you know how I stayed warm?" he smiled.

"How?" I said.

"I thought about you. Every time I thought of you and how much I love you, my body temperature would rise and that's exactly what saved me from freezing to death," he said.

"Really?"

"Really. Finally I couldn't take it any longer. I had to get back to all of you, so I got a ride on a sleigh that was pulled by a team of big dogs that were part wolf."

"Part wolf?" I asked with wide eyes. "Weren't you scared?"

"Well, it was like being cold. If I just thought of you, I wasn't scared."

"Wow. So were the wolf dogs nice?"

"Oh yes, they were nice but they took their job very seriously. They knew I had to get back to see my girl. But they were part of the reason it took me so long to get home because they had to stop and rest every few hours. It's not the same as traveling in a car."

"I'm so happy you're back!" I jumped onto his lap and hugged him hard. "I love you Daddy."

"I love you too."

We left the bedroom and went back to join the rest of the family. Dad brought out a bag and pulled from it, a gift for each of us. Angie and I got little dolls, Tim and Toby got trucks, and Mom got a glass vase.

My Alaskan doll had real leather moccasins and a brown leather poncho. Her long, black hair was braided and tied with colorful strings that matched her dress. Dad said her name was Kewook and she was exactly what a real Alaskan Eskimo girl looked like. I vowed I would cherish Kewook for the rest of my life.

chapter six

Blossom Drive

I had cherished Kewook for about a week when it was time for us to move again. Dad said moving so often was like test-driving a car; if it didn't work out, we tried another one. In the following months of summer, Dad was away playing in the band while our gypsy camp was relocated three more times. We lived in a house made of stone, cool and dark, which was nice in the heat of summer. But shortly after that, we moved to The Barn House. It was like a barn because it smelled like wheat and tires and didn't have any windows, just walls made of wood planks.

Two months before my sixth birthday we had to leave our Barn House loft for a "fresh start." Dad was going to get a real job so he could stay closer to home.

Our new place was a small, green house on Blossom Drive, in the outskirts of Salem. The August air had swapped its heat for a swirling September breeze. I was glad we were going to a house that had walls and windows.

When we drove to our new place in the low-riding Chevy, Dad serenaded us with "Let It Be." We turned off Blossom Drive and pulled into the driveway, in front of the garage. I had never seen a garage connected to a house before. I wondered how you got in the garage because it had no handle. I also wondered what was behind that mysterious garage door.

We all sat in the car and looked at our new home. Dandelions covered the front yard and outnumbered yellow clumps of dead grass. A cracked concrete walkway led to the front door of the little two-story house the color of canned peas. There was one dormer and one front window.

"This is nice!" I said.

"Yeah," said Tim. "Look, we have neighbors all around us!"

Even Mom twisted around to look at the other houses on the street. She looked pretty with her hair in a French twist and nice makeup, but she was frowning.

Dad put his arm around Mom's shoulders and she turned toward him. We all quietly watched them from the back seat.

"I promise you, this time it's going to be different," he said. They just stared at each other for a long time. Then Dad said, "I mean it. I'm going to get that job at the furniture factory. We'll have more money and things will be easier for you." He put his hand to her cheek and smiled at her. From the side of her face I could tell she was smiling too.

"It's so litto," said Toby, pointing at the house and clutching his blankie.

"A little house makes us extra lucky," said Dad, "because we have very little to put in it."

I looked out the car window at the surrounding houses and the cars parked on the street. A yellow cat slinked around a telephone pole. He sat, looked up, and licked his lips at the overhead wires that swayed under the weight of a dozen chatty blackbirds. I saw that only an overgrown hedge separated us from the house next door. We hadn't had close-by neighbors since the Mollala House so long ago.

Dad kissed Mom slowly on the lips, and then they opened their car doors at the same time. "Everyone carry your own stuff," Mom ordered without turning around. We each had a pillowcase stuffed with our belongings. I held my pillowcase loosely and Kewook tightly.

Angie yanked her blanket out from under Toby's foot and stuck her thumb in her mouth.

"Don't touch my blanket," she mumbled, "It's *my* soft spot." We all piled out of the car for yet another household inspection. Both Angie and Toby looked a little scared, but Tim and I were excited to get inside.

Tim shoved his way past me, jumped up the two concrete steps, and pushed the front door open. We stood in a tiny living room that was furnished with a TV, a vinyl couch, and an upright piano. Next to the piano, narrow stairs led to our bedrooms. We kids scrambled up on all fours. Angie and I ran into our bedroom to find matching wrought iron beds. I looked out the milky window at the alley below. After seeing their room across the hall, Tim and Toby rushed into our room, ran to the little window, and opened it. Toby grabbed Angie's blanket and dropped it out, watching it fall to the garbage cans below. Angie began to cry. "My soft spot, gimme my soft spot."

We thundered downstairs and the boys ran outside to retrieve the soft spot. At the base of the stairwell I stopped to check out the bathroom, which had a real door. There was a bathtub, and a metal showerhead, and even a shower curtain rod. A medicine cabinet with a clear beveled mirror hung over the porcelain sink. I ran my fingers over the dip in the sink that would soon hold a bar of our soap. In front of the medicine cabinet I stood on my tippy toes to see my reflection, but only got a glimpse of the top of my head.

I went to investigate the kitchen, hoping to find some food. When I saw the green-and-white-checkered linoleum floor, it made me want to play hopscotch on it. I was surrounded by green striped wallpaper that smelled like rubber. I touched the green stove, rubbed my fingers over the green floral contact paper that covered the refrigerator. This was just like The Blue House, except whoever had lived here before really liked green.

I quietly opened the fridge but it was empty except for a box of baking soda. I could hear my family outside, but the kitchen curtain was closed so I couldn't see them. I crawled up on the counter by the sink to open the white curtain trimmed in rickrack. When I slid the curtain back, there was no window. I hopped down from the counter and looked at the entire striped wall. Right in the middle of it was a brass doorknob. I put my hand on the knob, but then decided against turning it.

About two weeks after we had settled into the Blossom Drive House, I asked Dad, "Why is Mom's tummy poked out so much?"

"That bump is her reward for swallowing a spoonful of pure clover honey," he said.

When Mom suddenly got a stomachache, Dad urged us to gather our pajamas as fast as we could. In a whirlwind, I grabbed Kewook and my nightgown. Angie grabbed her soft spot, Toby clutched his blankie, and Tim pulled me by my sleeve. We piled into the car and Dad drove full speed while Mom rubbed her swollen belly. We four kids were quickly dropped at Gramma and Grampa's.

The next day Mom and Dad brought home a new baby boy named Max, a sweet, quiet little guy with a fuzzy brown head and sleepy blue eyes. As Mom put him in the crib in her bedroom I could see she had puffy eyes, like she had forgotten to sleep, but her belly was flat under her pretty yellow dress and her blonde hair was styled perfectly.

As soon as baby Max had fallen asleep in the crib, Dad left for work at his new *real* job. He was going to work at a company that made furniture, which meant we would get to see him more than ever before. He said as part of his plan for a brighter future, the first thing he was going to make was a table for Mom to set her coffee on when she watched *General Hospital*.

We nicknamed Max "Babus," and things seemed to be going along all right, with seven of us packed tightly in the Blossom Drive House. All right—until the night I heard the crash.

I was sound asleep when the house shook violently, like a big rock had landed on it. My heart pounded in my chest. I sat up in bed, face-to-face with darkness. I clutched Kewook and tried to trace Angie in the blackness. She lay in her bed, hugging her soft spot and snoring softly. I slid out of bed, tiptoed out of the bedroom and into the hallway at the top of the stairs. The boys' bedroom door was closed. I wanted to wake Tim and ask him what shook the house. I put my ear against their door, but it was dead quiet. I crept down three steps, peering toward the bottom of the stairs. In the silence I tried to adjust my ears and eyes to the dim light on the first floor. The bathroom door was open and I could just see the living room. I went down three more steps until I heard the soft flow of water inside the bathroom. I knew Mom was in the bathtub. I imagined her, soaking shoulder deep in foaming milk bath. I crouched lower on the stairway, waiting to see if she was going to do something about the crash. The kitchen door slammed. Footsteps were coming closer. I ducked back into the shadows, squeezing Kewook tightly. The footsteps were soft and slow. It had to be Dad, but I stayed hidden.

When the footsteps came through the living room, past the piano and the bottom of the stairs, I could see it was Dad. He went into the bathroom.

I heard the water splash as Mom sat up.

"What the hell was that crash?" she screamed.

"Nothing really," Dad said.

"Goddamn you, Ted! What happened?"

"Just a little bump."

"What do you mean, a little bump? The entire house is still shaking!"

"I drove into the garage, but I . . . I couldn't stop the car in time," he said.

"You WHAT? YOU DROVE THROUGH THE BACK OF THE GARAGE?"

"Shhhh, don't wake the kids," he said.

The running water stopped. Their voices lowered to angry whispers.

"You've been drinking, haven't you?" she said.

"Well, a little."

I leaned closer.

"I hate you when you drink!"

I could suddenly hear things loud and clear and I shivered from my earlobes to my toes. I sat down on the step and covered my feet with the bottom edge of my nightgown.

"You hate me, and everything about me." I'd never heard Dad sound like that.

I could see his shoes and the back of his pant legs shaking. He was tapping his toes nervously.

"Why did you just take off?"

"Because I can't fight with you anymore, Gloria."

"Where have you been?"

"I had to go for a drive. I had to get some space."

"YOU need space?" she moaned.

"Yeah. I'm so tired of this."

"You make me sick. Look at you."

"Gloria, please stop."

"You're hopeless."

"Oh, darling, I love you."

"You're hopeless and you're pitiful." She said it like she was growling through her teeth.

"Please. I've had enough. I can't live with this ridicule."

"You can't live with *anything*," she said.

He began to cry.

When I heard Dad cry, my heart cracked. I chewed my lip and wound Kewook's braids around my fingers.

"Oh God, now you're gonna fall apart?" she said.

"I—I'm—I can't. Why can't we just stop this?"

He backed out of the bathroom and went to the living room. I silently wiped my nose on my nightgown and stuck Kewook's poncho between my teeth to keep from crying. He sat down at the piano and began to play, soft and deep, like velvet.

Mom must have been in the tub still, because suddenly loud splashing drowned out the piano.

"What about ME?" she screamed. The music stopped.

He didn't answer. I could hear nothing but the thudding of my heart. The eerie silence made me want to pee.

"What the hell are you doing out there?" she shouted.

I edged forward on my butt until I could see Dad sitting at the piano with his face in his hands. I knew if they caught me I would be in giant trouble. I was so scared and knew I shouldn't be there, but I couldn't help myself. I held my breath.

"Answer me, you coward!" Mom called out.

Dad stood up so fast the piano bench tipped over and crashed to the floor. Sheet music fell all around his feet. He charged into the bathroom. I knew Dad had lost control. He was real mad. He was the kind of mad that Mom was when she went crazy sometimes, the kind of mad that made things get broken and someone gets hurt.

I moved down a step closer to see the bathroom sink and the edge of the tub. Mom stood there with a towel around her. Dad lunged toward the sink and grabbed the sides of the medicine cabinet. He tore it off the wall and threw it at her. She raised her arms and fell backward. She crashed against the tub as the mirror shattered over her hands and arms. I backed up the stairs as fast as I could and froze. I saw Dad's shadow slip by the bottom step, then heard the front door open and slam shut.

"Tim! Help me!" Mom screamed.

Tim's bedroom door flew open. He ran out of his room and as he passed me in the darkness he hissed, "Get back in your room and don't come out."

I stood still at the top of the stairs. I waited to hear the baby cry, but he didn't. I listened for Angie and Toby, but they were still asleep. I got on my knees and tried to bend far enough to see what was happening. Mom was crying to Tim. Suddenly, there was a thud on the bathroom door. I bolted into the bedroom and leaped into bed.

I lay there shaking and whispering to Lightbug. I hugged Kewook and cried quietly. I heard water running and fabric ripping, the broken glass being swept up. I heard Mom sobbing, Tim mumbling, then a rumble that shook the stairs and the floorboards.

I cried for all of us. I cried for Dad out there, walking in the darkness and for Mom downstairs in the bleak and painful aftermath of their fight. I cried for the stains on the bathtub and the shards of that beautiful beveled mirror. I cried for Tim, who was too young for the bloody, wet broom and his unfair duties. I cried for the Blossom Drive House with its splintered garage and its mistreated walls. I cried until the noises of my heart faded into blackness.

The next morning I was hungry, but afraid to go downstairs. Angie wasn't in her bed. I heard the sounds of morning and smelled something sweet and delicious, then crawled off the bed and put on two pairs of socks and a sweater. I stepped down the stairs, my eyes peeled in anticipation of seeing the bathroom. I was relieved to see the bathroom door was closed. At the bottom step laid the coffee table Dad had made. It was split down the middle and one leg was broken off. I carefully stepped around it, feeling sick to my stomach from fear and hunger.

I glanced toward Mom and Dad's room and saw Mom lying on the bed in her nightgown, nursing baby Max. His tiny head of hair was dark against the white cotton bandages on her hands. I slipped by unnoticed.

I found Gramma in the kitchen making pancakes. The other three kids were watching cartoons. Dad was still gone.

"Hiya, honey," said Gramma.

"Hi, Gramma," I said. I went to her and buried my face in her apron.

"I bet you're hungry." Her hands, stroking my head, felt warm and good.

"Yeah. Gramma, what happened in the night?"

"Oh, just a little accident, but everything's okay now."

"Where's Daddy?"

"It's gonna be just fine. He had to go away for a while."

"Where'd he go?"

"I'm not sure, but he should be home soon."

"When?"

"I don't know, honey, but don't you worry. Now come on and have some breakfast."

We all sat down and ate pancakes with warm Karo syrup. Mom didn't come out of her room. I guessed that she and Max had fallen asleep.

After breakfast Tim motioned for me to step around the broken table and come upstairs. We sat on the floor at the foot of his bed. He told me what had happened to Mom.

He said when he heard Mom scream he ran down to find an awful mess. She had cuts on her fingers and wrists. She was so upset that she kicked the bathroom door with her bare foot and hit the wall with her bloody fists. She told Tim to rip up a sheet and tie it around her hands. She made him pick up all the glass and the broken cabinet, and put it in the trash outside. He said it was scary in that dark alley and he almost peed his pants when that old yellow cat jumped out from behind the trashcan. He told me how he swept the floor and rinsed the bloody bubbles out of the tub. When he was done, Mom told him to throw the piano out the front door with all Dads' stuff, but when Tim wouldn't do it, she kicked the coffee table across the room, leaving it mangled at the bottom of the stairs.

"Don't say anything, 'cause Mom doesn't want anyone else to know," he said.

"I won't," I promised.

"And you know what else?" he said.

"What?"

"In one week you're gonna start school with me and Tobe."

"I am?" I said. "I thought I wasn't old enough."

"Well, it's your birthday today, but you're not 'sposed to know that either."

"My *birthday*?"

"Yep, your birthday and their anniversary."

I ran into my room and threw myself on the bed. I wanted Dad to come home and sing to me. I wanted Mom to feel better because I knew having bed sheet bandages really hurt. But mostly, I wanted a chocolate birthday cake with a big blob of vanilla ice cream.

I had been six for exactly seven days when I started first grade. Toby was in second grade and Tim was starting fourth. Angie and Max stayed home with Mom while the three of us walked a mile and a half to Salem's Hayesville Elementary School.

The wind had shifted from a gentle swirl to a freezing gale. Snow was on the way. We wore stocking caps pulled down to our necks as the invisible icicles speared our hands and cheeks. Tim and Toby wore matching Levi jackets, compliments of our grandparents. I had secured my stocking cap with a safety pin under my chin and wore a sweatshirt that just wasn't cutting it. Gramma had sewn me a blue gingham pinafore that I wore over a thin layer of courage. Under my sneakers I wore two pairs of knee socks to keep my toes from freezing and to bring me good luck.

Before leaving the house, Tim had reprimanded me because I had Kewook stuffed under my pinafore.

"You can't bring your doll to school," he said.

"Why not?" I asked.

"Because dolls don't go to school, stupid. And it's already embarrassing enough to have to walk you to your classroom. If you have a doll with you, everybody's gonna think you're a baby, not a first-grader."

"Yeah," said Toby, "only babies carry dolls to school."

Tim turned on him. "You shut up. Only babies have blankies."

I ran back and left Kewook on my bed. We kicked a can from Blossom Drive all the way to Hayesville. As we chased the can, Tim explained that with Dad still gone, Mom was upset and forgot to register us for school. He said we would be coming in six weeks after the rest of the kids.

When we arrived at Hayesville, Tim walked me to my class and left me standing there. The teacher looked down at me and said, "Welcome to first grade. My, you're a skinny little thing, aren't you?"

By the time spring came, Dad had returned. I had decided I needed to gain some weight and straighten my teeth and be extra good if we were going to keep him around.

Standing in the kitchen alone, I was trying to make an orthodontic apparatus out of a Mason jar lid ring. I was pounding the ring with a tablespoon, trying to bend it, when Dad walked in from the garage.

"Hi, sweetheart," he said.

"Hi, Daddy." I looked up at him.

"What are you doing?"

"I'm trying to make a mouth brace."

"What exactly is the purpose of a mouth brace?"

"It's to make my teeth straight."

"Well, why would you want to mess with your natural beauty?"

"'Cause the boys keep teasing me and calling me Bucko. They said my teeth are bigger than a horse's teeth and that my mouth looks like a dog's butt."

"Well, I have an idea," Dad said. "When you go to bed tonight, you do this." He put his thumb on one of his front teeth and his index finger on the other. "Just lie on your stomach and prop yourself up on your elbow with your fingers like this," he instructed. He leaned his elbow on the kitchen counter with his fingers on his front teeth to show me the proper position.

"Like thith?" I asked.

"That's precisely right, but you need to do it every single night until your teeth get straight," he said solemnly.

"Okay. I will."

"One day you're going to wake up with perfectly straight teeth, and you know what your brothers will say to you then?" He smiled a gentle, knowing smile.

"What?" I asked, looking into his deep-water blue eyes.

"They're going to tell you your arms are too hairy or your legs are too long." He shook his head. "What you need to know, Eve, is that you are very special. You have a loving spirit, which neither your brothers, nor anyone else can break or take from you. Your teeth are special too because God made them different from anyone else in the whole world. Just think about that, there are more than a jabillion people on the planet and you are the only one with this smile." He took my chin in his hand. "Plus," he added, "you're prettier than your brothers anyway."

I set the jar lid ring down and put my arms around Dad's neck. I hung there giving him a tight squeeze.

"Mmm, you smell like fresh wood," I said.

"Mmm, you smell like a dream come true."

"Well, you smell like a fluffy cloud in the bluest sky," I said.

"You smell like a sugar plum."

"I love you, Daddy."

"I love you too," he whispered.

Since we were all alone, I asked, "Will you play "Fly Me to the Moon"?"

"Absolutely," he said. He went to the piano, sat down, and did what only Dad could do. His magic hands glided over the keys. The words danced from his lips and filled the air.

After he played and sang "Fly Me to the Moon," he did "Mrs. Robinson." I twirled around like a jewelry box ballerina with her hair all messed up.

"Yes, ma'am. I am going to put you in the Pinochle Theatre," he said.

Although I had never seen the place, I knew it was special. Dad had told me the Pinochle Theatre was a big place with a huge crystal chandelier, and decorations on the walls. He played there, and at a cool club called Arbuckle Flats. Dad promised me that one day I would not only play the piano, but be a dancer on stage all lit up in color. He said it was just a matter of *logistics*, and he would figure out how to teach me piano and dance without causing *marital discord*. I wasn't sure what that meant, but probably it had something to do with Mom hating music.

chapter seven

John Ruby

We moved from Blossom Drive to a place we called The Cinderella House. It didn't get its name from a beautiful fairytale, but because it was made of cinderblocks all piled into a single story like a factory. It was a cold, cement-gray color with steel bars over the back windows. Of the four stall-like bedrooms, Tim and Toby had one, Angie and I had one, and Max got his own stall, but he always squeezed into our room for company.

Dad said the good thing about The Cinderella House was that it had great acoustics. When we yelled, a vibrating echo bounced off the ceiling and walls. The Cinderella House came with an upright piano that was sadly out of tune because of the damp concrete floors, but Dad played it anyway when Mom wasn't around, and I tried to play it too.

One winter morning the four of us were waiting at the bus stop. Toby and Angie were a few yards away, trying to crack ice in a mud puddle. Tim came over and patted the top of my head—a big brother's consolation for the rough morning. Mom had thrown me out the front door.

"You gotta watch your butt," he said.

"I don't get it," I said. "I try to be good."

"Well, like I said, just watch it. There's something that doesn't work with you and Mom. I'm not sure what, but it just isn't right."

"I think she hates me, and I feel terrible because I can't make her like me."

"Well, I feel terrible because I can't make her like you either. You know I'm sorry about not being able to help you more. You just gotta be strong and stay out of her way."

"Maybe I'm from a different litter than the rest of us," I suggested.

"Nah, I know for sure you were born from them, because I was there when they brought you home from the hospital."

"How would you remember that?" I asked.

"The same way you remember all the stuff that's already happened to you," he said.

"Yeah? Like what?"

"Like how you remember things that we already forgot, like the names of all the houses we've lived in."

"Yeah?"

"Yeah. Say 'em. Name as many as you can remember."

"Well, there's The October House where I split my head, and The Rat Shack, The Blue House, and The Mollala House. Then, remember when we had those three right in a row, The Birdhouse, Rock House, and Barn House?"

"See, I forgot about The Birdhouse," he said.

"That's because we only spent a couple nights there. Remember all those sparrows were trying to pull out our hair?"

"Yeah, that was freaky. Anyway, you get my point. You remember stuff and you're smart, so just use your head."

"I will," I said.

"You just keep doing good in school and just stay out of her way, the best you can."

I nodded down at my shoes. "Dad said we all came from a spoonful of clover honey. Maybe Mom made a mistake with me and instead of honey, she choked on a hard lump of sugar."

"Naw, more like a bucket of nails," he said.

I kicked a stone and watched it slide across the frozen pavement.

Tim grabbed my shoulders and shimmied me around until I started to giggle. "Hey, you got a boyfriend yet?" he smiled.

"Well," I stopped laughing and looked down at the ground. "I kinda like a boy in my grade called John Ruby."

"Well now, that's a nice name," he said. "Mrs. John Ruby."

"Be quiet!" I swatted at him.

"Does he *kinda* like you back?"

"I don't know. How do you tell when a boy likes you back?" I looked up at him.

"Oh, you can just tell," he said.

"Well, he chases me."

"That's definite proof of kinda liking someone," he said.

My face got warm at the mere thought of it.

"Here comes the bus." He gave me one more shake and let me go. "Keep me posted."

"Tim." I pulled on his sleeve. "Please don't tell anybody I like John Ruby."

"Okay, I won't."

When we got to school I was excited by what Tim had said. After all, he was eleven years old, definitely old enough to know about such things.

When I wasn't chasing John Ruby on the playground, he was after me in hot pursuit. We devoted our entire recess to running underneath the monkey bars and around the four square players. We ran and ran but never caught each other. Although we had never spoken, we had mutual respect for one another's skill of the high-speed chase.

John Ruby had straight, shoulder-length brown hair that hung in his eyes when he wasn't running incredibly fast. He wore red high-top tennis shoes and a jean jacket, which I thought elevated him to rock star status.

Only a couple of hours after confiding in Tim, I was standing on the playground and noticed that my heartthrob was missing. Maybe he was sick, I thought, or maybe he missed the bus, or maybe both. I imagined him bundled up in his jean jacket, a red scarf, and a stocking cap with a Kleenex plastered to his nose. I imagined him speed-walking to school, cars zooming past him, just to get to me by recess. I just knew after a failed attempt at hitching a ride, he would find another way to reach me. I scanned the horizon looking for a white stallion with the fearless John Ruby on its back, bounding over obstacles and galloping full-speed ahead to where I awaited in fervent anticipation.

I was knocked out of my romantic trance by a sudden blow between my shoulder blades. I stumbled forward and landed in a bony pile, then craned my neck to see Leslie Brune standing over me with her hands on her hips.

"Stay away from John Ruby!" she boomed in a voice of authority. Leslie was also in third grade, but much bigger than me. She had long, brown hair and a huge mouth that took up most of her face. Her big hands hung on arms that were longer than my legs. She traveled in a pack at all times, including now. They all glowered down at me. "Yeah, stay away!"

"He's mine!" Leslie Brune screamed into my face.

"Yeah, he's hers!" they chimed, like an all-girl boys' choir.

"He's mine. One hundred percent mine." Her jaw stuck out and her face was red.

I just couldn't take it. She had no claim on my John Ruby, and I knew it. After all, I had never even seen him chase her.

I jumped up so fast that the girlie circle dispersed like a water ring in a mud puddle. I got right in Leslie Brune's face, even though I had to look up. She grabbed my hair and started pulling. We ended up rolling on the cold, wet ground in a screeching, scratching ball of limbs. She didn't let go of my hair until I heard a rip inside my head. I let out something like a demonic scream. I heaved myself up on top of her chest and pinned her shoulders to the concrete with my scrawny knees.

She looked up at me, clutching a blood-tinged clump of my hair. Her face looked like it was caving in. I drew back my fist to blast her right in the nose. Then I stopped, my arm suspended in mid-air. Except for our hoarse panting, the world was silent.

I looked into her dispirited eyes. They began to fill with tears. She was really scared. Her freckles mirrored mine. I felt Lightbug heat up inside me. I had a vision of Mom's fist coming toward me. I couldn't do it. I could not hit Leslie Brune in the face because I knew firsthand what it would feel like. I had no right to hurt her just because she liked John Ruby.

I dropped my arm limply at my side and pushed myself off her. I stood over her and saw the road rash on her elbows. I looked around at the accumulation of three-foot spectators. Then I said to Leslie Brune with composed authority, "You can keep the hair."

When the bell rang, the playground monitor promptly took us straight to the principal's office. As we sat there, I felt a special bond between the two of us. I had experienced my first catfight. *Wow*, I thought, *I can't wait to tell Tim.*

In my heart I proclaimed my commitment and undying love to the fabulous John Ruby. I wondered what he would have said about the battle on his behalf. I also wondered whom he would have chosen as his betrothed.

Lucky for me, the principal didn't call home. As soon as I saw Brother Tim, I told him the story. He listened with a closed-lip smile, put his hand on my shoulder and said, "Way to go, Ruby." The name stuck with me.

chapter eight

Cliffside Ride

We were bombing down a long gravel road through the Willamette countryside, distancing ourselves from Salem Suburbia. At the wheel, Dad caught sight of me in the rearview mirror and gave me a wink. He had a bright orange lipstick mark on his cheek from Mom's recent kiss. Her orange fingernails caressed the back of his hair. Each time we hit a bump in the road, they bounced off the seat, making Mom's plastic pumpkin earrings swing back and forth. Angie and Max sat securely between Mom and Dad, completely unaware we were moving again.

Crammed in the rear of the station wagon, wedged between a box of dishes and the broken coffee table, I readjusted myself to see out the back window. Grampa, Tim, and Toby followed us in a hay truck loaded with the rest of our stuff.

I scooted closer to the back window and felt the coldness on my nose. My breath left a foggy spot on the pane. I drew a heart shape on the steamy glass and filled in the secret message "I love J. Ruby." I was sad knowing I would never see John Ruby again. I stared at the dripping letters and silently bid him goodbye, keeping his name and the sweet memory of the first boy I ever liked. I wiped the past off the window with my sleeve and waved to Tim through the wet smudge and the flying rocks.

We pulled up to a two-story farmhouse surrounded by fruit orchards. Grampa's truck lurched to a stop in front of the mailbox as Dad pulled the loaded Chevy into the dirt driveway. When I saw my brothers jump out of the truck I pounded on the window to get them to let me out, but they ran straight to the house. Dad came around and opened the back of the car. I fell out with a dustpan, a basket of curlers, and a bag of diapers. Stumbling to my feet I regarded the new home before me.

Without a neighbor in sight, the peeling white house on Juniper Road sat back from the country road, behind a grove of huge walnut trees. A walkway sprayed with fresh grass cuttings led to a rambling front porch. Holding Max like a football, Mom marched onto the porch and pushed open the weathered double doors with her shoulder. We all paraded into the large dining room. I stared up at the high ceilings and thick crown molding. Off the dining area was a spacious living room with two doors leading to bedrooms. I ran from room to room on the squeaky hardwood floors, which spread throughout the entire house. It was old, but it was big.

The bathroom had a tall cabinet with a large shelf and a mirror above it. I supposed Mom would put all her makeup, perfume bottles, and earrings up there where they would be out of our reach. The bathtub had feet shaped like lion's paws.

The oversized kitchen had countertops above my shoulders. *Am I getting smaller or are our houses getting bigger?* I went to the pantry and gazed at four rows of painted wood shelving. I imagined the shelves stacked to the ceiling with food: cans and jars and loaves, sacks and boxes and bags of food. My stomach lurched and growled at the empty planks. I backed out and headed up the curvy, narrow stairs to see our new bedroom, the one Angie and I would share, across the hall from Tim and Toby. Dad said the extra room was for storage and that Max would sleep downstairs.

From my bedroom window I saw that rain was on its way. Rows of trees and fields stretched out under the metal-gray sky. In back of the house was an old barn brimming with hay, orchards with two different kinds of trees, (Dad said they were apples and cherries), and an open field that went for miles. Dad told us we were in the middle of acres and acres of clover, but it had been mowed down, and there were just dirt clods and clumps of yellow stems left. Farthest away I saw a forest, with plenty of trees that looked like they were built for climbing.

Dad said that even though we had rented the only house around, we were lucky because we might get to witness the nature of man in the works, the construction of a housing development. He said that such a development was a benefit to the future of the countryside. I didn't understand how a pack of houses would be good for a place that had nobody else around.

"What about the orchards and stuff?" I asked.

"Oh, the orchards and the clover fields will all be safe, they'll just be surrounded by brand new houses with white and lavender garages," Dad assured me.

"White and *lavender*?" He knew lavender was my favorite color.

Mom overheard him and said that there were no such things as lavender garages.

I curled in bed that night, sandwiched between good and evil. Above me the rain fell softly on the roof, while below the angry voices of my parents pressed up through the floorboards. I didn't understand why they had to fight so frequently, so bitterly, and so often at night. Suddenly I heard something smash to smithereens, and my heart quickened. I pressed my feather-ticked pillow against my ears, drowning out their voices with the loud crackle of goose quills.

When I uncovered my head, stilled my breathing, and listened, the argument had gone from paint colors to divorce. Although I didn't know the true meaning of the word, I suspected it was bad. I climbed out of bed and laid my ear on the cold floor.

"Gloria, I can't do it anymore," said Dad.

"You don't have a choice!" Mom screamed.

"Divorce is the best option," he said.

"It's a chickenshit option!"

"The only way out of this misery is for me to leave. You'll be much better off starting over with a clean slate," he said.

"There will never be a clean slate. Don't you even think about leaving. If you do, believe me, I'll put those kids in the station wagon and run the whole mess over a cliff and into the ocean!"

An icy shiver shot through me. I sprang up so fast that I bit my tongue. I jumped back into bed and bumped my forehead on the mattress 122 times. As things quieted down on the lower level, I convinced myself that their fight would end like it usually did, and that they had already kissed and made up.

We were at Hazel Green School for just one week when I got the feeling we were there to stay. Mom and Dad seemed happy enough in the farmhouse and I loved being so far out in the country. The kids in my class were pretty friendly compared to some I had met. Angie and I walked to school when the weather permitted, past strawberry fields and filbert orchards.

We came home from school on a Tuesday afternoon and something was wrong. Mom sat at the kitchen table, staring at the back of her hands.

"Your dad left," she said without looking up.

Then in a slow whisper she went on to say that he wasn't on a trip to play music, he was really gone. Scared, I went up to my room until Tim and Toby came home. When they got home Tim tried to talk to Mom, but she went into a weird sort of trance.

The next night it was dark and rainy, and I had just fallen asleep when Mom shook me hard. "Get up! *Get up!*" She got us all out of bed and told us to get in the back of the car, lie down and keep quiet.

I was in the back seat holding Max tightly bundled up. We all lay hidden under our coats and blankets like a heap of drowsy puppies. Mom drove for what seemed like hours, all in the dark and rain. Phasing in and out of sleep, I heard the tires splashing through mud puddles, then gradually the drone of the Chevy engine changing pitch.

Out in the wet darkness the rhythmic slapping of the windshield wipers seemed to urge Mom to drive faster and faster. My ears popped—I knew we were climbing up that coastal road she had threatened to drive, high above the ocean cliffside.

Suddenly we were sliding from side to side, crashing against each other. Mom was driving out of control, tossing us about the car. "Mom!" Toby yelled from the floor. Over the seat, I could see her clutching the steering wheel and staring hard through the windshield, charging headlong into the stormy night. I was scared to death and scared to die.

I gnawed my lips so hard I could taste blood. Tim uncovered his head and looked at me through the blackness. He looked as terrified as I felt.

"Stay down!" Mom said in a voice I didn't recognize.

All at once I saw Tim's face and the mound of blankets flare up in flashing blue and red light. Sirens shrieked as we sped on and squealed around curves with the colored strobe lights on our back bumper. I held back the bile in my mouth and braced myself for the upcoming cliff. I smashed Max to my chest and clenched my teeth. Crushing my eyes closed, I turned to the light barely flickering within me. *Lightbug please save us.*

We began to slow down and the transmission downshifted, bringing the car to a gradual roll. The sirens stopped but the lights stayed on us.

"Pull over and stop the car!" a voice blared through a loudspeaker. Mom stopped the car and turned it off. She dropped her forehead to the steering wheel and began gulping defeated sobs. I had never heard Mom cry like that before and was surprised and saddened that she cried so loudly.

"Remain in the vehicle." The command blasted through the rain. Mom kept crying and rocking her head back and forth.

There was a sharp rap rap rap on her window. It was the cop tapping with his pistol barrel. She slowly rolled down the window to look out at the state trooper. In the flashing lights he looked huge, in a slicker shiny with rain. He asked her to get out of the car. She obeyed by cranking up the window weakly and almost falling out of the car, now whimpering instead of sobbing.

Mom and that trooper stood out in the rain with the silent flashing lights for an awfully long time. She had plenty to tell him, and he appeared to be interested in what she was saying. Tim, Toby, Angie and I, shaky and silent, craned our heads up to watch, but in my lap Max was fast asleep.

Somewhere in the middle of it all, more troopers arrived. Over the blasting wind, their radios spat and hissed about *armed and dangerous* and *secured positions*.

Eventually, the car door opened and the trooper leaned in, flooding us all with his blinding flashlight. He looked at us briefly, nodded and backed out, encouraging Mom to get behind the wheel.

"I will follow you," he said in his deep officer's voice.

"Okay, thank you," Mom said.

She started the engine and took a long time to maneuver the car in a u-turn, with the assistance of the trooper's incandescent floodlight.

The wind howled and rocked the car as we crawled back down the cliffside road. The state troopers followed close on our tail, but much slower than before. I could tell we were a long way from home and was afraid of where we were going. Eventually I got up enough nerve to raise my head and ask, "Where are we going now?"

"Home," Mom said, completely spent.

Relief, so great, swirled around my insides and spilled out all over me. I rubbed my lips to remove the crusty bile from the corners of my mouth. Then I covered my smile when I realized I had actually saved that moment to pee in my nightgown.

chapter nine

Berry Patch

Dad came back before the summer started. He arrived in a white car with three other guys in it. They pulled into the driveway and he rolled out of the back seat and onto the ground. The driver backed up, honked, and sped off. Dad stood up, brushed off his pants, and came waltzing back into our world.

After settling in, Dad got busy setting up a wood-working shop in one of the sheds. I hung around every chance I got just to hear him sing while he worked. I knew he remembered about teaching me to play the piano because when he saw me leaning on the door jamb, he always winked as if we had a secret. He and Mom were doing fine and we were all extra happy to have him back. Mom said instead of just standing around gawking and being worthless, we were all going to go to work. There was bean picking, she said, and filberts, and berries galore.

The main job we had was on a strawberry farm about a mile and a half away, and the strawberry season lasted a good portion of the summer. We headed out walking toward the wet, leafy rows with luscious red berries hidden beneath them. With the heavy morning dew on the strawberry bushes, I got off to a slow start—I didn't like getting my shirt sleeves wet or getting my bare arms wet and itchy. I marveled at how Brother Tim would just rush in there and start picking, while I stood and tried to figure out some way to change the course of nature by evaporating the drops off the leaves. Angie usually found a little boy to play with and Toby spent the majority of his time eating enough berries to get a bellyache. Tim had made a friend named Steve Henry, an obnoxious thirteen-year-old. He always wore tank tops that he called muscle shirts. He had a long, ropey scar down one arm that looked like a melted snake.

"Hey, Tim, your little sisters are cute, but if I had my choice I'd go for the blondie," said Steve.

"Henry, back off. She's only nine years old, you jerk," said Tim.

"Who are you calling a jerk? Jerkoff!" He pegged Tim in the face with a fat berry. The row boss saw it, blew his whistle, and Steve Henry was promptly kicked out of the field.

"Screw you all!" he screamed at the kids who had stopped picking to stare at him. As we watched him march away kicking up dust, Tim turned to me and said, "You stay away from him. Steve Henry is nothin' but trouble."

"Then why do you pick in the row next to him every day?" I asked.

"Because I thought he was my friend," he said.

I shrugged, pushed my berry cart ahead, and started plucking berries with both hands. I was making up for my slow kick-start by working extra fast. I wanted to earn more than just enough for school clothes. In Gramma's Sears Roebuck catalog, I had seen a pink bicycle, which I knew was destined to be mine. I convinced myself I would make enough money to get that bike. It had a white vinyl banana seat that sported hot pink daisies to match the frame and white-walled tires that would make me go faster than the speed of light. With the white rattan basket on the front I could carry in the mail or maybe even a little dog, or a bouquet of flowers. The best thing about the pink beauty was that it had long pink and lavender tassels flowing from the ends of the stingray handlebars that would make me look very cool, like a bike racer and a cheerleader all wrapped into one. I couldn't wait to ride it to school.

That whole summer, the crystal-clear night skies over the farmlands left a blanket of morning dew and heated up the day like an open inferno. It was on one of those sweltering days that the row boss found me passed out from heat stroke beside a stack of berry flats and alerted my mother to come and get me.

Mom pulled up in our station wagon as the berry boss carried me out from the field. She didn't get out, just sat there staring ahead while the engine ran. The berry boss got the back door open and laid me down on the seat. He barely closed the door when Mom peeled out. My nose had been bleeding and as we drove home, I felt like a fuzzy, hot blob.

"You just wait 'til I get you home," Mom fumed. "I get one chance to become somebody and you blow it. I had my first customer appointment to be a successful Avon Lady, and you screwed it up." I struggled to sit. I saw she was clasping the steering wheel tightly; her fingernails were painted like ladybugs.

"I'm gonna throw up," I mumbled, my mouth filling with saliva. Out of compassion and the kindness of her heart, she pulled over and let me barf in the roadside ditch. She was hovering over me, her shadow shielding me from the sun. My knees were wobbly and my brain was pounding against the inside of my skull.

I looked up at her silhouette.

"Thank you for letting me puke. And I'm really sorry I messed things up for you."

She put her ladybug fingertips on my cheek for just a second and looked past me.

"Get in the car," she said.

I fell asleep in the back seat and woke up in the car, parked in our driveway, well after the sun had gone down. I finally crawled out into the cool evening, surrounded by the thick chirping of crickets. I had my mind on food as I headed for the porch.

I stopped when a little dog scampered down the steps. He was a brown and white beagle mix with buggy eyes. He jumped up on my legs. I sat down on the step and petted him all over while he wagged his tail and pushed his squirming body against me.

"What a sweet little doggy you are! When I get my pink bike, you can ride in the basket!"

I asked him where he came from. I didn't know if he was a neighbor's dog—they were all so far away. But I was glad I could hug him. He wagged and shook and licked my face. I kissed him on the nose and quietly went into the house to find out if we could keep him, and to forage for food. I stood there amid the family commotion and blended right in—no one even seemed to notice I had been missing. I shoveled in hot macaroni and cheese and four slices of bread.

"Hey, Tim, whose sweet little doggie is that?" I said.

"He's ours now, Ruby. We named him Saddle because of the brown patch on his back."

There came a huge sigh of relief from all four of us: Me, Lightbug, and the two angels hovering above my shoulders. I was the luckiest girl alive.

I told Dad all about the pink bike I wanted. He said even though it was a mighty big undertaking for a nine-year-old, I could get it if I earned the money.

"But you better be careful working so hard out in the hot sun," he said.

"Oh, I will," I said.

"You know there's a condition called 'heat stroke' that causes a person to pass out if they get overheated."

"Yeah?" I said.

"Yes, ma'am. Plus, it's more likely to happen to someone with a special combination like yours, Swedish and Norwegian."

"Yeah," I said, "I saw it happen to someone already this summer."

Dad smiled.

By the end of the summer I had met my goal and was able to give my cash to Gramma, who ordered my pink Trailblazer. I watched her fill out the order form and write a check to Sears. The form had an additional line amount for shipping and handling, which I wasn't prepared for. Gramma paid for the shipping and handling as my early birthday present. The pink beauty would be delivered to Juniper Road within ten working days.

"Did you order your bike?" Dad asked me that evening.

"Yeah! I can't wait. I'm so excited! It's supposed to come within ten working days. But what exactly does that mean, 'working days'?"

"That means it will take the bike-making factory ten days just to polish it. Every day when the people come to work, an entire team of talented agents is chosen whose only job is to shine your bicycle, so that by the time it arrives, it will be sparkling like a diamond. The polishing people devote all their time and are actually paid an additional bonus for doing a good polishing job on your bike."

"Wow!" I said.

"And it's all because you are *so* special," Dad beamed.

chapter ten

Fire

Steve Henry said I burned down the barn but that wasn't entirely true. Part of the house, the surrounding orchards, the clover field, *and* the barn all burned. And anyway, Steve Henry was a liar.

It was late August when field harvesting wound down. The hay and wheat had been cut, baled, and bucked. Farmer John, as we called our nearest neighbor, had worked almost every day for two weeks, stacking truckloads of hay to the rafters of his shabby old barn. The long, hot days of summer had dried up the whole countryside. The burning rays of the sun were toasting the roofs of all the buildings.

The day was sultry and suffocating with no relief from the wind that blew on me like a hairdryer on the medium setting. I was being lazy, slumped on the porch step, rubbing an ice cube on Saddle's belly. He smiled up at me, a doggy grin that showed his little white teeth. Everyone was gone except for me and the Babus Max, asleep and sweaty in his bed.

Steve Henry and two of his friends rode up on bikes looking for Tim and Toby. They threw their bikes to the ground in a cloud of dust and lumbered up to the porch.

"Making a dogsickle?" said Steve. He had freckled white skin that had been burned pink, and brown hair hanging in his face. His eyes were big and dark. His scar looked tight and wrinkly, and I wanted to ask him how he got it. Maybe he had been caught in a bear trap or escaped from a torture chamber.

"Poor Saddle, he's got the hot belly sickness," I said.

"Your brothers here?" asked Jerry.

"No, I think everyone went to town."

"Why'd they all go to town?" said Steve.

"I don't know. They've been gone all day. My dad's with them."

"Maybe your brothers are going to buy bikes," said Jerry.

"I doubt it." I shook my head.

"Maybe they're gettin' ice cream," said Jerry.

"I doubt that too," I said. "I just hope they aren't out looking for another place to live, because I like it here."

"Yeah, and you haven't even lived here that long," said Jerry. "I've lived in my house my whole life."

"Well, you're lucky. We lived in more like fifteen houses in my life," I said.

Saddle licked my toes and I giggled.

"How can anybody live in fifteen houses in nine years?" said Steve.

"It's possible," Daniel said. "If you do the math, it's an average of about one new house every seven months."

"Sounds about right," I said.

"So why did you have to move so much?" asked Jerry.

"I have no idea. It's always for a different reason, but mostly we don't talk about it, we just do it. I'm pretty used to it by now."

"Do you remember all those houses?" said Steve.

"Yeah, it's easy. One year we moved five times, every time on the first day of the month, so we named the houses after the month we lived there."

"You've got to be kidding me," Jerry half-laughed. "You mean you like lived in a house called *January*?"

"Yep. And The March House, and June, all the way up to The October House, which was actually named after a storm, then we switched to The Rat Shack."

"You lived in a *rat shack*?" said Daniel.

"Yeah, it was pretty cool, but really noisy."

Steve shook his head. "Unbelievable."

"My dad says it's an adventure. He tells us time is short, so eat candy whenever you can and live life looking out through many different windows."

"Well, I guess that explains it," said Jerry. He smeared the grimy sweat off his forehead with the front of his even grimier T-shirt.

"It's hotter than a witch's tit out here," Steve sighed.

"Witches' tits are cold, stupid," said Jerry.

"Whatever. It's hotter than hell," said Steve.

"I know, really," I agreed. I was feeling very grown up being around those big boys, also a little worried that Mom and Dad would come driving up and I would be in trouble for having them there, even though I didn't invite them. I felt Steve Henry eyeing me, felt my cheeks heat up.

"Well, you want to go for a swim in the hole?" asked Steve.

"No, I can't."

"Why not?" he said.

"Because I'm babysitting. The little guy just went down for a nap."

We all looked at each other, fading in the heat and the lull in the conversation.

Steve broke the long silence. "I got some matches."

"Oh," I said. My bare feet rested on Saddle's ribcage.

"We could smoke some straw," he said.

"Have you done it before?" Jerry stared at me.

"No, um, but I bet I know how. The barn just got filled up with straw. Come on, I'll show you." I jumped off the step. Saddle turned over as if he finally realized we had company, and began wagging his tail at the three boys.

"What about your baby brother?" said Daniel.

"Oh, right. He was pretty hot and cranky when I rocked him to sleep so he's probably out for a while. Hold on while I go check."

I ran into the house, which was much cooler than outside. Baby Max was sleeping with a tiny wisp of hair stuck to his face. His thumb rested on his lower lip in a stringy spot of drool. His skin was pink in the hot, humid air, thick as a damp blanket. I leaned over and blew softly on his face to cool him off. He didn't flinch so I ran back outside.

"Okay, follow me!" I said. Callused feet and tennie runners pounded over the crunchy grass as I led the troop through the orchard, across a field, into our neighbor's barn.

The barn was stifling inside. Dusty rays of sunlight shot through the wallboard cracks like gold X-ray beams. Hay was meticulously stacked to the ceiling, leaving just enough room for Farmer John's forklift. It was parked in the center, done for the day, with only the huge clover field left to harvest the next morning.

It felt like it was twenty degrees hotter inside the barn, and I started to get dizzy. I leaned against the forklift. Steve yanked four thick stalks from a bale and said, "Okay, let's smoke some straw."

We each put the pretend cigarette to our lips.

"Who's going first?" I asked, weak and nervous.

Those three boys were all thirteen years old, and why they wanted to involve a punk kid like me in this was the enigma of a lifetime. Steve pulled out a box of matches and handed it to me. I quickly handed it back and said, "No, you go first."

He struck the end of the matchstick and the match ignited with a *fwoooof*. He passed the flame by his straw, then held it to the golden piece stuck between the split in my front teeth. I closed my lips over the straw tube and sucked in just a little, creating a flame and a puff of smoke from its end. Steve shook the match and dropped it to the barn floor.

My cheeks puffed up like I had a mouthful of cherries. I let out a blast of heavy white smoke from my lips.

"Wow!" they exclaimed.

"Now, let me light yours," I said to Steve. He handed me the matches. We all took three turns, until our straws were burned down to our fingertips. I licked my lips, needing a drink to wash out the taste of smoke.

"That was way cool," said Steve.

Daniel and Jerry nodded, but they didn't look real happy. Their faces were purple and puffy, and mine felt the same.

"Come on. I'll make us some Kool-Aid!" I squealed, and we raced out of the barn and into the orchard. Instinctively, I stopped at the third tree and turned back toward the barn. Smoke was rolling from the barn doors, slowly pouring low to the ground.

"Fire!" I screamed.

We ran back into the barn to find a baseball-sized pile of straw smoldering on the barn floor. We frantically stomped on it and hacked lugies on it until the smoking heap was officially out.

"Good job!" I said.

"I thought I was gonna have to piss on it," said Steve with a cocky grin.

I flushed the image out of my mind.

"That woulda been a major bummer if the barn caught on fire," said Daniel.

"Well, you're right about that," I said, with the smile of a satisfied smoker.

Back at the house the boys sat in the shade of a tree while I went in to check on the baby. He still slept soundly. I blew my smoky breath on him and went to the kitchen. I gathered cups, a pitcher, and a packet of grape Kool-Aid. The front door opened and Steve popped his head in.

"Hey, man, can I use the head?"

"Sure, you guys can come in. I'll have this made in no time." I felt naughty—I knew I was doing something wrong—but it was exciting too.

They slunk in, took turns using the bathroom, and stood around watching me create the purple nectar of the gods. I scooted a kitchen chair into the pantry and crawled up to the third shelf to get some sugar. Perched with one foot wedged between the rungs of the chair and the other teetering on the middle pantry shelf, I leaned into the third shelf and grasped the open sugar bag by the top flap. As I pulled it toward me, the paper bag ripped and gave way. Four pounds of generic label, fine granulated sugar poured out in a white avalanche over the shelves, the jars of canned tomatoes, the chair, and me. As the sugar sack hit the floor I looked down at the crystalline mess and said, "Oops."

No one said a word.

I quickly got a cup from the counter, scraped three cups of sugar off the floor, and dumped them into the pitcher. After ripping open the Kool-Aid packet with my teeth, I sprinkled it in and added tap water. The boys licked their lips as I stirred it up in a swirl and carefully poured each one of us a cup.

"I smell smoke," I said.

"It's probably your breath," said Steve.

I got the broom and dustpan and swept up the snowdrift as the boys slurped down their sugar high. I picked up the torn sugar bag and wondered if I could tape it. I knew I'd be in a world of hurt for wasting. I saw that the bag read "565 servings per container," which qualified as a severe waste. It took me half an hour to sweep the shelves, the chair, and the floor. The boys kept slurping as I gathered the dirty sugar up in the dustpan, poured it in a grocery bag, and stuck it back on the pantry shelf.

"Want some more?" I said.

"Sure," they chorused.

I refilled their cups until the Kool-Aid jug was empty. After Steve let out a loud burp, I went to see if he woke up the baby, but he was fast asleep.

"I can't believe he's still asleep," I said. "Come on, let's go outside."

When I opened the front door a blast of hot smoky air belted me in the face.

"Who turned up the thermostat?" joked Steve, but I didn't laugh.

I looked toward the barn and shrieked when I saw searing red and orange flames lashing out of the doorway. We ran into the orchard, but a wall of heat stopped us in our tracks. I stood there in shock bracing myself against the trunk of a cherry tree. The old barn was cracking and popping, huge bursts of black smoke shot out from the barn door. The roof began to quiver like the lid of a kettle on full boil.

"Call the fire department!" Jerry yelled.

I ran back into the house, grabbed the phone from the wall and, with shaking fingers, dialed O. In what felt like five minutes, the operator answered, "Operator. How can I assist you?"

I screamed into the receiver "The barn is on fire!"

"I'm sorry, what is your exact location?" she asked.

"I'm in the kitchen!" I cried.

"Which fire department may I connect you with?" she asked with her well-trained calmness. I was hysterical, I couldn't think.

"I don't know…Just anybody that can help us!" I began twisting the phone cord around my arm.

"Do you know your address?" she continued, with incredible control.

"No!"

"Is there an adult available?"

"NO!"

"Are you closer to Hazel Green or Salem?" she asked.

"Hazel Green, I think. No! Salem. I think… No, I don't know! Just hurry!"

I unwrapped myself, dropped the handset, and left it swinging from the wall. In a blur I ran out into the yard. I desperately looked for the boys through the thick smoke starting to sting my eyes. Despite the heat, I felt a chill down in my bones when I realized Daniel, Jerry, and even Steve Henry had deserted me. My heart cramped in my chest. Acrid smoke sent my lungs into a coughing frenzy that knocked me to my knees.

Looking up, I could see the sky closing in, covering me with an enormous blue-black lid. Balls of fire punched holes right through the dark barrier and into the void beyond.

The crackling roar was getting closer; Queen Anne cherry trees stood bravely in the orchard, bombarded with hot shards of burning barn splinters. A thunderous boom shook the ground as the barn gave way and imploded. Its disintegrated contents, blackened hay, and shredded baling twine spun through the air. Deafening cracks ricocheted off my body. I clasped my hands over my ears and screamed into the space behind my burning eyes. My nostrils stung with the smell of destruction. My tongue felt thick with the taste of carbon and doom.

Then, faintly . . . horns and sirens in the distance. Through my delirium I ran to the road thinking I could get someone's attention, maybe alert the fire trucks as to which house to come to, as they probably didn't have the right address.

I looked back at our house in terror and saw a blazing sphere hit the rooftop, igniting a fire above the front porch. I panicked remembering Max, ran into the house, and grabbed him up. I clutched him to my chest in the quietness of the nursery and whimpered like a puppy. I didn't know where to go for safety.

The blaring sirens finally drew me out the front door. There were four fire trucks and more than fifteen firemen marching about. A colossal fireman strode across the lawn and stood towering over me. He wore thick leather gloves up to his elbows and a shiny red coat covered with bright yellow reflectors. I scanned him from his massive boots, all the way up to his huge helmet. His face was distorted behind the hazy safety mask.

"Is there anyone else in the house?" he boomed.

"No, Sir," I said meekly.

"Any animals inside?"

"No, Sir, there's only our dog, Saddle, who's probably under the house." I was trembling so hard I was making the baby shake too.

He leaned down and peered into my face. "Are you alright, young lady?"

"I'm sc-scared." I began crying again.

Then, he asked the question that unleashed my remorse to the fullest. "Do you know how this happened?"

I looked at the kind eyes so far behind the plastic windows, held his gaze, and hiccupped, "M-M-Me, Sir." I began bawling, dripping tears on top of the baby's head.

"Who do we have here?" he asked.

"This is my little brother," I blubbered.

"Well, we're going to have the two of you stay right over here by this truck," he said.

He guided us to a safe place and I sat on the ground with my legs crossed. I laid Max in my lanky nest and he accepted my dirty finger to chew on. I bobbed him up and down and rubbed his fuzzy head. He stared at me wide-eyed, but kept quiet considering all the commotion.

The firefighters wore massive suits of combat armor. They pulled forcefully on mighty yellow hoses that carried water from the huge truck tanks. The hoses stretched half the length of the property. I watched in a daze as the fire chief spat orders into his walkie-talkie and firemen bellowed to one another. They worked together manhandling hoses that spewed great geysers to soak the roof and the house and all around where the flying sparks hadn't reached yet.

The fire could only take half the credit for the damage because truly, the best helper was the relentless wind. It lifted, carried, and dropped firebombs as far as the eastern clover field. My stomach lurched—it was all happening because of my stupidity. I turned away, pressed my forehead into the oversized truck tire, and pushed against the hard rubber spikes until I felt the pain I deserved. When my head was throbbing, I turned back to the reality before me. Cars of spectators lined up alongside the road, swallowed up by the sea of smoke. I recognized some of the faces staring at me.

In the smoke I thought I saw a giant daffodil. A slow-moving, bright yellow shape crept into my line of vision. Out of the gray cloud Mom emerged. She was wearing crayon yellow hot pants with a navy blue patent leather belt cinched around her narrow waist. She stopped in front of me, but my stinging eyes fixed on her strappy blue sandals and her toenails. They were polished bright yellow with blue smiley faces. It was truly the cheeriest thing I ever recalled seeing.

I finally looked up. Her expression was murderous. I thought I would vomit up my heart and leave it to lie blackened at her feet. Without a word she put out her arms for the baby. I could no longer look her in the face. I mustered enough strength to offer up her baby, who naturally began crying with fear and most probably, hunger. She snatched Max from my arms, turned on her heel, and the blue smiley faces disappeared behind the veil of smoke. I looked to the fire chief for help, but the smoke had swallowed him too.

Then the forklift's gas tank exploded. With a roar, a massive green-ringed dome rose up from the barn like a pulsating mushroom. Sparks shot out like roman candles and were carried by the wind over the rooftop and into the apple orchard. Some trees caught fire, but stood bravely as dead grass smoldered around their trunks. When the dry, cut clover began popping with isolated flares, two fire trucks roared to the field to get them under control. I heard a fireman on his walkie-talkie, calling in a helicopter team to dump water from above if they couldn't defeat the fire from the ground.

I stood up, wanting to run to the house and make sure Saddle was safe under the porch, but my legs wouldn't move.

Little by little, the field fires were drenched, preventing them from connecting to one another. One complete acre of clover was annihilated by fire and water. The wind eventually began to subside, which aided the firemen considerably in their efforts. The longer the crew worked, the sicker I felt. They didn't lighten up in the fight until the wet, blackened trees, field, and rooftop were completely out and the remains of the barn were smoldering in a water-soaked heap of charcoal and seared metal.

I stood there dazed in the tail end of the pandemonium until I saw Saddle slinking toward me, low to the ground with his stub tucked between his legs. He was bug-eyed and his ears were pinned back, but he looked unharmed. "Saddle! You're okay! Good boy." I fell to my knees and he licked the tear-streaked soot from my face. Snorting and slurping and swinging his haunches from side to side, he whined, rolled his lips in and grinned up at me. I patted him all over. "Oh, Saddle," I whispered, "We have to find a shovel. I need to dig myself a grave."

Two days passed before Mom approached me. I was sitting outside, petting Saddle and examining the insides of his ears for general interest. For a solid forty-eight hours I had existed in the shadow of impending doom. I worried myself sick, inventing endless forms of persecution. If Mom gave me what I deserved, I figured she would cripple me. I would be wheelchair ridden for the rest of my life, being pushed around with Saddle on my lap. But when she came to me, I could tell by the look on her face that no punishment would suffice except for getting it over with by ending of my life right then and there.

"Come with me," she said.

I stood, looking at the ground, holding my hand between my legs.

I followed her to the gravesite of the barn. She picked up the blackened remains of a plank. Unfortunately for me, I was wearing shorts and a tank top.

I hurt for a week and my humiliation had never run deeper, but the punishment paled in comparison to the talk I got from the fire chief.

After the fire was completely out and miraculously Jerry and Daniel returned to the scene of the crime, the fire chief sat us down and spoke to us about fires. He told us about little kids getting their whole bodies burned and scarred for life. He talked about playing with matches and how animals suffocated in forest fires caused by uncaring people who never learned right from wrong. He told me how fortunate I was that I didn't have the loss of our entire home and all its contents to haunt me. He said that although we were incredibly irresponsible, I fortunately had enough sense to call the fire department and get the baby out of the burning house.

The fire chief was a great man who changed my life with his speech. For one thing, I knew I would never play with matches again. Also I knew, as stupid as I had been, now I was somehow older, wiser— my tears were different from before. I cried from deep remorse and also gratitude that things weren't worse and I was lucky I didn't kill anyone. I was also glad that poor Farmer John didn't keep any other pieces of his valuable machinery by the barn. I really couldn't have lived with myself knowing I had destroyed a hardworking man's livelihood.

"What the hell were you thinking, Ruby Jane?" Tim scowled.

I told him the whole story, the truth about Steve Henry and the boys, the sugar spill, and smoking straw. I hadn't dared say anything to Mom or the fire chief, but I knew Tim would believe me. When I was done, he ran all the way to Steve Henry's house, knocked on his door, and beat the crap out of him right there on his front porch.

One week later I was standing in the kitchen peeling potatoes for dinner. Mom was in the bathroom cutting Angie's hair, the other kids were watching *Gilligan's Island*. I looked out the window and saw a white van pull into the driveway. It said Wassons Delivery and Pick Up. I panicked, assuming it had come to pick me up and take me away to an institution for horrible children.

Dad went outside to talk to the driver of the van, who was holding a clipboard. The driver looked somber and professional. I imagined it must be a sad job to have to transport bad children to dark, ominous places. I watched as Dad signed the paper, surrendering me to my life sentence. I supposed it had been planned ever since the fire but no one wanted to tell me ahead of time. I wondered if Tim knew about this. I wondered how I would ever get to say goodbye to Gramma. As my heart began thudding harder, I heard the Skipper call Gilligan an idiot, and I wanted to run to the couch and hug everyone goodbye.

I began to worry about what I would have to eat in a jail for rotten kids, maybe just porridge, like Oliver in the orphanage. I dropped the potato in the sink and continued to stare at the van. Dad and the man walked around to the back of the van and opened the doors. I supposed I would have to ride in the back, tied to a big metal hook on the van floor. I shifted from foot to foot.

From the back of the van, the Wasson man and Dad pulled out a big, flat box that said "Pink Bonanza" and "Assembly required." *It's my bicycle!* I had completely forgotten about it. They laid the big carton in the yard and the delivery man drove away.

I ran out the front door and jumped up and down. "My bike! My bike!" I squealed. Dad took my hand and we walked back to his shop together to get a box cutter and the tools for assembling my dream come true.

I assisted Dad as he put the bike together piece by piece. I admired the pink and white pedals and the shiny kickstand.

"Crescent wrench, please," he said as he put out his hand.

I carefully handed him the wrench as if we were performing surgery. When I wasn't assisting I was fondling all the pretty pieces of plastic and metal. The banana seat smelled of factory new vinyl and was more fantastic than it had looked in the catalog. Dad was right about the polishing people because that bike glistened brighter than the North Star.

When the bike was complete, Dad steadied it while I got on. The banana seat between my legs made me giggle. I put my bare feet on the bumpy pedals and Dad pushed me gently back to the shop. Even riding slowly, the tassels fluttered from the ends of the bar grips. When we stopped at the shop, I looked up at him. He seemed sad. "What?" I asked.

"Hop off, sweetie," he said. "I have to take the bike."

"What do you mean, you have to take it?"

"Your mother says you need to pay for what you did and you can't have your bike."

"Forever?"

"We'll see."

He took two giant horseshoe-shaped bolts and I stood and watched him bolt my broken dream to the shop wall, right above the workbench. When he was done, he shook the bike to make sure it was securely fastened; I could tell it was going *nowhere*.

"You know what concerns me the most?" he asked, softly.

"What, Daddy?"

"Well, I just hope you aren't going to be too hard on yourself over this whole fire thing. I mean, yes it was wrong and it was a disaster, but the truth is that Farmer John had good insurance and he's going to be able to build a brand new barn and he may even paint it lavender in your honor. See, he's not mad at you and I'm not mad at you. You've taken your punishment quite well and I'm sorry it has to continue, but it's your mother's wish and I respect that."

My face crumpled. "I'm so sorry, Dad, I really am. I didn't mean to do any of it. It all happened so fast and I—I didn't know it would be so horrible. I know I was *so* bad, I'm sorry. I'm really sorry."

I covered my face with my arms, then wiped my nose with the back of my hands.

"Now listen to me," he said.

He knelt down on one knee and gently tilted my chin up. "When you think you did something bad, you really take it seriously, especially because Mom punishes you. But you need to forgive yourself, sweetheart, and move on."

"How am I 'spose to move on when Mom hates me and everybody thinks it's all my fault?"

"She doesn't hate you. And moving on means you leave a bad thing behind. This was just an unfortunate incident, but you'll forget about it one day. Before you know it, you'll be riding your bike down Juniper Road faster than a shooting star."

"You really think so?"

"Absolutely, because you've got resolve."

"What's resolve?" I squinted.

"Remember a long time ago, when you were trying to straighten your teeth, and I told you that you have a spirit that no one can break or take from you?"

"Yeah."

"Well, that *spirit* means you have resolve, a special way to make it through challenging times. That spirit is what you call your Lightbug. It's what will always make things right. It's the ability to have enough faith in yourself," he nodded.

"Does that mean Lightbug will get my bike back?"

"Not only will it get your bike back, it will guide you in the right direction."

I looked up at the bike. It was already getting dust on it. The tassels hung motionless from the handlebars. I glared at the strong metal bolts that held me away from the beautiful thing I had worked so hard for all summer.

"I hope so," I mumbled. "I just feel so bad inside."

"Well, I know you have learned a valuable lesson from this. You are not bad, Eve. You are a good girl. You're my girl and you're special, like I've told you since the day you were born. I love you and don't forget it. Ever. Never." He rested his fingers on my bare foot.

"'Kay," I muttered.

"And you know what else?" he said.

"What?"

"I know what it's like to feel bad and what it's like to lose something you truly care about."

"You do?"

"Of course. We all have things in our lives we love, including people and animals, even music . . . and sometimes they get taken away and it hurts," he sighed.

"Yeah," I sighed too and turned my eyes to the empty banana seat.

"But even when you lose something you love, you have to remember that it will still be with you in your heart forever. Nothing can take away a good memory."

"Nothing?"

"Nothing," he smiled.

"Ted! What are you two doing out there? I want these potatoes peeled!" Mom hollered from the back porch.

"Coming," Dad said loudly.

I looked up at the bicycle for the fifth time in a series of about four thousand. I would continue to view the great wall ornament every day for the next seven and a half months.

"One more thing," said Dad, "I want you to also remember that your kisses are special and you don't go giving them to just any bloke, you understand?" He winked at me and I leapt up and kissed him smack on the lips and he said "Weeeeeeeee! See what I mean? That kiss has impact!"

"Impact," I repeated.

"Utterly astounding impact," he said.

"Utterly astounding," I said, grinning like a hedgehog.

chapter eleven

Leap Year

Summer faded away and autumn filtered in before us, bringing shorter days and a new school year. Like a devoted worshiper, I visited my bike in bondage each morning before we left for school. We four kids walked to school, passing filbert orchards and wide, barren fields.

"Tim, tell me again, why did we have to live in so many houses?" Toby asked, hopping sideways next to us.

"I already told you," Tim said.

"Yeah, 'cuz Mom had salmonella, so we had to find a house where she didn't have salmonella," said Angie.

"Not *salmonella*," said Tim.

"Yahuh, you said so," said Angie.

"I never said she had salmonella. I said we had to keep moving because she had *insomnia*," said Tim.

"What's somnia?" asked Toby.

"It's when you can't sleep," said Tim.

"Yeah," I said, "it's when you're unsettled inside."

When winter arrived, we traipsed down Juniper Road through a world asleep. A wall of icy air hung between the dull-chrome sky and gray earth. Our breath blew out white and fluffy. We ran and jumped and made every effort to keep warm until we got to school each day. What we really longed for was the outdoors to warm up enough so it would snow, but the snow didn't come that winter of my tenth year.

February 29th was a silent, frozen night inside the Juniper Road farmhouse. In the shadows before sunrise something woke me up. Angie was crying softly from her bed on the other side of the room. I blinked to see Mom sitting on the edge of Angie's bed.

Mom pulled back the covers and said, "Go get in bed with Eve."

"Why? What is it?" I asked.

Angie sniffed. "Mom said . . . Dad's gone."

"He's gone? Where'd he go?"

Mom stood, and I could barely see the outline of her face. "To Heaven," she said.

To Heaven? I sat up. "Why?"

"Because God needed him," Mom said.

I couldn't breathe, I couldn't see. I felt Angie climb up and press next to me. Mom was saying that Dad was *dead.*

"I hate God!" I screamed. A geyser of anguish blasted me and threw me back onto the pillow. I melted into the sheets with Angie beside me. I tried to cry but I couldn't get a sound out. Mom walked out and closed the bedroom door. I heard the boys' bedroom door open and Mom say something to them in a muffled voice. Then Tim's low mumble, and a high-pitched cry from Toby, like a scared girl. We lay there and hugged and shook, and shivered, until Angie somehow fell back to sleep. It was the coldest morning I ever remembered. I didn't want to see the light come.

Eventually I got up and put on three sets of clothes. I went downstairs by forcing my legs to bend at each step until I got to the kitchen. With numb hands I tried to make the sandwiches for our lunches until Mom's friend Leta came into the kitchen and told me we weren't going to school that day.

I followed her cautiously into the living room, which was filled with women sitting around, drinking tea. They were talking and dabbing their tears but they were laughing too. Mom sat on the couch in the middle of the women; some of them I knew, some were strangers. They were perfectly polite, apparently there to assist Mom, who sat with a vacant look. Without her careful makeup, her face was white and her eyes were scary. I thought of the words I had heard somewhere: She was visibly shaken to the core.

Did I even have a core? I tapped on my stomach to get a response from my hollow self. I felt boneless, like an empty shell, unable to sense anything except the icy feeling that surrounded me.

I hung back against the wall, trying to gain information and absorb some comfort from anyone who could offer it. Where were Tim and Toby and Max? I thought they had come down the stairs before me, but my mind was too blurry to remember. I looked at Dad's piano and then at his bench, where he wasn't sitting and never would again. A sharp inhalation cut the air from my windpipe. I grabbed my throat and squeezed tightly, trying to breathe again. I listened to the low droning of voices slowly circling the living room.

I peeled my ears for answers and gradually heard what my mind couldn't handle. Dad had committed suicide. My dad killed himself on a day that only comes every four years. He had destroyed all photos of himself, hoping he would not be remembered. *Daddy, how could you?* I listened to Mom tell the story. She spoke softly, her head cocked to one side, her eyes drained of their usual vitality. I promptly rediscovered my heart when I felt it split in half.

I learned that after a fight the night before, Dad went into the bathroom and mixed up a medicine cabinet concoction of rubbing alcohol, hydrogen peroxide, tap water, and a bunch of other things. He put it into a syringe and tied a shoelace around his arm. He injected the deadly serum into his bulging vein. He cracked the glass syringe in half and dropped it behind the bathroom bureau.

He came out of the bathroom and went to his piano to play a song for Mom. She said she did not want him to play, she wanted to finish the argument he had walked away from. She said he started talking as if he had two tongues. His last words were "I love you, but this world is gross." She helped him to their bedroom and he fell back onto the bed. As he took his last breath, his eyes rolled back in his head and white foam came out of his mouth. I bit my tongue until I tasted blood. I bit harder, hoping to taste white foam too.

Mom said that as the ambulance arrived, every dog around the farmlands howled in sorrow, and I could understand because I felt like howling in sorrow myself.

After she finished saying this, I took off running. It was a good thing I had three outfits on because it was beyond freezing outside.

I ran out the door and down Juniper Road, leapt over an irrigation ditch and stumbled through the bumpy field. I ran from the misery of emptiness, searching for the solace of isolation. I didn't stop until I was deep in the frozen woods. I fell back onto the forest floor and crushed my knees to my chest. Following the outline of a dead tree branch, I searched for Dad. He had to be here somewhere.

It just could not be true. He always left but he always came back. I knew he would come back. He had to because he loved me. Besides, if he was going to kill himself he would have told me his plan and I would have talked him out of it and then he would kiss me in gratitude for being his girl.

I looked at the gloomy sky above the trees. Could it be true that God would take away somebody's dad if they didn't behave properly? If I had been better, he never would have done it.

Panic launched me to my feet and out of the woods. I ran until I reached the middle of the white, plowed field. I frantically kicked the frozen dirt clods, but they didn't budge.

I put my hands to the sides of my mouth, tilted my face to the great, drab sky and screamed "DAD!!!!!COME BACK!!!!"

But he didn't answer me.

Five days after Dad was ripped from our world we went to the memorial service. There were a lot of adults milling around our house and I listened to them quarrel about which of Ted's kids should attend the funeral and who should be allowed to see the open casket. In their wisdom they decided that the four oldest kids would attend the service and the viewing. I went with Gramma and Grampa.

The night before the funeral we all met at the funeral parlor. I had never seen a dead person before and didn't know what to expect. Gramma said I didn't have to look if I didn't want to, but I insisted I would be okay and besides, I wanted to see Dad just to . . . just to know I couldn't pretend any more.

The funeral parlor had two open doorways, one where you entered the viewing room and one where you walked out, probably crying. I was the last one in the family line-up as we filed in silently.

A red carpet led the way and bouquets of red gladiolas sat on top of white plastic columns. The small room was dimly lit, the elevated coffin illuminated by a soft yellow light. I looked down at my feet and made an impulsive decision not to look at the display on the stage. I kept my head down, following right on the heels of whoever was in front of me. We stopped momentarily, and then continued toward the exit. I stopped in the doorway, turned around and tiptoed back to the coffin.

At eye level I saw Dad lying there, all the oxygen gone from his cells. His face looked as if it had been painted with a coat of pale porcelain. He had makeup on and his hair was unnaturally puffy. His cheeks had been brushed with rosy powdered rouge and there was a hint of mascara on his long, curly eyelashes. He reminded me of Snow White asleep in her glass casket with hair as black as ebony, lips as red as cherries, and skin as white as snow. His long, slender fingers were intertwined and rested peacefully on his chest. He was wearing a suit and a tie, which I recognized from his high school graduation photo that sat on the piano at Gramma's.

I kissed two fingers on my right hand and hovered them directly above his puffy lips. I wanted to set my goodbye kiss on him, but was blasted by a bolt of something—so instead I ran out of the room.

chapter twelve

Welfare Kids

The funeral was awful. We were in a Catholic church that we had gone to a few times with Gramma, even though Mom hated it. It was suffocating, like they had the furnace all the way up. Angie and I wore matching dresses that Gramma had made us, but I couldn't get comfortable in the church, in the dress, or in my own skin. I knew whoever sat behind me had a close-up view of the monster tangle in the back of my hair. Gramma had tried to pull it out with a hairbrush but it had been matted for so long, it was part of my neck.

I sat scrunched between Angie and Gramma in a row behind Mom, her friend Leta, Tim, and Toby. Mom's shoulders shook like hot kernels of corn were popping inside her. The pews were stuffed with sad people, blowing their noses into hankies and nodding mournfully at the preacher, a ghoulish man, taller than a road sign, who stood at the pulpit speaking about Dad. My dad was a well-respected man, beloved son and husband, devoted father of five, accomplished musician, and above all, a child of God. I stared at the side of Angie's head, my tongue clamped between my teeth. *I hate God.*

As if she felt her cheekbones burning, Angie craned her neck to look at me. Her pretty face was ruddy and her eyes held a pool of pure sorrow. I gently touched her leg. I felt hollow—I knew I had *nothing* to make her feel better. I couldn't bring him back. Where had God taken him anyway? Last night he was lying in the box, pale and polished. *The polishing people. It was the polishing people who scrubbed his skin, painted his face, and shined the box.* But where was the box? Had the polishing people closed the lid? Had they worked overtime buffing and putting a bolt on it, like Pink Beauty?

Mom's popcorn shoulders began shaking harder. Toby dropped his chin and stared at his lap. Tim watched the ghoul guy as if his droning was important. Grampa covered his face with his hands. Leta put her arm around Mom and pressed her lips to Mom's cheek, making them both bob up and down.

I scanned the room for the box. A few faces I recognized . . . Mom's brothers and sister, aunts and uncles we barely knew. There were no cousins, and no other kids being forced to sit through this weird, scary ceremony. My eyes wandered up to the stained glass window, a brilliant dove. Below its blue and green wings, Jesus was speared to a giant golden cross. His thorn-crowned head hung lifeless, dark red blood streaked down his bare chest. The bloody nails through his hands and feet made my stomach turn. *Poor Jesus. I wonder if God did that horrible thing to him. I hate God.*

When I spotted the shining wooden coffin, not far from the dead Jesus, my head began to spin. Through the blur I saw that the lid was closed and covered with red roses and white gladiolas. It *was* the work of the polishing people. I put my head down and watched my own hot tears drip into the pink fabric of my special occasion dress. I scooted closer to Gramma's side for warmth. Although it was stuffy and hot inside the church, an icy breeze drifted into me because I had a hole blown through my heart.

Back at home the stench of decaying flowers made my temples pound. I didn't get why everyone thought sending flowers to a dead person was a good idea. It made me sick. It also seemed senseless to cover the kitchen counter with desserts and casseroles when even I had no appetite. I hated that people I didn't even know looked at me and raised their eyebrows or shook their heads. I heard someone whisper to another, "such a shame, widowed at thirty-three." They were supposed to be sad, these strangers, yet they chatted among themselves, nibbled on cookies, and drank coffee from the china cups that Mom's grandma had given her when she was little. "Don't you ever touch those cups!" Mom had scolded us many times. Now she was letting complete strangers drink out of them. Even with her blotchy makeup, Mom still looked pretty, wearing a black dress with a black fur collar, and black gloves. I wondered if she had on black fingernail polish to match. I wanted to hug her to stop her from crying, but I couldn't get to her through Leta and all the other women. She was ignoring me, but I knew that was because she had more important things to take care of. We had all lost the love of our life.

After the service I knew Mom needed Tim—he was fourteen and the man of the house now. Angie, Max, and Toby needed Mom. And more than anything else I needed to be at Gramma and Grampa's. It was sheer relief when they finally took us away from the wake, leaving Mom shaking in Leta's arms.

Grampa stopped the Ford in his driveway and we all slumped out, swollen-eyed and dazed. I felt Lightbug stir when I looked at the front door. The A-frame would always be my real home. When we walked in and the screen door banged shut, the frozen air was left at the doormat and the warmth of the woodstove embraced us. As always, the woodstove stood crackling in the kitchen with a rocking chair on either side, each with a hand-sewn seat cushion, brown calico for Grampa and blue for Gramma. We often had rocking contests to see who could make their rocker squeak the loudest.

A dark pine dining table nudged one wall and a well-scrubbed farmers table sat in the middle of the room, surrounded by four chairs with red vinyl seats. Those happy, familiar chairs instantly made me feel better. I thought of how we had surrounded that table playing board games, cutting quilt pieces, kneading bread dough, and spilling out the big glass button jar, marveling at buttons from Gramma's childhood. A thousand times, Angie and I had counted and sorted them by shape, size, and color.

The accordion door to the living room was kept closed to keep the kitchen warm, but on the other side Dad's upright piano stood solid with his music book, Bach's *Inventions*, still resting on the music stand. Next to the piano an open staircase led up to Gramma and Grampa's bedroom. Across the hall, the spare room had a bed, a dresser, and a bookshelf with my three Laura Ingalls Wilder books. I had always slept in that room and loved how the springs creaked when I rolled on the bed.

I wanted to open the accordion door just to have another look at Dad's graduation picture on top of the piano. He would be smiling serenely back at me, as if to say, "I'm sorry I left you. You're still my girl. Always remember, you can't forget a good memory." I could just hear him singing "Fly Me to the Moon" and it made me want to blast the moon out of the sky and erase all the stars, just like God had erased Dad. Poof! Gone. *I hate God and I hate the moon. In fact I hate the night. Bad things always happen at night.*

Grampa quietly went off to change his "goin' to town" clothes and headed out to feed the cattle. The kids gathered around the big table while Gramma uncovered a plateful of oatmeal raisin cookies, but I still wasn't hungry—for food. I nestled into Grampa's rocker and motioned Max to sit on my lap. I rocked him while he smacked on a cookie and gently kicked my shins with his mismatched-stocking feet. Poor little guy was only four years old and had no idea what was going on. He had stayed with a neighbor while we went to the funeral.

I pulled my fingertips through his messy hair and flicked a wet, plump raisin off my knee. The wall clock clucked like a tired chicken. Through the kitchen window, clouds rearranged the sky, probably making room in heaven for the new arrivals. In slow motion, dim sunlight moved across the room, playing tag on the downcast faces.

We had all changed somehow. Tim's face was set hard in a pained scowl. His blonde hair hung straight to his shoulders, quivering over his ears as he ground his teeth. His fingers and knuckles were white, pressed together like Dad's were in the coffin.

Toby had acquired a twitch from agonizing day and night for the last week. He and Angie looked more alike than ever with their curly, dark hair, and round, sad features. Angie's red-lined eyes, with lashes as long as nature would allow, showed a hopelessness greater than any eight-year-old deserved and I worried she was so fractured that she might slip away. And Gramma . . . rocking, staring, rubbing her rosary, clinging to the God she believed in, and praying that he would heal her unspeakable wound.

Gramma snapped out of her trance and tried to sound cheery. "How about a game of Yahtzee?" she said to the general gloom in the room. "Or Scrabble?"

"Scrabble," I said.

"Okay," said Tim, "Let's play Scrabble."

"I hate Scrabble," said Angie.

"That's because you can't spell," said Toby.

"Shut up, Toby," said Tim, "You can't spell any better."

I let Max pick out my seven letters and place them on the wooden stand so no one else could see. I arranged them: DDLLFEA. When my turn came I placed the D on the triple word score and spelled DEAD.

"You can't spell that!" Toby cried. Gramma looked up from her rocker and bit her thumb nail.

"Yes, I can," I said, "plus it's triple words. AD, DEAD, and DAD." Toby began to sob.

"Triple word score doesn't mean you make three words, it just means you get more points," Tim said.

"I can't believe you made those words . . . Dad—is—dead," Toby squeaked.

A spiky, icky feeling crawled up my arms. "Angie, your turn," I said.

She glared at me, then at Toby. "I pass."

"So do I," Toby sniffed.

Max smacked me on the shoulder. "What?" he yelled, "Dad is *dead*?"

Gramma began to rock harder, so the only sound was the squeaking of the rocker. I felt hot and nasty, like a rotten pile of manure. Then to make matters worse I began to laugh. There was no way out of my body and no way to take back the trill that escaped my mouth. I knew it was mean, but I couldn't stop it.

"What's so funny?" Tim yelled. I couldn't talk. I covered my mouth and pinched my cheeks, but I couldn't stop snickering. Angie said, "I quit. I hate you." I sucked in the side of my cheek and sawed it raw with my molars, welcoming the taste of blood.

Finally, my nervous laughter lulled to a breathy snort. I picked up my other Scrabble letters. Using the A in DEAD, I spelled FALL, and scooted away from the table. Toby stood up, slammed the Scrabble board shut, and threw it back in the box.

When we came home the following day, I set out looking for Saddle. He must have been so scared with all the strange cars, people coming and going, and none of us kids there to feed him. I found him on the back porch, curled tightly with his nose nuzzled under his hind leg. He looked up at me and tried to smile, but I could tell he was confused and cold.

"Hi, Saddle. Good boy." He stretched out a skinny limb, jumped up, and shook from his ears to his stub, shedding dusty dog hair.

"You're so cold, aren't you?"

He wagged and snorted and grinned at me. I bent down, grabbed his muzzle, and kissed him right on his wet nose holes. He licked his nose, shook his head violently, and sneezed in my face. "Oh, nice job," I said and scrubbed my face with the front of my sweatshirt.

We jumped off the porch and ran to the shed to say hello to Pink Beauty. She looked brave and strong up there, protecting Dad's workbench. I picked up an old feed sack filled with wood scraps from one of Dad's projects, and dumped the sawed-up chunks on the shop floor. Saddle watched intently, smart enough to know I was doing something for him.

I snuck in the back door; no one noticed I had Saddle wrapped in the burlap bag. I crept up the stairs and into our room. Angie was kneeling on the floor, cramming a Barbie foot into a tiny plastic go-go boot. I plopped Saddle on my bed and arranged the sack and quilt into a doggy nest to keep him warm. He turned around three times and settled down. Angie stopped playing with her Fashion Barbie and looked over at me.

"You're gonna get in trouble for that, you know."

"Not if you don't fink on me. Saddle was freezing out there."

"But Mom said he's supposed to stay outside."

"Please don't say anything, Ang. I'm just going to leave him here for awhile. After supper I'll put him back out."

"'Kay, I won't tell." She clicked her tongue and shot me a look that said I owed her one.

"Why are you such a sneak?" she said.

"Better a sneak than a fink."

"Supper!" Toby yelled from the bottom of the stairs.

I wedged Kewook under Saddle's chin and patted him between the ears. "You're a good boy. You can sleep with my doll, because I know you've been lonesome."

Angie rolled her eyes.

"What?" I said.

"Like he's gonna like sleeping with your doll."

"Hey, it's better than your ol' Barbie doll. Those things stink like plastic."

"So what, I like 'em better than those other ones. They have nicer hair, better clothes, and more shoes and purses to play with. Gramma said we're gonna make some more Barbie clothes as soon as she finds the wedding pattern. We're gonna make a bride's gown with a veil and then I'll have Bridal Barbie, which is the best one of all." She had a defiant look on her sweet face, like she was trying to pick a fight. But I saw the hurt in her eyes.

"Hey, that's nice, Ang," I said.

Angie pulled the miniature comb hard through Barbie's silky hair and slid three purses up her arm. "When are you gonna get that rat out of your hair?" she said. I thought about using her Barbie comb but knew it would probably do about as much good as a Yahtzee pencil.

"I don't know and I don't care."

We closed the door behind us, leaving Saddle there, snug as a foot in a sock.

After I washed the dishes I ran back up to check on him. He was still in the same place, but had turned into a hairy monster! He was covered with gnarled black hair and had strands of it coming out his ears. I covered my mouth and gasped. I was afraid to go near him, thinking he had rabies, like Old Yeller.

He stood up on the bed and his black grizzly fur fell around him.

He smiled, baring a mouthful of multi-colored teeth with a shredded piece of leather stuck to his tongue. *Kewook! You ate Kewook.*

I looked over at Fashion Barbie sprawled on the floor, clutching her purses. I could smell her new accessories from across the room. I sat on my bed and picked the strands of horsehair off Saddle and untangled the thread from his teeth. He had completely eaten her face and most of her body. I pawed through the stuffing, half expecting to find Kewook's beating heart. I pulled apart the remains of her poncho and the fringe of her leather moccasins.

I didn't cry. I thought life couldn't be worse right now and nothing would help, especially crying. Saddle jumped off the bed and stood there with a guilty, knitted brow, panting like he was ready to go. I wrapped the slobbery remains in the sack and rolled it into a ball. I squished the wad to my stomach and headed for the outside. Saddle nudged my heels so hard he practically knocked me down the stairs.

In the backyard the air was thin and chilling. Finally the frozen world had begun to thaw. We squished through the mucky lawn to the compost pile, made up of lightly iced leaves and rotten potato peelings. I kicked at a soggy spot until I made a hole deep enough to bury the sack with its sacred contents. I stuffed it down and covered it with earthy mush, then one hard stomp for a dent and another for a good memory. When I was done, Saddle sat on my foot, saliva dripping off his tongue, onto my shoe. I crushed my eyes tightly, but still didn't muster a tear. *No morbid funeral service here. They got to be together in Alaska and now they get to be together in Heaven.*

The next day we were supposed to go back to school. I tried to prepare myself, to get my mind on studying instead of what happened to Dad. Tim went to his junior high, but Toby and Angie refused to go to school. Mom said because Toby, Angie, and Max were more sensitive than Tim and I, they could stay home for an extra week.

Tim and I scuffed down Juniper Road, past a filbert orchard and a cherry grove exploding with the first fruit blossoms of spring.

"We got wheels today, Ruby."

"What do you mean, wheels?"

"Me and Tobe have been helping Steve Henry fix up a Chevy Malibu. So he's gonna teach us how to drive."

"He's not old enough," I said.

"Steve's stepdad got him a fake ID. You know, like a driver's license with his picture on it, but with a different birthday."

"What kind of dad gets their kid a fake ID?" I asked.

"A way cool dad, that's who."

I daydreamed about Dad, lying in the coffin, buried in a giant compost pile. *The frozen lid thaws, and then opens. He flies up to heaven with wispy white wings like an angel, wearing a soft crown of cherry blossoms.* I looked up to the sky, but no Dad. Only papery clouds, floating like crinkled tissue.

"What if you get caught?" I said.

"We won't. And if you nark, you die."

"Understood," I agreed. I knew the rules.

"Here he comes. Right on!" Tim waved his arms at the speeding car.

I hurled myself into the ditch, but Tim dug in his boots and put out his hands, as if he would hold the racing car at arm's length. The Malibu thundered forward and skidded to a stop right in front of Tim's fingertips. Steve Henry beamed behind the wheel, his arm resting on the door like he was Evil Knievel. He revved the engine, spewing black exhaust.

"Hey Henry. Nice work," Tim said.

"Get in, nimrod," Steve said.

Tim opened the passenger door, dulled by Bondo and gray primer. "You comin', Ruby Jane?"

I grabbed a clump of crabgrass and crawled out of the ditch. "No, thank you. I'll walk."

The tires spun, scraping a black semicircle in the gravel as they peeled out. Stinky black fumes and sharp rocks flew over my head and into the ditch. The green Trouble-mobile swerved out of sight. *That Steve Henry is bad news.*

When I got to school I was given a card to bring home to my family, *In Deepest Sympathy*. It had been colored and signed by all the kids in my fifth grade class, my teacher, and even the school principal. It said "Sorry for your loss" and "God bless you," which made me mad at God all over again.

After I read it, my teacher handed me a similar card and asked me to sign my name. It was for the DeCarlo family. Robbie DeCarlo, who was a fourth grader, had died the same week as Dad. They said he died because he had a hole in his heart. I signed my name and drew a big smile and a bug next to it. Then I stole into the girls bathroom and locked myself in a stall for the rest of the afternoon. I sat on the lid of the toilet seat with my hands over my chest. I was afraid I was the next to be taken by God because of the hole in my heart.

In the days that followed we became the Welfare Kids. The Oregon State Welfare System was as dire and bleak as the state's January weather forecast.

Being a Welfare Kid provided us with some noteworthy benefits and one of them was the privilege of hot lunches. We had never bought hot lunches at school because we always made our own lunch and Mom said that spending money on school-made food was assinine.

When a kid purchased a hot-lunch ticket at school, it was a small tan colored stub that came off a big roll, like a ride ticket at the State Fair. But when a Welfare Kid got a ticket, it was fluorescent orange and the size of a dollar bill. It had to be hole-punched with a special device that was kept in the ticket drawer and made a loud popping sound. It was so embarrassing to dig out my ticket, holding up the lunch line while the ticket monitor took forever to find the ticket punch. Everyone stood there and stared at me like I had a huge sign hanging above my head that said "Hi! I'm on Welfare!"

On Thursdays, Mom went and stood in her own line at the Welfare Food Distribution Complex. She came home with two plain, corrugated boxes, one for the "perishables" and one for the "other" food substances.

The perishable box never had much in it because anything that would have normally required refrigeration had been miraculously and chemically engineered, resulting in an other food substance of some sort. Even the cheese wasn't classified as a perishable because it resembled a loaf of Velveeta, but they added plastic to make it last longer. *For preservation*, the label said.

All the food came in plain brown boxes with a white label or a black stamp. A box stamped "powdered eggs" replaced fresh eggs. The powdered eggs were a brilliant invention, for all we had to do was add water, and presto! Egg product.

Tim and I secretly made fun of the "monkey meat," which came in a square tin can and mysteriously was not labeled. It had a Spam-like consistency and was covered in an inch thick coating of something between lard and monkey fat. But like a precious gem, the true beauty lay within, because when you cut the monkey meat with the side of a spoon, the shiny little grease pockets were exposed. This globby, pinkish-brown mass was slightly prettier than diseased innards and was our protein staple for many months.

Once every few weeks, Mom would replenish the "bulk can," a sizeable metal canister of bulgur. Next to monkey meat, bulgur was the nutritional source that kept us alive. Bulgur was very versatile, Mom said, because we could have it for breakfast with powdered milk or cold for a snack, or we could eat it for dinner, steamed and slathered in pretend butter. Tim and I made fun of the mealy grain and secretly called it vulgar bulgur. Mom's household mantra was "You're lucky you aren't starving." But I *was* starving. I had an empty stomach and a huge hole where Dad was supposed to be. I wondered what he would have said about powdered eggs and powdered milk and dehydrated potato flakes.

The bread was wrapped in a waxy brown paper package labeled "Bread." It was white, hard, and unleavened. The bread was the one thing I wished would have been powdered.

I fantasized about adding water to a whitish floury mixture, stirring it up, placing it in a gently greased bowl, covering it with a kitchen towel, and setting it in a warm place to rise. After it had risen I imagined the sheer joy of washing my hands, drying them thoroughly, getting up on a stool and carefully raising the cloth from my lovely, precious dough.

I dreamed of the freedom I would feel when I raised my elbow high, made a strong fist, punched that big puff of dough and watched it collapse.

I would stare at the shrunken dough and understand how it felt to be a star on the rise. It had better times to come. It took its hard punch knowing it would turn out all right in the end, and even bring happiness to others. I imagined tenderly lifting it from the bowl and placing it on a lightly floured countertop, where I would dust it gingerly and begin the kneading. I could just hear Gramma sing her praise, "Knead it until you hear the mouse squeak."

Then I thought of how perfect my daydream would be when I shaped the dough into a loaf and placed it in a loaf pan, let it rise again, and popped it into a hot oven of 350 degrees, just like Gramma taught me. When the house was filled with the mouthwatering smell of homemade baking, I would present it to the family— a feast of warm, soft, puffy bread that the butter would nestle into like a slow, melting kiss.

But instead the Welfare bread was hard and the weather was harsh, the days were gloomy and my soul was shaken. I ached for Dad's arms around me and his gentle voice telling me I was one of a kind. I spent hours convincing myself he was on another trip and if I just rearranged my bedroom and counted my blessings, he would reappear, swoop me up, take away all the pain and make everything perfect again.

Sometimes I heard sirens in the distance and hoped the ambulance was on its way back, delivering Dad safely. The neighborhood dogs would raise their heads and bay a welcoming howl for his return. Saddle and I would join in, howling a duet sweeter than a love song and Dad would clap and whistle and tell us how talented and special we were.

But as the sirens diminished in the distance, so did my false belief.

My hopes were squelched by the reality that *dead* is final. He was gone. Forever. Never to return. Never to play another song or put me in the Pinochle Theater. Never to open the pickle jar or bounce me on his knee. He would never teach me to play the piano or kiss me goodnight. Never, ever, again.

chapter thirteen

Saddle

Gramma sent Angie and I an Easter card with postage stamps inside so we could write to her. I wrote back straight away, telling her about school and how different it was without Dad around. I told her about Robbie DeCarlo and the hole in his heart. I wanted to tell her that I hated God, but somehow it didn't seem right. Gramma had always said she was *a woman of God*. I wrote her a poem about butterflies and lightning bugs, and sealed it with a kiss.

On my way to the mailbox I snuck into the pantry searching for food. Behind the sparsely filled shelves I found my empty jelly jar. I filled it with a handful of potato flakes, a smattering of powdered milk, and a splash of warm tap water. I screwed on the lid, shook it like a Yahtzee cup, and gulped down the mealy mashed potatoes. The glob stuck to my tonsils then slowly slid down my throat until it hit bottom. It was like patching up a hole with wallpaper paste. It tasted more like wood chips than potatoes, but it beat cold bulgur, which looked like dried earth worms and smelled like river mud.

As I was putting the flag up, Saddle crossed the road to squirt his turf. From a distance, I heard the whining engine of a speeding car. It looked like Steve Henry's green Malibu coming way too fast down Juniper Road.

"Saddle, come!" I yelled.

As Saddle obediently leaped toward me I screamed "Saddle, stop!"

But it was too late.

The massive metal body swallowed him up. The shriek of the brakes matched Saddle's scream as he rolled further under the car. The front tire crushed his leg and pitched him to the rear treads. Flung from

the undercarriage, he kept rolling. He cried and whirled like an eggbeat-
er. He yelped and howled, spun and crunched and cracked right before
me. Blood, slobber, and poop squirted in every direction. His shredded
tongue jutted out the side of his mouth, exposing broken teeth and a
torn lip. His eyebrows were ripped off, dirt and bloody gravel stuck in
the gashes.

I was sick. Each time he shrieked I screamed "NOOOOO!"

The car lurched into the driveway and rocked to a stop. Wild-eyed,
Steve Henry jumped out and lunged toward me. On three legs, Saddle
dragged past me, crooked, crying and trembling like he was escaping an
electric fence. He fell on his side by the porch, trying to lick himself with
his mangled tongue. His hind leg was bent like a pretzel. A thick patch of
dirty blood and pebbles covered his raw belly.

"Oh Saddle," I cried. "Oh my good boy, I'm-I'm so-so-so-sorry."

Yowling, he flopped onto his back, his right hind leg splayed beside him, like it belonged to another animal. Hanging off his bloody belly
were two pieces of his wiener, split and skinned like a raw, sliced sausage.

Tim, Toby, and Mom came running out of the house. Saddle's
cries were deafening. "What happened?" Mom screamed. I looked at her
hopelessly and through my snotty tears, I blubbered, "It was my entire
fault. I took him out to the mailbox and I couldn't stop him . . ." I turned
to Steve Henry for help. He was gone.

"What hit him?" Tim asked.

"A car. A fast-green-car," I said.

Saddle quieted his crying and slithered under the porch. I got
down on my stomach and peered into the black hole under the step, my
elbows stuck in bloody dirt.

"Here, Saddle, come on boy, come on good boy, come on."

In the faint light I got a glimpse of him licking his fractured body.
He flashed me his wet, bug eyes and wagged his tail weakly. "That's a boy,
Saddle, good boy."

Suddenly I saw a shadow pass over me. Mom stood there shaking
her head. She lifted her hand and slapped me on the top of the head.

"Tim, go get the gun and shoot him."

I went hot. "No, Mom, please," I said. I turned away from her and heaved up a milky pile of potato glop.

"You can beg all you want, but it won't change things," she said.

I scrabbled through the dirt, feeling all my organs spasm into a big ugly mess of worthlessness. I was a horrible, despicable, wretched murderer.

I crawled up onto my feet, covered my ears, and took off running.

"Eve Elizabeth! You get back here!" I barely heard Mom through my hands. I ran my route, through the yard and the orchard with no intention of ever stopping. I kept my ears covered while yelling, "Ahhhh-hhhhhhh" so I wouldn't hear the gunshot.

At the river's edge I collapsed. I had not yet uncovered my ears for fear of hearing my best friend's execution; another death because of me. As I stared blankly at the gray, gurgling water, it was clear that I had no way out. Saddle was going to die. Why Saddle? Why Dad and Robbie DeCarlo and Kewook? Why? I seethed with hatred for the unfairness of it all.

I sat by the muddy riverbed until the sun went down. When shadows and hunger jabbed at me, I knew I had to head back before I made matters worse. *I am a killer. I could be a killer if I could get my hands around Steve Henry's neck. What a chicken he is. He ran from the fire and now he thinks he can just take off . . . wait . . . I took off. I have to go back and face it.*

Trudging back to the house I felt Lightbug flutter and buzz inside me. I stopped and spun slowly around in a circle, holding my arms to my stomach. Looking ahead, I started cautiously toward home. I began to pick up the pace as the buzzing turned to an inner trembling that whirled around and spread through me like a flash of warm light. Things were going to be different from now on. Lightbug morphed into *Flash.* Flash was an inner light more intense than I had ever experienced. Flash assured me everything was going to be fine.

I stumbled through the field and picked up more speed through the dark orchard. As I pounded into the yard I slowed—something was different. In the driveway was a big car, a shiny purple Impala. Tim sat on the porch. *Poor Tim, this must have been so hard for him.*

Out of the shadows, Tim said "Hey, Ruby Jane. It's okay." In the mystery light that wasn't day and wasn't night I could see Tim, the rifle propped up next to him, and Saddle's body lying in a blanket. My breath hung in the air around my face. I stepped onto the porch. Tim cleared his throat, put his hand on the blanket and looked up at me with a half-smile.

Saddle was alive! It looked like he was sleeping peacefully. His leg was splinted with a stick and his body wrapped in ripped sheets. His ears twitched when I stepped closer.

"I didn't shoot him," Tim whispered, "and Mom said if I fixed him up, we could keep him for another life. He's been banged up enough to be more like a cat than a dog . . . having nine lives and all."

"I'm so happy, I would wag my tail if I had one!" I said.

I pulled off my mud-caked tennie runners and lay down beside our brave dog. I petted him by his ear, the only place that wasn't wrapped up or oozing.

"Do you think he's in pain?" I whispered.

"Nah. Mom crammed a pain killer down his throat."

"That was nice," I said.

I suddenly liked Mom more than ever before. I wished I could just run in the house and jump into her lap like I did with Gramma. I wished I could kiss her and thank her for her kindness and tell her what a nice mom she was. Then she would smile at me and tell me everything is going to be all right. *Go get the brush and I'll brush that big rat out of your hair*, she'd say and I would skip to the bathroom and come back with her soft brush.

"Yeah," Tim said, "but she said you're gonna get a beatin' for takin' off."

"That's okay," I whispered to Saddle. "I'll just try to be as brave as you are."

I kissed him softly on his nose. "I love you, good boy." I got up slowly. "Thanks, brother."

"You're welcome. Hey, good luck in there. I know it sucks." He shook his head.

I looked out at the purple car in the purple light. "Hey, Tim, what's that car doing here?"

He shrugged. "You'll see."

Then I went in to meet my mother and one of her good friends, the leather belt with the brass buckle. I stood before her and took it all in. Her hair was perfect. She had on thick blue eyeliner. Her nails were painted like Easter eggs. I looked at my own hands. I looked at the belt wrapped tightly around the colored nails. My heart thudded as I envisioned my bony wrists and knuckles split open because I put my hands out to protect myself.

She scratched the belt with a pink-dotted fingernail, opened her mouth, then shut it. I closed my eyes and turned to Flash for help.

It took about six weeks for Saddle to heal completely. He licked his weeny several times a day and it miraculously grew back together so he was able to squirt like he had before.

His leg never was functional again so he kept it tucked up underneath himself like a flamingo. We called him "Three Legs" for the rest of his lives.

chapter fourteen

Nuptials

June morning sunlight poured through the wavy window panes of our bedroom. It cast squares of kaleidoscope color onto Angie's angelic mop of curly brown hair, dappled her bedspread, and fell onto the beat-up wood floor.

I had gotten up early and made my bed, picked up Barbie doll clothes, washed the dishes, and swept the front porch. I also finished my job of wrapping a wooden spoon in a wet rag and scraping the sticky fuzz off the bottoms of the kitchen chair legs. Dressed and ready for school, I stood by Angie's bed watching her doze. She had a tiny, fluffy snore like a baby hamster underground. I couldn't decide if she was prettier asleep or awake, but it didn't take a high voltage brain to know she and Toby got Dad's good looks. Tim and I were definitely out of Mom's mold and Max could go either way.

"Angie, get up. It's the last day of school and we can't be late." She twitched her lips like a dreaming cat, and then squinted up at me standing there in the new day.

"Come on, move it," I said.

"Where's Mom?" she moaned.

"She's still in bed and her bedroom door's shut. Max's asleep and the boys just took off in Steve Henry's car, so come on, get up. I made us breakfast."

She stretched her arms and let out a croak, stuck her thumb up her nose, and dug around until her eyes were officially open. It looked like she suddenly remembered her dream about twin boys she liked in her fourth grade class; she perked right up. Little folded paper triangles surrounded her head and stuck in her hair. She had fallen asleep with love notes under her pillow so she could remember all the swirly words from David and Paul Brown.

"I see you slept with all your love letters again."

"Shut up."

"I didn't mean anything bad by it, just that they seem to be piling up. Pretty soon you're gonna need something bigger to hold them all, like a boot box or a Barbie Camper Case."

She scooped up the notes and slipped them into her pillowcase, safe from burglars and spies and the likes of me. She crawled out of bed to get dressed and I went downstairs to put pretend butter on our toast.

The kitchen smelled sweet and fresh and felt steamy and sticky. Jars of Queen Anne cherries, gold with a red blush, covered the countertop. We had picked cherries for a week and Mom had canned for two days straight. I popped the crispy bread out of the toaster and slathered greasy yellow stuff on both sides. I tore one piece in half, opened the back door, and tossed it to Three Legs, who gulped it down without chewing. He nodded his head up and down as he swallowed, like a duck pushing a dry hunk down its gullet.

"You be a good boy today, Three Legs. When I get home I'm going to work on your special project, all right?" He smiled and snorted and shook his butt.

I went back in the house and wrapped my half of the toast in a napkin and stuck it in my sweater pocket. When Angie came down the stairs, I handed her the other piece. "You ready to hit the road?" As she opened the kitchen door, I grabbed a steak knife from the utensil drawer and stabbed the top of a quart of cherries. *Sssspptt,* the seal broke and sugar juice shot out of the punctured lid.

"You can't do that," Angie said.

"Watch me."

"But Mom says we're not 'spose to eat them yet because they're for special."

"This *is* special. It's the last day of sixth grade. I'm a graduate today and I will celebrate by eating these delicious cherries."

I clutched the dripping jar to my chest and pulled Angie along the hall. Mom's door was still closed. Through Max's door I heard a rhythmic boy's snore. Unlike Angie, Max really let it rip. I didn't have time this morning to bid Pink Beauty goodbye out there in her deserted prison, so I blew Dad's piano a kiss and rushed out the door. When we stepped out into the yard, the grape-colored car caught my eye.

"There's that purple car again. Who's here?" I asked.

"Oh, it's Larry," Angie said, walking away.

"Who's Larry?"

"He's the electrician guy."

"What do we need an electrician for?"

"Mom say's the lamp on the piano needs fixin'."

"Did anyone try changing the light bulb?"

"I don't know. I only know that Larry is a real pro when it comes to electricity. He works at Sears and Mom's real happy she found him to come help her."

I grabbed her sleeve. "Wait, so how come I've never seen him?"

"Well," Angie said, "probably 'cause every time he comes around you're out runnin' around with the dog or stayin' with Gramma and Grampa. Everybody else's seen him. He's nice."

I looked long and hard at the shiny car, trying to imagine a nice electrical guy in the driver's seat. "Come on, I guess I'll meet him later."

When we were out of sight of the house, I stopped, set the cherry jar on the road, and gouged my fingernails under the rim of the lid until it popped off. I took a long chug of the sweet syrup and rolled a mouthful of plump orbs into my cheeks. Angie took the jar, reached in, and pulled out a dripping handful, forgetting we were committing a criminal act. She crammed the cherries in her mouth. Even in a green Salvation Army jumpsuit, she looked so cute. We walked and kicked at the gravel, flat and dull like old nickels. A fat red-breasted robin sang a spring solo from the tip of a filbert branch.

"Listen, Ang—it's a robin."

"So what?"

"Gramma says that's good luck to have a robin sing to you. Do you remember from the bunches game what you call a bunch of robins?" I asked.

"Um, a pack or somethin' like that?"

"A flock. Okay, you ask me one," I said.

"Oh, I know. What's a bunch of cows?"

"A herd. What about a bunch of geese?"

"A killing?" she looked frustrated.

"No. It's a gaggle of geese. You're thinking of a murder of crows."

"Where'd you learn all those bunches again?"

"Our Plurals assignment from Mrs. Davidson."

She rolled her eyes. "I don't wanna play anymore. I hate this stupid game."

As we walked down Juniper Road eating cherries, I had a good feeling about the day.

"This is the last time I'll walk to Hazel Green Elementary," I declared and spit three cherry seeds over my shoulder. "Then it's Whitaker Junior High, here I come."

"I'm glad I get to stay at Hazel Green 'cause that's where David and Paul will be next year too," Angie smiled.

"Who do you like more, David or Paul?"

"Well, I love Paul, but David loves me."

"How do you even tell them apart?"

"Oh I can tell. It's the way they look at me."

"Well, doesn't it make sense you would choose the twin that loves you back?"

"Love doesn't work that way," she said. *The expert.* Angie burped and said, "What're you gonna do with that jar? You're gonna get caught and be in huge trouble, I just know it."

"No way," I said.

I grabbed an armful of feathery Queen Anne's lace from the roadside and stuck it in the sticky jar, a farewell bouquet for my teacher.

In the afternoon there was an assembly in the cafeteria to celebrate our graduating class. I got a pencil with a frog on it and a pink cupcake topped with Red Hots. I felt awkwardly special and a little nervous when the principal gave a speech about moving on to Whitaker Junior High

School. "You are the future of this country, so make us proud." My heart galloped at the thought of such an enormous responsibility. How was I going to make an entire country proud?

When my teacher handed back our biggest report of the year, mine displayed an A plus. I had done a seventy-five page report titled "Canines of the World." Each of the fifteen chapters consisted of five pages of research covering a different breed, complete with illustrations either cut out from a magazine or hand drawn from my imagination.

Of course Three Legs was my inspiration. After his near-fatal accident I changed my topic from the Nation's Deepest Lakes to Dogs.

"You did an exceptional job on this, Eve," my teacher said.

"Oh, thanks."

"I found the last diagram very imaginative. Is this something you have actually constructed?"

"Well, I'm in the process."

"And it looks here as if your *canine wheelchair invention* is motorized?" She arched her eyebrows. Considering all the teachers I ever had, I liked Mrs. Davidson the most and was embarrassed that I had an overwhelming urge to reach up and yank that big hair out of her chin. I averted my eyes and scratched my neck.

"It was actually my brother Toby's idea to put the engine on it. He is going to be a professional automotive specialist. I figured out how to attach the cart with the wheels to the back of my dog. This piece right here is where his messed-up leg will rest." I pointed to the diagram. "My brother's idea is to hook it up to a lawn mower engine, which would give Three Legs enough power to keep up with me when I ride my new bike."

"Fascinating." She stared at the drawing while fingering her whisker.

"There is just one problem," I said.

"Oh, and what might that be?"

"The noise. A lawn mower engine is one of the loudest motors around. Since Three Legs is rather sensitive to roaring sounds, we might not be able to use the engine. He's skittish on the account of a speeding car splitting him in half."

Mrs. Davidson cringed and I got the notion I better just take my report and get out of there.

"Well, good luck with your endeavor," was the last thing she ever said to me.

The final day of sixth grade was the first day of freedom. Angie and I ran all the way home and into the arms of summer. As we approached the house I spotted a cloud of dust and flying gravel going the other direction. It was a big yellow truck rocking from side to side down Juniper Road, busting with a heavy load. Since the truck hadn't passed us, it could only mean it had come from our house. I got a sick feeling that maybe Mom and the new electrician had moved away and left me to take care of the family. I began to panic when I remembered the cherries and hoped Mom didn't realize I jacked a jar. I wondered if she counted the quarts after we left for school. Inside my head I suddenly heard her screeching in my ears. When she screamed it was as if a murder of crows flew out her mouth and cawed and dodged all around the room trying to pull my hair and peck my eyes out.

When we got to the yard the purple Impala sat right where it had been that morning.

"Oh good, Larry's still here," Angie said and ran into the house.

When I walked into the living room my skin rippled with goose bumps. Something was very wrong. I looked to Dad's piano— and it was gone. In its place was a stack of boxes taller than me with labels that read *Cotillion, Brocade, Dazzle, Tawny,* and *Peachy Dream.*

Mom was sitting on the couch with Max at her feet. Angie ran to the boxes. "Look! Mom's Avon stuff came! Mom's gonna be a real Avon lady now!"

"Where's the piano?" I mumbled.

Mom's bedroom door opened and a guy walked out holding a light bulb. I looked blankly at him, then at Mom.

"We sold it," she said. "Larry knew someone who wanted to buy it for fifty dollars. Eve, this is Larry."

"Hi," I croaked.

Larry nodded, but didn't say anything. He looked to be slightly older than Tim, maybe already out of high school. He had thick, dark hair like hot fudge that drooped over his ears, parted way to the side so it covered half of an eyeball. Just like Steve Henry, he cocked his head and threw it back quickly to get the hair out of his face, which immediately fell back over his eye. He seemed jittery, moving his feet but not going anywhere. I wondered if he had to pee. He wore jeans and a blue-collared shirt that had *Sears* stitched on the pocket. The pocket held a plastic insert with pencil-thin tools I didn't recognize, like metal jabbers probably used to electrocute bad guys or hotwire a car. He rolled the light bulb in his hands and looked helplessly at Mom.

I felt like I wanted to go upstairs and change out of my skin. *They sold the piano.* They loaded it into a fat, ugly moving truck and hauled it off to somebody who probably didn't even know how to play it. For fifty dollars they blew the remains of Dad down Juniper Road and beyond, as if a piano dolly and a truck ramp would completely erase all memory of him. Well, it wouldn't and nothing could. Inside my heart and my ears I still heard "Fly Me to the Moon," even louder than shrieking crows. I bit my lips to hold back a tub of tears and headed for my room. As I sulked away I heard Angie ripping open a box. "Look!" she said, "Avon even has *Leg Makeup!*"

Gramma and Grampa came to pick us up that very afternoon. Angie didn't want to go when she found out Gramma still hadn't found the Barbie dress pattern she was hoping for, so she stayed home with Max and Mom and Larry. Tim and Toby were busy painting orange and yellow flames on the sides of Steve Henry's Malibu. Toby said it would take two and a half months to buff out the Bondo, detail the car, and trick out the transmission. He told me Steve Henry wanted to show me what was under his hood when they were done.

From the back seat of Grampa's car I watched rows of strawberries fly by, perfectly even like bristles on a gigantic toothbrush.

"How was school?" Grampa asked as he drummed the steering wheel with his thumbs.

"Oh, good. I'm all done with grade school now. I'm going to Whitaker in the fall. I got good grades and my teacher said I'll probably stay at the top of my class if I keep reading. I'm so happy we don't have to move anymore and I'm making a little car for Three Legs so he can get around without getting too tired. Mom got a bunch of supplies to be an Avon lady and she's getting that red glass lamp fixed by a professional electrician. His name is Larry and he's fixing the lamp that was on top of the piano except that . . ." My leg started bouncing and my tongue felt like it had turned to moss.

"What, honey?" Gramma turned around from the front seat. "Except what?"

I didn't answer her. "Well, honey, that's wonderful about your grades. I have some more books for you to take home. Mrs. Arnold is trying to get rid of them since her husband passed. He left behind a lot of the classics. You'll enjoy reading them."

"Thanks, Gramma. Mom sold the piano."

Grampa stopped tapping and looked out his window as if the song of joy had just been sucked out of his fingers.

When we got to Gramma's I was even more determined to teach myself to play the piano with the music books that were in the piano bench. All behind Mom's back of course. On the twenty-three mile ride there I schemed up a plan, but it was a secret that only Flash knew. Someday Mom would be walking around the streets of Portland, selling Avon from the back of Larry's car and they would run out of gas right in front of the Pinochle Theatre. The wind would start to blow blue frost so icy it would force her into the beautiful chamber for safety, only to look up on the glittering stage and see *me* (with straight teeth) sitting at Dad's piano playing a haunting minuet in E minor. Beautiful fancy ladies would dab their eyes with silk handkerchiefs and boys in white starched shirts would stand protectively in the aisles ready to assist anyone who was too moved by the music to ever leave the theatre. Mom would listen and watch in utter amazement and when Larry came to check on her she would say to him, "Shhhh."

"It's a shame you couldn't get yourself some lessons," Grampa said.

"You're doin' good, but it's better to have a background in music theory."

"Yeah, I know. There's this lady, Mrs. Frazier, who teaches piano about two miles from Juniper Road. I know because there's a sign in her window that says 'Piano lessons here.'"

"Oh, honey, you should pay her a visit," Gramma said, and bit her thumbnail.

It was almost the Fourth of July before I could get away and walk over to Mrs. Frazier's house, on a warm, clear day, with the fields perfuming the air. I asked her if I could do chores in trade for lessons. She said that since I was almost eleven years old, she did have the perfect job for me to do on Saturdays.

Because I didn't have school until September, I managed to sneak away for eight lessons. Mrs. Frazier was a nice lady with neatly styled white hair and silver-wing-tipped eyeglasses. We sat at her spinet upright piano in a living room that smelled like chicken fried steak and shoe polish. She was gentle on me, with a faraway voice like there was a breezy meadow between us. I had a hard time looking at her eyes because they were wet and milky, the pupils like guppies swimming in a clouded pond. I worried she was nearly blind and wouldn't be able to see if I made a hand position mistake. Her fingers were crooked and knobby and everything curled on her. She had curly arms and bent legs from the wavy bones under her support hose. She picked at her earlobes, which, flipped up as if she had set them in a pin curl with bobby pins. Even the hem on her housecoat curled up.

On top of the piano sat a cut crystal bowl with peppermint and butterscotch hard candies so old they stuck together. I really wanted one, but she never offered.

I fibbed my way around Mrs. Frazier by asking if I could please leave my music book at her house until we got a piano. I added that the music book needed to be safeguarded from all the little kids in my house who might destroy it. I also told her we didn't have a phone, just in case she ever tried to call and blow my cover.

Mrs. Frazier told me I had a gift and natural musical talent, which made it all worthwhile when I had to clean up the mountains of poodle poop from the floor of her two-car garage.

When I went to Gramma and Grampa's I practiced the piano as much as I could. My favorite music books were the yellow books from *Schirmer's Library of Musical Classics*, like *Clementi's Sonatinas* and *Bach's 15 Inventions*. When I wasn't playing piano or cooking something at Gramma's, I explored outside in holes and mounds, looking for creatures of any sort. Down at the creek I hunted crawdads and caught things that hopped and slithered, like mud frogs and baby snakes.

Back at home, life was looking up because Mom seemed to have gotten herself something to occupy her time, other than just fighting for survival and surviving to fight. Larry was twenty-four years old and Mom was thirty-three. He worked at Sears in Salem and Mom had increased her Avon route to go all the way to Chemeka Community College, where she sold tubes of coral lipstick and Skin-so-Soft to the Native American Indian students.

Larry didn't say much, but he seemed nice enough and Mom didn't fight with him, at least not in front of us. Tim thought it would be insane for a guy that age to take on Mom and her five-pack of banshees, but the day I saw Larry out back with a can of WD 40 was when I knew he was the perfect guy for us.

Three Legs and I were on the back porch working on the Dog Runner, as Tim called it. I had vetoed the engine idea. Two wheelbarrow tires, a coffee can and an old cow collar attached to a wooden apple box. It scared Three Legs to look at it and I began to believe he would travel faster on his own. He was doing an amazing job running pain free and he could even leap in the air, propelled by one back leg.

When I noticed Larry, he was standing in the backyard, next to Pink Beauty with a lug wrench slipped through his belt loop. He had broken my bike out of her death sentence! I froze. Three Legs started springing up in front of me like a circus dog. Larry carefully removed the spray tube from the side of the WD 40 can, inserted it and began spraying the bike chain. He sprayed the pedals and checked the brakes while I stood petrified and praying to Flash that he wasn't preparing it to sell for fifty dollars.

"Um?" I said. Without a word he lubed the kickstand and wiped the excess drips with a shop rag. Three Legs and I stepped closer. I didn't look up at Larry because I was ready to burst into tears with my bike on the ground, so close to me, a step away from being mine again.

Larry held the handlebar and knocked the kickstand with his boot. I reached out for the banana seat with both hands. He let go and I stood there supporting the shining Trail Blazer. Bending over, I laid my nose on the grip, and took a long sniff of the factory-made vinyl. Then, with my cheek pressed to the brightly colored daisies, I wrapped my arms around the entire frame. I was lost in the moment when Three Legs let out a happy yowl. He was so excited he squirted on the tire. I looked up and Larry was gone. I walked Pink Beauty to the front yard and to the driveway. I mounted her and took off down Juniper Road.

Once we got up speed, my hair whipped behind me and the lavender tassels blew up and tickled my elbows, a sensation greater than I had imagined all those months. Three Legs ran alongside me without the help of the Dog Runner. The weeds on the side of the road danced with my reeling heart. I put my feet up on the handlebars and screamed, then burst out laughing when my ears filled with tears, because I knew Dad was watching from some glorious place. Flash reared and soared and almost exploded. *See kid, I told you it was all gonna be just fine.*

That was one of the best summers of my life. We were still on Welfare but I didn't mind so much. I was grateful for all I had. I played the piano, rode my bike with Three Legs beside me, ate canned cherries without sneaking, and picked berries and beans. But best of all, we didn't have to move to a different house and Mom didn't get mad at me for almost six weeks straight.

School was about to start and I was anxiously awaiting seventh grade at Whitaker.

It was a Saturday in September when we kids were outside shucking corn that a neighbor had dropped off for us. It was well past corn season, so I suspected the corn was mealy, but I was appreciative it wasn't powdered.

"You ask her," I said.

"No, you ask her," said Tim

"No, YOU ask her," I said.

We were all curious as to whether or not Larry was Mom's boyfriend and if he was, were they going to kiss and if they were going to kiss, would that mean they were going to get married. Tim still didn't think it was possible but I thought maybe Larry saw Mom as an angel of light or a movie star or a Bridal Barbie. She was pretty after all— when the crows weren't flying around her head.

I argued that if you kissed someone, you should probably marry him, but no one else seemed to agree with my view on romance.

Angie piped up, "I've kissed a hundred boys and I wouldn't marry any of 'em." Toby rolled his eyes.

"You ask her, Ruby Jane," Tim demanded.

Tim thought that in order to get these questions answered, someone had to ask Mom directly and *that* someone was going to be me. I inhaled deeply and brushed the corn silk off my lap, and set out to do my duty.

Mom was in the bathroom standing in front of the mirror, picking at the tease job on her head with the pointy handle of a rat-tailed comb. This was an indicator that my chances for success were greater because Mom was happier when her hair was fixed up. Her hair was teased high into a beehive. She wore garage sale chandelier earrings and her mouth glistened with pastel pink lipstick. She was what Gramma called "singing in the key of G," which meant she was glowing and something good was about to happen. "Mom," I blurted out, which caused her to jump and drop her comb.

"You scared the crap out of me!" she said.

"Sorry," I mumbled, staring at the floor like a moron.

I bent down, picked up her comb and quickly offered it to her. She snatched the comb out of my hand. "You want something?" she said.

"Nah, I was just going to ask you a question, but it can wait." I walked away.

My loyalty to Tim overrode my fear, so I stopped, turned around, and rushed back to the bathroom, making my feet slap loudly on the linoleum.

"Mom," I said, "are you going to marry Larry?"

She held her gaze on her glamorized reflection and said, "We're already married."

I ran to the backyard and yelled, "Mom and Larry are already married!"

"You liar," Toby and Angie yelled.

"It's true. She said so herself."

Toby's eyebrows rose like baby caterpillars over his wide blue eyes.

"Well," he said, "this guy is either really stupid or really nice to be taking on a woman with five kids. If they're married then that means we should call him Dad."

"I'm not calling him Dad," said Tim. "He's young enough to be our brother."

We all put our fists together and made a pact that we would try our best to be Larry's children, except for Tim. He said he was just plain pissed off about the whole thing.

"What kind of a mother would go off and get married without even telling her own kids?" Tim fumed.

"Our mother," I said.

chapter fifteen

Homesteading

Four days before seventh grade, Three Legs, Pink Beauty, and I were racing down Juniper Road faster than a swarm of mud swallows. I pedaled barefoot and reckless, gravel flinging up, stinging my legs and pinging off the spokes. We were smiling, me and Three Legs. Warm wind whistled through the spaces in my front teeth. Three Legs bounded beside me, ears pinned back, tongue flapping out the side, and white froth flying over his nose and onto his chest.

With summer tumbling right into autumn, the familiar smell of fresh-cut hay filled the hot air—without the smoke of a burning barn. I felt as light and bright as a morning glory gracing her delicate vine. As always, Flash had been right. All my disasters were far behind me, as if they had been gobbled up and dissolved in the belly of a goat. Something about learning to play the piano and starting junior high rumbled inside me, a feeling that tickled and pinched at the same time.

As we flew toward the house, I heard a scraping sound by my feet as if the bicycle chain was slipping. When the grinding got louder I realized it was Three Legs growling deep in his throat. In the driveway sat Steve Henry in his Chevy Malibu, smirking and smoking like James Dean. He slid his mirrored sunglasses down his nose, looked straight at me, and revved the engine. The car backfired, causing Three Legs to arch and fall on his belly. He covered his ears with his front paws, yelped, then tore for cover under the porch. Tim and Toby ran out the front door.

"Hey, Henry, what's up?" said Tim.

"Hey, what's up, longhairs? I came to give ya that jump ya asked for. I got jumper cables right here."

I stood straddled over the banana seat, watching them.

Toby said, "Eve, come and check out the detail job we did on this car."

" 'Kay," I said.

Squeezing the handlebars tightly, I baby-stepped closer. Steve Henry got out slowly, dropped his cigarette butt and ground it out with his Beatle boot. When he tossed his shades onto the front seat, they clinked against an empty beer can. He looked at me again, put his hands up like parentheses, then ran his fingers through his long hair. After a flip of his head he said, "Hey, where's Bridle, your dog?"

"His name's not Bridle. His name *was* Saddle, but now it's Three Legs," I said.

"Yeah, Henry, thanks to you," Toby drawled. "You dumb shit."

Steve Henry walked around to the front of the Malibu and lifted the hood, cool and deliberately like he was taking off his shirt. The three boys hovered over the motor under gobs of lank hair. I parked Pink Beauty and walked over to get a closer look.

Hot air rose up from the engine as it purred in neutral. Toby explained the belts had all been replaced, as well as the sparkplugs and gaskets. The muffler had been designed for the full hotrod effect, complete with a killer backfire. He proudly pointed out the gleaming grille, the spotless transmission, and explained the difference between an eight cylinder and a one-horsepower—like my bicycle.

"This V8 baby has enough force to jump a canyon," Steve grinned. I noticed his teeth, straight and white with thread-sized gaps in between, like a nylon zipper.

"Yeah, well don't try it, numb nuts," said Tim. He walked over to Dad's old green station wagon, which had been ignored since the purple Impala had arrived months before. Dad's faded car had sat in the driveway like a burnt-out freezer thrown in the dump. A riff of *Dad sad* breezed through me, a forlorn feeling set off by things that reminded me he was permanently gone. The feelings were getting less frequent, like Gramma had said they would. She said *the pain will lessen, but the memory will never fade.* So many of his things had gradually disappeared—tools, the piano, his comb. At least we still had his car. Toby was going to fix it up, but Mom said he had to do it at Grampa's, not in our driveway.

Tim opened the squeaky door and snapped the hood release. The hood popped up and he lifted it, heavy and creaking, until it stuck open like a huge, dirty mouth. He secured the rusty hood rod, brushed a nest of cobwebs off the battery with a pocket knife and wiped it on his jeans.

"Looks like the cables will reach," he said.

I watched the boys hook up the jumper cables, as if they had done it a hundred times. Toby got in the driver's seat of the station wagon and Steve Henry in the Malibu. It looked like a car club in the driveway with Larry's souped-up Impala and the gleaming Malibu with fluorescent flames painted on the sides. I wondered if those flames reminded Steve Henry of the barn fire. Maybe that's why he painted them, because he really wasn't as heartless as he appeared and although he never mentioned it, he really was terribly sorry. Maybe I should have given him a little brown and white stuffed doggie to hang from his rearview mirror instead of those silly dice he had, that swung even when the car wasn't moving. Between driving around covered in flames and a swinging beagle in front of his face he would have to admit he did some serious damage and owed me an apology.

Steve Henry revved the Malibu three times and Toby made the station wagon start. He kept his foot on the gas pedal to charge up the old battery. Steve Henry got out of the car and lit another Camel. He pulled the clamp off the battery and turned his head to wink at me. I got nervous, lost behind rings of thin smoke that spelled "oooo." I looked at the battery then at his black-lined fingernails, his gnarly scar, and strong forearms. I didn't want to stand so close to him or stare, but my face was stuck and my eyelids were forced open like they were pinned to my eyebrows. My eyes traveled up his arm, stumbling over wispy brown hairs, up to rippled muscles that sparkled with sweat. I stared at the solid shoulders that popped out from under a ragged orange T-shirt, one I was sure he had ripped the sleeves off with his bare teeth.

Behind a screen of smoke and hair he whispered, "When you start junior high, I'll give ya a ride to school."

I felt all fuzzy and dumb.

"And," he straightened up and smacked his lips, "I'm gonna put this baby in the Salem Speedway. If you play your cards right, you can sit next to me when I race. Your brothers say you like cars and you like to go fast." He stared at me, tapping a ragged fingernail on the radiator cap.

Off the rumbling engine came a hot breeze that rose up under the hood, fanning the smell of stale beer and the musty animal scent of Steve Henry's armpit into my nose. My face heated up and my bare toes lifted off the dirt as if my blood cells had filled with air bubbles. I had never smelled a boy like that before.

Suddenly the front door of the house flew open and Mom stood on the porch holding a broken high-heeled shoe. Her hair was jet black, set in pink curlers the size of hairspray cans. Her face was smeared with white cold cream. I braced myself when I saw her mouth fly open.

"Hey, Leonard Steven or Henry Grimes or whatever the *hell* your name is—you better put that cigarette out or your ass is grass!" Mom hated cigarettes.

Steve grinned slowly, his teeth clenching the wet end of the smoldering Camel. Tim and Toby looked at each other, then at Mom. She screamed, "You can stay the hell off this property unless you're cruisin' for a bruisin'! And Eve Elizabeth, you get your boney ass away from there and quit pesterin' your brothers and hangin' around out there. Get in here and pack it up!"

She slammed the door. I grabbed Pink Beauty and beat it to the backyard.

Sneaking in the back door I smelled warm dust rising up from the floorboards. I sneezed and ran up the stairs to our room. I shut the bedroom door and leaned against it, clutching my chest. I wanted to tell Angie about how I got the boy smell in my nose because she understood boys who weren't brothers, and I obviously didn't. She was born with that quality, like other people were born with cousins or freckles. What was dizzyingly disgusting was this: As rank as Steve Henry smelled, I think I liked it.

Angie was stuffing her pillowcase with Barbie clothes, socks, love notes, and her beloved soft spot.

"What are you doing?" I asked.

"What's it look like? I'm packin'. Mom says we're all goin' on a trip and you're 'spose to pack everything into your pillowcase but you can't bring your pillow because we don't have enough room for all of us, plus the pillows."

I heard the Malibu peel out and blast down Juniper Road. When it backfired, I secretly took it as my own personal goodbye from Steve Henry. *Flash, he's going to give us a ride to school . . .*

"Where are we going?" I asked.

"I don't know." She picked her nose and batted her lovely, long lashes.

"What about school?" I said. "How long are we going to be gone? Whitaker starts in four days. Are we even going to get any school clothes?" I started pacing.

"Shut up and quit askin' me everything."

She slung the case over her shoulder and opened the bedroom door. I grabbed my pillow, shoved it down and added a nightgown, a pair of jeans and a book, and followed Angie down the stairs and outside. Mom was bent over, getting behind the wheel of the station wagon with Max and Tim beside her. The cold cream was gone, replaced by sparkling turquoise eye shadow, pink blush, and pearl lipstick. Her hair was black and perky and fell over her shoulders in four huge ringlets. She was wearing lavender hot pants with a strapless top to match and white plastic, loopy earrings. We stood there watching her wriggle into place. Her earrings swished back and forth as the engine rattled and the car shook.

"What stinks in here?" she scowled. Tim shrugged.

"The rest of you ride with Larry," she shouted out the window.

We squished into the grapemobile and backed out of the driveway. Mom led the way and we followed behind. Larry was silent and I was hungry.

As we drove through the countryside I knew we were headed to Gramma and Grampa's. I began to salivate just thinking about what

Gramma would have for us to eat. My cravings took over . . . a hulking roast beef, mounds of mashed potatoes with rich, dark gravy. (Whoever got the bay leaf in their gravy had to help wash the dishes. I would fish it out first so I could do the dishes with Gramma after supper.) There would be creamed corn, coleslaw dusted with paprika, and golden fried chicken for Toby, who couldn't chew meat so well. Gramma would open a can of pork 'n' beans so Angie could chew the little gooey clump of fat. I would eat three servings of everything without Mom seeing me. We would finish off with freshly baked blackberry pie with a flaky, fluted crust sprinkled with sugar. Grampa would blow on and sip strong black coffee and I would wash everything down with a giant glass of milk and cold well water right from the kitchen tap.

When we got to the ranch, Mom parked the car. We pulled in behind her.

"Stay put," she yelled and walked to the front door. Gramma came out on the porch wearing a gingham apron over her housecoat. From the back seat I could see Mom explaining with her elegant hands and long pink fingernails. Larry must have fixed the heel on her shoe because she shifted easily from hip to hip on the hot pink spikes. Gramma stood looking concerned, frowning, nodding, and biting her thumbnail.

Mom came to the car, opened the backdoor and said, "Eve, get out. Bring your bag." I looked at Angie and, true to form, she stuck her tongue out at me.

I jumped out and ran to Gramma. I fell into her big, soft bosom and wrapped my arms around her sides. She smelled like Chantilly powder and oatmeal. With one eye I saw Mom walk away in a flash of lavender, legs, and bouncing black ringlets.

"Want a cookie?" Gramma said.

"Yeah!"

Gramma and I went into the kitchen where she offered up a plate of warm oatmeal raisin cookies and a mug of milk. The house smelled like Sunday dinner and was cool compared to the hot September air outside. We took our places in the rocking chairs. I smacked down the cookie, bounced my legs, and yakked all at the same time.

"How are you, Honey Girl?" She rocked back and forth slow and evenly like she was listening to a song. Her thick, silvery hair was brushed nicely, as if she was expecting company, although I don't think she knew we were coming. She smiled at me with her whole face. I was wound up and whenever I got Gramma alone I couldn't shut up because I knew she was genuinely interested in what I had to say.

"I'm great. I'm so excited about school, it's only four days away, well actually now it's closer to three if you don't count the rest of today. Angie says we're going on a road trip, but we're bringing Dad's car here first so Toby can fix it up and trick it out. You should see what he did to Steve Henry's Chevy Malibu." Gramma shook her head slowly at the mention of Steve Henry's name. She had never met him, but after the fire incident she referred to him as *that kid*. "He put a sawed-off muffler on it which looks cool, but it's really loud. It scared Three Legs to death. Well he didn't actually die, he just ran and hid under the house. He recognizes that car even though it's painted differently now. It has bright orange flames like they put on the cars in the drag races."

"Oh my, that sounds pretty fancy." She continued rocking slowly.

"We followed behind Mom in Larry's purple car. I call it the grapemobile, but he doesn't know it. He's a nice guy although he doesn't talk at all." Gramma laughed and it sounded like music. "It's like Mom talks for him and he understands and agrees with everything she says, even when she's yelling but I don't mind, he gave me my bike back."

Gramma got up to put the tea kettle on.

"Excuse me, Gramma, I'm gonna go see what everybody's doing out there."

I opened the front door and looked at the driveway. The Impala was gone. Dad's Chevy sat empty, parked up under a fir tree. The whole family had driven away. My beat-up pillowcase leaned against the porch screen. I picked it up and went inside.

"Where did they go? I asked.

"To Washington state" said Gramma, sadly.

"Why Washington?" I whispered.

"Your mom says it's time to move on. She said they're homesteading."

"What? We're moving *again*?" Gramma's head moved in a slow circle, telling me yes and no at the same time.

"How long have you known about this, Gramma?"

"Honey, this is news to me too. Your mother just now told me. Just then . . . only a minute ago. Right out there. Right there on the porch. Then she left. I didn't even have time to say anything, honey."

My guts began to bubble like molten lava. I could see Gramma's mouth move, but I couldn't hear. On top of the stove I watched the red glow of the electric burner, the tea kettle releasing silent, hot steam. I clutched my pillowcase and squeezed my eyes closed. I saw Mrs. Davidson holding my canine report and Mrs. Frazier handing me two peppermint candies stuck together. I was running down Juniper Road in glaring, warm silence. The rocks under my bare feet were sharp and hot from the sun. I saw Three Legs eating corn on the cob by Dad's casket, and Robbie DeCarlo riding a bike with straw sticking out of the hole in his heart. The filbert orchard was in bloom, light and white under an indigo sky that turned black with crows. The silence dissipated with millions of crows screeching and ripping the baby buds off the trees, circling and diving, their mustard-yellow eyes glinting. When I heard Angie laugh and Steve Henry's Malibu backfire, my eyes shot open. Gramma was hugging me.

She knelt down and looked into my eyes. We were both crying. She took a folded white hankie out of her pocket and dabbed my face first, then hers.

"Are they ever coming back for me?"

"Oh yes, honey, they're just not sure when at this point. Homesteading means finding a new place to live and getting set up."

"Oh, yeah, we've homesteaded lots of times," I said.

"Yes, I know you have. Anyway, you get to stay with us until they come back."

"You really didn't know about it?" I asked.

Gramma's eyes watered up again. "No, honey. It's a surprise and a shock to me too. Pop is gonna be beside himself."

I hugged Gramma too hard. "I love you, Gramma."

She handed me her hankie. Gradually my rolling intestines slowed to a swish and my stomach groaned, starved for something I could tear apart with my hands and cram down my throat until my belly bloated.

"I love you too, Honey Girl. You know, I remember it like it was yesterday when they brought you here to stay the first time. Your poor dad was so upset. He said he was worried you wouldn't make it. Gosh, you weren't even five weeks old. They took the boys and headed down to California. Can you imagine that? Leaving you here with us like that. Well, of course I was happy as pie to have you but scared half to death at the same time. You were such a measly little thing. You wouldn't eat. I took you to see Dr. Konofsky there in Canby and he thought you were the cutest little thing. He had me feed you sugar teats. I'll never forget when he said—he shook his finger at me—and he said, *Remember now, Mrs. Chanteau, you can't keep her forever.*"

Gramma dabbed her eyes with the corner of her apron and shook her head. I had heard that story many times and never got tired of it. It made me feel like I really did belong somewhere, with someone, like there was a certain plan for every baby ever brought into the world.

I blew my nose. My ears were ringing, but I got up, took the pillowcase, and tucked it under the rocking chair. "Gramma, can we bake some bread?"

"You bet we can."

"Can we have mashed potatoes for supper?"

"Sure can. I have a nice roast in the oven. Pop should be back from feeding soon. He'll have a real nice surprise for you."

"What?"

"You'll see."

I went upstairs to put my pillowcase in the room I loved, and came down to the bathroom to wash up. The mirror on the bathroom door was full length and I always stood in front of it, amazed how much *me* I could see. I stood there in cut-offs, scrawny and smiling with bare feet, white powdery knees, skinny ankles, and hairy legs. I had a solid rat at the nape of my neck and chapped lips. This is what Steve Henry saw this morning with one exception: my cheeks were now streaked with pink, freckled lines from tears sliding through a layer of road dust. As I tried to wash off the memory of the morning I began to fret over Pink Beauty and Three Legs. What was going to happen to us?

I knew it. I knew all along deep in my heart that I would be dumped, but I always figured it would be in a dark cave or maybe a roadside ditch or a deep canyon that would take several weeks to crawl out of. Mom had told me many times that she didn't choose me—that I chose her to be my mother and someday I would understand why. So I was lucky. She left me at one of the greatest places on earth—here with Gramma and Grampa.

The screen door slammed and I heard Grampa taking off his boots and talking to somebody. I splashed cold water on my face, scrubbed it with a hand towel, and ran out to see him.

"Hi, Grampa!"

"Well, hi there, Eve. Howzit goin'?"

The whole world brightened like someone had just turned the lights up when two little hairy dogs jumped up on my legs.

"Who's this?" I squealed. I fell down on the ground and let them lick my face and gnaw on my fingers. They bit into my hair and started shaking their heads, trying to yank it out of my head.

Over the puppy growls I heard Grampa say, "This here's Buddy and Choppy. Someone left them at the stock sale two weeks ago. I found 'em in a burlap sack rolling around under my truck so I brought 'em home. They're good little ranch hands, real good with the cattle . . .so far."

"Oh, they're so cute! Why would someone put them in a sack? Mmm, their breath smells like cherry popsicles. They look like a mix of Collie and German Shepherd. I bet they're gonna get huge, look at the size of their paws!"

Grampa whistled through the slant in his teeth and went inside the house. I stayed on the lawn and wrestled with the pups. We gurgled and rolled around and chewed on each other until I was green with grass stains and covered with slobber.

I was on my back with a pup in each arm, looking up at the clean, blue sky when I heard Grampa yell. This was a sound you didn't hear unless he was calling a cow. I unwrapped myself and went to the screen door. The exhausted dogs rolled up together and closed their eyes. I opened the door quietly and stepped into the kitchen.

"That damn Gloria, who does she think she is?" Grampa stood at the window with his back to Gramma, gripping his Blue Willow coffee cup. Gramma had apparently explained what she knew of my situation and as she predicted, he wasn't taking it very well. She rocked hard in the chair.

"Oh, Pop, please don't swear." She had tears in her eyes again.

"Gloria still rules the roost. Ted never would have put up with this, taking the whole lot of them five hundred miles away from here. She gets a bug up her butt and off she goes. She's moved those poor kids a hundred times and never for any reason other than she makes up her mind to go and off they go." He slapped the countertop. Gramma dabbed her eyes and looked over and saw me. I stood still and she looked back to Grampa.

"Gloria said they had saved a little money and that the Ouija board told her to homestead to Washington," Gramma said softly.

"The WHAT?"

"The Ouija board. Supposedly it's some kind of fortune-telling thing that spells out the answer to your question. Gloria asked it if they should move far away."

"That's the most ridiculous thing I've ever heard," he growled. I didn't know if it was ridiculous or not, because I didn't even know what a weejee board was.

"I know, Pop, but you know Gloria, she's always got some strange notion and like you say, there's no changing her mind when she decides to do something."

"So why does she just leave Eve here without even calling first or talking about it or anything?" he said.

"I don't know. It's like I told you, they just showed up. She said they didn't have enough room for all of them to ride. They left Ted's car out there and took off." Gramma turned to me as if she was apologizing.

"Ted never had any backbone when it came to that woman," Grampa shook his head. "She gets away with more crap because nobody stands up to her. Wait till she shows her face around here again. I'm fed up and I'm gonna let her know it too." He rinsed out his coffee cup and sloshed the water into the sink. Slamming the cup down, he walked into the living room and turned on the TV.

"Supper'll be in about twenty minutes, Pop," Gramma said. He turned the volume way up. I stood there picking at the tangle in my hair.

Gramma shook her head. She wiped her eyes and tried to look cheery.

"You wanna make Grampa some of your nice biscuits, honey?"

"Sure."

Gramma had taught me to make baking powder biscuits when I was little. It took one cup of flour, a third cup of shortening, a dash of salt, and one teaspoon of baking powder. When Gramma wasn't looking I put in two heaping tablespoons of baking powder so when they came out of the oven, the biscuits were three times their regular size.

When we sat down to supper that evening I could tell Grampa was still mad because he didn't talk and chuckle like normal and he didn't remark on how big the biscuits were. We ate quietly until our plates were empty. I had thirds because I could.

"Well, look who got the bay leaf," Gramma said when she saw it sticking out of my mouth. Grampa shoved his chair back and went into the living room. When he clicked on the TV I hoped Walter Cronkite would make him feel better.

Gramma put the dishes in a pan overflowing with bubbles, and scrubbed hard. "It's a shame he gets himself so worked up over your mother. He always has, you know. From the time Ted first brought her around, Pop thought she was trouble. He claimed she was too pretty to be a good wife. Can you imagine thinking that way? Of course as time went by, I knew he was right."

"How'd you know?" I took a dish and wiped it with a cotton towel.

"Oh, your mother. She's forever mad or jealous about something and she's not afraid to let anyone know it. Your father once said, You name it and it's happened to Gloria and I never really knew what he meant by that. He loved her, we sure knew that, but oh, she has a temper that won't quit."

I fidgeted, knowing I shouldn't listen to these stories, but I always

wanted to hear them. Somehow it made me understand Mom a little better and I got a guilty little thrill knowing she got mad at other people, not
just me. For some reason I felt like laughing, but I bit my lip and kept my
mouth shut so as not to hurt Gramma's feelings. She talked as if these
things happened only a minute ago, she remembered it all. Then we were
sitting at the table again, even though the dishes weren't finished.

Gramma had a funny look on her face, like she was sad but angry
at the same time. "Eve, there's things we always knew about Gloria, but we
kept it to ourselves because we loved your dad, and his life didn't need to
be any harder. But maybe it's time to tell you some things. One time here
when she was pregnant with you, we were having a nice Sunday supper.
I roasted a fat chicken that day and baked boysenberry pie for your dad.
Well, your mother got in such a bad mood she just couldn't shake it and
she would not stop picking on your poor dad. She was saying bad things
about the baby inside her.

"Oh I worried for you, honey, I worried she would do something
crazy to hurt you, but there was nothing I could do about it. This was
toward the beginning of fall, in September. It was September twelfth. I
remember because that would have been the Sunday of my Aunt Nina's
one hundredth birthday, had she still been living. Mind you, she made
it to ninety-nine without ever taking any medication. You were born in
November, so your mom was pretty far along in the pregnancy, but you
wouldn't know it because she was as thin as a string bean.

"Oh, I worried for you. She didn't come close to plumping up
the way she did when she was carrying the boys. Anyway, your mother
jumped up from the table like a monster and headed for your dad with a
fork. Can you imagine? We thought she was going to stab him with that
fork. Tim and Toby saw the whole thing, the poor little dears. Your mom
was screaming and Toby started to cry. When Grampa jumped up to stop
her she cleared this whole table off with her arm. Right here. This table.
Food, plates, glasses of milk all over the floor."

I chewed the bay leaf hard until my mouth burned. I looked at the
floor, imagining all the broken glass and smashed potatoes.

"What did you do after that happened?"

"Pop stormed out first. He took off up the mountain and stayed up there till after dark. He said later he couldn't trust himself when he got that mad. He did the right thing by leaving. Gloria just smiled at the mess like she had accomplished something good. Mind you she still had the fork in her hand. It was frightening, not knowing what was going through her head. Then she set the fork on the table and picked up those boys, one in each arm and kicked the door open. She drove away fast, we could tell, and left me and Ted sitting here speechless. After a long while I finally just cleaned up the whole mess. None of us even had supper that night."

"That's just terrible that you all missed supper. Weren't you starving?"

"Oh, she was ornery, your mother, but maybe she wasn't treated so well by her daddy and she's still mad about it. At least, I suppose so. You know how your dad called me Ma? He once said *Ma, sometimes Gloria is the light at the end of my dark tunnel.*"

"That was nice of him to say, Gramma."

A clear round tear rolled down her cheek. "*But Ma*, he said, *there are other times when I feel like she is the dark tunnel itself. The one I'm trapped in.* It just broke my heart."

She smiled and wiped her eyes with a hankie. "He hated it when I cried. He would say, *Ah, come on, Ma, please don't cry,* and I would get so mad at myself because you know how easy I cry, especially when it comes to you kids and your dad. Oh, honey, I miss him so. He had such a short life. He deserved light, not darkness."

"I miss him too. A lot."

"Well, honey, remember the pain will lessen, but the memory of him will never fade."

"I know. Sometimes I feel so sorry for Mom. I want to hug her or talk to her but I can't even get close to opening my mouth around her. Sometimes she walks by and I duck. Then she slaps me and says, *Why are you flinching? You think you deserve a slap?* And I get so mad because she's completely unfair and there's nothing I can do about it."

"I know, honey. I understand what you're saying and it's *not* fair." She didn't say anything for a minute. I could hear Walter Cronkite telling

Grampa the news, and the kitchen clock ticking, and an owl outside in the dark. I wondered if Grampa was going to bring Buddy and Choppy in. Gramma stood up stiffly, like her back hurt, and started on the dishes again. "But we shouldn't be talking about her behind her back. She is your mother and she has many good qualities."

"Well, you're right about that. Did you know she's a champion Avon lady? She sold a record amount of lipstick to the Indian College girls. I was really proud of her for that." I spit the ground-up bay leaf into my palm and got up to finish clearing the table.

I stayed with Gramma and Grampa for almost four weeks without a word from the family. I was sick about missing school, even though Mom had said that educated people were *retarded.*

I trained Buddy and Choppy to do tricks and the three of us swung on the tree swing. I played the piano every day and fell into a comfortable routine with lots of chores and walks and all the good food I could eat. We went to the little town of Lebanon to buy toiletries at Woolworths and fabric at JC Penney. Grampa sat in the car and people-watched while Gramma and I looked at McCalls, Butterick, and Simplicity sewing patterns.

We went to the Catholic church in Scio every Sunday, and Gramma and I helped the church ladies do good for those less fortunate than ourselves. We gathered on Thursdays when Grampa went to the stock sale.

I got tucked into bed and kissed goodnight every single night, not like at home. Where *was* home anyway? I tried to count all our houses and say the names at night to put myself to sleep. I dreamed of what I thought Washington state would look like, but in my dream I was always cold and wet from raindrops the size of apples, since the two things I knew about Washington was that it rained and there were lots of apple orchards. I wondered if they had a Whitaker Junior High up there. I wondered if Steve Henry had won the race at the Salem Speedway and if he still smelled the same.

For most of every morning Gramma and I worked on a block quilt all in blue fabric. In the evenings I trudged off with the dogs in Gramma's size ten rubber boots and helped Grampa feed the cattle. In addition to the dogs, Grampa also brought home a pair of horses from the Thursday stock sale. There was a smallish red one named Korky, who was sold because he was old, but I figured he couldn't be too old if he could still walk. The other horse was a giant, especially standing next to Korky. She was a Quarter horse that came with a low price tag of forty dollars and a sticker on her saddle that said *Hay there, my name is Pam.* She didn't look like a Pam to me. I pictured a Pam to be more like a hairdresser than a horse, but since that was her given name, we kept it.

On a blustery autumn day, when the wind rustled high in the trees and carried maple leaves the size of Grampa's hands, I decided to ride bareback. I knew Korky was nervous from the wind because his ears were back and he pawed at the ground. I thought a ride before a storm would be plenty fun.

"Seriously, Korky, it will be great. The wind only sounds scary, but it won't hurt you," I said. I lifted his lip and slid my fingers along his slimy teeth. He stuck out his big brown tongue and flared his nostrils, his hot breath covering my face and hands. Just as I was about to snap the bit in his mouth, the purple Impala swung into the driveway. It was Larry and Tim.

The wind stopped. I thought I was hallucinating at first. I had pretty much given up on ever seeing them again. Gramma and I had watched *Oliver* for the third time, and *Anne of Green Gables*, which convinced me that it really was possible to be ditched by your own parents and raised by someone else.

I dropped the bridle, jumped over the fence, and ran to the driveway.

"Hey there," said Brother Tim as he got out of the car. Larry walked toward me with a closed-lip smile.

"Hey!" I shouted. I ran and hugged Tim first, then Larry. It suddenly dawned on me that they hadn't come for *me*. They were probably just coming to get the Chevy or bringing me my bike so I would have something to do for the rest of my life. Maybe they had a little framed picture of all of us together so I could remember that I really did have a family even though I would never see any of them again. Maybe they came to tell me that Washington had flooded and Mom and Angie, Toby and Max were swept away and that it was just going to be the three of us from now on. When Larry looked at me I felt embarrassed and too eager, like an orphan jumping up and down with her hand in the air yelling, "Pick me! Pick me!"

Buddy and Choppy started barking and Gramma and Grampa came out the front door.

"Hey there!" said Tim. "I see ya got some dogs."

"Yeah," Grampa said, "Eve thinks she can train these maniacs to have some manners," he chuckled. Gramma hugged Tim and Larry and invited them in.

We all sat around like strangers since Larry still didn't talk. Tim explained they had driven down Interstate 5 for exactly six hours to get here. They left at five in the morning.

"Yep, it's a long drive, but not bad with a decent rig. Larry's Impala is smooth plus it's got good tunes." He looked so different to me, even though it had only been a month since I had seen him. It was his nose. His nose was bigger and he had a zit on his chin and white fuzz above his top lip.

"Well, Ruby Jane, are you ready to roll?" he said.

"Roll? Roll where?" I said.

"We're takin' you home. Back to Squalicum Lake, Washington," he said.

A lump came up my throat. I looked at Gramma. She said, "Oh Tim, do you have to go right back? Can't you at least stay the night? That's way too much driving to do all in one day. Larry, you must be exhausted. Won't you stay for supper at least? I could get it going right away. Eve can peel potatoes and we could have meatballs and gravy. I have some hamburger and we could make some slaw . . ."

"We gotta go, Gramma. Mom says so," Tim said. "Larry's gotta work in the morning."

"Tomorrow is Saturday," I said.

"Yeah, I know," said Tim. "He works pretty much every day now, with mom. They'll have to tell you all about it."

Gramma bit her thumbnail. "Very well. You go ahead and get your things, Honey Girl. Hurry now. I don't want you traveling so far in the dark." She dabbed her eyes.

I went to the piano and took two of Dad's music books like Gramma had told me to and ran up the stairs to my room. Standing there I felt ripped. I put the books in my pillowcase and put my jeans on. I was excited and confused and scared and mad. But a more pressing problem was I couldn't get my jeans buttoned. I rolled the waistband down and tried to hide it with my shirt. I wondered when I would ever get Gramma's delicious mashed potatoes again.

Standing outside Gramma cried and Grampa talked with Tim and Larry about the hubcaps on the Impala.

"Did you get the music, honey?" Gramma said. Her eyes were puffy.

"Yes, I did, Gramma. I'll take good care of it."

She handed me a paper bag heavy with goodies. "Here, take this along for the road. It's not much, but it'll get you far enough until you can pull over and get something to eat."

"Thank you, Gramma."

"I wish I had some dishes to wash. I always love washing the dishes when you kids leave because it gives me something to do instead of just cry."

"Oh, Gramma, please don't cry. I'll be back—I promise."

"Play the piano every chance you get. Play. And write to us. I put some stamps in that bag too."

"Let's hit it, Ruby!" said Tim, already in the front seat.

I crawled in the back, determined not to cry. Larry backed out slowly. I rolled the window down and blew kisses by the handful. We were half a mile down the road and Gramma and I were still waving to each other.

On the long drive in the cool car, Tim reported that Larry got a bunch of money when someone in his family had died, enough money for our family to buy our first home ever. It was way up at the top of Washington state and we were already moved in. He said Three Legs loved the property and it had ten acres and the boys had fixed up an outbuilding for their own place with a wood-burning stove and everything.

Tim said we would be going to a school called Mount Baker High School and he hoped I would be happy there being so far away from our grandparents. He said that it was his and Larry's idea to come and get me because Mom wanted to leave me in Oregon.

"Forever?" I asked.

"I suppose so," he said.

We cruised all the rest of the day in the purple Impala to get to the top of Washington state and out to Squalicum Lake Road before dark. Squalicum Lake Road was long and winding with only a few little houses tucked back in the fir trees. Tim pointed out the Canadian Rocky Mountain Range, which was a beautiful row of snowcapped peaks. In the east, Mt. Baker reached toward the heavens, surrounded by a snowy Cascade Range.

When we neared the driveway I was happy to see a small, spotted horse grazing in a field. I rolled down the window and yelled "Hi, little horse! How are you today?" Tim rolled his eyes, as if horses didn't talk. He told me that was the neighbor's horse. I stuck my head out the window and felt the air was bigger and bolder being so high up on the map.

A long driveway led from Squalicum Lake Road to our new house. When I saw that it was such an eye-catching shade of green, I decided to name it the Granny Smith Apple House. In front of the house was a field of tall, wild grass. Behind it were miles of evergreens.

As soon as the Impala pulled to a stop, I jumped out and ran to Three Legs, who lay curled up on the front porch. I started to cry and fell down on my knees. He lifted his head and smiled at me. I kissed him on the nose as Tim and Larry stepped around us and pushed the front door open. I saw Mom with curlers in her hair, raking a green shag carpet.

"Hey, we made it," said Tim.

Mom kept raking, leaving straight, even lines in the carpet. Her hair was platinum blonde and set in blue sponge rollers. She was wearing a red and gold Chinese robe with shiny silk slippers. She looked like a rich person in a small room.

"Hi, Mom," I said. "Nice house!"

"That's right," she said, not turning around. "We own this place and we're gonna keep it nice. Your room's upstairs. Go look."

"Okay," I said.

"Your nose is bigger," she said, still raking. Touching my hand to my nose, I wondered just how big it was. I hadn't noticed anything out of the ordinary in Gramma's bathroom mirror.

Tim pulled me by the sleeve and we ran off to find my new bedroom. When he opened a door off the hallway we were in a small room under the stairs. In the corner sat an upright piano with a sheet over it. Tim explained that in the olden days the house had been remodeled. He said the room had been built around the piano, so that in order to remove the piano, the walls had to be knocked out. He said it was an oversight on the builder's part, because if the walls got knocked out, the upstairs would cave in. He added that Mom had it all figured out as to how they were going to get that piano out of there as soon as possible, but in the meantime she would keep a sheet over it.

We climbed up the narrow stairway to the upper bedrooms. Tim explained that the folks would be downstairs, Max would be upstairs in one room and Angie and I in the other. In our room sat two cast iron beds painted hot pink and lime green. A window with six panes looked out to the field of wild grass below. I went over to sit on my bed and welcome myself to a new world. Angie, Toby, and Max came running up the stairs.

"Angie!" I screamed. I threw my arms around her. "Wow, you look so beautiful. Your hair has grown so much."

"You look kinda fat," she said. "Why are your jeans all rolled up like that?'"

"She don't look fat," said Toby. He came over and hugged me tenderly. That was Toby, gentle and sensitive. He looked different too. In just one month he had gotten taller and darker and older. Both he and Tim had hair past their shoulders, but Tim's was straight and blonde like mine and Toby's was dark and curly, like Angie's. I could still pick up Max, so I did. He grunted and smiled at me.

"You're just as cute as a munchkin! I missed you guys so much."

They showed me Max's room, where the biggest thing in it was the window, and then we all tromped down to see the rest of the house.

The Granny Smith Apple House was one-fourth the size of the Juniper Road farmhouse; that's why Tim and Toby slept in another building. Our living room was small and green with gold accents. It held an antique china cabinet and a floral couch I didn't recognize. There was one bathroom with an oval sink, a built-in bathtub, and a toilet with a daffodil-colored seat. Mom and Larry had the nicest bedroom I had ever seen, with a cherry wood dresser and a giant canopy bed. The bedspread and curtains were made of heavy fabric with a pattern of flowers and autumn leaves. Mom had wrapped artificial vines around the bedposts.

The kitchen was apple green, small and confusing with three doors leading outside and two more that were nailed shut. A bright yellow linoleum floor with green speckles clicked when we walked on it. The cupboards had glass doors so you could see the dishes and the peanut butter jar on the shelves.

The best part of the kitchen was the sink, right under a big window that looked out onto all that was lush and wild and green—our very own piece of the great Northwest.

That night we all crowded into the built-in benches around the small kitchen table. Mom had made grilled Velveeta cheese sandwiches and Campbell's Tomato Soup mixed with extra water. For special we had crisp celery sticks and Tang. Even though my entire life and surroundings had changed again, some things were exactly the same. Angie still slurped her drink while twirling her hair around her thumb, Toby ate slowly and I ate fast like someone was going to steal my food. Max pulled the crust off his grilled cheese, Tim dunked his sandwich in his soup and Larry was so quiet you couldn't even hear the celery crunch when he bit into it. Although no one actually said so, I felt like they were glad to have me back in the family. Anyway, I was happy to be home. I tried real hard not to think about what Gramma and Grampa were having for supper.

When it looked like we'd all scarfed down enough to stave off death by starvation, Mom was the first to talk. "We opened a resale shop out at Nugent's Corner, about twelve miles from here."

"Yeah," said Angie, "the shop's got a giant cornucopia over the door."

"What's a cornucopia?" I asked.

Angie rolled her eyes dramatically. "Everybody knows it's a horn of plenty."

I looked at Mom and smiled. "That sounds very original."

"Of course it's original," she said. "Everything I do is original. And creative. I came up with the design and a professional sign maker carved it out of a piece of wood that I found in the dump. It's the size of a garage door." Mom patted her mouth with her paper napkin and spooned more soup for herself. She said with disgust, "People must have shit for brains to throw away a good piece of wood like that."

"Why does it have to be so big?" I asked.

"Don't be a dimwit," Mom frowned. "The bigger the sign the better the business. The Canadians have the big bucks and they're comin' right over the border to buy gobs of our stuff. We can hardly keep the store stocked. As soon as the OPEN sign goes up, that parking lot is swarmin' with cheese heads lookin' for a bargain," she said.

"Cheese heads?" I said.

"Yeah," said Toby. "Around here that's what they call the Canadians. Cheese heads and Hosers. Go on, Mom. You were talkin'."

"The name of my shop is Amalthea's Horn. We have everything from used nylons to Depression glass. I got a book on antiques and soon I'll be able to be an appraiser of furniture and dishes. For something to be a real antique it has to be a hundred years old," she nodded.

"That's interesting. I didn't know that," I said.

"I knew it," said Angie.

"I get most of the things from garage sales. In Washington people have garage sales on Friday, Saturday, *and* Sundays—not like in Oregon where most of those idiots don't appreciate secondhand things and can't even tell their ass from a hole in the ground. I found a Franciscan vase today at a yard sale. The lady wanted fifty cents, but I told her I'd pay a quarter and she took it. Three hours later I sold it in the shop for a hundred and twenty five dollars!"

"Hey, Mom," said Tim, "is it cool if we go to the 'Bummer the Burn Out' pad? We got homework, dog stuff, etcetera." That's what Tim and Toby called the outbuilding they had fixed up to live in—"Bummer the Burn Out"—whatever that was supposed to mean.

"Yeah," said Mom.

"Thanks for the eats."

Toby edged his way out of the booth and hugged Mom. "Thank you for the mighty fine dinner, Mom. And welcome back, Eve. I love you."

I felt embarrassed about crying, but I just got up and hugged him and said, "Thank you, Tobe. I love you guys, too."

They went out one of the doors and we shifted to fill in the spaces. I wrapped my arm around Max and he leaned into my side and snuggled closely. Feeling Max so warm against me, I was ready to fall asleep. Mom continued talking. "I sold enough last week to pay the rent on the shop *and* pay off the van. Larry doesn't even have to do his electrician stuff because he's so busy strippin' furniture for resale. At this rate we're gonna need more space real soon. Isn't that right, Larry?"

He nodded and began scraping a dried noodle off the table with his fingernail.

I wrote to Gramma as often as I could and she wrote back, always sending me stamps, as we weren't allowed to call long distance. I managed to stay out of Mom's way, which I attributed to the fact that she was happy for the first time in my life with her first real home, a growing business, and a new husband.

She and Larry worked every day at Amalthea's Horn. They took us all there so I could see the massive cornucopia sign for myself. The carved horn of plenty had flowers, grapes, boots, and books spilling out among a stack of one hundred dollar bills and an old-fashioned bottle of witch hazel. The longer I stood and stared at it, the more things I found carved into the sign. Mom said she had designed the letters to be bright purple lined in real liquid gold to symbolize wealth. She said from now on she was thinking big and nobody was gonna stop her from getting what she wanted.

They frequently drove over the border and came back with boxes full of stuff they had bought at estate sales and auctions. Sometimes we had to step around the boxes that sat on the porches or in the basement before they could go through them and price everything. Mom said her favorite part was bidding on a container without knowing what was in it. She said she had a gift of being able to get the most valuable items for the least amount of money and she was on her way to getting rich. I knew it had to be true, because it hadn't even been two years earlier that we were eating dehydrated Welfare potatoes.

As life carried on at the Granny Smith Apple House, I continued with all my chores, keeping the place clean, cooking, and going to school. I attended seventh grade at Mt. Baker High, which was a mountain-based school for grades seven through twelve. Tim was a sophomore and Toby was in eighth grade. Angie and Max went to elementary school and rode a separate bus. Tim, Toby, and I caught the bus at the end of the driveway and rode thirty-eight miles to get to school.

The first friend I made at school was Lori Mezo. Lori was from a family of eleven kids and most of them had been home-schooled. Age-wise, Lori sat right in the middle of the clan and her parents were already in their seventies. She had an eighteen-year-old brother named Delbert, who didn't attend school because he was mentally ill. Lori said that Delbert had a harelip, which made him talk funny; People were mean and called him "Retard" and "Spazo."

"Golly, Delbert is just the nicest, most kindest person you could ever meet," said Lori. "He's such a good helper to my ma, but my dad gets pert near crazed and embarrassed over 'im. He gets real mad at Delbert fer takin' off all the time. Sometimes Delbert'll be gone the whole dang day and nobody but nobody can figure out where he's been. Delbert don't even know where he's been. Well, my ma is always sayin' he was doin' somethin' real worthy, like pickin' perty flowers fer 'er or savin' baby birds who fell outa their nest or turnin' over turtles that got stuck on their backs. But not the ol' man, he thinks Delbert is just out stompin' around and freakin' people out 'cause if ya ain't used ta lookin' at 'im, he might scare ya a bit on the count of 'im havin' the deformed face and funny walk and all."

Lori said this all without taking a breath. I guess she had to talk fast if she had ten other kids in her family. When she drew air, I rushed in with a question.

"Where are you from?" I asked.

"Well, we live on a hundred-acre place up there outside Nugent's Corner. My great ol' aunt lef my ma the land when she died. Originally we was set up in Arkanas, where my dad's folks is from. Ma dint care fer it much out there 'cause the ol' man kept Delbert in the cheekin' coop and Ma heard from her ol' aunt that sorta thang jis ain't allowed in the state of Worshinton. We dint none of us go to school in Arkansas 'cause there was jis too many of us to git there ever mornin' so comin' out here is gittin' us a good chance fer education. Ma done taught us all at home fer a long time now."

"Utterly astounding," I said.

"Udder ass what?" she drawled.

I giggled. "Speaking of udders, do you have any animals on your hundred acres?"

"Hell yeah, we got damn near any animal you could think of."

"Do you have a chinchilla?" I asked.

"Yep."

"What about a gorilla?"

"Not yet."

"Do you have stock?"

"Whatzat?"

"Stock. Cattle. Cows."

"Hell yeah. We got everthin' fer eatin', cheekins, goose, ducks, pigs, 'n cows. We got them fur ball nutrints fer skinnin' and a snake pit fer rattlers. They're good eatin' but the ol' man says it's takin' too much 'lectricity to keep 'em warm enough to grow right."

Lori told me that every Sunday her mom cut the head off a live chicken and dressed it for supper. She said supper at their house was really good and I could just imagine it was something to behold, although the thought of eating a rattlesnake made my stomach flip.

As Lori and I got to be better friends, I knew that the chances of ever going to one another's house probably weren't very good. I truly enjoyed her zoo-life stories, but didn't want to tell her too much about myself. I figured if word got out that I had my head dunked in a toilet or caught our place on fire, kids would think I was a weirdo.

Before long, Lori and I became inseparable. Because I started school in the middle of the term, she was my welcome buddy and showed me the ropes of the 'Mount Baker Mountaineers.' I helped her refine her western accent. She said she'd rather talk like a cowboy than a hillbilly. I didn't mind the way she spoke because her smile made up for it and she was as nice as she could be. I just thought maybe she could swear less and she asked me if I would snap her with a rubber band every time she swore.

Angie got a boyfriend straight away at school. Max fumbled along in first grade, glad to be at the same school as Angie. Tim and Toby made friends quickly, but they still talked about a visit from Steve Henry. They insisted Steve Henry was on his way to see me.

"He's coming, Ruby Jane," Tim said. "He wants to apologize in person for the fire and the dog, and show you his new '73 GTO. It's blue."

"Blue's my favorite color," I said.

"Yeah, he knows," said Toby. "He says he wants to see how you're turnin' out."

This information made my heart prance around in circles and I didn't know why. Thoughts of Steve Henry sat on the ledge of my life, teetering like they may stay forever or fall away at any time. I tried my best to forget about him and concentrate on school.

The third of June brought a most beautiful baby girl into our lives. She was Larry and Mom's prize package and they named her Amber. I was enamored of her from the first sight of her perfect little face. As she grew, it was apparent she would turn out to be a raving beauty like Angie and Mom and hopefully be blessed with the gentle disposition of her dad. I hoped she would talk more than he did. Mom didn't fuss much about her, and she was added to the batch as if she had always been there. I loved changing her diapers, feeding her, and packing her around like I was a twelve-year-old mama with my very own blue-eyed baby. I told Lori all about her and wrote to Gramma about how fast she was growing and all the cute things she did, like sit or drool or stick her toes in her ears. Every day when I got home from school I took Amber out to visit the neighbor's horse. I was trying to get her to talk way before she was ready. I tried to teach her to say our names, Tim, Toby, Max, Eve, Angie, Amber, but all she said was "lee."

Steve Henry called Tim from Olympia, Washington, to say he wasn't going to make it to Squalicum Lake because he was in jail for driving under the influence. When I asked Tim what influence Steve Henry was under he said, "Love and alcohol." I couldn't wait to tell Lori how excited and scared I was about Steve Henry. If the day ever came that I got to ride beside Steve Henry in his GTO, painted blue in my honor, I might actually forget how to breathe. Given my history, I decided it best to keep the secret to myself in case things didn't pan out the way I had hoped.

By eighth grade I still liked English the most. Lori and I had math and English together and she struggled terribly. Our English teacher's name was Mrs. Laverne Dupree, which I thought sounded stately, yet romantic. She was small and dainty, wore her blonde hair in a loose knot at the nape of her neck, and spoke kindly to her students. I admired her handwriting, whether it was scrolled delicately on the chalkboard or marked artfully on my term paper with lavender ink. She looked like a woman who wore white, lacey dresses on her days off and called her husband "darling." Lori accused me of being in love with Mrs. Dupree and maybe she was right. I sat in class and daydreamed about being her only child. We would live way out in the country in a small, white house with pale yellow walls inside and a garden gate with a cheery bell that rang when we opened it. We would sit in the cutting garden in white wicker chairs sipping lemonade with mint leaves floating on top. Mrs. Dupree would have a small, soft dog the color of an apricot sleeping on her lap as she read a romance novel. I would pet a gray rabbit named Dutchess, while doing a word-search puzzle out of the book she had given me just for being me.

When Mrs. Dupree asked me to stay after the bell rang, I worried she knew I loved her and I was going to get in trouble for it. She sat at her desk as the classroom quickly emptied out. Lori waited by the door looking perplexed until I gave her the sign to go on without me.

Mrs. Dupree stood up and walked toward me. She was so graceful and calm she could have easily been surrounded by butterflies.

"I've been watching you, Eve," she said with a slow smile.

"Me?"

"Yes. I have observed your writing. You seem to be quite advanced, your descriptions vivid and seemingly beyond your years."

It was the first time I had ever heard something like this, and I was sure it signaled something wrong. "Is that bad?" I asked.

"Oh, no. I am not insinuating you have done anything wrong. I am merely suggesting you enter our annual high school spelling bee. It would be an invaluable experience, and I believe you would do quite well."

"When—when is it?"

"It will be in the spring, so you have a couple months to prepare. I will be happy to give you guidance in regard to the expectations and what you can anticipate from the panel. It has been the policy that participants are at least freshman level to enter, but I could waive that, given the circumstances."

"Do you have to call my parents for permission?"

"No. The spelling bee is during school and in order to attend you will be excused from your regular classes. The majority of the high school students will be in the audience. It is quite a fun and engaging event. They even give a prize to the winners." Her slender arms were crossed over her chest casually. "So, what do you say? Can we count you in?"

Mrs. Dupree's hazel eyes, like jewels, were so penetrating. I blushed and stared down at my beat-up shoes.

"Sure," I said. But, *Yes, Mrs. Lovely Laverne Dupree, anything for you*, is what I meant.

Two months later, on a wet spring day we had the spelling bee in the auditorium. I felt sorry for Lori so I considered letting a ninth grader, Marsha Tidwell, beat me so I wouldn't seem like a showoff. But when Marsha made a screwed up face at me I decided to keep spelling until she was out. After a grueling two hours I got her on the word *sabotage*. I won the first place ribbon and a new spiral notebook with a picture of a kitten on it, but the best part was that Mrs. Laverne Dupree hugged me and told me she was proud of me. She said she hoped I would be in her English class next year.

At recess Lori and I were standing under the eaves, watching the mist swirl. The sky was light gray with soft white lumps, like it might break into a sunny day any minute.

"Here, you can have it," I said, handing her the notebook.

"I ain't takin' it. You won it fair 'n square."

"No, seriously, I'm more of a dog person than a cat person anyway," I said.

"My cousin skinned a cat and ate it once," Lori said as she took the notebook.

"That's gross," I said. "Here, take the ribbon too."

"Now fer sure I ain't takin' the ribbon. Nobody but nobody would believe I won a friggin' spelling bee. That's hilarious." She busted up laughing Lori Mezo style, slapping her thigh and sticking her front teeth way over her bottom lip. She had a snort to go with it, something she had learned from living with so many animals. She finally agreed to keep both the notebook and the ribbon.

When we got home from school that day, the weather had turned. The sky was mottled, dark, and rumbling like it held something that shouldn't happen in the springtime. *Oh no Flash, what's up?*

Stay cool, Kid. It's gonna be just fine.

Tim, Toby, and I went through the front door to find Angie and Max sitting in the kitchen with Mom and Larry. Amber sat on the floor, chewing on the corner of a plastic sign that said "Rummage Sale."

"Baby girl," I said, "don't put that in your mouth, it's covered with bacteria. Here." I handed her a wooden spoon, which she rubbed on the floor, then licked. Outside the rain began falling softly at first, then grew to a rattling spray against the windows. The moment the thunder cracked and lightning flashed on our faces, we got the news.

Mom and Larry were selling the farm. They had been working very hard they said, climbing the economic ladder and it was time to get a bigger, better house in Bellingham.

"Well, that really sucks!" said Lori, when I told her.

"I know. What am I going to do in Bellingham? There aren't any horses and I'll have to go to Bellingham High," I said.

"Well, it ain't like it's a hundred miles away so you can always come 'n visit."

Lori was right, Bellingham was only twenty-five miles from where she lived at Nugent's Corner. We promised we would keep in touch and stay friends, no matter what happened.

Mom had bought a royal blue Econoline 500 van to haul the furniture they bought and sold for a living. For three days, several trips were made in the van to town relocating us to "Walnut Street."

The Granny Smith Apple House was finally emptied out and I was left there to finish cleaning. I wanted to leave the place sparkling clean because it had been sold to a couple with a new baby. Scouring the bathtub I realized I was alone and needed to save the music books I had hidden under the piano. In the hallway I kneeled down and retrieved the book of *Bach* and *Clementi* from the space between the piano and the floor. The bed sheet had been removed from the piano and the bench remained.

I sat down and began to play a goodbye song to Lori. I sang farewell to Mt. Baker High School, Mrs. Laverne Dupree, and the neighbor horse. I was singing so loudly I didn't hear the hall door open. Mom stepped behind me.

"Are you trying to *haunt* me?" she yelled.

Tell her no, said Flash. Our eyes met and the world stopped for one brief second. Outside a robin chirped.

"No," I said.

When I picked myself up off the floor, I saw that Mom was wearing an animal print turban on her head and a burnt orange pantsuit. She inhaled sharply and heaved out a breath. I walked past her and went back to scrubbing the tub. She went out to the van and loaded up the vacuum cleaner.

When I was done we got in the van and hauled the last load to the new house. Crammed in the very back between the cleaning supplies and the nightstand from our bedroom, I opened the drawer an inch and pulled until I got a hold of my notepad with the daisies on it. I found a pencil and wrote Gramma a letter.

Dear Gramma,

How are you? I'm fine. I am sorry to say that we have to sell the farm. I am sad about leaving the Granny Smith Apple House and Mt. Baker school. We had an early graduation ceremony for my eighth grade class. Mom came to the cafeteria and left me eight blue carnations. I ran after her to thank her but she drove away before I could catch her. Everyone else is happy about moving to town but I'm not. I will especially miss the piano and the neighbor horse. I promised him I would ride him to town one day so he could get his teeth cleaned. (Sorry for the messy handwriting, we keep hitting bumps.)

Next Sunday is Father's Day. Could you please put some red roses and snapdragons on Dad's grave for me? (You can put any color snapdragons you want.) Also could you please tell him I love him.

Love,

Eve

P.S. The good news is we will be 13 miles closer to you! Please kiss Grampa, Buddy, Choppy, Korky, and Pam for me.

chapter sixteen

Louanne Berg

My family was thrilled about the move to Bellingham. During the two years at Squalicum Lake Road, Tim and Toby had ventured into Bellingham enough to have friends there, so they already knew their way around. Angie got a new boyfriend in town and Max and Amber each had their own bedrooms in the new house, so they were happy. Three Legs was confused, so we had to keep him locked in the garage most of the time, which made my heart hurt.

My deep cravings continued. The food was no better in our seemingly wealthy new lifestyle, but the ambiance had changed drastically. Everything was bigger, busier, and scarier, removed so far from the rural countryside I had always known. I knew no friends in town. Mom and Larry were busy selling antiques in their new shop, located in downtown Bellingham and remodeling the biggest house we had ever lived in. Remodeling and moving in general was a messy proposition, so my lifting and cleaning duties were tenfold. I learned all about crown molding and how to clean it. I learned how to clean beveled glass without scratching it and how to use lemon oil on highboys and lowboys.

Mom's new antique shop, *Old n' Oak,* was located in Bellingham's old town district and had two stories stuffed with furniture. Mom and Larry prospered and grew so fast in the antique furniture business that the used nylons, secondhand shoes, and the Amalthea's Horn sign were cast aside, making room for early American oak pieces and carved European dining sets.

The Walnut Street House was a century-old Victorian that was not only beautiful, but had the admirable characteristic of sitting across from Elizabeth Park. The park was my favorite place to be, full of big trees, with a fountain, a basketball hoop, tennis courts, and a playground. The Walnut Street House had two stories with five bedrooms on the upper floor. Angie and I still shared a room, as did Tim and Toby, and we had a bathroom on both levels, which was a first for us. The ceilings were higher than maple trees and all around the edges was dark-colored crown molding. The open staircase looked like something a young prince would come down, with a runner of burgundy carpet over mahogany steps polished to a high shine. There was an entryway in the front and one in the back, off the kitchen. It was the first house we had ever been in that had two staircases and windows with bevels where the sunlight made rainbows, all in panels set in lead.

Mom and Larry furnished the house with European antiques, grand pieces elaborately carved with falcon claws and lion's heads with brass rings in their mouths. It wasn't uncommon to come home and see that all the furniture had been sold and replaced the next day by an entirely new shipment. If a customer came in and asked for a specific piece and Mom didn't have it in the shop, she would send Larry home to load up something from the house. She said she could convince anyone to buy anything. She said she could sell a dead bat if she wanted to and that she was well on her way to getting rich. I didn't see anything great about getting rich. It seemed like a whole lot of work getting things that weren't even important, like mother-of-pearl spoons you couldn't eat with or a silver-inlaid toilet seat you couldn't sit on. We had a house full of things you couldn't touch because they were too valuable.

The phone rang constantly and we were allowed to answer only if it rang ten times. The home phone and Old n' Oak had the same number and rang at both places. This is how Mom and Larry stayed connected and how Mom checked up on us.

I entered Bellingham High as a freshman and tried to make my way around as best I could. I wrote to Gramma a lot, looking for encouragement on becoming a city girl and liking it, but she was no help. She just kept praying for me and sent me a medal of the beloved Virgin Mary to sew inside my coat to protect me. Each day I walked thirteen blocks to school. Bellingham High was a big, old, two-story brick building, painted white. The school was fast-paced and charged with high energy. The hallways were off-white, the classrooms were stuffed, and the kids ran in packs. Gramma said *Change can be good. Do your best.*

Flash and I didn't even try to fit in because there wasn't any spot I cared for except the park. The girls at school all wore too much makeup, and my clothes were extra hokey in the city lights. I missed Lori and it seemed like I needed money but didn't know how to get it. I was always hungry for food and for a piano, which was nowhere to be found.

Bellingham High sold food in their cafeteria, not like Mt. Baker where you could take what you wanted. I found that after I finished my lunch from home and was still hungry, I had to stay completely away from the lunchroom so I wouldn't be tempted. They had cinnamon rolls the size of a dinner plate for a dollar and your choice of chocolate milk or Orange Crush.

My lucky day came when I met Louanne Berg. I observed her from a distance when she hung out in the park with her friends. I suspected Louanne wouldn't waste her time on me because I was much younger than she was and I didn't hold a candle to her style and fashion sense.

She was a junior and had her own car, a red Honda Civic. She lived in a tasteful yellow house in one of the better parts of town. I thought Louanne was so cool because she came from a nice family, had pierced ears, and wore braces on her teeth. She had a mass of auburn hair with blonde streaks and eyes bluer than robin eggs. Her skin looked happy to cover her. When she laughed, it bounced off the trees like a boomerang.

One day I was walking home from school. I looked up at the teal blue sky, striped white like Father North and Father South were tossing a roll of toilet paper back and forth. As I turned onto Walnut Street I heard a splash of laughter douse the trees and knew it was Louanne Berg. She was heading into Elizabeth Park with her friend Jamie McBride. They were wearing tennis outfits and had matching gear bags perched on their shoulders. I tried to get by them without being noticed, but then Louanne spoke to me.

"Hey," she said and shot me a shiny metal grin.

"Hey," I said nervously.

"Would you like to watch us play tennis?" she asked.

"Sure," I said.

"Maybe you could hit a few balls if you'd like," she said.

"That would be great. Thanks!"

I followed them to the court and she and Jamie began a friendly rally, which gradually became more intense. They swung with such concentration and hardly missed a shot. I had never even held a tennis ball, let alone a racket, so I just watched, mildly confused. Occasionally one of them would grunt, or curse when they missed the ball or hit it out of bounds. They played a set and I watched in hopeful anticipation that Louanne would beat Jamie.

Twice, the ball rolled toward me so I retrieved it like a good dog and threw it back to Louanne.

"Nice toss!" she said, and I felt proud taking a forward lunge up the steps of social acceptance. When they finally stopped playing, I didn't know which one had the higher score, so I said "You were both great!"

"Oh! Thank you!" they said.

Jamie picked up her tennis bag and, jingling her car keys, said, "Gotta go. Good game, catch ya later," and she was gone.

"Are you ready to hit some balls?" asked Louanne with a pink-cheeked grin.

"Well, yes, but I've never done it before," I said.

"That's cool. Come on." She jumped up and tossed me a bright green Penn.

"What's your name anyway?" she asked.

"Eve."

"Cool. I'm Louanne Berg."

"Yeah, I know," I said.

"It's a pleasure to meet you," she said.

She was patient with my amateur tennis ability. She hit the ball to me while asking me questions. I spent most of the time chasing the balls. Afterward I thanked her and ran home with the thrill of a new friend coursing through my blood.

After that day, Louanne acknowledged me at school with high-fives, which made me giddy. I loved her friendly nature and her spirit. Louanne was a champion ice skater and an accomplished piano player. She told me she respected me because I got good grades.

Eventually we became very close, even more so than Lori and I had been. I told her about my family and Mt. Baker and the situations I had gotten myself into. I went to her house sometimes and felt more at home there than I did in my own house. She had a sister a year and a half younger and two older brothers, like I did.

Mrs. Berg glowed just like Louanne. Their yellow house was nicely decorated and smelled like carnations and fruit cocktail. Louanne had her own room and kept a locked journal under her pillow. She taught me how to play "Heart and Soul" and "Stairway to Heaven" on her baby grand. When we both sat on the piano bench and played duets, her dad would turn the volume down on the TV until we were done playing. Her mom offered us snacks and gave us drinks with colored ice cubes. It was hard to believe a family could be that nice. I wrote to Gramma all about the Bergs.

Louanne and I met in the park and talked about everything. I told her about Steve Henry and she told me about Jim Wade.

I was making Kraft macaroni and cheese when I heard the phone ring. I counted to myself and on the tenth ring I yelled, "Someone get the phone!" Mom and Larry were at the shop and everyone else was watching TV. Tim answered the phone.

"Hello?" I half listened while stirring in the orange powder and water.

"Henry! What's up?" My heart skipped a beat.

"You comin' up?" said Tim. I burned my thumb on the pan.

"Oh yeah, for sure she's ready." Who's ready? They were talking about a car. Maybe they were talking about me. I didn't know. I ran my thumb under cold water. When I turned the faucet off Tim had hung up the phone.

"Was that Steve Henry calling from Oregon?" I asked, blowing on my hand.

"Yep. He's comin' up."

"When?" I suddenly had to pee.

"He's hittin' the road in the GTO first thing in the morning. If he doesn't get arrested for speeding he'll be here by noon."

I set six bowls of mac and cheese on the table and poured five cups of water. I set Amber in her high chair and yelled, "Supper!"

We gobbled it down and by the time I had the dishes done, Mom came through the door wearing a short mink coat. Her hair was dyed brown to match. She had a bright red purse, bright red lipstick, and a broach made out of a broken teacup pinned near her shoulder.

"We're going to Canada for the night," she announced. "Eve, you watch the kids and don't anybody talk on the phone. And don't even think about going outside or you'll be sorry."

I was bummed out because Louanne and I had plans to meet in the park after dinner so she could show me a note she had gotten from Jim and I could tell her about Steve Henry coming to Washington. Mom left and as I watched their van go down the street and out of sight, I spotted Louanne standing in the park holding the sacred note. I waved to her and she waved the paper, which told me to hurry up and get over there. The kids were watching TV, laughing at *Get Smart,* so I ran out the back door barefoot. The air was crisp and cold, but my focus was to get to Louanne and deliver my message. We hugged quickly.

"I'm sorry, but I'll have to read the note another time," I said.

"Why?"

"Because. I'm not supposed to be outside. Mom said so. I can't use the phone either. They went to an auction in Canada for the night."

"I know," she said, "I saw the van leave. Here, just let me read you the first line." She pressed the crinkled paper to my back and smoothed it out. She cleared her throat dramatically and said, "Hey, Louanne . . . Oh shit!"

I turned to face her. "It say's, *Oh shit?* That doesn't sound very romantic."

"No! I mean look! The van's coming back!"

"Oh no!" I took off running toward my house. I stopped at the edge of the park and hid behind a tree directly across from our back porch steps. I watched them park the van.

Run! said Flash, and I sprinted to the back steps, leapt up two at a time, made it through the back door and onto the carpet just as Mom was opening the front door. We were all lying on our stomachs in front of the TV. My heart thumped hard in my chest.

"We decided not to go," Mom said.

She walked over to us and placed her hand briefly on the sole of each kid's bare foot, one by one. When she got to me she said, "Oh, what do we have here? Very cold feet. You went outside, didn't you?"

"Yes, I did," I said.

"Go to your room."

"Okay, sorry," I mumbled and ran up the stairs. I got into bed and kicked my feet under the sheets, not just to warm them up, but because I was so excited I didn't get in more trouble than that. I turned over onto my stomach and bounced my forehead on the mattress, not knowing until the next day it was too good to be true.

chapter seventeen

Scio

In the darkened hours between dusk and dawn, the Walnut Street House stood silent in waning moonlight. Lying on my stomach with my arms tucked under my pillow, I was dreaming of Louanne and Jim driving through Elizabeth Park in Steve Henry's GTO. They were both squeezed into the driver's seat and clutched the steering wheel, arms, legs, and hair flipping about. Louanne was laughing hysterically at Three Legs and me riding on the hood with our noses and tongues smashed against the windshield. Steve Henry's elbow bounced on the blaring horn, wreaking havoc and blasting blue jays out of the maple trees.

My eyes shot open. At first I thought it was the horn that jarred me awake, but it was a thump in the hallway. Blinking hard in the dark, I scanned the room. Predawn light from the windows cast black-purple shadows that blanketed the room and outlined Angie lying motionless in her bed. From the hall I heard a floorboard groan underfoot. A slow creak sent spikes zipping down my spine.

Angie smacked, swallowed, and sank back into her silent world. For reasons unknown, we had a rule in the Walnut Street house that after nine o'clock at night, no one was allowed to get up; therefore it could only be an intruder out there. Petrified as wood, my lungs shrunk up in an attempt to stay as quiet as possible. A slat of yellow light shot underneath the bedroom door and heavy, deliberate footsteps were coming down the hall—getting closer. The steps slowed and stopped just outside our door. I felt, more than heard, someone's hand on the knob. I pinched my lips together to keep from screaming and abandoned myself to the knowledge that a killer had finally come for me.

Mom kicked the door open and flipped on the light switch. I

reared up in the overhead glare and braced myself as she lifted a metal trunk above her waist and hurled it. The trunk slammed against the footboard and rocked by my feet.

"Pack it up, sister," she said and disappeared.

Angie sat up clutching her *soft spot* and scowled.

"*What* are you doing? It's still dark out."

"I don't know what's happening. Mom threw this and told me to pack, but—where am I going?" I was shaking all over.

"How am I 'spose to know?"

"What should I take?"

"Don't ask *me*. Just quit makin' so much noise. God! You totally woke me up."

She stuck her thumb up her nose and squinted at her plastic mouse clock.

"It's only 4:30!"

She had a point. The only ones up at this hour were milk cows, paper boys, and lunatics.

Yanking the blanket over her head, she plunged back into her pillow. From under the covers she groaned, "God! You're so annoying!"

The familiar, mixed feelings came over me: the strong urge to kiss Angie tenderly and apologize for waking her up, or clobber her on the head for being such a selfish brat.

I moved my feet from under the heavy brown trunk. The sight of the dirty thing made my skin crawl. It looked old and creepy like it held ugly secrets from a hundred years ago. My imagination churned up possibilities of where I might be headed. *Am I in trouble, Flash? What happened last night? Oh yeah, the cold feet. I knew it. I knew it was too good to be true. Mom had to think of something original and creative before she punished me; that's why it took her all night. Maybe I have to move into the garage to live with Three Legs . . . that wouldn't be so bad, just a little cold, but what would I eat? Or—I know . . . maybe she sold the dresser and I'm going to keep my clothes in this trunk. That won't be so bad either.*

My eyes darted to Angie, who lay completely still. Outside the window the neighbor's chimney rose up against the black cherry sky. *No,*

*wait! Maybe I'm going to live out my years on the top floor of Old n' Oak
Antiques . . . like a twenty-four hour watchman or a starving guard dog. Or
what about Bellingham High, in the basement . . . with the electrical panels
and the janitorial supplies . . . Oh no, I won't be able to tell Louanne where
I am because no one will know except Mom and she's too mad at me . . .
again . . . and Steve Henry is coming today . . . oh, I wish I could talk to Tim,
he would know . . . what to do.*

I slid off the bed, pulled my nightgown over my head, and rolled
it into a ball. In the fuzzy light I grabbed clothes and quickly got dressed
in jeans, a sweatshirt, knee socks, and my worn desert boots, although I
knew I wouldn't be going to school.

Straightening the quilt on my bed, I whispered, "I wonder if I
should take my pillow?" and grabbed it for good luck. Gramma had em-
broidered my name on my pillowcase in variegated blue letters, bordered
by perfect buttonhole stitching. I couldn't risk losing it, so I peeled off the
pillowcase and wrapped it around my nightgown.

I looked at Angie, asleep with her soft spot and her small rodent
snore. She could never get in this much trouble if she begged for it. Everything she did was cute and no matter what came out of her mouth, it was
acceptable. Unlike me. I made a career out of digging my hole deeper and
deeper. How could we be so different when we came from the same place,
had the same parents and, as Gramma said, were made out of almost the
same ingredients?

I watched the door, waiting for Mom to barge in with a noose in
her hand. I supposed she was finally fed up with me. I wasn't *trying* to
blow it. The truth was I put tremendous effort into being good but it always backfired and appeared the opposite. I considered either hiding in
the trunk or jumping out the window, but neither option was promising.

I'm scared, Flash.

*Don't be, kid. You need to save your energy for more important
things than fear.*

I poked at the trunk, then opened the rusty latches and examined
the inside. It smelled musty, like the boxes Mom had brought home from
the auction. Torn black fabric lined the bottom, patched with a strip of

yellowed newspaper and old scotch tape. Some ancient person had tried to mend it, maybe a soldier from World War I or a forgotten child from Oliver's orphanage. Who else would carry such a monstrosity? I stuck my fingers inside a furrowed pouch hoping to find a ten dollar bill, but it was empty except for a piece of gray lint.

The mouse clock said 4:42 and I knew time was running out. Mom would be back soon and I better be packed up, *sister*. I pulled out my two dresser drawers and dumped everything I owned into the trunk, grabbed my journal/address book from the dresser and threw it on top of my clothes, and shoved in the nightgown and pillowcase. I took a look around and snapped the three latches shut.

"Well, bye," I said to Angie. I watched her little form rise and fall with her soft growl and felt terrible for having thought of her as a brat. *What if I never see her again? She may cry her eyes out when she realizes I'm gone, or maybe she'll just push our beds together so she can have one big bed to jump on in a bedroom all to herself.*

The sky had turned deep violet when the first bird of the morning chirped. I slowly opened the bedroom door and stepped into the blackness. Peering left, then right, I switched off the bedroom light and waited for my eyes to adjust to the darkness. I tried to lift the trunk, but the plastic handle broke and it thudded to the carpet. I shoved the fake ivory piece in my back pocket, balanced the trunk in my arms, and tiptoed down the hallway.

Passing by the boys' room, I felt a sad longing to be with them, safely asleep without a worry in the world. I wanted to wake Tim, but I knew I would get in more trouble for it. I looked behind me, toward Amber and Max's rooms and felt like dropping to my knees and bawling. I wanted to hold Amber and play *totsie*, a game we invented where I tossed her up in the air and she squealed and burped at the same time.

In the darkness I heard a door open and close downstairs and an icy breeze passed through me; not from fear of the unknown as much as a fear that all my belongings were stuffed in a dead person's trunk. I made it to the bathroom where the morning light had finally arrived. Through the window, the horizon was splashed with a brilliant lavender hue that announced the coming of a new autumn day. Gramma always said that each day was a gift from God and provided us an opportunity to do something good with it. I had mixed feelings about what this new day and I were going to offer one another.

There's an element of safety in a softly lit room, so without turning on the light I brushed my teeth and splashed water on my face. I pressed a towel hard on my temples hoping to generate some understanding of what was going on. My ears were muffled in the towel but I felt the air temperature change at the base of my neck. Mom appeared behind me. Her presence was overwhelming, as if she carried a climate of her own. I looked at her dim reflection in the mirror and saw her face was hard, pale and slick, like a winter squash. She said, "Get in the car," and walked away.

I wrangled the suitcase down the back stairs, grabbed my coat, and stumbled out the door. The moon was nearly sunk into Bellingham Bay and the air had an October chill that would linger even after the sun cleared Mount Baker.

From inside the garage came a scratching sound.

"Can I let Three Legs out?" I asked.

"Hurry up," Mom said. I ran and opened the garage door. In the dark, Three Legs' white teeth glowed like a strand of pearls. He snorted and jumped up, pawing the air.

"Oh, good boy! Go pee!" He bolted out and sprang into the park.

I muscled the suitcase into the car and got in the back seat. My pulse pounded hard behind my eyeballs. Looking over at the van parked by the garage, I felt like throwing a rock at it. Mom started the car and hit the gas, jerking us from the curbside. Glancing at the Walnut Street House behind me, I was stricken by another familiar feeling . . . *What if I never see this place again?* As Elizabeth Park flew by, I began counting our houses in my head. *October House, Rat Shack, Mollalla House, Blossom Drive, Rock House, Birdhouse, Barn House, Juniper Road, Granny Smith Apple House* . . .As the street beat back behind us and not a word was spoken, the names of our past houses and the memories attached to them roared in my head.

Mom clenched her teeth and gripped the steering wheel. Her hair

was dyed the color of a pomegranate and she was wearing a maroon ve-
lour pantsuit with a zebra print scarf knotted at the neck. Exotic animal's teeth wrapped in copper wire hung from her ears with a bracelet to
match. Her fingernails were painted gold and her cuticles were stained
brown with furniture varnish. I knew she worked too hard, refinishing,
hauling, and selling furniture. I felt sorry for her that she looked mad so
early in the morning. I was starving.

In a few hours everyone would be waking up for school. Ninth
grade at Bellingham High had just begun and I liked it more than I'd
anticipated, especially after meeting Louanne. I could hardly believe she
still wanted to be friends with a buck-toothed thirteen-year-old. I wished
there was some way to tell her I was going away, although running to the
park to deliver the last message was what got me into this mess in the
first place.

We passed Kentucky Fried Chicken and Fountain Drug Store.
Bellingham Bay was dark and calm, dotted with San Juan Islands and
fishing boats. We passed the red brick City Hall where the tower clock
read 5:10. I opened my mouth to ask where we were going at this hour,
but decided against it. Nudging closer to the window, I removed my image from the rearview mirror and chewed my lips. I wondered if Louanne
was sleeping on her side like a pretzel. It was comical how she wrapped
her legs around her shoulders when she slept. I went to visit her once
when she was sick. Her mom let me go in her room and my friend was all
wound around herself. When she woke up and saw me looking at her she
burst out laughing and shortly after that she was all better.

My stomach growled when we passed the Old Town Café. I had a
ball of bubbles in my guts from nerves and no food.

The silence was abruptly broken. "There is one thing I want you to
remember," Mom said, "and that is you picked me to be your mother, I
didn't pick you. I had nothing to do with it. We all choose the womb we
enter through and you chose mine for a reason."

I remained silent because I had heard those words before. Also,
if I ever got my ears pierced I would be cursed forever by demons, and I
was going to end up huge from eating so many mashed potatoes. Trying

not to think about food, I looked at the side of her face and saw her jaw moving tensely like she was crunching clam shells. I tried to see myself standing in front of a lineup of moms, pointing at her and saying, "I'll take that one." She was right. I would pick her.

"And don't you for one second think I'm stupid. I know what's goin' on with you and that shit-for-brains Gregory Steven from Oregon. I heard it all on the shop phone. 'Is she ready?'—that's what he said to Tim. I heard the whole conversation between the two of them and you were probably standing right there gettin' an earful. 'Is she ready for me?' Well, he's not about to find out, because you're outa here."

Wordlessly, my mouth flopped open and closed.

"You're so goddamned stubborn, you have to learn everything the hard way. I'm beyond disappointed in you, Eve, and I'm going to teach you a lesson. You leave me no choice." As my fret level shot up, I had a strong desire to wrench the door handle up and jump out of the car.

Morning traffic got heavier. I felt relieved that Bellingham was finally waking up and I had company. We sped around a corner and wheeled in front of the Greyhound bus station. The car slammed to a stop.

"Get out."

I grabbed the trunk and crawled out, following Mom into the depot like a nervous dog dragging a cow bone. The depot was similar to a meat locker Grampa had taken me to, big and freezing with voices and humming noises bouncing off the walls. I could see my breath and taste the air, thick with the smell of oily corndogs. Between cement and steel, passengers with rolling suitcases milled about, their wheels and shoes clicking on the concrete floor. My cheeks heated, knowing mine was the biggest and ugliest suitcase of all. Gigantic florescent lights hung overhead, too bright, too early. Speakers sputtered and a wall clock the size of a stop sign read 5:30. On a nearby bench a man lay with a dirty backpack under his feet. His head was wrapped in a torn corduroy coat.

"Sit there," Mom said, pointing to the man. I squeezed in between his greasy boots and the metal arm of the bench. With my trunk on the floor beside me, I perched on the very edge of the seat so as not to disturb him. From underneath his coat came muted snoring. Out of hearing range, Mom was talking through the bars at the ticket agent, who looked like a hard-working man, accommodating her at 5:30 in the morning. I saw her clicking her nails impatiently on the counter and hoped she was speaking kindly to him. I imagined his surprise when she told him she needed a bus ticket to the city dump so she could dispose of her rotten kid.

Oh, Flash, what if she's sending me to Timbuktu? She's threatened to send me there, as well as China so I could see how lucky I am. Little kids starve in China you know, and Mom says in Timbuktu they eat horses. No—the Greyhound wouldn't go to China. I'm not old enough to join the Army; she's talked about that too. She says that everyone has to suffer in order to succeed. I looked at my bench partner and hoped he wasn't going to miss his bus. I felt sorry for him but glad he was asleep so I could check him out. Where had those boots been and where were they going? Where am *I* going and is he going with me? My thigh almost touched the brown paper bag that stuck out of his backpack. I readjusted myself and felt a sharp poke in my bottom. I pulled out the broken trunk handle from my back pocket and held it up to the light. *Maybe this was carved out of a real elephant tusk and traveled across several oceans in the hull of a stolen slave ship* . . . The handle was suddenly shadowed by a ticket agent hovering over me. His black mustache looked like he had a dead bat hanging off his nose. He held out his hand, offering the ticket to my destiny.

I darted my eyes around the depot searching for Mom. She was gone.

"This is your ticket, young lady. Your mother asked that I make sure you get on the correct bus. She had to hurry and leave because of the little ones in the car, as you know."

"Oh, "I said.

"*Flash, she can't do this! I don't even know where we're going.*" I thought about chasing after her or running back across town to Walnut Street, dragging the trunk behind me. If I hurried I could probably make it by lunchtime. Tears stung my eyes and my lips began to wobble.

"Here you go, here's your ticket." The agent waved an envelope in front of me. I wiped my eyes and took it. Inside, the ticket was paper-clipped to a five-dollar bill. I read the print:

September 26, 1972 Depart Bellingham, WN 6:00 a.m. Arrive Salem, Oregon 3:00 p.m.

I tried to scratch off the red letters—ONE WAY.

"Your bus is boarding in lane number three," said the agent. "Right out that door."

"Thanks." I stood in a scene where Three Legs should have been, or Brother Tim, or Gramma. I needed a dose of comfort.

You've got me, kid, Flash hummed.

I picked up my luggage, which was gaining weight, and we boarded Greyhound Number Thirty-nine Southbound. I stopped and stood before the bus and suddenly felt Flash expand inside me, pushing my chest out and stretching my core. My chin lifted and I drew upward right there in the bus parking lot—because I needed to, in order to take the next step forward.

The driver stood outside the bus taking tickets.

"Can't bring that on board, girlie," he said, shaking his head. "It's gotta go down below."

As I handed over the dead man's trunk, my stomach growled like a motor.

"Do I have time to get something to eat?"

"Sure do. The snack bar's right inside there. We leave in twelve minutes."

I hurried back into the icy depot and went into the restroom. Looking at my reflection in the mirror, I tried to smile but the corners of my mouth felt like lead. I suppose if you're just plain bad, these things happen. Everyday some kid must get bounced out the door for being a pain in the butt, although Gramma would say there are no bad children and we are all special gifts from God. *Maybe I get to go to Gramma's. No, Salem is too far away from Gramma's and they couldn't drive that far to get me. Flash, why does it all have to be such a stinking mystery? I'm buzzing so hard I feel like falling in the sink.*

"*Eat.*"

I bought an overstuffed egg salad sandwich with black olives and a bag of Lay's potato chips. The lady behind the counter stuck a dill pickle wedge in the sack and winked at me. I clomped up the big metal steps and onto the bus, which smelled like wet rubber. There were only five passengers on board so I went all the way to the rear, settled into a well-used cloth seat, and opened my snack bag. As the bus pulled out I devoured the sandwich and pickle and vowed to make the potato chips last.

For nine hours I watched the interstate and the people who traveled it. The Greyhound cruised in the slow lane with big rigs and RVs. We droned along from one dumpy station to the next. I studied the freeway for Steve Henry's GTO headed in the opposite direction and crunched a chip each time we pulled into a new station. *What will happen to Steve if he does make it to the top of Washington? Will Mom yell at him? Will she call him by the wrong name and scream that his ass is grass?* If only I could have explained to her that we weren't doing anything wrong. I admit the thought of riding in his car, like in my dream that morning, would be exhilarating, but it shouldn't warrant the ejection button. I didn't even like him that much anymore, did I? Angie would know. She was genius when it came to boys. I shook away the image of her jumping on the bed.

South of Mt. Vernon the sky began to spit water. It rode up onto the bus' windshield, where giant wiper blades swiped it back down to the cars below. The freeway glistened and hissed beneath us. Although the heavy clouds had darkened the day considerably, the bus driver wore sunglasses. Several times he downshifted, switched lanes, and lurched into empty Greyhound stops. Three of the stations were barren bus stops on the side of a street. At one such stop a lady got on with two little girls, each with a hand in their mother's coat pocket. I bet she had pockets full of M&Ms. As they took a seat up front I felt bad for them that they had been standing out in rain. The mom patted their damp heads with the tip of her scarf. Perhaps they were travelling to Salem to visit a pack of cousins, or maybe they were being sent to Portland to perform in the Pinochle Theater—they were cute enough. And certainly their beloved mom was also their talent agent. Watching the little sisters nestled beside their mother made me shiver. I thought of Angie and Amber and my ears grew hot. I bet the lady adored her daughters and told them so every ten miles. She probably washed their hair with lavender-and-rose scented shampoo and used the point of a pencil to tenderly work through their tangles. They surely bathed in sparkling bubbles up to their necks, listened to magical bedtime stories, and got two scoops of sugar on their oatmeal.

I got off the bus twice to buy food. Seattle depot had the best selection. I bought a fat baked potato and asked the guy in the white paper hat to please give me the largest one with extra butter and sour cream. In the back seat I ate it with a plastic fork and listened to the driver announce the names of the towns we passed through. When I was the only one left on the bus he kept speaking into the microphone as if he had a full audience.

In Kelso I was hungry again so I raided the vending machine for another bag of chips and a Payday bar, which left me with sixty-five cents.

We pulled in and then out of Portland with several new passengers. A shriveled-up man wobbled toward the back and I felt sorry for him that he was so crooked. As he came closer I realized he was going to sit next to me. I had managed to sit alone the entire day and felt uncomfortable when he sank down, too close. He smelled like spoiled fruit and his pants were wet around his lap. I tried to keep my gaze out the window, but he leaned into my side and nudged me. I turned to him and saw how dark and crinkled up he was, with small wet eyes and decayed teeth that looked like Cracker Jacks.

"Yer perty," he said, spraying rotten fruit spit onto my cheek. I thought he was twiddling his thumbs, but when I looked down, to my horror, his pants were unzipped. He panted hot, sugary breaths and mumbled something inaudible.

"*Get rid of him!*" Flash flared.

By some miracle I looked straight at the raisin man and shot him the look of a possessed monster child. Within three seconds he staggered up and away to another seat. I wiped the sweat off my palms and looked out the window to see the Tillamook exit sign speeding by.

I felt alone in the world. Was Louanne searching the school hallways for me yet? And what had become of the guy with the dirty boots in the Bellingham station, and what was going to happen in Salem? I laid my head back and counted my breaths until I slipped away with the engine's roar and the driver's voice in the back of my mind.

I woke up just as we pulled into another depot. I rubbed on the foggy window and looked through the clear spot. Outside, people waded in ankle-deep steam from the sun beating down on the concrete. The bus hissed and slowed to a stop.

"Salem!" the speaker popped. I jumped up, searching for anything remotely familiar. The engine rumbled to a halt and the door swished open. "End of the line."

As the passengers filed off one by one, I stood there like a fence post. When the bus was empty, the driver stood up and walked toward the rear, checking the floor and seats for items left behind. He took off his sunglasses and smiled at me. The sunlight caught his one gold tooth, giving me the impression he was famous; maybe a trumpet player.

"You get off here and call your grandmother. The phone number is here." He held out a piece of paper with Mom's handwriting on it. My hands went straight to my chest.

Call her grandmother from Salem.

(503) 394-5671.

Put her on the bus to Stayton.

I instantly needed a toilet and the driver looked as if he knew it.

"Come on, I'll show you where to go."

First he led me to the restroom and waited outside. When I came out, we rushed through the crowded Salem depot. It was loud and buzzing, and smelled like body odor and rancid popcorn. I stayed beside the driver, tripping over my desert boots, but he seemed not to notice. I kept glancing up at him, a man with a mission moving swiftly forward. Weaving through the mob, he said cheerfully, "Excuse us." I noticed two bumps on the back of his shoulders and decided they were angel wings. I had forgotten all about my trunk.

At the *Star Transport* ticket window, my famous trumpet-playing angel driver leaned in and said, "One way to Stayton please."

"Yes, Sir!" the ticket lady chirped. My, she was perky. "That will be seven-eighty, please."

I jammed my hands into my pockets, clutching the four coins. *Oh no.*

A little tune slipped through his lips as he pulled out his wallet and handed her some cash. She produced a ticket and a yellow grin. Sliding Mom's note to her, he said, "Would you be so kind, it's almost local."

The ticket lady batted her eyelashes, which were clumped with blue mascara, and he smiled broadly, showing her the gold nugget. *I think they like each other, Flash.* While licking her lips, she picked up the receiver, pressed the numbers, and passed the phone through the window. The famous, smitten bus driver motioned me to take the phone and I crushed the electronic purr to my ear. We stood there a long time, each of us showing our distinctive teeth. Nine rings later Gramma answered. It had been more than a year since I had heard her voice.

"Hello?"

"Hiya, Gramma." My voice was too high.

"Hiya, honey! How ya doin?"

"Um, good."

"We've got good reception. I can hear you as clear as a bell. It makes me feel like you're closer."

"I am. Closer. I'm . . . I'm in Salem."

"What, honey? *Where* are you?"

"I'm at the bus station. Um, in Salem. Did Mom call you?"

"Salem? No, she didn't call! Are you okay?" She was using her worry tone.

"Yes, I'm getting on the Star bus to Stayton right now. Could you come pick me up?"

"Right now? Yes—yes, of course honey, we're on our way. I'll go tell Pop. Are you sure you're okay? Are you alone?"

"Yes Gramma, I'm fine. I'll explain it all when I see you."

"You get on the bus now. Don't miss it. And we'll see you in Stayton. I'll tell Pop and we'll be right there to get you. Oh dear, is it safe there? Are you out of the cold?"

"Yes, I'm safe, I'm not cold, and everything is fine. I'll see you soon. Don't worry, I'm good, Gramma." The phone cord bobbed. The ticket lady and driver smiled at each other, pretending not to listen.

"I'll get Pop and we'll be right there. I mean in Stayton. By the time you get to Stayton we'll be waiting. We're leaving right now."

"Okay, I love you. Well, bye," I said.

I handed the phone back to the nice lady. "Thank you very much," I said.

"Oh, you are quite welcome." I glanced at her and knew she meant it: I was *quite* welcome. I shook away the vision of myself wandering around, lost in downtown Salem, scraping the trunk along a wet street, too afraid to stick my hand out, and worst of all, starving.

The driver and I went outside to get my luggage. The trunk had taken even more of a beating, riding in the bowels of the bus all day. He hoisted it up to the Star driver.

"Alright then, young lady, here you be." He flashed his teeth.

"Thank you for all your help, Sir."

"It was a sheer pleasure," he said.

"That was so nice of you to buy my ticket. I can pay you back."

"Oh, don't you even have such a thought. A fine young gal such as you ought to be cared for and we're all here to help one another. Good luck to you and God bless," he said. He put his big hand on my shoulder and patted it softly.

I stepped up into the bus. My trunk and I were the only passengers on Star Transportation eastbound for Stayton. I felt bright sitting in the chartreuse vinyl bench seat with Gramma and Grampa just forty minutes away. The bus started up and I looked out the window to see my driver waving up at me. I mouthed "Thank you," and he mouthed back "Good luck! Jesus loves you." As the Star began to pull out I saw for the first time, his nametag. "Colton Green." I decided in lieu of paying him back for the bus ticket and all the help, I would name my firstborn son after him.

Under a cloudless Oregon sky, the city soon turned to the country-side. We passed the Oregon State Correctional Institution set far off the road, surrounded by barbed wire and razor blade fencing. I wondered if anyone officially got corrected there. I now understood how easily a person could be sent away and forgotten.

We made it, Flash!

Yep. Hello, mashed potatoes!

The bus pulled into the Stayton station, which consisted of the parking lot next to Foster's Freeze. I spotted the blue Corolla with my grandparents in the front seat. I jumped off the bus and ran to them.

Grampa got out and rubbed the top of my head. "Heya!" he boomed, "You got taller." He looked exactly the same. When Gramma opened her arms I fell in. Silently, she held me like she had all the time and patience in the world. The bus driver scuffed over, dropped the trunk by the car, and walked away. He looked like all the fun had been washed out of him. What a grump he was compared to the shining star, Colton Green.

We went into the Foster's Freeze to get a Buster Bar. I ate two, plus a Dilly Bar. Sitting across from Grampa, his shoulders began bouncing up and down.

"What's so funny Grampa?" I asked.

He took a bite of his cone and said, "That damned Gloria. I'm surprised she didn't make you *walk* from Washington."

"Now, Pop," said Gramma.

Driving back to the ranch, I chatted about my day, the events leading up to it, what I ate, and the people I saw. I avoided the raisin man episode and for Gramma's sake, invented several more kids than the two little girls. Gramma sniffed and dabbed her nose and Grampa rapped the steering wheel and shook his head. I explained how I had once again let Mom down but this time to the point that she had to get rid of me. I could hear myself defending her beyond reason until Flash told me to shut it. I added that I was scared I had done far too much damage to repair it.

"Repairing emotional damage is not the responsibility of a little child," said Gramma. I put my head against the window and thought about the little child I had left behind. Somewhere on the interstate I had packed her away, preserved her for safe-keeping. Looking at the back of

Gramma and Grampa's heads, I felt safe for the first time all day.

My grandparents' income came solely from raising cattle. Grampa kept thirty-three head of stock at a time. He ran his cattle business by anticipating the price per pound on the hoof. He also knew how many calves were expected each season. Grampa said the cattle business gave them just enough money to pay the land taxes and put food on the table.

Grampa's cattle were Herefords, which are big brown and white beasts that lumber along, chewing their cud and grazing their lives away. Grampa said the Willamette Valley was stocked with Herefords because they liked the weather there. He told me there was no better breed for beef production and because they also thrived in many other parts of the world, it was a testament to the hardiness of the breed. Herefords were known for their gentleness and their excellent maternal qualities. The "Mamas," as we called them, were built for birthing.

Grampa's prized bull had the cushy job of eating well and making calves with the thirty-two cows. Most of the calving took place each spring, but some were born in the fall and even a few in mid-winter. When I got to stay with Gramma and Grampa, I would wake up and rush out to see the new calves each morning, sucking their mama's milk and wobbling in the pasture. Sometimes the herd would leave the lower grazing pasture and plow up the mountainside. Their ton-weight bodies stomped on saplings, devastated trails, and nearly destroyed the vegetation. Whenever the herd disappeared up the mountain, Grampa said not to worry. "The damn fools'll be back when they run into a dead end and finally figure out how to turn around and get back down where they belong."

I had been with Gramma and Grampa almost a month when the ninth fall calf was about to be born. Grampa and I were in the pasture giving the herd a salt block. I looked out across the Gap. The valley below us had a low, thick blanket of morning fog. When we heard a Mama bellowing, it seemed to be coming from underneath the fog. Her painful bawl told us she was in trouble—probably hip-lock.

Hip-lock was a serious situation in which a partially delivered calf got stuck in the birth canal. A heifer, which is a very young cow, was pre-disposed to hip-lock because she was too young for the trials of delivery.

"Where the heck is she?" Grampa said.

"It sounds like it's coming from up on the mountain," I said.

Grampa cupped his hand to his ear. He dug his boot heel into a hard clod and squinted up to the sky. The cow's cries rolled down through the woods and floated into the fog.

"Come on, Eve!" Grampa said. He grabbed his rope from the fencepost and we took off toward the mountaintop.

It has been argued that cows are stupid. Grampa had said so himself. But Gramma believed they just innocently got themselves into trouble, and I agreed with her. Trotting behind Grampa, I said a prayer for the Mama and asked Flash to give me extra strength to help her.

The air was moist and cool, with low clouds hovering at the mountain's crest. We trudged up the main trail, straight toward the clouds. The Mama's lonesome bawl had changed tone and had gone from a *mwoo* to a hoarse *mraa*. I had to run to keep up with Grampa and tripped several times in Gramma's big rubber boots. As Grampa crashed through the tree branches, I held out my arms to protect myself from the switches that sprang back in my face.

On the middle ridge we found the Mama on her side, trapped in a bramble of blackberries that covered a hollowed log. Twisted spikes impaled her hide, thorns skewered her ears, and her tail was bent and knotted. Her massive side rose and fell as her eyes rolled upward. I saw a tiny hoof sticking out of her birth canal. Dark red blood leaked out around it.

After hours of being down, the Mama was exhausted. If she would have been a horse Grampa would have shot her right there. As I made my way through the thorns, she let out a guttural moan. A thousand-pound animal in distress puts off a load of heat. Thick steam was rising from her hide like rain on a hot rock. I patted her massive rump and she blew hard out her nostrils. Grampa tied a fast tug-knot in his rope. He bent down and stuck his fingers inside the cow. When he removed his hand the little hoof slipped farther out revealing a calf's leg.

"All right, now, Eve, you're gonna have to reach inside her 'cause your arms are skinnier."

"Okay."

"Here. Stand behind her and as far back as you can. She's gonna kick." He handed me the rope. "You reach up there as far as you can until you feel the head. You'll probably feel something rough. That's the tongue."

"Okay, Grampa." I took the knotted rope and slid both arms up past my elbows into her warm, squishy insides. She began to slam her hind leg against the log. I closed my eyes and grunted. My fingers were feeling for the tongue but instead I felt soft, hot fur and something very slick. I kept my eyes closed and tried to imagine what was in my hands.

"Well? You got it?" He was at the Mama's head trying to calm her down.

She tossed, snorted, and moaned. The briars jammed deeper into her body and her nose began to spurt blood.

Sadly, there is a humanlike character in a cow's cry, and its tears are as big as fifty cent pieces. How I wanted to take away her suffering. I rolled the rope around and tried to figure out what I was looping. I felt a head. I felt an eyeball. I felt warm mush, but still no tongue. Then I realized the calf was horribly contorted. I was able to identify its small, lifeless head lodged under its back leg. I opened my eyes. Everything was blurry.

"It feels dead, Grampa."

"Well, we have to get it out, or we're gonna to lose her too. Can you get the rope around the neck?"

"Yeah, I think so."

I twisted the rope until it slipped over the calf's head. My arms sailed out, streaked with reddish-brown mucous.

"Grab the rope and on the count of three pull for all your worth."

We counted, pulled, and tugged. The Mama bawled with every bit of strength she had left. We yanked, strained, and prayed. When she deflated before us, Grampa wrapped the rope around the closest tree to gain leverage. The failing Mama was too weak; she could do nothing to help. Steam rose off our backs and a vessel broke on Grampa's face. We counted louder and wrenched harder until my hands were raw with blisters. Suddenly, from within the cow came a crack. She let out a deafening yowl and a hiss. The suction broke, releasing a slushy satchel of dead calf—hide, hooves, and all.

I looked at the bloody mess and then at the panting Mama. "Poor girl," I said. I felt so sorry for that Mama lying there after such a horrible ordeal and no baby to show for it. I started to cry, but Grampa wouldn't have any of that. "We have to get her some water," he said. "Let's go back down and get supplies. We need a shovel and we gotta cut those briars off her. Come on."

Following on Grampa's heels, I sniffed hard all the way back down the mountain. At the barn we grabbed what we needed: a blanket, a bucket of water, salt, bag balm, clippers, and a shovel. We turned around and carried the supplies back up the trail. I wanted to run back to the house to tell Gramma about the dead calf, but Grampa said there was no time and he wanted to make sure Buddy and Choppy didn't get wind of what we were up to.

We clipped away enough briars to set the Mama free, but freedom was more than she could handle. She was unmovable. Grampa dug a deep hole and buried the calf. We covered the fresh mound with a pile of big rocks to keep the coyotes away.

Grampa took off his gloves and slapped them hard against his thigh. "Come on now, it's gonna get dark here in about an hour."

"Oh, Grampa, can't I please stay with her? She's gonna be so lonely and scared."

"Ah, she's a mess. It's best to leave her be. There's nothin' you can do for her right now."

"Please, I just want to talk to her, you know, let her know she's going to be all right." The Mama let out a slow stream of air, like a punctured tire tube. Grampa shook his head and began picking up the tools.

"Okay, then. You can stay up a bit, but no longer than a half hour. We don't want Ma all in a tizzy and supper'll be on the table soon."

"Okay, Grampa. I'll be right down, after I tuck her in."

He tromped back down the trail.

I dubbed her "Mama Brave." I covered her with a blanket, cleaned off her bloody nose, wiped her eyes, and picked the crud from her eyelashes. Her tail crackled when I straightened it. I pulled out a bucketful of thorns and dripped water onto her giant, parched tongue. The evening air cooled as broken sunlight beamed from the top ridge. I laid myself over her huge, warm body, moving up and down with her slow breaths. It was like floating on gentle river rapids.

Singing to a cow is quite relaxing, and soon we both closed our eyes.

When an owl hooted above us, I stood up.

"Listen, Mama Brave, I have to go now. I'm so, so sorry about your baby. You did the best you could and I'm sorry we couldn't save him. It was a boy, you know. The important thing is that you get rested up so you can have another baby soon, maybe a summer calf. I'll be back very first thing in the morning, I promise."

When I heard something snap in the trees, I quickly kissed her goodnight and stumbled back home as fast as I could.

I woke while it was still dark and, just in my pajamas and Gramma's slippers, hurried out with Grampa. Buddy and Choppy were thrilled. As the sun was breaking over the eastern ridge, we bounded up the wet mountain. We were all panting when we got to the middle ridge. Ahead we could see Mama Brave still lying in the briars.

The dogs raced toward her, then suddenly stopped and whined. Mama Brave was completely still. Her udder was swollen and red. I knew then that she was gone.

Grampa was a man who knew how to treat a pie. On my fourteenth birthday Gramma made a Himalaya blackberry pie and stuck a matchstick in it. Grampa clacked two forks together and whistled Happy Birthday through his teeth. When we finished eating the entire pie and drinking a whole pot of hot coffee, Grampa leaned back in his chair and patted his stomach. "Now that's whatcha call a birthday belly." His shoulders rode up and down, making his chair creak. Gramma cleared the table, then brought me a gift nicely wrapped in a JC Penney box. Inside were two yards of paisley knit fabric to make a skirt and the newest edition of *Betty Crocker's Cookbook*.

Being fourteen felt very different, but I couldn't pinpoint what it was, exactly. For one thing, my clothes were too small. My hair had grown to my waist and Gramma's size ten boots fit me better each day. Although my teeth were still huge, they seemed less worrisome than before. My bones were stretching, so Gramma sent me to bed each night with a hot water bottle to sooth the growing pains in my legs.

In spite of all the changes, living on the ranch with Gramma and Grampa was like blooming in a garden of love. I soaked it up, devoured it in fact. In contrast was the home I once knew in Bellingham with my family, which I missed terribly, especially the kids. I wrote letters to Tim, Toby, and Max. I sent cards and drawings to Amber and Angie, telling them all about the animals, and asking them to kiss Three Legs on the lips for me. I wrote to Louanne and my old friend Lori Mezo, but Louanne was the only one who wrote back. Every time I began writing a letter to Mom, it turned into a soggy mess of apologies or a stream of questions. I reread what I wrote her over and over, then tossed the crumpled paper into the woodstove. As I watched the flame rise up through the isinglass window, I knew as hard as I tried and as deep as I dug, I had no words to suit Mom.

Louanne wrote that she had recently seen Angie in the park, and she told her that Steve Henry had indeed arrived the very day I had left on the bus so long ago.

"Now, who is Steve Henry again?" Gramma tilted her chin up.

"He's that friend of Tim and Toby's from Salem."

"Is he the one who was involved in the fire?"

"Well . . . yes. There were actually four of us. He's the one with the cool cars."

"Oh, honey, your mother would have your hide if she knew you were even talking about him."

"I know," I said, and a thrill slid through me.

Gramma rocked slowly and shook her head. "I miss him so," she said.

"Who?"

"Your dad. Today would have been his thirty-seventh birthday. Imagine that."

"Yeah, I know. I really miss him if I think about him too much. There are so many things around here that remind me of him. His piano for one, with his picture on top of it. Every time I play, he's smiling down at me. It's not a big, happy smile though, like you should have if you finally graduated from high school. He looks almost like he's not sure if he should be smiling or not."

"He was self-conscious about his teeth."

"What? His teeth were perfect!"

"I know, honey, but if the truth be known, he wasn't crazy about them."

"Well, you can see by the look in his eyes that he's such a good person. I love that picture."

"I do too, Eve. I can't put it away. Pop thinks I should, but it's all I have left of him. Oh dear, if he would have lived, he never would have allowed any of this crazy business with your mother. He stood up for you every chance he got, I know he did. He loved you so much it just burned Gloria up. She always had a storm brewing in her anyway and then when you came along and she saw how he adored you, she just couldn't manage it. She just couldn't share."

"Well, it seems to me that there ought to be enough love in a family to go around," I said.

"It's a shame. These could have been the best years of his life, watching you all grow up. He left you kids when you needed a father the most. I know Angie suffers so because of it, you all do. Children need their parents, *both* parents. I just don't understand why he did it—how he allowed that awful darkness to swallow him up. And he was so talented. Mind you, they wanted him in that jazz band when he was just a kid. He was that good." She blotted her nose with the back of her hand and gestured toward the sink.

"When he was just a little tyke, I would be standing there, washing dishes, and he would be right by my legs. I could hum a bar of any song there is and he could repeat it with perfect pitch. Oh, he had an ear."

I looked at the sink and imagined my dad as a little guy tugging at his mama's apron.

"I bet he was cute," I said.

Gramma sniffed. "I know it was God's will, but it's not fair for a child to pass before a parent."

"No, Gramma, it's not fair. Some things just aren't fair."

She tugged her hankie from her housecoat pocket and roughed up her nose. A light snow had begun to swirl outside the kitchen window and I knew it was time to break away from this beautiful sadness.

It was time to check on the cattle.

By the end of January, Grampa and I had welcomed twenty-nine newborn calves and successfully helped two more Mamas with hip-lock. Grampa said I had "stupendous nursing capabilities," which simply meant I had the fortitude to reach inside a bellowing cow and stick around long enough to help clean up the mess. I learned a lot about the texture of healthy bovine afterbirth, the normal heart rate of a cow, and how best to avoid getting impaled by a horn.

In the still, dark days that followed, the sky showed no movement. The valley had crusted over with frozen snow. It was too cold for snowflakes and too early for the first rain of spring.

Inside the warmth of the house I had a pleasant routine of cooking, sewing, playing the piano, and reading. I read Gramma's *Prevention* magazines and tried recipes of things made with carob, honey, and whole wheat flour. Grampa called it tasteless hippie chow. We rooted houseplants off clippings and saved egg shells in a gallon jar of water to fertilize the houseplants. Every Thursday when Grampa left for the stock sale, we watered all the indoor plants with the "organic shell protein." Grampa called it "Stinky Thursday." The egg water was putrid enough to make your nose burn, but *Prevention* claimed the natural fertilizer would make our coleuses brighter and our prayer plants turn to velvet.

Gramma and I worked on a crazy quilt for my bed. We bordered each random quilt piece in blue featherstitch. This project took two quilting hoops, plenty of room in the kitchen, and good eyesight.

I was sprawled out on the floor, licking my embroidery thread, about to poke it through the eye of a needle when Grampa came in with the mail. Holding two envelopes between his teeth, he stomped the ice off his boots and pulled them off with a grunt. He stood the boots by the woodstove and set the mail on the table. From so many years of performing on stage, Grampa had a special gift for livening up a room. He grinned at the two of us stitching away like old farm ladies.

"Looks like you got a letter, Eve," he said.

"I did? From who?"

"Dunno."

"Thanks," I said, as he handed me the letter. It had Mom's handwriting on the envelope. I slowly opened it and began reading to myself. Gramma stuck pins in the fabric and pretended not to watch me chew my lips.

Eve Elizabeth,

I am writing to tell you that everything has been so nice since you left. Your brothers come in before their curfew and your siblings don't fight anymore. The whole neighborhood is quiet now. I want you to realize the trouble you have caused and how peaceful it is without you here.

You will get what you deserve in life, just remember it is all up to you.

Your Mother

My back teeth bit into the inside of my cheek. I sucked at the blood and set the letter on the table. I went into the bathroom and closed the door. Looking in the mirror, I opened my mouth and watched myself bleed. My tongue streaked red. Wetness rose over my pupils. I swallowed, blinked, and started again. My brows furrowed, my forehead scrunched up. Drops came out my nose and slid off my chin but I wiped nothing away.

It took sixty-eight breaths to stop crying. Other than the burning in the back of my throat, it was a good, raw feeling, kind of like soaking your feet in warm water after walking barefoot in the snow. It was a comfort and for once, Flash had no comment. I washed my face with cold water, dried off, and came back into the kitchen.

Grampa cleared his throat in two beats and rolled a glance to Gramma, who in turn looked at me. After a moment of silence I gave them a wide, fake smile, but they knew better. There I stood with a fat red nose and swollen eyes and one of Mom's corkscrews stuck through my heart. How could it be true? How could I have such a rich and wondrous life with Gramma and Grampa and never get in trouble? Why is it I awake knowing I'll see Gramma and Grampa looking at me with love, and yet I am such a miserable burden to my very own family? Why is it that of all of us, I am the one to bring such ugliness into the world? How did I get the rotten job of giving my brothers and sisters such joy by disappearing? I missed them all so much it was like swallowing thistles to think about it. Suddenly Flash appeared: *It will work itself out, Kid. Get on with it.*

A quiet eagerness rumbled deep inside me. "Okay. I'm going to make some mashed potatoes," I said, then gathered a handful of potatoes and the paring knife. Grampa shook his head and went to the living room to read his mail. Gramma began putting the quilt away. "Did your Mom send news?"

"Yeah, she said everything's fine." I concentrated on keeping the potato peel in one long spiral.

"We're not going to lose you now, are we?"

I set the knife down and reached for the letter. "It doesn't sound like it, but here . . . you can read it."

It was my turn to watch Gramma sit in her rocking chair and read silently. Tears welled up in her eyes and she shook her head quickly, causing her thick, white hair to fall over her face.

"I'm sorry, honey, you just don't deserve this."

"Well, what do you think she means? Do you think she's saying that I'm going to live here the rest of my life?"

"That's the problem with your mother." She pushed her hair back tiredly. "She's so unpredictable, you just never know what to expect."

"I wish I could stay here forever."

"Oh I know, but your family misses you so, I know they do. You kids are supposed to be together. You all need each other. God made you for one another, I'm sure of it."

"Yeah, but Mom doesn't think so, does she?"

"Like I said, I don't know what she has planned. She won't return my calls. We had no idea she was sending you down here four months ago and we still don't know what she's thinking. Oh, it aggravates Pop so." Gramma dropped the letter onto her lap and rocked hard.

"Have I been here four months already?"

"Actually, almost five now." I felt like I had been punched in the shoulder.

"I think I'm going to go for a walk."

"What about your potatoes?"

"I'm not so hungry anymore."

"Oh, honey, you go ahead, but bundle up good. I'll finish up the spuds and fry us up some drumsticks. It's already four-thirty. I know that appetite will come back, so I'll make some coleslaw and biscuits and gravy. Don't stay out too long."

"I won't."

I put Gramma's coat over my own and stepped out into the late wintery day. Buddy and Choppy ran circles around my legs and whimpered.

"Come on, doggie dogs, let's go for a walk. Look! I can see your breath."

We tore out the gate and ran across the icy field. The creek was still solid. It had been frozen since before Christmas, but I stomped on it anyway in hopes of dislodging its first trickle and getting on with a new season. I was done with winter and ice and ruthless, hurtful letters and no kids my own age to hang out with. I couldn't wait to get back out in the sunshine and hunt things that slithered. I kicked at a river rock stuck solid in the earth and wished I could make a fire pit, boil water, and cook crawdads. In the fall Grampa had let me build creek-side fires as long as I was careful and Gramma had let me use her old cast iron pot. She said she didn't much care for eating the bottom-dwellers and when I offered one to Grampa, he said, "Ah Eve, I can't eat an ol', musty crayfish. That thing'd give me heartburn. But now if you'd roast me a raccoon, I'd gobble him right up."

Buddy and Choppy sniffed around until there were icicles hanging off their whiskers. I picked up a crystallized stick and tossed it across the ice. "Fetch, you crazy dogs!" They smiled and took off running. They brought the stick back to me, side by side, each with an end in their teeth. I cracked the stick in half and gave them each a piece to gnaw on.

"I know what the problem is, doggers. I need to go to school before my brain curdles." They crunched their sticks and wagged their bushy tails. "Come on, let's get out of here before a polar bear eats us!"

We ran back across the crackling earth and to the front porch where the dogs collapsed by the screen door. I went in, hung up the coats, and put my boots by the fire to thaw. The aroma of chicken and biscuits filled the warm kitchen. Grampa was asleep in his chair and Gramma stood at the stove stirring rue into hot poultry stock. I went behind her and laid my head on her back.

"Oh my, I can feel your cold cheek right through my housecoat."

"I know, that's why I don't want to touch you with my hands. It's freezing out there."

"Yes it is. That sky looks so dark and heavy."

"I know. Like it could cave in, any minute now."

Gramma sunk a bay leaf in the gravy and rapped the whisk on the edge of the pan.

"There we go, we'll give those legs about ten more minutes in the oven, and then supper will be ready." She leaned to put the whisk in the sink and I leaned with her.

"Gramma?"

"Yes, honey?"

I pressed my forehead into her shoulder blade.

"I want to go to school."

"Oh, dear," she said, and dropped the whisk.

The next day Gramma went into town and signed me up for school at Scio High. She said there were some details she had to work out about parental signature, proof of residency, and custody stuff. She said the bottom line was that Mom had to be notified that I was enrolled in Scio High and that we had to wait six days for my transcripts to be sent from Washington.

When the school secretary called to tell us the paperwork was in order, I ran upstairs and tried on my new skirt and corduroy vest again.

Early the next morning Grampa and Gramma drove me to school, five miles on the icy road. Scio High was a small brick schoolhouse that sat at the end of Main Street under big, barren maple trees. A white wood sign over the door read Scio High School Built in 1910. There was a dusting of snow on the ground and the crisp air was filled with the sound of tires swishing on the street and car doors slamming. Kids tromped up the steps, laughing and yelling to one another. I hadn't heard so much noise in months.

"Well, bye, Grampa." I patted his shoulder.

"Now don't be runnin' for president on your first day," he grinned.

"No need to worry, my fine grandfather. I shall be on my best behavior. Bye, Gramma."

"Oh, honey—don't you think I should go in with you?"

"Nah, it's alright."

"You sure? What if you need something?"

"Well, remember the secretary said we were all set?"

"All right then. Bye, honey. We'll be here to pick you up at 2:50."

"'kay. I love you."

"We love you too."

I got out and closed the door. Grampa pulled away in slow motion.

Here we go again Flash—the new cat on the block.

No worries, Kid.

I went to the office to get my schedule.

Flash, they're all staring at me.

Those are just eyes, not bullets. You'll be fine.

I had seven classes ranging from history to metal shop. Lunchtime came quickly and I was ready for it. Gramma had made me a triple-decker chicken salad sandwich with homemade dill pickles, a boiled potato that was still warm, celery sticks, apple slices, two devilled eggs, and a brownie with extra walnuts in it. Sitting by myself at a table in the corner of the lunchroom, I ate my lunch in less than four minutes, then spent the rest of the lunch hour in the bathroom, retying my shoes, plucking at a hair on my arm, and waiting for the bell to ring.

Gramma and Grampa were there to pick me up after school on the first day and after that I walked down to Gut Ripper Road to catch the school bus.

I started school on a Monday and by Wednesday I felt settled in. I met a girl in my geography class named Sandra. She dressed like a rainbow, had long red hair and the smallest hands I had ever seen on anyone over the age of eight. I wrote to Louanne about Sandra's opossum hands and her purple shoes.

Each night I sat at the kitchen table and did my homework and reported to Gramma about my day and the things I was learning. She took it all in, claiming that it rejuvenated her mind, like she too, was a schoolgirl again.

"I got *Grapes of Wrath* at the library today."

"Oh, honey, I'm so glad you get to read all those stories. But as I recall, that Steinbeck in particular is pretty depressing."

"Yes, but I like it because it's real. I read it in seventh grade. Those poor people had to go through a lot to survive in their new world. It makes me want to go to California some day."

"California is a long way away."

"I have an idea, Gramma. How about I check out two copies if they have them and we can read them at the same time? I get to keep library books for two weeks."

"Wouldn't that be cheating?"

On Friday of the second week, the dark sky finally cracked open and sunshine spilled out over the valley. Tiny buds began to appear on the maple trees and every blade of grass bent toward the warm light. In geography class, Sandra passed me a note that said, "Ronnie Underwood likes you." I wrote back, "Who's Ronnie Underwood?" She began coughing and choking, and then scribbled back, "He's only like the cutest senior in the entire school."

After school that day I jumped off the bus and ran up the driveway, chasing my shadow. I patted the dogs and flew through the front door, excited to give Gramma a Steinbeck book and to have the weekend to read together. Gramma was sitting quietly in her rocking chair. Taking a seat in the other chair, I flashed her a breathless grin.

"Did you see this day? It's beyond belief!"

"Yes, honey, it's lovely. Let's hope it holds."

"Gramma, I brought you a book and Ronnie Underwood likes me."

"Oh, thank you. And who is it that likes you?"

"He's a senior, but I've never seen him."

"Oh my, a senior? Seems to me he ought to keep his wandering eyes closer to his own age."

"Now, Gramma, I remind you Grampa is fifteen years older than you."

"Well, yes, you're right about that. I remember my father just about died when Pop asked for my hand."

"But obviously he said yes."

"Yes, they turned out to be good friends actually. Since neither Pop nor I had siblings, he probably thought we could take good care of each other. God rest dear Dad's soul."

"That's nice," I said.

"Well, isn't this a coincidence? A young man called here this morning about ten o'clock asking for you."

"Really? Who?"

"It was that Steve Henry fellow from out Salem way. He was nice enough. Said he heard from Tim that you were living here and he asked if he could come visit on Sunday."

"What did you tell him?"

"Well, I said I didn't see why not."

My heart pounded in my chest. I wondered what Angie would do. Surely having the attention of two boys was something she had encountered many times.

Oh Flash, this feels almost dangerous.

Yep, Kid, we got some danger on the horizon. Closer than you know—and not what you think.

The front door opened and Grampa came in with the mail and a blast of fresh air.

"Letter for ya, Eve," he said and handed it to me. "How was it down there at Scio High today?"

"It was good, Grampa . . . Oh no."

"What, honey?" Gramma asked.

"It's from Mom."

I opened the letter very slowly and read it out loud.

Eve,

It is time for you to come back and prove that you have learned a lesson. We will be going on a trip and you will be running the household while we are gone. I will see you this Saturday. Take the train.

Your Mother

"What?" I cried.

Gramma got up and went to the sink. "I knew it," she said, shaking her head. "I was afraid that would happen once she heard you were in school."

Grampa stomped into the living room, his boots still on.

"Oh dear, I can tell Pop is upset," Gramma whispered.

The sun blared through the window and the shadow of a hummingbird shot across the kitchen counter. I dropped the letter. The wall clock ticked like a marching band. Shaking my head, I yanked at my earlobes.

"Gramma, I don't want to go back. You have to help me. I *do not* want to go."

"Honey, I wish we could keep you, but we can't."

"Why not?"

"Like Dr. Konofsky used to say when you were little, 'Remember now, Gladys, you have to give her back. She's not yours to keep.'" Her eyes filled.

"It's getting worse. The older I get, it's like the bruises get deeper or something. Can't I please, please live with you and Grampa? I love you so much and I love being with you."

"Oh Eve, I'm so sorry."

"Gramma, I have never said this, but I'm afraid of Mom. I keep getting in trouble and I don't know how to please her. I'm afraid of what she'll do if I mess up again."

"I know, honey, but she *is* your mother. She's a tough bird. I think she sees strength in you that reminds her of herself. I also believe she's jealous, and jealousy can lead a person to unthinkable things."

"That's what I mean, Gramma! I love her more than I know how to say, but I can't tell her because . . . I just can't. And if I try to talk to her about it, she won't listen to me. Nobody knows some of the things she's done and probably she would just say I was a liar if I told, but you're not supposed to hurt your kids. She doesn't do it to the other kids and I just don't understand it!" I closed my eyes and clasped the arms of the rocking chair.

"Oh, this is going to burn Pop up. But we have to do what your mother asks, honey. We have to send you back."

The next morning, misty fog covered the fields and hills. Grampa's mountain was barely visible through the vapor that crept through the valley like a silent, mournful creature. From the pasture below, our cows lowed like distant foghorns. I stood on the porch in my paisley skirt and coat, trying to squint a hummingbird into sight or at least a single ray of sunshine left over from the previous day. The dogs were curled up, reluctant to romp on a soppy lawn after the warmth of the day before.

Gramma wore her town coat and a plastic babushka tied under her chin. She held my "luggage," a paper grocery bag with my clothes, food she had made , and a music book. "Come on, Pop, we need to get to

Penney's before we go to the station."

"I'ma comin'," he said. I watched them walk to the car.

Feeling weak, I bent down and kissed Buddy and Choppy on the ears. "Bye, doggie dogs." Buddy huffed a cloud of dog breath in my face.

"I'm gonna miss you, burlap breath."

I went to the car and fell into the back seat. Grampa turned the key and the engine whirred. As we pulled out, I watched my favorite front porch and my best buddies disappear like steam.

We crawled along through the fog, the wipers slapping hard and slow and the defroster blasting cold air. Stinking Saturday.

"I hope the train is safe in this thick fog," said Gramma.

"Ah, Ma, train travel is the safest way to go. Those engineers are used to all sorts of harsh conditions."

"Gramma, can we just go straight to the train?"

"But we need to get you some decent luggage," she said.

"I really don't need any. The sack is fine."

"Oh, honey, you can't travel all day with a grocery bag. It's disgraceful."

"There won't be any church ladies on the train. I'm just happy that old trunk finally fell apart. And I don't have too many clothes that fit so it'll be easy to carry this."

"Yeah, she'll be all right, Ma. Let's just go to Albany and wait for the train. JC Penney won't even be open this early."

Gramma bit her thumbnail and loosened the strap under her chin.

"All right, but she deserves better." She clicked her tongue, which made her soft chin tremble. "How I hate being rushed like this. Barely a day's notice and we're supposed to get her packed up and off and running at the drop of a hat."

"Don't worry, Gramma. We'll manage just fine," I said.

"Yeah," said Grampa, "that damn Gloria thinks ya gotta get up and lasso the sunrise just to learn a *lesson*."

"Now, Pop."

I leaned over the back seat, hanging between them. "Grampa, I think that's very poetic."

Gramma shook her head again. "We planned on baking a pie to-day, for your friend."

"Yeah, well you still can and if he shows up tomorrow, tell him hello for me."

Gramma opened the glove box, clicked it shut and turned around to face me. Her eyes were rabbit red, which made me want to punch something. She had most likely been awake the entire night, worried sick. She pointed her finger more at the roof than me.

"Now you make sure you don't talk to anyone. And stay on the train. Don't get off even if they ask you to. And pick a seat where the porter can help you if you need it. Get a seat close to the bathroom. But not so close that people will be passing by you every minute. You just never know."

I nodded and shook my head.

"Try to get two empty seats together so you can stretch out and have a nice nap. You should rest while you can. Keep your bag close to you so if you do fall asleep you'll keep it safe. You just never know. And don't start a conversation with anyone."

"I will, Gramma. I mean I won't. I will stay on the train. And I won't get off until I get there. And I'll pick a good seat."

Gramma continued, "I sewed another medallion inside your coat to keep you safe, and you have a whole fried chicken to keep you busy."

"I didn't get to say goodbye to Pam and Korky. Will you kiss them for me, Grampa?"

"Now you know if there's anybody's gonna kiss a horse for you, it'll be me. I'll take over where you left off—barebackin' and Kodakin'."

"Thanks, Grampa. Will you send me pictures too?"

"Of course we will, Honey Girl," said Gramma. "Oh, and there's stamps in the bag too. Make sure you write. Your letters have kept me going for a long time. I want to hear all about what you're all up to. Oh and read. Read and write."

"Do you promise to finish the quilt without me?" I said.

"You bet I will. I'll finish it if it takes me five years."

"Oh, I'll see you way before five years."

"Now, Eve," said Grampa, "don't get the notion your mom would send ya back here if you get into trouble. Gloria's a hell of lot smarter than that."

We pulled into the Amtrak station, where a shining silver train stood on the tracks. The engines roared like a massive waterfall. After Grampa hurried to the counter and bought a ticket, there was little time left for goodbyes. I hugged Grampa, then Gramma, clutched my Scio Food Center bag and boarded the train.

Flash, how can I do this?

Keep moving, Kid. Just keep moving.

I stepped up onto a yellow plastic crate pushed against a narrow metal platform. Inside was a dark enclosure with shelving for luggage and a steep, curving staircase that led up to the passenger seats. Engines boomed all around inside the steel walls. Signs were posted in every direction, *Place luggage here, Watch your step, This way to Observation Car, Warning! High Voltage!*

Upstairs, the train was sheer luxury compared to the Greyhound. The seats were clean, and the passengers were shinier. I set my bag into an empty seat, rubbed a filmy spot off the window, and waved at Gramma and Grampa. I rapped my knuckles on the pane and blew kisses but knew they couldn't see me through the tinted glass.

Keep it together, Kid.

My heart turned to water when I saw Grampa put his arm around Gramma, her plastic cap shaking, scrunched into his chest. *PSSHSHST*, the train began to rock and move forward and my favorite people disappeared.

I looked at the bag sitting next to me. In bold red print under Scio Food Center, it said "We're proud to be Western Family." I looked at the ticket in my hand with the same bold print. ONE WAY.

The train rapidly picked up momentum and trees sped up, backs of houses flashed like a movie. A porter came by collecting tickets. I handed him my ticket and watched him hold onto the seatbacks and swagger to the next car. I was alone except for an elderly couple four rows ahead. I stared at the back of their silvery heads. Gramma had never been on a train, or a bus, or a boat, or a plane.

I'm going to ride everything, Flash. Even an elephant and a camel.

That's the right attitude, Kid. Keep looking forward. And keep your eyes wide open.

The train bounced and creaked along hundreds of miles of rigid train track. We rolled in and out of dark forests, over bridges, through populated areas. Backyard clotheslines and empty cargo cars whizzed by. Children, dogs, even cows were flying. The shadow of the train smacked against barn sides and rippled along acres of wet pastureland.

I got up and walked from car to car, slamming my palm on the flat gray knob that said "Push" to open the dividing doors. Train tracks thundered underfoot, earth spun through the cracks, and heat rose from the friction of metal on metal. After stumbling all the way to the dining car and back, I fell into my seat and opened my grocery sack. Inside, safety pinned to a pair of socks, was a plastic baggie with ten postage stamps, twelve one dollar bills, and fourteen dimes.

Hours passed and passengers bobbed by as I counted phone poles until I was dizzy and read the Amtrak schedule in the seatback pocket in front of me.

How was the pie for Steve Henry coming along? What shoes would Sandra wear on Monday? Would Amber still smell like a baby? I ate everything Gramma had given me. I spoke to almost no one.

Flash, we're getting closer to Bellingham, and I don't feel so good.

Could it be because you ate an entire chicken?

I'm scared.

I'm here.

In the early evening the train screeched into the Bellingham Amtrak station. This was the end of the Northwest run. I grabbed my scrunched-up bag and stomped down the stairs and out the door. Outside the air packed a punch cold enough to sting my lungs.

I looked around, wondering where everyone was.

What were you expecting, a Western Family welcoming committee?

After searching in and around the station, I went back out into the cold, dropped the sack on the concrete and sat on it. I rubbed the medallion inside my coat and tried to figure out what to do. Was this Saturday? Was there more than one train? There wasn't more than one train *station*. Did I mess up? Are we early? I wanted to cry, but I was too cold. I had forgotten about the temperature difference this close to Canada. I did remember one thing, though: my phone number. I went back inside the depot and found a pay phone.

"'Lo?" said Tim.

"Hi, brother."

"Ruby Jane?"

"Yeah, it's me."

"Where are you?"

"I'm at the train station in Bellingham."

"Well, I'll be damned. I didn't hear anything about you coming back."

"Really?"

"No shit."

"Is Mom there?"

"Nope. I'm the only one here. Haven't seen anyone else all day."

"Well, can you come pick me up . . . or . . . should I start walking?"

"No, you stay put. I'll be right there."

"Thanks."

"No problem. I'm glad you're back."

"Sure is cold up here, compared to Scio."

"Ah, you'll get acclimated just like before."

"You think so?"

"Sure."

"Tim?"

"Yeah?"

"What day is it?"

"Saturday."

"Please deposit ten cents for the next three minutes."

"Gotta go. I'll see you soon," I said.

I hung up and ran to the bathroom. Looking in the mirror, I opened my coat and leaned closer to see the side of my neck bouncing where my pulse pounded.

I'm really going home, Flash. I'm going home and getting acclimated. Keep your eyes open, Kid.

Tim pulled up in a gray and white Ford pickup. I ran to his door and jumped up and down until he opened it and got out. I threw my arms around him and hugged him.

"Wow, Ruby. You look bigger."

"You too. Your hair's so long!"

"Yeah. Man, it's good to see you." He roughed up my hair. "You look like you're about fourteen."

"That's because I *am*."

"I'll be damned. Get in."

"Wait, I need to go back in the station for a sec."

"Did you forget something?"

"Yeah. I need to call Gramma and let her know I made it and you're picking me up."

"You got money?"

"Yes, she gave me fourteen dimes and I used two on you."

"Here, I'll go with you."

We rounded the corner and came to the front door of the depot. "That's smart thinkin', Ruby Jane, to call the grandparents from a phone booth. Mom finds a long-distance charge on her phone and you'd be in for a good butt beatin'." He smiled and held the door open for me.

"So," I shrugged, "things haven't changed much?"

chapter eighteen

Sixteenth Hole

I made it to Father's Day.

After Tim brought me home from the train station, we were alone in the Walnut Street House. We came through the back door and went up the stairwell.

"I gotta take a whiz," he said. "Check this out." He opened the bathroom door and I saw the room had been completely redone. "That's Mom's hundred-year-old cast iron bathtub." The nails on the claw feet were painted red.

Tim closed the door and I started to get reacquainted with the place.

The house was more like a mansion than I had remembered. Every piece of furniture was darker, larger, and scarier. Green-eyed gargoyles over the doors guarded the entrances to each room. I went up the steep front stairway and saw that the upstairs hallway, long and dimly lit, now had ethnic masks covering the walls. The masks stared back with no eyes, real teeth, and tufts of human hair sprouting from their ears. The floor creaked as I proceeded to go where I knew I should not: Mom's bedroom.

The door was open so I stepped in. The carpet and walls were fire red, surrounding an ancient Chinese wedding bed with bright red and gold stain. Satin and silk panels draped the windows and walls. Out one window was a view of the bay and what looked like an extension of the room. I crept forward to see that a new structure had been built: a high, arched thing that was taller than the house.

"Ruby Jane!" Tim stood in the doorway.

"God, you scared me."

"Whataya doin'?"

"Oh, just checking it out. This place is creepy."

"Yeah, the folks are getting way out there with the décor. They've been getting into the Oriental and African stuff. See all those beaded things on the wall? Those are from cannibals."

"Gross."

"Larry just finished this add-on. It's called a cupola, which is a turret for looking out. Mom says she needs to keep her eye on who's coming in and out of Puget Sound."

"Is she a sea captain now?"

Tim laughed. "Well, as you know, Mom's capable of anything she sets her mind to. She's gearing up to go to Russia to look for antiques and make peace with the Russians."

"Peace. She's amazing. You're right, there's nothing to stop her."

"Come on," he said, "let's get out of here before they catch us."

The reunion with the family came slowly, like blobs of ketchup dripping from a bottle. First, Three Legs peed on himself, then came Max, who had grown into his nice big teeth. Toby's hair was well past his shoulders and his voice had gotten even deeper. My teeth turned ugly again when I saw that Angie was cuter than ever with a mouthful of braces. Amber screamed "Myeve!" when she saw me. I scooped her up. At almost three years old she still smelled like a baby.

As the days went by I was back to being part of the family. Larry was still a quiet man. Mom was quite a businesswoman now, with her cropped, copper-colored hair and shoulder-length earrings. She and Larry spent most of their time at the new shop, "Gloria's Web," which was inside an antique mall. The door to the shop had been designed by Mom and built by Larry, a four-foot-wide wooden spider web. Mom said the idea was to make the customers feel like they were trapped inside and had to buy something in order to get out.

I was back at Bellingham High trying to catch up and pass ninth grade. Louanne was still the same—all bubbles and butterflies and in love with Jim.

I sat on the couch with Amber on my lap, her head resting on my chest. I rocked her and caressed the soft, fuzzy spot at the nape of her neck. After I spelled "I love you" over and over on her silky skin with my finger, she went limp in my arms and I laid her next to me. Leaning close, I sniffed her sweet breath and stared at her slack little mouth with drool weeping out the side, her tiny, plump cheek smashed against the cushion. Although I knew in my heart something goes wrong for everyone eventually, if they live long enough, I wanted to protect her from everything bad in the world.

Mom walked in the room and announced that she and Larry would be going to Europe on a buying trip. They would begin in London and then go on to Wales and Scotland. Mom said they were going to get even richer. They were going to ship their first container of antiques back across the ocean, increasing their profit margin by three hundred percent. They were scheduled to travel and shop three days in each country, returning by the middle of June. Tim was supposed to handle the money; my job was to babysit Amber, get the little kids to school, cook, clean, and be the fourteen-year-old general manager. The plan sounded fine—except that I would not be able to finish the last three weeks of school.

Two days later, Tim and Toby helped Larry put the new suitcases into the van.

"You better be good, or you know what," said Mom. She stood by the doorway, looking like royalty of her own country. She wore a full-length dress made of scarlet crushed velvet under a calico fur coat and an ecru scarf fringed with rabbit's feet. She glimmered with iridescent maroon eye shadow, lipstick, and nail polish. Her short hair was pinned back in a band of pheasant feathers, exposing her lovely jaw line. It seemed unfair that someone could look that glamorous, confident, and cool.

I held Amber up so she could be kissed goodbye. Angie wrapped herself around Mom's waist, and Max petted her coat and gazed up at her. Larry jiggled the keys in his pocket. "Bye," he said to the room in general.

"Have a wonderful, prosperous time," I said. *Flash, why do I always have to say something so stupid?*

You're fine, Kid.

"Come on, Larry," said Mom. "Get in the van. Tim, you're drivin' us to the airport."

So it went like that for more than a week. Running the household, caring for the needs of people under four feet tall, and dreaming about going to school. When Sunday came—it was Father's Day—we went on a treasure hunt in the park and around the yard. Instead of wheat germ, I put a crushed up Milky Way bar in the pancake batter for the kids.

After dinner that night Tim said, "Hey, man, I'm havin' the dudes over for some jams."

"You better not, Tim," I said. "You know the folks wouldn't approve. You're not 'sposed to touch Larry's stereo. And besides, there's school tomorrow."

"Well, how in the hell will they know, anyway? They're not coming back for another week." His eyes were floating in Budweiser.

"I know, but I don't feel right about it."

"Screw it, Ruby Jane. I'm almost eighteen and I can do whatever I want. Toby's been gone every night, out with his girlfriend."

"Yeah, I noticed. Whatever, Tim—just keep it down when we're asleep."

The back door opened and in walked Steve Henry. I lost my breath. He smiled, shook the hair out of his eyes, and stepped toward me.

"You remember ol' Steve, don't you, Ruby?" said Tim.

I stood there as if I were lost, like I'd possibly walked into the wrong house.

"Ah, yes. Yes, hello, Steve Henry."

He stepped forward and set his hands on my shoulders. He stood more than six feet tall and still smelled like beer, only . . . better beer. As I looked up, he leaned down and kissed me softly on the very corner of my mouth. "Hello, Eve," he said.

Tim laughed, "God, Henry, moving in kind of fast aren't you? She's only fourteen."

I looked around, worried the other kids might have seen, especially Angie. But no one else was there to bear witness.

"Come on, Steve, let's go get some more beer," said Tim. Steve Henry pointed his finger at me and said, "I'll be back to talk to you."

I got nervous and ran upstairs to write Gramma a letter. I opened the last letter she'd sent to get the stamps, just when Max called for me to help him get something off his closet shelf. I crammed the stamps in my pocket and went to his room.

By nine o'clock, Angie, Max, Amber and I were in bed. It had been two hours since Tim and Steve left and I was still dressed in jeans and a sweatshirt, hoping they would come back. When I had brushed my teeth and cleaned my face, I made sure not to wash the spot he had kissed.

I heard rumbling below then music blared up through the floorboards. Pink Floyd— *Dark Side of the Moon*. I crept down the back stairs and saw there was a house full of teenagers. Steve Henry was in the kitchen and motioned me to come to the door. We went out and sat on the back porch.

The black sky winked as if it knew. High above the park lay a white spray of the Northern Lights. Three Legs came up and sat on my bare feet.

"Remember Three Legs?" I asked.

"How could I forget? That was one of the worst days of my life when I ran over him."

"Oh, but I know it was an accident."

"You do?"

"Well, sure. Why would a person hit a dog on purpose? You know, he's a special dog. He's been hurt many times but he always survives. Nothing can break his spirit. He just keeps on going."

"Just like you," he said.

"Like me?"

"Yeah, your old lady said you're too strong-willed and you have to be chiseled down a bit."

I turned to his face. "How would you know that?"

"Tim told me. He told me your mom brought you home to straighten you out." He shook his head and his hair fell back over his face.

"Do you think I need straightening out?" I rubbed Three Legs' ears and thought about my buck teeth.

"Not at all. I think you're just right." He pulled out a Camel filter. "Want one?"

"No, thank you." I scratched Three Legs' nose.

"Sorry I can't offer you something better to smoke, like straw," he grinned.

"Funny."

The porch suddenly thudded under us. I jumped up. "I better go check in there. Tim promised me he wouldn't wake up the kids."

"Wow, you're so *responsible*." He gently pulled on my hand. "Hey, Eve. Sit down for a minute more, Okay? Relax." He lit the Camel and took a long draw.

I tried to sit but my legs felt too unsteady, so I stood with my hands in my pockets, touching the stamps. Three Legs nudged me.

"Tim and Toby have been keeping me up on you," he said. "I think about you all the time and I've been waiting for the day I finally tracked you down. I can't believe I just missed seeing you in Scio. I had a nice visit with your grandparents even though their dogs freaked me out."

"Buddy and Choppy?"

"Yeah, they're big and I have a thing about big dogs because my cousin got his face chewed up by one when we were little."

"Oh, how awful!"

"Yep, it happened in Oregon City. That's where I got this scar on my arm. Not from the dog, but from running away from him and I got snagged by a big bolt on the fence."

"That's awful."

"You know what the worst part was?"

"What?"

"My cousins, Victor and Ross, were identical twins. Victor's face was totally messed up."

He stood up and put his hand on my arm. "How come you didn't answer any of my letters since you've been back?"

"What letters?"

"I wrote you a bunch. One letter was thirteen pages."

"I swear I have never gotten a letter from you."

"You know that you and I are destined to be together some day, don't you?" He stared at me through the dark and I got scared he was going to kiss me again so I plunked my butt onto the porch. He sat next to me. He held the cigarette between his teeth and said, "I want to take you somewhere special tomorrow. I have a Camaro and I painted it blue just for you."

There he was—my destiny sitting beside me with a knowing grin and a blue Camaro. Somewhere between my tongue going numb and my blood heating up, an explosion came from inside the house.

"What was that?" I gasped.

We jumped up, knocking Three Legs off the porch. The back door flew open and bodies rolled out, arms, legs, beer bottles, masses of flying hair. I swam through the crowd and into the living room where Larry's new quadraphonic sound system hissed and spurted—speakers blown.

Standing on my tiptoes, I reached up to turn the stereo off. As I pushed the power button the front door opened behind me, about to let in another pack of partiers. Turning around, I suddenly knew I was standing on the dark side of the moon. Mom said, "Get your hands off the stereo and get these people out of my house. I'll deal with your ass later."

I ran into the kitchen and saw it was empty. I hurried to the window—the only vehicle there was the van. I looked around for Larry, but didn't see him. I listened for Amber crying, but the house was quiet except for the hissing in my ears. Peeking into the front hall, I saw it was empty so I scrambled up the stairs, three steps at a time.

"Stop right there!" Mom's voice speared me from behind. At the top of the stairs I turned around and looked down at her standing with her hands behind her back. I gripped the cool, smooth mahogany railing and stood like a statue.

Time has an uncanny way of stopping when you least expect it. In that one still lapse nothing moved around or within me, as if I were filled with quiet, weightless water. It was that frozen moment in time, after the bomb hits, just before the first scream.

All I saw was her mouth. Like a loaded gun. *No lipstick.*

"You get down here right now and take your beating."

The time has come to tell her, Kid.

A warm vibration began to shimmer from my core through my

arms and legs.

Flash, I'm too scared.

Tell her.

No.

Now.

"I am too old for a beating," I said.

"Is that right?" Her mouth turned into a sour pout.

Go on.

"Mom, I think we should just be able to talk about this. I didn't have that party. Those weren't even my friends, you can ask Tim. I did everything you asked of me and . . ."

She shot up the stairs like an arena bull going in for the kill. My words turned into a mouthful of mud, my ears stopped working. I put my arms up over my head. She attacked with something I couldn't see, but it was hard enough to do some damage. In blind silence I rolled down the stairs in contorted somersaults and hit the front door.

Grappling for the doorknob, I opened the door and took off running. It was cold and it was dark, but I kept running and didn't look back. A sharp pain shot through my left ankle. I ran into the park and crouched down into the bushes and waited.

She would surely come after me with a flashlight and a rope.

No, maybe she'll call the neighbors or tell Larry to find me and drag me home by the eyebrows. Knowing how clever she is, she'll get Three Legs to find me. That's what I would do if I was looking for me. When my breathing slowed down the shakes took over.

I suddenly craved warmth. I needed Gramma. I longed for understanding, a fair chance to speak, an answer to it all. My face was wet. Was it tears or blood? My nose felt too big. I wanted to find my destiny, ride in a blue Camaro, have socks and shoes, and punch Tim in the guts. I wanted Dad to be home for Father's Day and tell me I was special and everything would be all right. I wanted the Earth to stop moving underneath me, to stay in one place with my family. I wanted Steve Henry to kiss me again and overcome his fear of dogs. I needed my ankle to stop swelling, to hold my baby sister, and have a normal life without it falling apart every time the seasons changed.

And as if an angel heard me, there came laughter from the fountain. Everything was too sharp, too clear. The air pressed on my skin like cold metal, I saw porch lights twinkling through the trees surrounding the park, the earth smelled like night underneath me and the sound of the fountain was loud and alive. The laughter came again, the giggle of a girl mixed with splashing water.

I crawled onto my stomach and looked toward the fountain. On the park bench were two lovers. It was Rachael Steel and Wesley Ross, seniors who spent many nights kissing in the park.

I crawled out from under the bush. "*PSSSST.*" Rachael screamed and covered her mouth.

"Rachael and Wesley," I whispered.

"Who's there?" said Wesley.

"It's me, Eve."

"What the hell are you doing in the bushes?" he said.

"I'm kinda in trouble."

"Are you hiding?"

"Yeah, I messed up big time." I got to my feet and limped toward them. They were under a big blanket, wrapped around each other, their faces lit by the underwater fountain lights. Rachael covered her mouth and screamed into her hand. "Oh, my God! Look at you! What happened to your face?"

My hands went to my face and I realized my nose was bleeding.

"I accidentally fell down the stairs."

"Where's your shoes?" asked Wesley.

"I left them in the house."

"Something isn't ringing true here," said Wesley.

I sat down on the bench next to them and when they nestled closer together I began to cry. They looked so safe and warm and in love, none of which were even a distant memory to me.

"Fess up. Tell us what really happened," said Wesley. "We saw a bunch of cars peeling out from your house. What was goin' on over there?"

Gradually I told enough of the truth to get some help. Wesley offered to let me stay at his place until I figured out what to do. Rachel said we should call the police, which I knew would surely get me killed. She explained that there were safe places to go when kids didn't get along with their parents. There were agencies that protected kids from harm. I talked about living in the park, walking right back through the front door of the house or running away from home, but all my options tasted like vinegar in my mouth.

Finally Wesley convinced me to get in his car. We got in his Volvo and drove first to Rachael's house. I stayed in the back seat and watched them kiss on the doorstep, something straight out of a romance novel. Wesley got back in the car and said, "Okay, little one, off we go."

"I don't feel very little," I mumbled. Then I sat up straight. "Where are we going, Wes?"

"Ah, don't worry. I got my own pad and my parents are totally cool. They even let Rachael hang out with me sometimes."

I touched the crusted blood on my face and felt the pounding ache in my ankle. I leaned on the window so I could see the stars.

We pulled in front of the Ross house. It was made of red brick and had ivy growing on an arch over the porch. The detached garage where Wesley lived was also made of brick and covered with ivy. The stone pathway to the front door was lit with copper lights shaped like tulips. I stayed in the car and watched Wesley's feet float through the strips of light and up the steps as he went in to see his parents. Through the kitchen window I saw Wesley talking to his mom and hugging her goodnight. I could tell he was a good son because she smiled at him.

He then took me to his room. In the light he looked at me and shook his head. "Man, this sucks a big one. You can sleep here," he pointed to a couch. "I've got lots of extra blankets and pillows."

"That's great. Thank you so much. Did you tell your folks I'm here?"

"No, but it's cool. Hey, my alarm is set for 6:45, but you can sleep as long as you want. You're gonna ditch tomorrow, right?"

"No. There's only a few days left and I've got to make up some tests."

"Okay," he said, "Come morning, I'll give you a ride. And hey, right here is some of Rachael's stuff. You can use whatever you want, she's cool. There's shoes and clothes and a bunch of things in the bathroom, chick things."

"Hey, Wesley, really, thank you so much."

"No problem. I'm just glad we were there when you came to the park."

"Well, goodnight."

"'Night."

Lying alone in the darkness the pain began to turn to shame. How could I do this to Mom after all she had done for me? But—how could she do this to me? I must have finally pushed her over the edge. What now? What if she's going berserk, wondering if I'm okay? I know the panic I would feel if Amber came up missing. Maybe this was my lucky night. Maybe that was the final act, the last hurrah, the blast in the plaster that brought the wall down between us. Maybe I should just go home and try to talk to her again. No, I better let her cool off. No, she's never going to cool off, that's what makes her Mom. She's special that way, always full of explosive surprises. I wonder if she's going to sock it to Tim. *Dear God, please bless them all, especially tonight, and please double bless Three Legs and Wesley and Rachael. And please Dear God in Heaven forgive me for hurting my mother and my family. Amen.* I closed my eyes and saw red carpet, baby drool, and rabbit's feet.

I slept until 5:59. When I woke up I could hardly move. My ankle was swollen and my muscles ached like I had the flu. I pushed myself out of bed and went to the bathroom. Wesley was sound asleep with an *Autoshop* magazine by his pillow. In the bathroom I looked at my thrashed face and thought I could just scrub the mess off with a hot shower, but I was wrong. Afterwards I put my clothes back on, borrowed a pair of Rachael's sandals, and a new toothbrush. Wesley woke up with a smile. "Seniors don't really have to go to school because we're about to graduate, but we're signing yearbooks today," he said.

"Cool."

When we got in Wesley's car he said, "Here, this is for you. I have two and I bet you could use it sometime." He handed me a small green box. I opened it to find a shiny red Swiss Army knife.

"Oh my gosh! Thank you so much."

"You're welcome. Just don't stab anybody."

"Oh don't worry, I would never do that."

When we got to school I sought out Louanne first thing.

"Oh, my God, girl—look at your face! Is your nose broken or what?"

"I just got a few bruises."

"Jesus, tell me what happened."

"Lou, I gotta go. The bell's gonna ring and I can't walk very fast. I don't want to be late."

"That's the beauty of a freshman," she said. "Meet me right here at first break."

"Okay, bye." I started to limp away and she reached for my hand. "Hey, this whole thing with your mom is messed up. She did this, didn't she?"

"I deserved it."

"When you say shit like that, I'd like to kick your ass myself."

chapter nineteen

Nooksack

Louanne and I met right after the first bell rang. She grabbed me in the hallway and shoved me into a bathroom. We were crouched on a toilet seat when she said she had just seen Angie, who told her I better not come home. She quoted Mom as saying, "I'm goin' to jail tonight for child abuse because when I get my hands on that girl I'm gonna break every bone in her body."

With the Swiss Army knife and Flash and Louanne, my plan was made. We ran out of the bathroom and to the parking lot. I squatted down on the floorboard of Louanne's Honda while she drove to her house. Both her parents were at work when we made the raid. It took us twelve and a half minutes.

When the car trunk was stuffed with supplies, we drove east on Mt. Baker Highway. My plan was to simply run away and live outdoors until I found somewhere else to go, possibly Canada.

For now, I had it in my mind to go to the Nooksack River, which came out of the Cascade Mountain Range around Mt. Baker near the Canadian border. It was seventy-five miles long and was fast-running and cold. There was a waterfall that dropped a hundred feet into a deep, rocky river canyon. I knew some kids from Mt. Baker High had hiked up to the waterfall, and it was considered a dangerous place which is why they did it. I thought I would go down the North Fork, the other way from the waterfall and find a place along the river, far from people.

The day was clear and bright, unlike my face. "Not a puff in the sky," I said.

Louanne looked at me and scowled. "Yeah, but you sure have a puffy face."

I popped open the mirror on the visor, but the vision scared me and I immediately snapped it shut. "Charming. I look like a warthog. It'll heal. It always does."

"Aren't you afraid of anything?" Louanne asked.

"Well, obviously I'm afraid of my mother, but my biggest fear? You know."

"Oh, yeah—starving to death."

"That's right. And I don't expect to have the experience anytime soon."

When we got to Nugent's Bridge, Louanne took the steep dirt road leading down to the river. We parked under the bridge, out of sight.

"Good job," I said. "Hard to hide red paint."

We unloaded the trunk. Together we carried camping gear, an ice chest packed with food, and my lifeline; a ten-pound sack of Russet potatoes. We climbed down the sandy path and scaled the riverfront. Each time we stopped to rest, Louanne said, "Here?"

"Nope."

The river meandered, flowing with bubbling ripples and pounding rapids. We passed quiet, swollen pools, log jams, and keeper-holes. The light breeze smelled of river water and summertime.

"I can't wait to catch some crawdads."

"Gross!" Louanne squeaked. "Are we gonna walk all day? You don't even have shoes on."

"Probably," I said, "you're squeaking again."

"How's your ankle?"

"Sore, but sticking it in the water feels good."

Along the rock and sand shore were clusters of bear grass and thick, green river willows. We wrestled our way through acres of rocks and wispy limbs until we finally came to a small clearing.

"My new home." We dropped everything and fell to the ground.

The clearing was smooth with fine, gray sand, protected by a circle of willows standing around us like old friends. On one edge of the clearing, a massive fallen fir created a wall. I walked toward the roar of rapids and came out at the river's edge. The Nooksack raced by, deep and dark with the opposite shore a good-quarter mile away. I was definitely far from human contact. My campfires would be well hidden and if necessary I could easily find my way back to Mt. Baker Highway. I walked up to Lou, who was draped over the heap of supplies. "Pretty cool," she said, "I can't wait to come back and hang out with you."

"So, are we clear on the plan?" I asked.

"Yep. I'll be back in four days."

"You've got the letter, right?"

"Yep, it's in my glove box."

"I left the shoes in your car. Don't forget to give them back to Rachael and tell her thanks again for the toothbrush."

"Got it."

"Oh wait, I almost forgot these." I reached in my jean pocket, pulled out the wrinkled stamps, and handed them to her. "Come on, I'll walk you at least halfway back. God, I miss my dog already."

Louanne left me with a long hug and a short "Good luck, you nut." She was on her way to an ice-skating competition in Seattle. She was hoping to take the gold. We agreed that to protect us both, after the competition she would ask permission to go camping with her friend Kris's family. Kris and her family had already left town, so we figured we had it covered. Louanne was going to tell her parents that she was joining Kris and their RV in Birch Bay, which was on the other side of the county from where we stood. I had become a conniving liar almost overnight.

My world had once again flipped. At home for so many weeks I was engrossed in chaos, kids, and chores, but here in my river rock hideout I felt like I could fly, so free and clear-headed. I would not allow lonliness.

That's because you're never alone, Kid.
Thanks, Flash.

The first day in the life of a river-dwelling runaway goes something like this: Oh gee, I guess I better build a house. It took the rest of the afternoon to gather enough long, thick, fairly straight sticks. With string, I tied them together to make a frame, attached it to the giant log, and draped it with an old tarp that belonged to Louanne's dad. I slit her uncle's heavy raincoat up the back and covered the entrance with it so I could zip it open and closed like a real tent. Louanne had convinced me that I wasn't a thief; I was merely borrowing some things that her parents and her dead uncle would never miss.

As I built my seventeenth house, I thought of him. He was an Army doctor, that uncle. He had died tragically by choking to death while driving his car and ran it straight through a civilian's house. He crashed through the front picture window while a family was eating dinner and was found slung over the steering wheel, halfway in their living room, dead and blue. Louanne never could remember what he choked on, but she said according to her father, he was a brilliant man.

So I had supplies and books from a brilliant dead man. Louanne had told me I could pick any books I wanted from their bookcase. I chose *Diseases of the Internal Organs*, *Northwest Botanicals*, and a brand new 1975 copy of *Shōgun* by James Clavell. I built a shelf of rocks and sticks inside my tent and placed the books there beside my paper and pencil. I laid out a mummy bag to sleep in and folded my sweatshirt into a pillow.

Finally the sun dropped below the canyon rim, but the summer sky reflected the light for a long time. When the temperature dropped, I dragged everything inside the fort and made three peanut butter sandwiches. I sat on the ice chest and ate them as the sounds of night began to blend with the rushing water. Frogs. *There are only frogs out there.* In twilight, I tidied things up and by dark I was zipped up and exhausted inside my new home. I closed my eyes, listened to the lullaby of the rapids, and counted houses.

I awoke early the next morning and crawled out, blasted by cool, damp air and a screeching blue jay above my tent. I looked up at him and said, "Good morning to you too. Thank you for not being a crow." At the river's edge I got down on my knees and stuck my face into the freezing water. It felt good on my nose. I put my foot in a swirling rapid and soaked it until it went numb. Far across the Nooksack, river willows, with their little unfolding leaves, gleamed in the early light, and the sky was already coming to life with a thin, bright streak that ran over the trees like fire. A thousand wild birds rose screaming into the light. I watched the crystal-clear sky shift to pale blue as the birds flew upriver until they disappeared around the bend. I brushed my teeth and went back to camp to make breakfast.

Before breakfast I built a cooking pit. It consisted of a circle of river rocks with a deep sand bottom and three large stones. Beside it, I tied three poles together for hanging a small pot, a frying pan, and a metal mug. Gathering firewood would be an ongoing job, but easy enough because there was so much of it. I started a small fire and set a pot of water to boil for hot chocolate. Louanne had left me a full box of Swiss Miss with miniature marshmallows. With a forked stick I toasted three pieces of bread and roasted a piece of bacon. The fire flared up as mouthwatering fat dropped off the stick. Grampa used to say everything tasted better outside and he was right. The bacon and hot chocolate were finished off with a tangerine, two bananas, and a Snickers bar.

After breakfast I cleaned the pot in the river and gathered more firewood. Sitting down by the swirling smoke, I assessed the supplies. No more clothes, but there were ten pounds of potatoes, which were far more important than clothes; a dishtowel, which would also be my bath towel, and a big box of wooden matches. No flashlight, but that didn't matter because I would be inside when it was dark. Books, paper, toothbrush, and a bar of Ivory soap. No hairbrush, but I had a corkscrew and a toothpick on my Swiss Army knife for keeping the tangles at bay. There was a tablespoon, a baggie of small nails, and a half-used ball of string.

We had made sure to bring plenty of food; the plan was that Louanne could replenish anything I needed for as long as needed. When the small amount of ice melted I would have the freezing river to keep things cold. There was a piece of tinfoil and a wad of paper napkins, which reminded me I needed to dig a toilet.

Throughout the day, the angle of the sun was my only way of telling time, but I soon realized it didn't matter. I ate when I was hungry, which came to be six or seven times a day. It took most of the second day to dig a toilet with a spoon and a sharp rock and to make a cover out of a heavy slab of wood. As the sun went for the hills across the river, I stood and surveyed my camp. Stones lined the entire perimeter of the camp and marked out the toilet, the kitchen and the entrance to the bedroom. The tarp was completely covered with branches and bordered by the biggest rocks I could carry.

By nightfall I was exhausted again. Inside the mummy bag I closed my eyes and gave myself up to the feeling of being part of the rapids themselves, swift, unrelenting, and free. They too, were river runaways.

Four days passed and there was no sign of Louanne. I began to doubt my sense of time. The river could do that to a person. Because the splashing sounds were constant and the light changed frequently, the dancing shadows became undefined by time. I stuck four sticks in the sand and made it a point to add one each morning to keep track of the days that passed.

On day five, after flossing my teeth with bear grass, I made boiled potatoes and hunted crawdads. After they were cooked up and devoured, I tossed the pink shells into the rapids and watched them get swept away. It gave me the idea to take a bath, but it was more like going through a carwash when I slipped naked into the bone-chilling water and twirled down the rapids until I got hold of a log jam and pulled myself out.

Where is Louanne? I let the sun dry my skin while I ate noodles, then in my underwear I walked further down the river until I found a calm, deep swimming hole. *When she finally gets here, I'm going to push her in.*

Each night before bed I wrapped a potato in tinfoil and pushed it into hot coals. In the morning I had a baked potato for breakfast. The bacon lasted almost a week. I saved some of the grease in a soup can and made French fries with it. I ate potatoes boiled, fried, baked, roasted, and even raw. I made mashed potatoes, my favorite, but that made me miss Gramma terribly.

Where could Louanne have gone? The plan was that she would mail my letter to Gramma from Seattle. I hoped Gramma didn't cry when she heard I had left home. My letter explained that I was in a safe place where I could get therapy on my foot and that I would write her again.

On the sixth day I ventured east into the woods. Marking my trail with broken branches, I eventually got out of the river willows and into deeper old-growth forest. It felt ten degrees cooler in a clearing where stumps and pieces of huge trees lay around covered with emerald green moss and dappled sunlight. I figured there had been loggers here a long time ago. There was a patch of wild strawberries and Miner's lettuce, which I ate by the handful. The earth was musty and damp under my feet. Decomposed fir needles covered the ground, trilliums were in full bloom, and sword fern taller than me sprang from the soft, rotted wood of the fallen giants.

The logs gave me the idea to build some furniture for Louanne. It took all day to roll three big stumps back to camp. I gathered twigs, grass, branches, and a long rock for pounding nails. By nightfall I had completed a three-piece dinette set that looked like something bears would own. A soup can full of wildflowers sat in the center of the table. I ate Kraft macaroni and cheese inside my tent, licked the pan half clean, and kept it inside my sleeping bag.

On the seventh morning I knew it was going to be a hot day. I added water to the leftover cheese sauce in the pan and made au gratin potatoes for breakfast. When I saw there was one potato left, I panicked. Where is she? I know she would have been here if something bad hadn't happened. She must have gotten caught with my letter. Or worse yet, what if Mom found her and nabbed her by the throat? I packed a big lunch and headed for Nugent's Bridge.

After walking two miles, my head was so hot I stuck it in the river. Then I sat down, took off my pants and cut the legs off with my Swiss knife blade and scissors. I hung the pant legs in a tree to pick up on the way back. Just reaching up to a high branch made me remember vividly the moment I had stood on my tiptoes to turn the stereo down. Chills ran through me and I peed a dab in my shorts when I heard a branch crack. I jumped into a thicket and covered my mouth.

There was Louanne's unmistakable laugh—and a guy's voice. I

jumped out and scared them. She screamed and jumped on me, knocking us both down. I began to cry.

"Where have you been?" I sniffed.

"Sorry. I'll explain. This is Jim."

"Hey," he nodded. He was tall with no shirt, baggy pants, and clean brown hair past his shoulders. He was carrying a framed backpack that I hoped was full of food.

"Hey." I wiped my nose on my wrist.

Louanne stared at me. "My God. Your freckles are like totally connected to one another."

I said, "I can't believe this, I mean I have been out here for a week without ever leaving camp except to go to the river or the woods and I finally decide to walk this way and here you are."

"Yeah, trippy, huh?" she grinned. Jim smiled slowly. He was as quiet as Louanne was silly.

"Come on, let's get back to camp," I said.

"Get ready," she said to Jim. "It's a hell of a long way to camp."

"Cool," he said and we started walking. I jumped up and grabbed the jeans legs off their branch and wore them on my arms.

"You've got to excuse her, she's a little weird," Louanne giggled.

When we got back to camp Jim set the backpack down and went to the river.

Louanne looked around and sat down on one of the chairs. "Wow, where did this furniture come from?"

"Do you like it? I made it from stumps in the woods."

"God, you crack me up! I hate to say it, but this looks like something your mother would have done. Pretty creative. Man, you've sure got this place neat and tidy."

"Yeah, well now you know what I do all day when you ditch me for days on end. Where the heck have you been anyway?"

Louanne caught me up on everything that had happened. For one thing I had been there for nine days, not seven. She had mailed my letter from Seattle. She took the bronze medal in skating on the first day and the silver on the second. She told her mom she had no idea where I was and got permission to go camping with Kris for three more days. I learned with satisfaction that my mom had called her mom and a bunch of other people, including the police.

"That makes me feel better," I said.

"Are you crazy?"

"I can't help it. It makes me feel like at least she cares enough about me to call the police. That means she wants me back, right?"

Louanne shook her head. "Not necessarily, girl."

"I'm rotten."

Jim came through the branches.

"No, you're not," she said. "How do you like it Jim? Pretty cool, huh?"

"Yeah," he sighed, "I can dig it."

Louanne and Jim stayed for the next two and a half days. They skinny-dipped and kissed. We ate steaks and drank A&W root beer, played cards, and told scary stories. The backpack was full of drinks and food, including hotdogs, frozen hamburger patties, potatoes, and M&M's.

"You ever see any wild animals out here?" asked Jim.

"Mostly birds. I saw an eagle one morning and a hawk flying with a snake hanging from its claws. I yelled at him not to drop it near me or I'd eat it."

"Cool."

"Aren't you afraid of bears or coyotes?" said Louanne.

"Well, I never stay out after dark. And like my grandmother says, it's the two-footed creatures you have to worry about."

On the day they left with trash in the backpack and another letter for Gramma, Jim and Louanne decided to take a look at the forest where I had found the furniture stumps. By the expression on Louanne's face, they wanted to go there without me. While they were gone I made lunch and put fresh flowers in the can.

When they came back Louanne was grinning and her cheeks were bright red.

"What?" she said.

"What, what? I didn't say anything," I said.

"Yeah, but you're looking at me funny."

"That's because your pants are on inside out."

For the next few days I studied *Northwest Botanicals* and *Diseases of the Internal Organs*. Collecting wild sage, thistle, and salmon berries took up most of the mornings. I found plants to ward off bats, attract butterflies, and make spaghetti sauce.

Dear Gramma,

First of all I am safe. I am at a place where we are learning about plants. My ankle is all healed up and I am getting lots of good food. I clean the kitchen, the living room and the bathroom. We all help with the gardening because it is the rule that everyone here has to pitch in.

I know I am very bad for what I have done, but I want you to understand I felt I had no other choice. I was in Mom's line of fire and I had to leave to save her as much as myself. Sometimes I think she is so much happier without me, yet I wish on every star that I am wrong.

I don't understand God's will anymore. Here you are Gramma, so angelic you are a direct line to Heaven and you lost your dear mother when you were only two. I on the other hand am given a beautiful, bold mother and I am a fishbone stuck in her craw. I have had a lot of time to think about it and have decided that I will do everything in my power to make Mom like me, even if it takes me the rest of my life.

Please give Grampa my love and beg him not to be mad at me. I will write again soon. I love you and miss you both.

Love,

Eve

P.S. Give Buddy and Choppy a hug for me. Xo and S.W.A.K (that's sealed with a kiss)

Louanne showed up a week later. I had given up trying to keep track of the days, but she said it had been seven since she and Jim had left. She said she could stay for two nights and that the search for me had been called off. We sat by the fire in a circle of yellow light, listening to the rapids and the frogs through the darkness.

"The funny thing is," she said, "that Gloria called my mom just yesterday and told her they found you in Oregon. She said you were back living with your grandparents."

"She really said that? Why?"

"I don't know. You know your mom. It's some form of psychological warfare to get you all freaked out."

"Well, actually, I wasn't freaked out until now. The whole thing is creepy. Poor Gramma, I wonder what Mom told her, that I'm home in my own bed writing weird letters?"

"I don't know what to think anymore. You want to roast marshmallows? We can get jacked up on sugar and tell scary stories."

"I'll roast a marshmallow but let's skip the stories."

"Yeah, especially since Jim's not here to protect us." She smiled and the firelight bounced off her braces.

"I wonder what Angie and Amber think," I said.

"Maybe they believe you're living with your grandparents."

"I miss them all so much. Max and Amber are going to grow up while I'm gone and Tim and Toby will probably be married before I see them again. Angie's surely forgotten about me."

"I doubt it."

"I was thinking earlier today, do you suppose we could get Jim to kidnap Three Legs and bring him to me?"

"You're crazy."

"No, I'm not. My first thought was to kidnap Amber, but I know that would be very wrong."

"Oh my God, I can't believe you sometimes."

"What was that?" I said.

"What?"

"Shh, listen." Something snapped in the dark, just outside the glow.

"Oh, my God!" Louanne screeched.

I jumped into her lap and covered her mouth.

"Stay calm," I whispered with my forehead pressed to hers. Right behind her stepped a black timber wolf with firelight in his eyes. I fell backward taking Louanne with me. The beast disappeared.

"Let's get in the tent. Now!" I said. A shadow fell over us. We screamed and wrapped our arms and legs around each other. I thought we were dead. Standing over the fire was a giant of a man with an axe over his shoulder. He put a huge hand out in front of him.

"Thoom, tho, tho, ith onay."

"What's he saying?" Louanne whimpered. She was pulling the hair from my temple.

"Shhh, stop it!" I sat up and tried to keep my voice from shaking. "Um, hello. Um, we're sorry, but you scared us. And the wolf. Is—is that your wolf?"

"Are you nuts?" Louanne yanked harder.

"I'n Nemoth," he said, patting his chest. He towered over us. His eyes were half closed, like a lizard.

"He's a harelip," Louanne hissed.

"Shut up." I grabbed her hand. "And stop pulling on me. Um, Nemoth, is that your name?"

Louanne blew. "He's gonna kill us!" she screamed.

He stuck his big fingers in his mouth and let out a piercing whistle. The bushes cracked and the wolf came crashing through the willows. When he got within the circle of light we could see he was a German shepherd.

"Oh, my God!" Louanne cried. "It's a dog."

"Ne, ne, themoth." He put the ax down and patted the dog on the back.

"Oh, my God," I said. "Are you Delbert?"

He nodded his head wildly.

"Who's Delbert?" Louanne squeaked.

"Lori Mezo's brother."

"Who the hell is Lori Mezo?"

"I knew her from seventh grade at Mt. Baker. They live on the other side of the bridge. It's a huge family with a pack of kids and a hundred animals," I whispered. "Lori said Delbert is as harmless as a church mouse."

"Delbert!" I said cheerfully. "Is that right? Are you Delbert Mezo?" He nodded again.

"Shit," Louanne jumped up. "I'm gonna have a heart attack. Why does he have an ax?"

"Delbert," I said, "why do you have an ax?"

"I'n chommin woon."

"Chopping wood?"

"Mmmm," he bobbed his head. He picked up the ax and walked into the darkness with his dog. We sat speechless, straining to hear over the sound of the rapids.

Delbert came back with an armful of fire logs and stacked them neatly on the woodpile. I tried to talk with him as best I could, trying to ignore Louanne muttering, "Oh, my God" like an idiot.

I tried to find out how long Delbert had known about us. Had he told anyone else? He shook his head violently. I asked him if he only came out at night—again the head shake. Then without a word, he lifted his ax and walked away toward the bridge.

We stayed up until the sky began to lighten in the east and we were sure Delbert and his dog, King, were gone. When the dark line of trees became visible and the birds of the river began to rustle above, we crawled into the tent and zipped it up.

Louanne yawned. "That was totally the weirdest night of my entire life."

Louanne left the next day with two more letters for Gramma. She would mail them from Everette, where she had a piano recital.

After Lou was gone, I stripped down and washed all my clothes in the river: tank top, cutoffs, underwear. Fortunately I had a dishtowel to wear when I came back to stoke up the fire. On the table there was a small woven basket with six brown eggs in it. "Delbert?" I called. No answer. I boiled the eggs, ate two soft-boiled, and cooked the rest to make egg salad sandwiches for lunch.

Three days later I saw the giant again. He walked up without King and handed me a small bundle. It was something solid, wrapped in a rag.

"Hello, Delbert. How are you today?" He didn't answer, but just looked at the package in my hand. "Thank you, Delbert. What is it?"

"Ith a nihun."

"A chicken?"

"Neth," he nodded.

"Oh, Delbert, how sweet of you. Did your mom chop its head off?"

"Neth," he said. When he smiled the tip of his nose dipped into the space where an upper lip should have been.

I unwrapped the cloth. There was a tiny chicken wrapped in wax paper. It had been plucked clean, the cavity stuffed with ice and salt.

"Would you like to stay and have dinner with me?" I asked. But he turned around and walked away.

chapter twenty

Independence Day

Loneliness hit hard the evening I roasted a dead salamander.

After finding the small creature belly-up on a rock, shriveled from the sun, I speared its wilted tail with the corkscrew and transferred it onto my roasting stick. I got the idea from *Shōgun* where they ate and drank the unimaginable and actually enjoyed it. Sitting before the stoked-up fire, a feeling stirred within me—something between a fast-growing meanness and pity for the dead thing. I held the stick tightly and bit my lip. When the heat from the coals hit the leathery skin, it puffed up, black blood bubbled out its mouth and it exploded all over me.

I marched to the river and washed the sticky mash off my arms and face. Then I began to cry, knowing that I could have easily been that salamander, withered away by nature's elements. A slow, lonely death.

Since meeting Delbert and King I felt that there was nothing out on the Nooksack that would hurt me, but as darkness approached I was restless and didn't want to retreat to my tent. I decided to stay out by the fire much later than usual. As I sat in my bear chair, the spaces between the trees began to fill in slowly until the grove around me was a spiked gray wall.

I stared into the endless dusk and realized that away from the fire, summer light faded without ever disappearing. In the shadows that cloaked me I conjured Mom's face, as if she were actually watching me. But I knew it was me who wanted to watch her from a vantage point other than just a child's memory. What was she like as a girl? Did she ever see the night sky? Did she keep secrets or tell lies? Did she ever make her parents mad or get into trouble like I did? Was she ever an innocent girl or did she just appear with a grown-up plan, a set of goals that no one or nothing could stop? The more I thought about her I knew I could forever try to figure her out and fill in the blanks—memories can always be dug up, rearranged, and dabbed with a brighter color when necessary.

What I really wanted to know was how I was going to turn this mess around and get another chance to start over. I had no idea when Louanne would return or how much longer I could go on with a frail spirit and very little food.

Then I heard a distant booming in the sky. At first I felt that after weeks of perfect weather, I was about to be dumped on by a summer deluge. The summer storms of the great Northwest were noteworthy. When it decided to rain, there could be a torrential downpour within two seconds of a thunderbolt.

But the more I listened, the less I was convinced it was thunder. I walked to the water's edge where the rapids rode by like dark constellations. In the moonless sky above the stars took on a faint glow each time there was a boom. The flash wasn't coming from storm clouds, but from the far western sky; the same sky that blanketed my family.

I stood and watched until the rumbling flashes eventually stopped, leaving just the music of the frogs and the rapids. I walked back and opened the tent, crawled in, and zipped myself safely inside. When I fell onto the mummy bag I was spent. In the darkness I rubbed my eyes and felt a smile jerk on my face.

I'll feel stronger tomorrow, Flash. I think I'm just tired.
Happy Fourth of July, Kid.

The next morning I awoke to my sunny-day routine, knowing the date for the first time that summer. It was a still, hot day and I had plans to wash laundry in the river and hang it on a branch to dry. I peeled my clothes off and then pulled my sweatshirt on in spite of the heat. At the water's edge I noticed I had scrubbed the dishtowel and undies with stones so many times, that they were threadbare. I whacked them hard, wrung them out, and held up the panties to see if the sun would shine right through them.

I saw a buzzard circling high overhead. I suddenly felt very small, as if I had transported myself into the sky and got the bird's view of where I was positioned on Earth. I saw myself as a tiny, meaningless speck that washed little ratty underwear no one else cared about. A weird feeling passed through me, one I had not felt before. With a crushing sense of failure, I wanted to give up.

I dropped the clothes to the ground and sat down with my feet in the river.

Flash, let's face it. No one cares about me except for Louanne. Gramma and Grampa are probably so disgusted with my behavior that even they have given up on me. I've been alone so long out here, I'm sure they all think I'm dead. Mom is probably happy that she's finally rid of me forever.

I began to get scared. Sitting in the wet sand with the foaming current roaring past, I started shaking. I confessed to myself and to God that I only wanted to prove to Mom that she could no longer mistreat me, and I was determined to wedge my way back into her heart. For weeks I thought for sure she would send out a rescue team to find me and bring me home. I was fooling myself.

Kid, you've got to pull yourself together.

I will, Flash, I sniffed. *I've decided to finally do it.*

Do what?

Steal my dog.

chapter twenty-one

Bathtub Bust

Louanne came two days later, packing a sack of apples and a bag of dripping ice and beaming because she had gotten her braces off. She looked radiant and kept going on about how big and smooth her teeth felt. I suddenly felt like my teeth were sticking out a mile and pulled my lips over them. I told her she looked beautiful and teeth *that* nice would certainly contribute to her skating and musical skills. She said I was crazy and giggled her Louanne trill. Then her face got serious.

"What do you want?" she asked.

"What do you mean, what do I want?"

"Well, like you've been out here so long, don't you need anything? You look kind of sad, like you might need something."

"Well, yeah. I mean we all need something sooner or later. Weird things have been happening that make me think I'm getting a sign."

"What kind of weird things?" She began shining an apple on her T-shirt.

"Well, like strange feelings inside me… and in the air. And, I've actually gotten kind of scared a couple of times."

"No shit. I don't know how you've done it this long," she smacked.

"You're just eating that apple because you can," I said.

She smiled, showing her teeth. "And what do you mean, you're getting a sign?"

"Lou, I've come to terms with a few things lately. One is that I don't see the benefit of staying out here until I'm grown up. No one is coming for me."

"Are you losing it? Have you been like, talking to your Jesus light or what?" She crunched down, and then spit out the stem.

"It's not my Jesus light." I swatted her shoulder.

"Sorry, your Kodak bulb?" she giggled.

"It's not funny. It's *Flash*, but you aren't supposed to tell anyone."

She threw the apple core into the fire pit. "I haven't told anyone a thing about you, trust me. So what does *Flash* have to say about all this, and what do the two of you want to do about it?"

"Well, for starters, I need my dog. If I can't have my sisters, I want my dog. Maybe if Three Legs disappears, they might start looking for me again."

"You nut. We've talked about this before. You can't steal your own dog and use him for bait! Did you ever consider just going home, or maybe calling your mom on the phone?" She arched her eyebrows.

"Of course I have. I've thought about everything. One day I was down in the dumps and realized I'm jonesing for a hot bath. So I spent the entire day building a stone bathtub and filling it with boiling water."

She squealed, "You filled a whole tub with that little pot? How did you make the water stay in it? Oh my God, you must have run back and forth a hundred times."

"You're not getting the point."

"What's the point?"

"The point is I probably could stay out here for the rest of my life, but I can feel myself changing somehow and I want to do more than just hide and exist."

"Oh my God! Did you start your period?" She clapped her hand over her mouth.

"No, I didn't start my period. I just mean that things are different than when I first came. I was full of rage and fear for so long, thinking like a runaway, like it's a big game to stay hidden. Then I realized nobody cares."

"Ah come on, I care." She put her hand on my shoulder.

"I know you care and you've been such a great friend. There's no way I could've survived without you, but I'm ready to make a move. I'm ready for my dog and I'm ready for a hot bath with bubbles in it."

"Oh, comfort. My Aunt Ellie says that's the desire of every woman;

that if a woman gets her needs of comfort met, she can do anything. So, do you want to come to my house and take a nice hot bath?"

I thought about it. "What if someone sees me?"

"No one's home. They left for the weekend to visit Ellie in Tacoma."

"Okay, let's do it." My heart jarred my breastbone.

We squirreled away the camping equipment, tucked things out of sight, and doused the fire completely. We had a lunch of cold noodles and ice cubes, since Louanne had been kind enough to pack the ice all the way to camp. I grabbed my dirty towel and we hiked back to the car.

It was culture shock seeing the bridge from beneath and hearing a huge logging truck rumbling over our heads. It felt strange just getting in the car. I had been out in the wild for more than seven weeks.

I slid down low in the front seat and Louanne cranked the new Eagles cassette, which sounded awesome. With "Desperado" playing, my eyelids felt heavy and I began to doze off. The last thing I heard was Louanne saying, "Anyone else would have looked in the mirror first." I fell into a deep sleep.

When we got to Louanne's house, she woke me up with a smack on the shoulder. I got out, clutching the dish towel. From above came a screeching *Aaww!*

"Oh no," I said and pointed up.

"What?" Louanne squinted.

"Look what's on the phone line."

"A crow? So what?"

"I haven't seen one since I left. It's not just a crow. It's a sign."

We entered the quiet, scented house, which then smelled like Pine Sol and fruit punch.

"Go ahead and help yourself. When you get undressed, toss your clothes out and I'll stick them in the wash." She went to her room and brought me out a clean pair of underwear, jeans and a tank top.

When I went into the bathroom I was shocked when I saw myself in the mirror. My skin was so dark and my hair so light, I looked like an alien. My eyebrows had grown closer together and my nose was bigger. Hundreds of freckles spattered my face. My buck teeth were shining a bright white, but my lips were dry and cracked. I pulled my top off and regarded the body before me. Platinum strands of hair fell past my waist, over a protruding ribcage.

Flash, it's time to turn this river rat into a civilized girl.

Go right ahead, Kid. Enjoy the comfort while you can.

I drew a long, hot bath and filled it with lavender-scented bath salts. I washed my hair with Clairol Herbal Essence Shampoo and massaged the fragrant crème rinse into my scalp. I did everything in slow motion to savor the good smells, the cleanness, the soft washcloth.

After I rinsed my hair, I let the water out of the tub, scrubbed off the ring, and filled it up again. I dropped in one of Louanne's soft bath oil balls and sunk down to my chin. I watched it slowly melt into the water, surrounding me with tiny islands of rose-scented oil.

I closed my eyes, lying back in a state of bliss. Suddenly, a strong fist hit the bathroom door and I jumped up, splashing water over the floor and the toilet.

"Yes?" I said to the door.

"Eve Chanteau?" said a man with a deep voice.

"Yes?" I could hardly speak.

"I'm with the Bellingham police. Open the door."

I got out, wrapped a towel around me, and opened the door a crack.

There stood a giant police officer in full uniform with a gun, a billy club, and a radio on his belt. I looked in his eyes and he said, "Get dressed. You're coming with me."

He had a purple mole over his eyebrow.

I started to close the door and he stuck his boot in the way. I was embarrassed at my half nakedness and pulled the clean clothes over my wet body as fast as I could. I rubbed my hair with the towel and stepped out of the bathroom. The officer put his hand down on my shoulder and I froze. He gave me a nudge and said, "Let's go."

As we walked through the house, all I could hear was the tick of the grandfather clock and the washing machine beginning its spin cycle.

When we got out to the driveway, Louanne's car was gone and a police car was parked in its place.

I didn't have to look up to know that my blue skies had turned to gray, and my riverbank world was gone.

chapter twenty-two

Juvy

Sitting in the backseat of a patrol car was more cramped than huddling on the floorboard of Louanne's Honda. The policeman drove downtown and pulled in front of City Hall. As many times as I had walked by the four-story building on my way to school, I had taken little notice of the Washington state and American flags flapping from the flagpole and the brass-lettered sign, "Whatcom County Courthouse, City Jail, Juvenile Hall."

The officer opened the car door and clamped his fingers around my arm. He didn't say a word. He pulled me out and led me along a concrete walkway and through a side door. We went up an elevator, the inside walls covered with gray-speckled carpet. The elevator opened into a hallway, bright with fluorescent lights. Jangling keys and slamming doors echoed down a long corridor leading to the entrance of Juvenile Detention.

A large man in uniform sat behind a glass window and buzzed us in. The two officers spoke quietly and filled out paperwork while I kept my head down, looking at my wet hair and bare feet. When they were finished I was handed off to a female officer who stared at me until I stood up straight and pushed the hair out of my face.

Flash, what do they think I've done?

Stay strong, Kid. It's gonna be just fine. And don't mention me or we'll be heading down a road we never dreamed of.

"Excuse me," said the lady officer. "You need to come with me to the exam room."

I followed her into a small room with white linoleum clear to the ceiling.

"Remove all your articles of clothing and place them in this bag."

I did as she asked and stood there naked. The officer lifted the back of my hair and examined my neck. She put her hand between my thighs and pushed my legs apart. With her palms, she turned me around, swept under my armpits, down my sides, and over my butt.

"Open your mouth and let me have a look inside." She peered in and seemed satisfied I wasn't hiding anything.

She handed me some blue cotton clothes that looked like pajamas. "Put these on. Here are your socks. The rubber bumps go on the bottom." She left a plastic basin on the chair that held a tiny bar of Ivory soap, Crest, a toothbrush, and a black comb. The basin had a yellow sticker on it that read "Chanteau, E. JD 3."

She walked out and shut the door.

I was locked into Cell Number Three with two other girls who had been there four days. The room was dull white with a cot against one wall and a set of metal bunks against the other. My eyes went to the tiny window, which had bars on it— just like in the movies.

One girl glared at me. She had tired eyes and short, bleached-blonde hair with black roots. She slumped in outsized blue pajamas, dangling one bare foot over the top bunk and gnawing on the side of her ring finger.

"I'm Pam." She spit out a piece of skin.

"Oh," I said, "I have a horse named Pam." They both stared at me like I was from outer space.

"Well, actually, she belongs to my grandfather, but I'm the only one who rides her."

"And I'm Ronna with an R," said the other girl.

"It's a pleasure to meet you, Ronna with an R," I smiled.

"Don't gotta be a smart ass," she sneered.

Ronna stood there like she had a dark cloud around her. She had thick black hair, a tattoo of a black cross on her wrist, and the remains of black nail polish on her fingernails. One sleeve was rolled up, showing a tattoo of a skull on her shoulder.

"What are you in for?" said Pam.

"Running away from home."

"Shit," said Ronna, "I split like three years ago and nobody even noticed. My ol' man is twenty-four and I'm gonna be eighteen in two days. We're gettin' married. I gotta see him soon or I'm gonna lose it."

"Do you mind me asking what you guys are in for?"

"Yeah," said Pam, "Ronna here was riding on the back of a Harley with her boyfriend and they pulled a gas 'n dash at the Chevron in Ferndale and it got 'em both sacked. And you don't even want to know what I'm in for."

Ronna stood there and stared at the floor. "I gotta see my ol' man."

"I wish you'd shut your trap about that," Pam said. "He's in jail, you're in juvy." She switched to her thumb, chewing on it like corn-on-the-cob, which reminded me how hungry I was. "Your little plan ain't gonna work, Ronna."

"What plan is that?" I said.

"Ronna thinks if we cause enough trouble, she'll get sent to jail 'cause she's almost eighteen, and like she'll get to see her *old man*. She wants to knock the bunk beds over, but we already tried and they won't budge."

Ronna looked up at me. "With little miss Rosy Sunshine here now, we could do it. What do you say, little Rosy with an R?" My skin prickled at the thought of misbehaving in a jail cell, but I was even more petrified to tell them no.

I started to bite my lip when the keys rattled the lock and the cell door opened. The officer who arrested me told me to come out. As I walked by Ronna, she rolled her eyes and snorted.

I followed him to the front station where he explained that I would be allowed one phone call. "Who do you want to call?" he said.

"I would like to call my grandmother, please." My heart began thudding.

"Number?"

"Area code 503 . . ."

"Nope. No long distance."

I thought about Louanne. She wasn't home when I left her driveway less than an hour ago. I thought about Ronna in there and how I did not want to go back into Cell Number Three. My head began to spin.

"*Who* do you want to call?" he said.

I thought about Pam and her bad hair. Mom would never have let her roots show like that. Mom. My beautiful mother. Some part of me deep down wanted to throw myself on the floor and cry, *I want my mommy.*

"This is your last chance," he said, trying to be patient.

"My mother, please. It's 676-2175."

The phone was hooked up to a speaker and a recording system. He dialed the number and we listened over the intercom as the phone rang at the house. Four rings . . . I felt like hanging up. Five rings . . . I felt like throwing up.

"Hello." I heard Mom's voice and my palms leaked sweat.

"Hello, this is Officer Nelson of the Bellingham Police Department. We have your daughter Eve in custody at Juvenile Hall. It is policy that she be allowed one phone call and she wishes to speak to *you.*"

"Eve?" she said. "I have two daughters. I have Angie and I have Amber, but I do not have a daughter named Eve." She hung up.

I stood there in shock, looking at the phone and listening to the dial tone.

A feeling began to bubble inside my guts, like the beginning of a rolling boil before you drop the pasta in. I clutched my stomach to make it stop. *How dare she! If she doesn't have a daughter named Eve, then who was the girl she beat up and threw down the stairs?* The bubbling built, erupted through my core and heated my blood with a rage that turned the room red.

The big red officer led me back to the cell and locked me in with a clang of the thick metal door. Ronna and Pam were waiting by the bunk bed as if I'd never left. I walked over and gripped the steel frame. No one said anything until Ronna clenched her teeth and hissed, "Let's heave this iron son-of-a-bitch. And remember, Rosy, *I* get all the credit. On the count of three." I tightened my hold. "One, two, three." We pushed with all our might and the metal mass crashed to the floor and shook the room like an explosion.

The cell door flew open and five uniforms rushed in. Pam and I stood completely still and pointed at Ronna.

"She did it!" Pam said. "We had nothing to do with it."

Just as Ronna had hoped, she was cuffed and carted off. It took four men to set the bunk upright. When they left I picked up the pillows and blankets and tried to tidy things up. Pam sat on the cot and picked at her toenails. We had nothing to say to one another. I crawled on to the white cotton cover of the bottom bunk and prayed for food.

Not long after Ronna had left, the cell door opened again and she was shoved into the room by a pair of strong hands. She threw herself down on the bed and sobbed into her pillow.

Eventually Pam said, "So, I take it you didn't get to see him."

Ronna rolled over, her face creased and wet. "What a bunch of fuckin' derelict pervs."

"What happened?" said Pam.

"They throw me in this cell, I mean *throw* me onto the floor that smells like piss 'cause there's a hole in the stinkin' floor for a pot. It makes this place look like a goddamned Barbie playhouse."

I felt sorry for her. "Did you get to see your boyfriend?" I asked.

"What do you think, Rosy Sunshine?" Ronna sneered. "Do I look like I've been on a fuckin' honeymoon?"

"Shut up, Ronna, she's just askin'."

"Well, the answer is no. I did *not* get to see him. Instead I got to see some filthy fingers attached to a creep next door who stuffed his shirt through the bars of my cell and told me to rub it between my legs and pass it back so he could get a good sniff!"

"Oh, gross," I said.

"What do you mean, *oh, gross*? It was fuckin' disgusting!" Ronna yelled.

"So," said Pam, "why are you back so soon?"

"Because I totally freaked out on the pigs and they couldn't deal with it."

The cell door opened and three trays were brought in. Applesauce never tasted so good.

     Pam and Ronna left the next day and I was moved to a single cell down the hall. For three days I stayed in my bunk and ate jailbird food. I could hear kids playing in the recreation room but I was restricted to my cell. I was too numb to feel really scared. I could only think about my little camp and what would happen to the tent and the food Louanne and I stashed. I didn't think about what would happen next—all I knew was that I was a criminal. There was no one to talk to. I was too afraid to reach Louanne and get her in trouble too, plus I didn't know how to get to her.

     On the second day of lockdown, I was taken into a closed room with a table and two plastic chairs. I was told to sit in a chair and wait for my evaluation. A lady wearing a brown suit and glasses came in. She introduced herself as Pat Moody, my probation officer. For an hour she asked me questions and gave me tests, which I later came to find out was referred to as a "Psycho Valve," short for psychological evaluation.

     Some of the testing was oral and some written. I answered questions like *How do you feel about expelling vomit into a toilet?* I was asked about colors and shapes and sleep habits. I was asked about my closest relationships and my sexual background, which made me blush. I explained that I never had a boyfriend except maybe John Ruby, but he probably didn't feel the same about me and besides, we were eight at the time. I thought about mentioning Steve Henry, but decided against it.

     Occasionally Mrs. Moody would smile the tiniest smile when I answered a question. Sometimes I would start telling an involved story and she listened and took notes, but she never said "Just the facts," like they did in detective stories.

     I said that my closest relationships were with my grandparents and my best friend Louanne Berg. When she asked me about Mom, I began to feel mixed up. I tried to explain how I had done my mother wrong and she stopped me mid-sentence. Mrs. Moody gathered her paperwork and left the room.

     On day four in the Juvy, I was let out of my cell and allowed to play ping-pong in the rec room. I played mostly with boys and we played every chance we had. Some kids played checkers and occasionally there was a TV show on, but I stuck to ping-pong, determined to beat every boy in the place.

That night I had a dream that Mom was walking slowly toward me. She had a purple mole over her eyebrow and a baby in her arms.

After the first week I asked permission to write to Gramma. They said yes, as long as my probation officer approved the letter before it was sent.

July 15th

Dear Gramma,

You probably know by now that I am a criminal. I lived out on the river for awhile and tried to figure out the right thing to do. Now I am in Juvenile Detention in Bellingham.

Even though I heard it with my own ears, I'm not sure whether Mom said she isn't my mother, or if she said I'm not her daughter. I can kind of understand how a person must feel when they lose one of their real important organs.

I'm wondering if maybe I can come back and stay with you if she doesn't change her mind and if you and Grampa can forgive me for being so bad. I'm going to be good from now on.

Love,

Eve

P.S. Happy Birthday two days late.

P.P.S. Kiss Buddy, Choppy, Pam, Korky, and Grampa for me.

Each day I waited for a letter from Gramma and got better at ping-pong. I had the urge to mop the floor of my cell, but an orderly, a small old man, cleaned each day when I was in the rec room. I thought he was nice although he didn't talk to anyone. I felt sorry for him, his back all hunched over, rolling that big bucket around, wringing out the mop, and cleaning up after everyone when he should have been on a porch, somewhere warm, rocking in a rocking chair with a little dog on his lap.

On the fifteenth and final day, I was back in the bare interview room with my probation officer who introduced my court-appointed caseworker, Beth Lombard. She was tall and slim, with her hair pulled back tightly in a bun. Both women wore suits of polyester and authority, but Mrs. Lombard's was trimmed in compassion; Pat Moody's was just brown.

They looked so proper sitting across from me. I was perched on the edge of a steel chair in my prisoner pajamas. I wondered what it was like to be them, to get dressed in the morning knowing you were off to work, where you would tell some lost soul she was about to be dropped into a system she couldn't get out of, no matter what.

I fidgeted, trying to get comfortable in my cold chair and my embarrassment. Glancing at the ground, I noticed Mrs. Lombard's shoes were very nice. I thought of complimenting her, but figured it was just best to keep my mouth shut and my ears open.

I didn't hear Flash during the days in juvy. Possibly because it was a time for me to adjust, find my own strength, and get ready for what was about to come, or maybe it was a way to protect me from being labeled as a disturbed child who appeared to be talking to herself. Whatever the reason, I was okay with it, because Flash could do that: lie low when necessary without really leaving me.

Mrs. Lombard began. ""Eve, we are here to explain some things to you."

"Okay."

"Let me begin by saying that you will be released today."

I blasted out a breath. "That's good. Do I get to go home?"

She glanced at my probation officer, then back at me. "Let me get to that in a moment. First I would like to give you some information regarding the court system."

"Okay."

"Adult Criminal Courts handle cases that are criminal in nature, unlike Juvenile Court, which is a civil court." I nodded to make her think I was following her.

"An Adult Court is designed for punishment, whereas a Juvenile

Court emphasizes protection of the community and rehabilitating the kids who have broken the law."

"And I've obviously—broken the law?"

"Bear with me, if you will. Juvenile Court also differs from Adult Court, in that Juvenile Court hearings are closed to the public in order to protect the child. Juveniles do not have the right to request jury trials and cannot post bail to buy their way out of detention."

"Wait . . . so are you saying, that I have to go to court?"

Mrs. Moody spoke. "No, you will not be going to court at this time. What Mrs. Lombard is explaining is most certainly a lot of information for a fourteen-year-old, but if you pay attention we will clarify everything so you will have full comprehension of your options."

"That sounds fine, thank you." I was relieved to hear I had options.

Mrs. Lombard continued, "Let me try to make this simple, Eve. The juvenile court system oversees two types of cases. There are delinquency cases, which involve kids who get into trouble, and dependency cases, which involve parents who get into trouble—because of the way they treat their kids."

"So which case am I?"

"That's a very good question." She nodded approval. "Some juvenile delinquencies can involve traffic violations—that doesn't apply to you—or an extensive list of crimes committed by juveniles."

"Is running away from home one of those crimes?"

"That also is a good question, but allow me to continue. This is where it gets a bit hazy. Dependent cases involve children who have been abused and who are dependent. These cases include child neglect, child endangerment and other acts of violence that fall into the dependency category."

"I'm not quite following you. Are you saying I am a dependency case?"

"Well," Mrs. Lombard tapped her pencil on her notepad. "Let me ask you."

"Ask me what?"

"Do you feel that you have been harmed by your mother or stepfather, or put in any kind of danger while in their care, or neglected in any way?"

How could I tell these women that being asked these questions was like being stuck by an electric prong? I felt completely helpless. If I were to say Mom was mean, they might take her away; they made that clear with the "parents getting in trouble" statement. If I denied it, maybe they would send me back home and I would just have to deal with it. If Mom still said I wasn't her daughter or she wasn't my mother, maybe I could go to Gramma's or Mrs. Berg's, or go live with Tim. Yeah, Tim had just turned eighteen; I could cook for him and help Mom by babysitting Amber while she was at work.

"Eve, please respond."

"I'm sorry. Could you repeat the question?" I began to feel good about this.

"Do you feel that you have been harmed by your mother or step-father, or put in any kind of danger while in their care, or neglected in any way?"

"No, I do not."

"All right, that being said, I just have one more question for you."

"Okay."

"If things were going so well, why did you run away from home?"

"Well, I didn't say things were going so well. In fact, because things were a little, um, *strained*—I felt I probably should give my mom a little break from me, so I went to the river. You know, to clear my head and try to figure things out."

Pat Moody picked up her clipboard and stood. Mrs. Lombard said, "That's enough for now, Eve. You can go back to your room. Your personal belongings are waiting. You can go ahead and get dressed and we'll chat again in a few minutes."

"Thank you."

I went back to the cell and slipped out of my loungewear and back into Louanne's clothes.

In the last chat with Beth Lombard and Pat Moody, I learned that

I would not be going back to my parents ever again. Also, I would not be going to my grandparents and I would not get to move in with the Bergs or my brother Tim. Mrs. Lombard said it: Because of the situation at hand and the lack of cooperation on my mother's part, I would, in a sense, be placed in the custody of a judge.

I was sitting in the steel chair and they were standing by the table.

"Does this mean I'm going to live in the judge's house?"

"No," said Mrs. Lombard. "You will be living in a foster home."

"What exactly is a foster home?" I asked.

"It's like a regular home, except children are often there temporarily, so kids may come and go during your stay. It's also probable that you may be placed numerous times in different homes, but at this time we are unsure."

"Just so I'm clear on this—you are telling me that I am in the care of a judge, but I'm going to live in a foster home?"

"Yes," said Pat Moody. "You are now a ward of the court."

"A ward of the court?"

"Yes, you are under the laws and legal protection of the State. You will be on probation during your time in foster care."

"Okay, I got it. So when can I see my family?"

"I'm sorry. There will be no familial contact under ward status, unless approved by the judge."

"Wait. Are you saying I can't see Tim or Toby or Max? What about Angie and Amber?" My lip began to bounce. I slammed one socked foot on the other to stop from crying. I was going to a motel for messed-up kids.

"For now, let's just get you to the Carlyle House."

"Is that my new foster home? The Carlyle House?"

Pat Moody nodded. "Yes."

"How long will I be in a foster home?"

Mrs. Lombard lifted her chin. "Approximately . . . four years. You will hold ward status until you are eighteen years of age."

The door opened and a County Sheriff stepped in. He nodded at Pat Moody, who tore off the yellow copy of my discharge paper and handed it to me.

"Good luck," she said, and then walked out. Mrs. Lombard looked at me. My head was roaring. *Never see Tim or Toby or Max, never hold Amber or pet Three Legs, never see Tim* . . . I think she left.

The Sheriff signed me out, hiked up his pants and opened the door. He said, "Okay, Missy, let's go." We walked out of Juvy and into the hallway.

As we stood waiting for the elevator, the old orderly shuffled over with a bucket of dirty rags. He stopped and looked at the lighted numbers, like everyone does when they're waiting for an elevator. I stepped a bit closer to him, thinking maybe his hearing wasn't all that good.

"Thank you for all you've done," I said. "You have worked very hard keeping this place so clean and taking care of all our trays and stuff. I just want you to know how much you are appreciated."

He looked down at the floor and said, "You can't take them socks."

chapter twenty-three

Carlyle House

My summer on the Nooksack River left me with two things I would keep for a long time: good memories and a juvenile criminal record.

I had not only broken the curfew laws and been booked on runaway charges, but my judgment read, "The child is incorrigible, beyond and out of the control of her parents."

Riding in the back of the Sheriff's cruiser, I held the wrinkled copy of the discharge summary. I read it again. *Incorrigible* sounded like a disease. I folded the paper into a small square and stuck it in my pocket. *How did I get to be an incorrigible and a criminal all in one day?*

I turned my attention to the bald spot on the back of the Sheriff's head. It looked checkered through the black metal poultry wire that separated the outlaw from the badge. I could see his face in the rearview mirror. He looked kind, and about as old as Grampa. I wondered if he could whistle through his teeth, and what he was doing before he got the call to pick me up. He was probably playing catch with his grandson, using a softball so the little guy didn't get hurt.

And how far away was my eighteenth house, anyway?

"Excuse me?" I leaned forward.

"Yes, Miss," he said.

"I don't mean to bother you, but can you please tell me where the Carlyle House is?"

"It's in the next county."

That was the difference between Washington and Oregon. Anything outside of Bellingham, you were in the county. At Gramma's, you were in the country.

An odd feeling came over me when we passed Kentucky Fried

Chicken and the doughnut shop: because my heart was racing so fast, I had no appetite.

We drove north on the Guide Meridian and passed a giant construction site.

"They're putting in a whole new mall," said the Sheriff. "Building it so the Canadians have a bigger place to shop. I guess K-Mart's not big enough."

"Mmm," I said, quietly, not sure if he was talking to me or to his radio.

We passed the last gas station out of town and pastures began to whisk by. I could gradually breathe easier being in the county. I craned my neck when we drove past a leaning mobile home next to a rusted out pick-up truck with "Sale Today" painted on the side. Someone had added a piece of plywood next to the tire that read, "Tomorrow too!" I wondered if the people in the crooked trailer had gotten any snappy customers like Mom.

As we got further out, I began to worry that the Carlyle House might be a trailer house too, possibly a double-wide to hold all those kids. The Sheriff put on his turn signal and we sat on the Guide, waiting to turn left, while oncoming traffic passed. It had never occurred to me that a Sheriff had to stop and wait for everyone else to go first. I wished we could just drive all day, around in circles or back and forth. I wasn't ready to get out of the cruiser with its poultry wire barrier.

On Wyman Road we passed three small farms and a pen of peacocks. The Sheriff turned left again on Bartlet Road, rolled the cruiser into a dirt driveway, and let it idle.

"This is it," he said, and reached for his clipboard.

The Wyman and Bartlet street sign stood at a slant on the corner of the lot, as if the Carlyle House could have either address. The property was big and rundown with overgrown juniper bushes, a broken fountain, and lots of weeds. It seemed like someone wanted the yard to be nice, but didn't have the time to keep it up. There were a few rock walkways going nowhere. A flag dangled off the wood mailbox that had Ca lyl 257 painted on the side. Weeds grew high around the mailbox and under the front windows.

The house was an old, single-story rambler. Maybe it had had a color once, but now it was just washed-out wood. Its shake roof was covered with moss so thick that it hung over the gutters. On the front of the house were several paned windows with chipped paint and closed curtains. The porch was small with rotted wood steps leading to a door that might have been painted a brilliant green maybe fifty years before.

The Sheriff called in to the station: "Bartlet two-fifty-seven, a seven-thirteen code, nine-fourteen hundred hours." I was glad to see there wasn't a double-wide sitting in the yard and a saggy couch on the front porch. I jumped when the Sheriff hit the "Whoop-whoop." I guess that's how he announced us, since there wasn't a doorbell from what I could see.

"Out we go. You're about to meet Mrs. Stella Mae Carlyle."

We walked up the steps and stood at the door. My heart started thudding like a shoe in a dryer.

The front door opened to the smell of must and pork grease. We were greeted by a short, round lady with beady eyes and hair dyed jet black, piled high on her head.

"Hello, Stella Mae," said the Sheriff.

"Hello, Sheriff." She had a wrinkled smile.

Stella Mae had drawn on her eyebrows in wide arcs, maybe to make up for her little eyes. She wore bright red lipstick that leaked into the lines around her lips. Her mouth looked too small in her round face and reminded me of a miniature red daisy.

"Well, are you just gonna stand there?" she said. Unsmiling, she stepped back and pulled the door wider.

I turned around and saw that the Sheriff had already left. I didn't even get a chance to ask him if he had a grandson. "Well, hello, I'm Eve," I said, stepping into the house.

"I know who you are," she said. "Come in."

We stood in the living room, which boasted five beat up couches and not much else. No coffee table, end table or lamp—just a 200-watt bulb hanging overhead with a light like the interrogation room at Juvy.

"You don't got no stuff?" she said.

"No."

"Where's your shoes?"

I looked down and saw we were standing on a dirty plywood sub-floor. "Um, I left them at home."

"Well, Eve, let's get one thing straight right now. This is your home, you hear?"

"Yes."

"Come on, I'll show ya around and introduce ya to the others. This is the living room." She pointed to a door in the corner. "Over there's the boys room. Girls ain't allowed."

"Oh," I said.

For only knowing her two minutes, I already thought of her as an odd bird. For one thing, she was noisy. She sighed and grunted and something clicked around her. I thought maybe her ankle bones were cracking, but then figured out it was dentures that didn't fit right. She sucked in her lips, then crunched down and the plates went click, click.

"Come on, this way."

We turned into a dark hallway. At the end of the hallway was a powder-blue bathroom.

"This is for kids to use," she said. She stepped in. "Have a look."

The toilet bowl was filthy, but even with the seat up, I could see it had a blue shag cover on it to match the rug fitted at the toilet base—the kind Gramma said was unsanitary. Rusty water dripped from the faucet and the showerhead, and there was a bottle of Prell Shampoo spilled all over the floor. I realized Stella Mae couldn't see the spill because her super-large bust was in the way. I had never seen such big ones before. They looked like they would surely throw her back out. Also she didn't have much neck, so she probably didn't look down often.

"Nice," I said. "Blue is my favorite color."

"That's good." She sighed like she was already worn out.

Next to the bathroom was the back door with a small window in it. I glanced out—and there sat a doublewide trailer about thirty yards away. It was connected to the Carlyle House by a line of half-buried concrete blocks, maybe used as stepping stones.

"My mother lives there," said Stella Mae. "Kids ain't allowed."

I opened my mouth but nothing came out. I was staring at the back door, and the huge lock that looked like it worked from the inside, and only with a key.

Stella waddled away and I followed her. The house had an open floor plan as far as the living room, dining room, and kitchen, but there were oversized steps down into the kitchen, making it like a big bowl. Stella grabbed onto a counter and stepped down. The kitchen was small, cluttered, and cheerless. Standing down in the hole, Stella Mae reminded me of a munchkin in *The Wizard of Oz*. She patted all the counters, one by one, like she was either nervous or staking her turf.

The house was spared from total gloom by more bright, hanging light bulbs. One hung over the dining table which was cluttered with stacks of newspapers and a pile of bath towels.

"Where are the other kids?" I asked.

"You'll see 'em soon enough. Everybody's in their room until you get a chance to meet my husband Clyde and get yourself settled in."

We passed through the kitchen into another big room. It was like the living room with a TV and couches, and it stunk like a skunk.

"This is Clyde," Stella said. "And this is Clyde's room. Kids ain't allowed."

Clyde stared at his TV and said nothing.

He sat there in a beat-up chair, whiskered and dirty, surrounded by a cloud of cigarette smoke. He had black-rimmed glasses cockeyed on his nose. His territory was marked with plates of old food and overflowing beanbag ashtrays scattered on a ratty green carpet dotted with cigarette burns. There were burn holes in his chair and even on the heavy, dank drapes, closed against the daylight. How could you get cigarette burns on drapes? Clyde had holes in his pants and holes in his socks. I later discovered that he had a hole through his upper lip, which was hidden by his nicotine-stained mustache. He gave me the creeps.

I would soon learn that Clyde repulsed me because he was yellow and mean. I didn't trust him from the get-go. His fingers were yellow and his eyes were yellow, although I never had direct eye contact or a conversation with him. He didn't talk because he didn't need to. He belched and coughed and grunted. He watched TV and smoked, when he wasn't drinking. Standing there, I vowed to keep my distance from Clyde.

Stella said, "You gotta go by Clyde's place to get to your room, but he don't care. *Clyde!* This is the new girl." He didn't even look up.

There were three doors in Clyde's room, which were more bedrooms. Stella Mae said one was pink, and that's where a foster girl named Barbara stayed. There was Stella and Clyde's bedroom, which always had its door closed. Last was a drab green bedroom with two double beds and a dresser. In the right corner was an attached wooden ladder that led up into a small opening.

"You'll stay up there," said Stella Mae, pointing to the opening.

I was going to live in an attic.

"Oh," I said trying to sound appreciative. She flipped a switch on the wall behind the ladder, and the attic lit up. "You can go up and look," she said.

I crawled up the cold rungs and peered through the entrance. The attic had been closed in with sheetrock to create a room that was about ten feet by ten, with an angled ceiling under the roofline. The room had been recently brush-stroked powder blue, just like the kids bathroom. There was a mattress on the floor with a bedspread like the ones at Juvenile Hall. Next to the bed was a nightstand with a lamp and a little window. Makeshift shelving on the wall would be my dresser.

I looked down at Stella Mae. "Can I go in?"

"I already said so, din I?"

I pulled myself up into the room. I could stand up without bumping my head as long as I stayed in the middle. I bent, and went to open the window to let out the paint fumes.

There was a braided carpet on the plywood floor that made me miss Gramma.

I climbed backward down the ladder.

"It's really cozy, Stella Mae. And I'm all moved in!"

She let out a cackle like she was laying an egg.

Today I'd meet the four other foster kids at the Carlyle House, three boys and that girl named Barbara. As I waited in the living room, trying to figure out how a rug would look on the bare floor, Stella would waddle in with each foster kid to be introduced.

The first kid I met was Bobb Hanson. He was almost eighteen. *If only I could be eighteen.* I closed my eyes and imagined traveling light speed through a time warp that would spit me out at age eighteen, all grown up and free from this place.

Bobb entered the room like a parade float, graceful and grand, with a huge head and rosy cheeks. At six foot three, he filled the shabby living room with shoulders wider than a linebacker's. He clasped his large hands together and said, "Welcome, Eve! It's great to meet you!" I felt my cheeks flush, not knowing if he was going to lunge forward and hug me or if I should just stand there looking stupid and feeling special. He shook my hand with a palm as soft as Gramma's.

"It's a pleasure meeting you, Bobb."

I would later learn what happened to Bobb when he told me of his mother, who passed away when he was six. Bobb came to live with Stella Mae when he was ten because Stella knew Bobb's father and they had made a deal.

After Bobb's mom died, Bobb took over his mother's role as home-maker and cared for his three-year-old brother. His dad wasn't a mean man, just helpless when it came to household chores, so Bobb handled everything from laundry to Lysol. He cleaned the house every day, made the beds, and cooked for the three of them. Bobb's dad brought home the groceries.

Like Cinderella, Bobb scrubbed the floor and dreamed of meeting his own Prince Charming one day. He became the woman of the house. He took long baths, soaking in his deceased mother's Calgon Bath Oil Beads. He dusted his body with her Jean Naté powder. He adored wearing her jewelry and touching her things. When he began to fold and re-fold her undergarments, Bobb's dad intervened and removed his wife's belongings. He confided in Stella Mae about his weird son, and Stella said she'd take Bobb for a price.

The next guy Stella hauled in to meet me was Dennis Devries. Dennis was a good-looking sixteen-year-old who totally outclassed the place. He winked at me and I knew we would be friends. He had happy blue eyes, sandy blonde hair, and straight white teeth.

Within a week I pretty much had his story. He told me he was "the privileged child" of parents who were both doctors; his father was a cardiac surgeon in Seattle. He grew up an only child, materially spoiled, and was ignored just enough to get himself into big trouble.

At the age of nine Dennis began stealing prescription drugs, more as a sport than anything else. He was kicked out of three different private schools for misconduct. Finally at age thirteen he was handed over to the authorities. The Doctors Devries maintained legal custody of Dennis but never let him return home. He was held tightly in the clutches of the legal system and had run through seven different boys' homes by the time he reached Stella Mae's.

Dennis had been diagnosed as a kleptomaniac, which in simple terms was just a thief. His beginnings as a pill kyper evolved into professional burglary, with armed robbery as his grand finale. He had a playful sense of humor and laughed at himself and everyone else. One of my favorite things about Dennis was that he had a smile and a nickname for everyone.

One day Dennis said, "This rat hole should be condemned."

"Oh," I said, "you're just spoiled. You should learn to be more appreciative."

"Now that's some good advice, coming from a girl who's basically lived under a rock."

After I met Bobb and Dennis, out of the boys' pad strolled Jim, another temporary placement kid. He'd been at Stella's for a week.

Though he had white skin, Jim had the physical likeness to a beautiful black man. He was lean and sinewy, with bulging biceps and deltoids. He wore snug Levi 501s and a black tank top that didn't say anything on it, which I thought was pretty classy. He had a tawny brown Afro, full lips and cool, blue eyes. When Stella stomped in with Jim in tow, he greeted me with such an engaging smile that the whole room took on some of his grace.

It was from Jim's story I learned terms like "pistol-whip" and "packin' heat." He had the classic case of the stepfather who was driven by raw jealousy, went berserk, and took it out on the kid. Jim had been pistol-whipped by his stepdad many times, which meant he used the butt of the gun to beat Jim instead of shooting him. Jim finally retaliated by pulverizing the guy with a baseball bat and leaving him for dead. Jim's mom found her husband in critical condition; her son was missing.

After Jim was arrested with an assault and battery charge, his stepfather refused to take him back and was making every effort to postpone the hearings as long as possible, hoping to get Jim tried as an adult.

Stella said, "Eve, you better watch it."

"Watch what?" I said.

"I'm no idiot. I can tell the way two people look at each other."

"Stella Mae, I'm sorry, but I don't know what you're talking about."

"Okay, Eve. That Jim may be handsome, but he could snap yer neck if he felt like it."

The last of my new "family" was Barbara, a fifteen-year-old hyperactive case of nerves who bravely crept out of her pink bedroom to say hello. A bristling halo of flame orange hair surrounded her head, which seemed stuck as an afterthought on a large, pear-shaped body. Her pillowy flab gave her an interesting bunch of dimples. She had dimples in her chin, around her wrists, and nestled in the knuckles of her hands. Rust-brown freckles had settled in the dimples, and dotted the pale skin of her arms and hands and kneecaps. It looked like she even had freckles on her teeth, but the little brown specks were actually stains from taking so many medications.

Barbara's voice was painfully shrill, especially during a bout of hysteria. I soon found out she was Stella Mae's pet because the two of them had a lot in common, like how they gulped food and talked loudly with their mouths full.

Barbara didn't really tell me her story. But Bobb and Dennis were good at filling me in. She had a mentally ill mother and three sisters, each of whom had different fathers. Barbara didn't know where her father was and that made her mad. She claimed she was going to find him through a "Father-Daughter Reunion Network" she was in the process of forming, but so far she was the only member. Barbara had been placed in many psychiatric wards and group homes, but never for very long. I would soon learn why, as she whined, cursed, complained, and screamed her way through life in the Carlyle House.

Dennis told me Barbara had borderline personality, ADD, and organic brain syndrome, which was the umbrella of her underlying symptoms. She suffered a host of disorders: bipolar, delusional, anxiety. She was taken from her home because of a diagnosis of "sibling rivalry disorder." Although Barbara was placed at Stella Mae's as a dependency case, she really qualified more as a psychiatric case.

By the time two days had passed, I was feeling down about the dump I was living in. I knew I had to write to Granmma, but I didn't have anything to write with.

"Hey, Barbara," I said. "Do you think I can borrow a pen and a piece of your paper?"

She narrowed her eyes. "Why?"

"I want to write a letter to my grandmother."

"I carry this notepad at all times," she said.

"That's very impressive, Barbara."

She ripped two pieces out of her documentation journal and handed me a pen with pink ink.

"Thank you so much, Barbara. I'm going to tell my grandma how nice you are."

July 24th

Dear Gramma,

How are you? I am fine. I am now in a foster home called the Carlyle House. It belongs to Stella Mae and Clyde. I have a room that's just been painted blue. The saddest thing of all is that they want me to swap families. They think I can just trade Tim, Toby, Max, Angie and Amber for Bobb, Dennis, Jim, and Barbara. Please ask God how he expects me to do this, because I ask him every night and he won't answer.

Stella's fat and messy and doesn't even cook. How can a person run a houseful when she won't cook or clean? I'm sorry to sound like I'm complaining, but I miss you so much my heart hurts.

Love,

Eve

P.S. Please scratch everybody on the head for me (even Grampa!)

It was a Monday morning when I found Stella in the kitchen with a mouthful of something brown.

"Stella Mae, can you please mail a letter for me?"

"Who you writin' to?" she said, as stuff slid out the sides of her mouth.

"My grandma in Oregon."

"Well," she smacked, "I'll have to read it first."

"Oh, no problem, I'll show it to you as soon as I'm done."

I crawled back up the ladder.

July 24th

Dear Gramma,

I'm writing to tell you how wonderful my new home is, especially Stella Mae. I can tell by the way the house smells and how healthy everyone looks, that Stella Mae is a great cook. I get the entire top floor of the house all to myself and it's our favorite color!

Clyde is super nice. He wears glasses, so he must read a lot.

I love you,

Eve

P.S. Tell Grampa we are close to a peacock farm and that I love him.

I knocked on the door to the bathroom. It opened with a swoosh.

"Barbara, sorry to bother you, but do you happen to have an envelope and a stamp I can borrow? I'll pay you back as soon as my grandma sends me some. I told her how nice you are."

"Sure! I'll get it right now," she said and bounced away.

chapter twenty-four

Saturday Special

As summer faded into autumn, I blended into the Carlyle house the best I could while trying not to become a product of my environment like the other kids had.

By the end of the first week, Stella Mae had explained the rules that applied to me as things came up—or as she invented them. There would be no phone calls, she said. In fact, I was not allowed to *touch* the phone, unless someone died. No contact with my family. No contact with Louanne Berg. No dog, no piano, no lollygagging around the boys or messing around outside. No going past the mailbox or to the trailer out back. No housecleaning or opening curtains. What Stella Mae didn't know was that with each restriction she laid on me, I began to make a plan as to how I was going to do it anyway.

Stella constantly told me that my *Ward Status* rules were different from the others because they were "Mandated by the court." Having Ward Status was equivalent to having skin. I could do nothing to change it, couldn't rub it off or just slip out of it.

It was a Thursday morning when I was standing in the dining room; the kids were in their bedrooms, and Clyde was pickled, slumped in front of the television. Stella Mae stood in the kitchen eating a fish stick wrapped in bologna, bread, and a thick layer of Miracle Whip. She smacked and yakked about the court, smearing her lipstick and leaving red and white goop on the back of her wrists.

"Ya best not be actin' up or you'll have the Judge to deal with, sted-da just Clyde."

"Well, Stella Mae," I said. "What exactly do you think I'm going to do?"

"I been in this business long enough to know the rules is the rules. I ain't sayin' you're gonna do nothin'. I'm sayin' you just better not *try* somethin'—or else." She swiped her tongue over her lips and continued munching. "For as long as you live here, you ain't spendin' the night nowhere but here or at the Juvenile Hall. That's a law come straight from the Judge hisself."

I tapped a finger on my lip and stared at her.

She wiped the back of her hand across her mouth. "You can't work no job or drive no car neither."

"Well, that being said, will you please tell me what I *can* do?" I snorted.

"I'll tell you what ya *can* do. You can take your patooty up that ladder for bein' a smart alleck. I ain't stupid neither. I know when yer flipper fingerz pointed at me."

I walked away, crawled up the ladder, and sat on my bed. The cubby hole was my favorite place to brew hate, make evil plans of destruction, then talk myself out of it. Stella Mae had her own set of rules, all right. The one that was going to drive me buggy was the "no cleaning" rule. She had caught me with a broom, trying to sweep the grubby kitchen floor and screamed, "No sweepin'! It just raises dust and makes the house dirtier. What fool sense does it make to lift dirt off the floor and put it on the window sills?"

I wrote to Gramma about Stella's quirky ways, like how she sloshed dishes around in soapy water, then stuck them in the oven and turned it on. She kept the refrigerator bins on the kitchen counter, filled with cereal. She scooped up fistfuls of Kellogg's Frosted Flakes from a bin that said "Meat" and shoved it in her mouth. She didn't care if she stepped on Frosted Flakes and took them to bed between her toes. Stella didn't believe in sitting at a table to eat—she stood over the sink or by the stove. She bought plenty of food, but rarely cooked. When she did make a big pot of something, she stuck it in the fridge when it was still hot; she had melted a milk carton more than once.

I also told Gramma about how Stella loved Miracle Whip more than life itself. She bought six jars at a time, in the industrial size, and put it on everything she ate. She cored out apples and filled them with Miracle Whip, she coated olives in Shake n' Bake and deep fried them, dipped them in Miracle Whip and ate them out of the pan.

Gramma wrote back to tell me that Stella Mae was a blessing. *Try to imagine what a difficult job she has, Honey Girl, with all those troubled children and a husband who doesn't work. Also, when a person gets nervous they sometimes eat their worries away. And consider, perhaps she is from a different culture.*

Gramma was right. I had to concentrate on how lucky I was to have a roof over my head and someone to care for me. I needed to follow Flash, my guiding light, and remember that my real family and my foster family held me in their hearts and I had to hold them in mine. I would survive and come out a better person, Gramma said, with God's will and my own strength, because God helped those who helped themselves. When I wanted to cry myself to sleep because my arms ached from not getting to hug Amber or pet Three Legs, I figured I could go deep within my soul and yank out enough strength to believe. Gramma wrote that this whole thing could possibly be a mistake and if so, I would find my way back to my real brothers and sisters and Mom would come to her senses and let me come home. She wrote. *I'll keep praying for you.*

I remembered what Louanne's aunt said once . . . a woman needs comfort. Well, I was on my way to becoming a woman. I had to figure out how to get some comfort. When I got to wallowing in my own misery I would reread one of Gramma's encouraging letters. What I wasn't about to tell Gramma or anyone else, was that the first chance I got, probably on a Saturday when Stella and Barbara were grocery shopping and Clyde was double-drunk, I was going to clean out Stella's slimy pink bathtub and have a luxurious bubble bath.

I heard Stella Mae's bones creak. Her teeth clicked as she stood below the attic. "Eve! You can get down here now."

I crawled over and looked down the hole. "What's up, Stella Mae?"

"Comeer. Ya got company."

My heart whopped against my ribs. I practically fell through the hole and hit the floor below. "Who is it?" I said. She waddled away and I followed her into the living room.

A lady who looked like she was twenty-something stood there wearing a long denim skirt, a tie-dye tank top, and macramé sandals.

"This here's Doola," said Stella.

"It's Darlene," the woman said.

"Hello," I said. I looked back at Stella Mae. Did she think I was supposed to know this person?

Stella grunted. "Doola's from the Probation Department and she's gonna take ya to get some shoes today."

I was so relieved I wanted to dance. When Stella waddled away, Darlene gave me a quick smile and rubbed a finger under her nose. It was probably the smell of the place. She opened the front door like she was ready to escape and I followed her. I didn't bother to put on shoes because I still didn't have any.

Outside, the day was hazy and hot enough to grill a bird. Walking out to Darlene's car, I thought how cool the air would be on the Nooksack right now. We got in Darlene's yellow Volkswagen Bug and putted out the driveway. I felt freer than I had in a week.

"I'm Darlene Parks. It's nice meeting you."

"Well, as you know, I'm Eve and it is a pleasure to meet you too. Thank you for breaking me out." She punched in the clutch with her foot, shifted, and our heads lurched forward and back.

"Just kidding," I said, "about the breaking out part."

What I learned on my way to Bellingham in Darlene's Bug was that before we went shopping we had to first get the money.

"Where are we getting the money?" I asked.

"We're going to go and get it from your mom," she said.

I cranked the window down so I wouldn't throw up on her crocheted granny-square seat cover. I was dizzy all the way down the Guide Meridian. I began to panic and plucked out blonde hairs from my legs, pinched each little hair between my fingers and pulled until I felt a sharp pain. I flicked them out the window. I counted fifty of them, trying not to think of what was about to come.

We drove silently for twenty minutes until we rolled into Bellingham, buzzing with traffic. The Volkswagen sputtered by City Hall where the flags hung limply, too hot to flap. We turned toward Old Town and Darlene pulled up in front of *Old n' Oak Antiques* and stopped.

When I saw my parents' van parked in front of us, I dropped my eyes and stared at my blotchy legs and bare feet.

"Come on, sweetie," she said.

I looked at her and found my voice.

"Darlene, I want to thank you so much for doing this for me. But . . . please, please don't make me go in there. My mom is mad at me I'm sure and she doesn't like to be bothered during business hours. Her work is *very* important to her and besides, you're not allowed in her shop without shoes."

"Eve, I realize this seems difficult or awkward or whatever, but I'm trained in this sort of thing and it won't be that bad."

"Have you ever met my mom?"

"No, I haven't."

"Well, she's not your average person. She has a . . . way . . . well, I just don't—"

"You can let me handle it, okay? We'll just go in, ask for the redemption of the voucher, and—"

"What voucher?"

She reached up, adjusted the rearview mirror, and flipped her long hair behind her shoulders. "It's a court order that your mother pay for your clothes and your shoes, but she's refused, so we have to present this form in person and get fifteen dollars from her." She waved the paper.

"I would be willing to bet she's not just going to hand you fifteen dollars," I said.

"I bet she does. Then we buy shoes for eleven dollars and go to Baskin Robbins for ice cream with the extra four bucks!"

She appealed to the kid in me. I hadn't had ice cream in a year. "Okay, but you walk in first. I'm staying behind you."

"Good girl." She pulled hard on the handle and slammed her shoulder against the door to open it. I opened my door and got out in slow motion. The sidewalk was scorching under my feet.

When Darlene opened the front door to the antique shop, a fog-horn sounded and scared us both. Mom laughed. She was standing in a corner next to a giant cash register. There were a half dozen customers browsing among the furniture and collectibles. The smell of furniture oil reminded me of the house on Walnut Street, of the quadraphonic sound system in the big carved cabinet. Walnut Street was only one mile away. It hurt to be standing this close to my brothers, my sisters, and my dog.

"That's the loudest doorbell I've ever heard," said a man looking at a Tiffany lamp.

"That's what I like about it," said Mom. "It scares the crap out of everybody. Hah!"

Darlene cleared her throat and said, "Hello?"

Mom glared at her, then at me. She looked different. She was plumper in the face and around the middle, or maybe it was the robe-like thing she was wearing. Her hair was bright blonde, piled up high, care-less and perfect at the same time. She wore glittery eye shadow, loads of bangles, and gold shoes.

My head closed up the way it does when I'm about to pass out. It was unclear what words they exchanged, but the next thing I knew, I was being pushed out the front door by Darlene. Mom was yelling something about trouble paying for itself. We ran to the car and jumped in. Dar-lene turned the key and shoved the Bug in reverse, the voucher crumpled around the gear shift.

A couple minutes later Darlene finally spoke.

"Jeez, now that I'm done shaking, I say we indulge in some ice cream."

"With what money?" I was shaking too. My legs were jiggling and my voice sounded far away.

"I've got my own money."

"So what did she say exactly?"

"Well, first of all, you were right about your mother. Although I see some very interesting family dynamics in my line of work, she is most certainly one-of-a-kind."

"That's an accurate observation. Are you my new probation officer?"

"I'm with Social Services."

"Oh. I thought Stella Mae said you were with the Probation Department."

"Well," she laughed, "she also calls me Doola. If you haven't noticed by now, the Carlyles are a real piece of work."

"I've noticed."

"Anyway, I do mostly field work, child advocate stuff. To answer your question, your mother essentially said she was *done*. She said that anyone who came through the door of her shop gave *her* money, not the other way around. When she began raising her voice—that was our cue to leave. I don't get hazard pay."

"Well, I'm glad you handled it so nicely."

"And," Darlene said, "you know what really blows my mind? She screamed at us like those customers weren't even there. Right in the middle of the whole thing, I could tell that one lady got so scared. She had a dish in her hand and was about to set it back on the shelf and get out of there. Your mom yells at me *Who do you think you are coming into my place of business* . . . then she looks at the lady and says *I'll take seventy five dollars—that's a Duncan Miller piece.*"

"Yeah, Mom has always been an excellent business woman." I put my face in my hands and shook my head. "I knew I would be scared, but I was like, petrified—it was like I wasn't even there—like it scared my body right out of my skin."

"I understand. Such emotional intensity can cause one to retreat within. It's an unconscious protective mechanism. Fear is one of our most powerful senses."

I noticed my legs had stopped shaking.

"Yeah." I looked out the open window, spotted my reflection in the side mirror. My face was thin, my straggly hair fluttered in the wind. "My mom looks different from what I remember. Do you think she's pretty?"

"Well, sure. A bit done up maybe, but don't value my fashion opinion that much; I'm somewhat of a hippie." She gave me a quick look and smiled.

"I like your style. It's nice you can dress like that for your job." I thought of the probation officer women in their suits.

"Right on. I like your style too. One of the reasons I chose this career is so I could make a difference somehow with kids like you. It's hard to handle, seeing parents and children split up and going through so much when the world is already such a mess. My parents are mere shells of themselves now because my little brother was hurt in Vietnam. He lost his legs."

"Oh, I'm so sorry."

"Yeah, it sucks. I hate war. But at least he made it home. There are so many who weren't so fortunate. Have you been following the whole 'Nam thing?" She rolled into Baskin Robbins and stopped.

"Not much," I said." I mean, I know how it supposedly ended in April, but I've kind of been raised without TV and sometimes I think the way I've grown up, I don't know much about the world around me. It's like life has just been one house after another and another—"

"Really? How many houses have you lived in?" She drummed the steering wheel.

"This is number eighteen," I said. "I'm going back to my eighteenth house . . . with no shoes."

"Don't worry," she said, "after we eat ice cream, I'm going to buy you some shoes and a new outfit for your first day of school."

Gramma's prayers were really working.

When Darlene dropped me back at Stella Mae's, she said she would try to come out again and take me to her house so we could bake cookies. I asked her if we could make mashed potatoes instead of cookies and she said we could make both. I told her I respected what she did for a living and that she made me want to be a "child advocate" one day. I mentioned again that I was sorry about her brother and thanked her for her generosity. And her bravery.

Darlene drove off and I walked in to see Dennis and Jim slouched on a couch and Barbara sitting at the table grinding crayons into a Disney coloring book. I saw that Clyde's Rambler was gone, Stella was gone, and

Bobb was in the bathroom.

I held my bag of new clothes. "Where's Stella Mae?"

Dennis grinned like he just couldn't help himself. "Nice shoes. Stella went shopping."

"On a Thursday?" I said.

"Guess so."

I headed for my room.

Dennis yelled, "Nice socks too."

Upstairs, I emptied everything onto the bed. The smell of new clothes filled the air. I was going to have to figure out a way to pay Darlene back for what she had done. She bought me a pair of jeans, three pairs of socks, underwear, two tops, and a sweater. I was wearing the suede shoes with knee socks even though it was the hottest day of the year. I pulled the price tag off the sweater first.

I jumped when a peacock screeched from the kitchen. That was probably what Dennis was smirking about—they had stolen a peacock from the neighbors. The shriek was loud enough to rattle the windows. I clomped down the ladder as fast as I could.

Running past Clyde's room and into the kitchen, I found Barbara slumped in the middle of the kitchen floor, puffed up and screeching. Dennis and Jim were standing over her, covering their ears. Dennis shook his head and grinned at me.

I screamed, "What's going on?" Dennis grabbed my hand and pulled me through the house and onto the front porch. We were hit by a blast of hot air. Jim followed us and shut the door so we could hear each other. Barbara would not let up. It sounded like she was being eaten alive.

"I called her a maggot," said Dennis.

"You didn't *call* her a maggot," said Jim. "You *said* 'maggot.'"

I looked at Dennis. "All you said was *maggot*?"

"Yeah, it's such a trip. She totally loses it just from hearing the word. And the even trippier thing is that no other word gets the same reaction." He smiled. "You wanna see?"

"No," I said. "That's so mean, you guys. What if her heart pops or something? Poor Barbara. You don't know what you're messing with.

Maybe she's had a horrible experience with a maggot. Wait, she's saying something. Is she saying hurt me?"

"No," said Jim, "She's saying she's thirsty. She always says that."

"Well, why didn't you give her some water?" I said.

Dennis shook his head. "She's not our problem, freakin' nut case."

"Come on," said Jim, "this may be your only opportunity to witness a maggot revulsion disorder."

"How long has Stella been gone?" I said.

Dennis shrugged, "I don't know. A couple hours?"

"I thought Barbara always went with her," I said.

"Apparently not today," Dennis smiled.

Barbara stopped screeching like someone had unplugged her.

"Come on, let's go make sure she's okay," I said, opening the door. Barbara was standing at the kitchen window, completely silent, staring trancelike. Her face was its normal pink again, but her ears looked like plums.

I approached her slowly. "Barbara? Why didn't you go shopping with Stella Mae today?"

She kept staring straight ahead.

"Barbara?"

"She forgot me," she said flatly.

"Did she give you your medicine before she left?"

"No," she whispered. Her eyes were swollen and red-rimmed.

"Would you like a drink of water?"

"No. It doesn't help. Nothing helps." Her pudgy face looked deflated.

Dennis said, "Mmmmmmmmm. Aggot," but she didn't respond. I smacked him on the arm. His face brightened and he winked at me.

Jim said, "Little white worm hatched from a fly, which feeds on decomposed flesh."

Barbara didn't blink, just stared.

Dennis got closer to her and said, "Starts with an M and rhymes with faggot."

She wasn't going to give them the satisfaction.

I took a coffee cup off the counter and was about to fill it with water when Stella Mae's Dodge Dart plowed into the driveway and rocked to a stop. We split like cockroaches hit by a bright light. I was in front of Barbara's bedroom door when I heard Stella yell, "Barbara, I refilled your prescriptions."

"Yay," she said.

"And," Stella Mae screamed, "I brought ya Kintucky Fried Chicken with lotsa gravy! They make a extra crispy kind now. I got us a sixteen-piecer."

"Double yay!" Barbara squealed.

September 25, 1975

Dear Gramma,

How are you? I'm fine. I started school at Meridian High. Bobb and I take the bus. The other kids don't get to go to school because Dennis and Jim have court dates coming up and Barbara can't handle school because of her "condition."

The best thing has happened! The choir teacher, Ms. Platt, said I can play her piano on my lunch break! I have six other classes I really like. This school is smaller than Scio High; they don't even have P.E. uniforms. The school lunches are really good though.

Bobb has a new friend named Bruce, but he likes us to call him Brucey. Anyway, Brucey is nineteen years old and drives a peach-colored Cadillac with a Texas license plate. He brings pizza over every Friday night.

Today in Home Ec. we put cupcake batter in a microwave and watched it expand right before our eyes. My Home Ec. partner's name is Tammy. She's really shy and wears a puffy blue coat all the time. Her father is a baker and he's never seen a microwave.

I've got to do homework now before Stella catches me "goofing off." I'm trying my hardest to like Stella Mae and see the best in her, but she tells me awful gossip about the other kids and it makes me want to scream.

God Bless You.

Love,

Eve

P.S. Tell Grampa I double-dare him to go on the tree swing with both Buddy and Choppy on his lap!

By my fifteenth birthday, I had been at the Carlyle House long enough to see how things worked. Stella ran the place with a vengeance. Clyde got drunk. He wasn't allowed to drink inside, so he went out the back door, got in his Rambler and drank around a country block. After doing it seven or eight times a day, he was plastered. He came through the back door tilted to one side, stumbled through the kitchen and into his room. There he sat and smoked until it was time to go out again or pass out for the night. But he was always in by dark, before Stella locked the back door and stuck the key in her bra.

Bobb told me that Stella Mae got paid one hundred dollars per kid each month. I wrote to Gramma and told her that all together, we were almost as valuable as one of Grandpa's beef on the hoof.

Stella Mae was irritable, nosy, and impatient. When she got mad, she slapped the counter and screamed "Clyde!" but he never responded. After Gramma's letter pointed it out, I could see that Stella Mae ate when she was bored, angry, or nervous. I suppose she ate when she was hungry too, but it was hard to tell the difference. It seemed to me she was happiest every Saturday, when she and Barbara left to grocery shop and eat junk food in Ferndale. They were gone five hours, sometimes six.

Saturdays became our rule-breaking day. Dennis called it "Saturday Special." As soon as Stella and Barbara were gone, Dennis made prank phone calls and pawed through the cupboards, Jim stole Clyde's Pall Mall 100s and smoked them, and I cleaned. We occasionally spied on Stella's mother, but all she ever did was eat canned clam chowder and sleep. She had a pile of empty soup cans on her front porch as high as the doorknob.

It was a Saturday in early February when the air had taken on a bite from the north. The house was freezing, especially the attic, and I wanted a hot bath. Stella and Barbara were gone and Clyde had passed out earlier than usual. Bobb and Brucey had gone to ceramics class, and Dennis and Jim were up to no good in the backyard.

I crept past Clyde, who had one leg swung over the arm of his chair and a cigarette burned all the way to his fingers. I didn't get how the ashes stayed so long without falling to the floor. He was snoring, his head half off the back of the chair. The room stunk like spoiled apples. I opened his bathroom door and looked under the sink for some Comet cleanser. I pulled out a dried-up sponge, a plastic bowl, and a crusty can of Ajax. I closed the door and locked it.

The bottom of the tub was lined with smelly green algae. I rolled up my sleeves and began scooping up the gunk with the bowl and plopping it into the toilet. When the toilet bowl filled up, I flushed it, but it was clogged so I opened the window and tossed the rest into the bushes. It took me an hour, but with the sponge and several wads of toilet paper, I wiped the tub until it was almost pink again. When I flipped the toggle to plug it and turned the hot water on, thick green froth bubbled up from the drain, more rotten than the first batch. Disgusted, I turned off the water, put the supplies back, and shut the window. I looked at myself in the grungy, splattered mirror. I decided my Saturday Special had to be kicked up a notch—and it wouldn't have to do with a hot bath.

Bobb wasn't too keen on the idea, but Brucey said he would be happy to help, as long as we didn't get caught.

Brucey had two jobs in Bellingham. He worked at the public library, filing, and he was training to be a makeup artist at Felton's Funeral Parlor, which was three blocks from the Walnut Street house. The first part of the Saturday Special was to get a message to Angie. As instructed, Brucey waited by Felton's until Angie walked by on her way home from school. There he introduced himself and gave her my note. He told me she cried when she read it. He said the following Saturday he would give me a ride to Elizabeth Park and wait for exactly twenty minutes, no more, while I visited with my sisters.

When Saturday came, Stella and Barbara were rushing out the door. Dennis was smiling at me, because he knew the plan.

"Dennis, whatcha smirkin' about?" Stella said.

"Nothing, Stella Mae." He grimaced at her. "It's just gas."

Barbara scrunched her face so tightly her eyes disappeared. "You're so gross," she whined.

Don't never mind 'im Barbara, jis git in the car. You kids best not be actin' up while we're gone," Stella said, and they left.

When Brucey pulled into the driveway, I ran out and jumped into the Cadillac. The car was clean and shiny and smelled like gardenias. A Barbara Streisand song played on the radio and Brucey sang along as we backed out. We listened to music all the way to Bellingham, the Bee Gees, Streisand, and Barry Manilow.

When we stopped a block away from Elizabeth Park, Brucey kept the engine running.

"Twenty minutes, no more," he said.

"Got it. Oh man, I should have peed first."

"You're just excited," he said. "I don't blame you."

"Thanks for this, Brucey. You're the best."

"Hurry up."

I raced down the sidewalk and into the park. There they were, Angie sitting by the fountain with Amber on her lap. I ran toward them, tears falling.

"Myeve!" Amber squealed.

"Shhhhh," Angie said.

We wrapped ourselves around each other.

"Group bawl," Angie said. "Oh my God, you look *so different.*"

"Can I hold her?" I said, reaching for Amber. She was warm and smelled as pure and sweet as ever. Twenty minutes, no more.

chapter twenty-five

Tammy

Jim was right. Rule breaking was more addicting than cigarettes.

The day was warm and sunny with the promise of a great Spring Break. I was running up the back stairwell on the way to my last class when my Home Ec partner stopped me in my tracks. Tammy was standing three steps above, and I got a good look at her for the first time. She had shoulder-length, oily black hair half-tucked into the neck of her puffy blue coat. A solid, dark eyebrow sat above black-rimmed glasses like Clyde's, which made me feel sorry for her. Her face was mottled. As long as we had been in Home Ec. together, I had never seen her hands—she always kept them tucked out of sight. She chewed nervously on a coat sleeve. We were all alone.

"Aren't you hot in that coat?"

She looked around, then peered at me through her thick glasses. "How did you get in your foster home?"

"Excuse me?"

"I wanna be in a foster home," she mumbled.

Was she mocking me? Who in their right mind would volunteer to live in a can like the Carlyle House? And how did she even know I was in a foster home? It wasn't something I talked about and Bobb had promised not to tell anyone. He said although he just loved "Mom," the Carlyle place "carried a stigma." He said it was hard enough being called *faggot* all the time without having the title of *lowlife* too.

Then it dawned on me: Tammy Vanzandt wasn't in her right mind. She was probably just crazy. Maybe she was retarded or chemically unbalanced like Barbara and that's why she always covered herself up— afraid of germs or air.

"I think . . . we're in the same Home Ec. class," she said. That proved it. She had memory loss or "recollection disorder." She was likely half blind; her lenses were as thick as glass ashtrays.

"Yeah, I know. I've seen you," I said. "Remember, we were microwave partners?"

She looked back up the stairs and behind me.

"I was wondering how you got in your foster home," she said quickly.

She stared at me, waiting for an answer.

"Look, I don't mean to sound like Dorothy or anything, but there's no place like home. Believe me, you don't wanna be in a foster home. I'm not there by choice, it just happened that there has been a grave misunderstanding and I'll soon be going home to my real family. Well, that's not entirely true. Actually, I am somewhat of a law breaker."

She cleared her throat and pushed her glasses up her nose. "Please help me," she whispered.

"Is something wrong? I mean are you in trouble?" I asked.

"I can't really talk about it, I just thought you could tell me how I could get to a place like the one you live at." I just stared at her, dying to know if she hid a broken arm under that coat. I felt sorry for her all over again.

"Please?" she said.

"Do you have a pencil?" She shook her head.

"Okay, remember this: Darlene Parks. She works for Social Services in Bellingham. I only met her once, but she's really nice. You can also try Pat Moody."

The bell rang. "I've got to get to Science," I said.

"Thank you," she said.

"Darlene Parks or Pat Moody. Good luck." When she stepped down the stairs, her coat brushed up against me. It didn't smell too clean.

If anything, maybe Darlene would buy her a new sweater.

On the bus ride home from school I was preoccupied with thoughts of Tammy Vanzandt. Bobb sat ahead of me, but I was glad to be by myself to think about the strange girl. What was her story? Where did she come from? Did she take the bus? Did she ever talk to anyone? She didn't appear to have any friends. She'd probably forget she had spoken to me at all. Perhaps I had been wrong to tell her about Pat Moody and Darlene. It was possible I had broken one of Stella's stupid rules or "a rule come straight from the Judge hisself."

I smiled out at the fields passing by, at the thought of Stella Mae always suspecting something, yet I had been to see Amber and Angie twice without getting caught. Our time in the park was spent laughing, crying, playing with Three Legs, and trying to persuade Amber not to tell. So far she hadn't.

The bus ride was one of the most peaceful parts of the day. Now that we would be out of school for nine days, I was going to sneak into town to see my sisters more than just Saturday. More than just twenty minutes. Angie's voice was like candy to me. She told me how everything had come to be. Mom had put police surveillance on the Berg's house when I was at the river. Angie had seen Louanne a few times in the park with her new boyfriend, Bob. Louanne was starting to show and her baby was due in February. Louanne told Angie she had gone back to the Nooksack and gotten my things and she was going to send them to me when she got an address. I gave Angie the address and told her all about the Carlyle House. She wanted to know if Brucey was cute and I told her he had fantastic lips and he could sing like a dream. She said Max had started fourth grade, Toby was an auto body genius, and Tim had a serious girlfriend named Jill. As for Angie, she was in-between boyfriends, still hated school, and didn't like having a bedroom all to herself.

"Does Mom ever talk about me? Like do you think I'm gonna come home one of these days?"

Angie was quiet.

"Well? Do you?"

"I don't know."

The bus stopped at Bartlett and rumbled. Bobb and I jumped out. When we opened the front door, Stella Mae bounded toward me.

She pointed her finger and clacked her teeth. Bobb said, "Hi, Mom! It's Spring Break." He waltzed past her and into his room.

Stella's cheeks were flushed and her hair had come unpinned on one side. Her white roots had grown out enough to make her look like an overfed skunk. Poor Stella Mae, she was really wound up.

I looked around for Dennis. With one look he could tell me if I was busted. Had Amber finally told? I dropped my book bag by the door. "What's up, Stella Mae? You look upset."

"Did ya talk to a girl named Tammy Vanzandt today?" she said. Stella's voice began to rise like it did when she talked to her son, Marlin, on the phone. He only lived five miles down the road but she screamed at him like he was a world away and nearly deaf. She started pacing in a circle. Before I could respond she said, "Did ya know she's coming here ? Did she tell ya *why* she's being brought here by the sheriff?"

I shook my head.

"That was 'sposebly a respectable family from out Lynden way."

"Stella Mae, I don't know anything about the girl, except that she's in one of my classes."

She glared at me. I could see where her makeup ended around her chin.

"And she wears a big blue coat. Where is everyone, Stella Mae?"

Stella stepped closer, her eyes as sharp as darts. I knew the story was coming and I wanted to cover my ears and say la, la, la, la.

Through Stella's panting and ranting, I found out about my school-mate. Tammy Vanzandt lived on a nearby farm with her father Elroy and her brother Tony. Elroy owned a bakery in Lynden. Their mother had walked out on them when Tammy was two and Tony was three. For the next five years, Elroy brought home a variety of women. The two children managed to get mothering in small doses, but no woman stayed long enough to make an impact. Tammy learned to read early and buried herself in books.

When Tammy was seven the women stopped coming around, and Tony began to work in the bakery with Elroy. They began work at 3:30

a.m. so Tammy was left alone at home.

After Tony was apprenticed, which took two months, Elroy dropped Tony off at the bakery and returned to Tammy around 3:45 each morning. Initially he approached her in her own bed and eventually forced her to sleep with him in the barn.

"Stella Mae, please stop telling me all this stuff. It's none of my business. And what makes you think she's coming here anyway?"

"Pat Moody called, that's what. That filthy man bit that little girl's fingers when he done thought she weren't cooperatin' with 'im. An' he took her glasses away so's she couldn't read."

"I don't care, Stella!"

"Well you'd care if yer own father told ya semen's a cure for poison oak and a gun's a cure for tellin'. An' this's been goin' on all these years right here in our own backyard."

I covered my ears and screamed, "Stella Mae! Stop!"

Bobb came out of the boy's pad. "Mom, that's enough. We all know there are bad things in the world. Let's just try our best not to dwell on them. Now, where are we going to put this girl when she comes? In the green room?"

I was beyond sad for what Tammy had been through. My own guilt washed over me for having had such a good childhood compared to her.

It was almost dark when the Sheriff brought her to us. He came to the front door with the paperwork. I wondered if she had a yellow copy in her pocket. I saw her from a distance, a lump of blue in the backseat.

I crawled up the ladder, laid on the mattress, and listened to the rustling below. Although she was bringing her things into the green room, we didn't speak to each other that night or for the next three days and nights. But our sisterhood had begun.

Tammy stayed holed up the first few days. I guessed that as each day passed, she found comfort in the quiet of her green room, and like an abused dog, it took some time for her to trust that she was safe in her new home. Because I had to walk through her room to get to my ladder, it was fortunate that we became friends instead of enemies.

I thought it was nice of Stella not to force Tammy out into the nuthouse too soon.

In the first few weeks of Tammy's arrival, I was actually excited to get home to the Carlyle House. She began to talk to me after the first three days. At first, she was unable to get certain words to come out of her mouth. Maybe she never had anyone to talk to, maybe saying those words made the ugly memories too strong. I knew what it was like—you could read a lot of books, but awful thoughts could just stay in your head and take over if you didn't have someone to talk with.

She started to speak more easily, and share interesting news about the progress of the case. She gave me daily reports. Tammy had bi-weekly meetings with her caseworker and Child Protection Services. It was put on *her* whether or not to press charges against her father. But the therapy was helping Tammy grasp what had really happened. Her biggest issue, she was told, was guilt.

Tammy said she liked my room because it was the smallest and furthest from anyone else in the house. We spent our waking hours talking about life, school, and cheerleaders. We shared our pasts and talked about our grandmothers. Her Grandma Hazel had died, and she didn't know if her mom was still alive. She had one aunt named Linda, who was being briefed on the actions of her only brother, Elroy. I told Tammy about my grandparents and my family. She talked about her brother, Tony, and I talked about Tim. As Gramma had been my saving grace, Tammy had her Aunt Linda. It was her Aunt Linda who brought her things once she had arrived at Stella Mae's. She bought her new clothes and, much to my relief, a new coat.

Tammy always came back from being with her aunt loaded with candy bars, chips, and Marlborough Reds.

"Why do you have to smoke?" I said.

"I have to do something with my mouth or I feel sick," she said.

"Well, why don't you just eat?"

She shook her head. "You wouldn't understand."

We were sitting on my bedroom floor and I asked, "What was your mom like?"

"I can't remember what she looked like, but I remember she smelled like smoke." She looked at the ceiling. "What about yours?"

"Well, I know what she looks like, but I don't think I've ever smelled her," I said.

"How could you not have smelled her?"

"I don't know. It's like I never got close enough to know what she smelled like. Either that or I just can't remember."

"You're blocked," she said.

"What?"

"My therapist says it's like putting your heart in a little box and locking it up. Because—it's hurt. But you can't fix it. I mean, you can't get to it unless you unlock the box and do the work." She shoved her glasses higher up her nose.

"I can probably tell you what color her nail polish was on any given day, though."

"Stella smells like a goat," she said.

"I know that's mean, but it's true," I said. "The funny thing about Stella is that you don't have to get very close to her to know what she smells like. She's surrounded."

"What do I smell like?" Tammy leaned toward me.

I sniffed her shoulder. "You smell sweet, kinda like a candy bar. In fact, I was going to call you *Pepper* because your hair's black, but I think I'll call you *Sugar*."

"I like that," she said.

I told her about my days on the Nooksack. She said she wished she would have known me then and we could have gone and lived there together.

"You could actually pass for a Nooksack Indian girl because you have those big, dark eyes," I said.

"Speaking of eyes, Aunt Linda's gonna take me to get contact lenses. The therapist said it would be a good thing to get rid of my glasses because they're attached to negative thoughts."

"Well, do you think so?" I asked.

"All I know is that it would be so cool to have contacts."

"Yeah, Cindy Shannon has contacts, you know."

"Yeah, but she has everything because she's a cheerleader," she said.

"She has nice clothes and pretty hair," I said.

"Well, I can't stand her. She thinks she's so cool."

"Well, when you get your contacts, you'll look just as cool as she does. In fact, you can get your hair cut and you'll be even prettier than any one of those cheerleaders."

"Yeah, right." She rolled her eyes.

True to her word, Aunt Linda took Tammy to get contact lenses. And she got reading glasses for evening. Sugar looked completely different without the black-rims.

"Well, how was it, getting rid of your glasses?" I said.

"It was good, I guess. The therapist told me I could do what I wanted with them, throw 'em against the wall or step on them."

"So what'd you do?"

"I thought. Then I got mad and everything turned black. Then I pulled the sides off and I threw them on the floor and smashed the lenses with my boot."

"That must have felt good."

"I wanna get a new haircut to go with my new eyes," she said.

"Sugar . . . do you ever cry?"

She looked away. "Never," she said.

We went into the bathroom, washed her hair in the sink, and combed it out until it was a thick, wet silky strand. She held her head upside down as I combed it all into a ponytail coming right out of the top of her head. I gathered it with a rubber band and she sat down on the toilet lid. She put a towel around her shoulders, and holding the ponytail straight up to the ceiling I snipped off her hair, leaving a four-inch spike on the top of her head.

When we took the rubber band out and dried her hair, she jumped up and looked in the mirror.

"Oh Eve, I love it! Now you want me to do yours?"

"No, thank you. My hair's too straight so it would never be that cute."

"Well, thanks. I really like it." She went to her room.

Dennis and Jim were in the kitchen.

"Hey, did you open your own beauty salon in the bathroom?" said Dennis.

"No, actually, I have higher goals."

Stella and Clyde were both gone when I was upstairs doing homework. I heard Tammy's drawl from the bottom of the ladder.

"Eve?" she said.

"Hey, come up." I was struggling with a math problem, surrounded by wads of notebook paper.

"I've got something for you," she said as she popped her head in the cubbyhole.

"What?"

"Well, I saw Tony earlier and he gave me some pot," she said.

I was disappointed it wasn't a bag of potato chips. "Have you ever done it before?" I asked.

"Yeah, Tony and I did it together," she said as she crawled in.

"How did you get to see Tony anyway? I thought it was a court order that you don't see them."

"I can see him if he comes to Aunt Linda's. She let us go for a walk in the woods and he brought his dope. He said it would help me have good dreams and that if I listen to "Dream On" by Aerosmith when I'm high, all my dreams will be in color."

"Wow."

"Stella and Clyde are gone," she said. "Come on." We crawled over to the window and sat underneath it with our legs intertwined. Sugar pulled out a tightly rolled joint, the first I had ever seen.

Tammy explained that getting high was really cool and anyone who was cool did it.

"And," she added, "Tony says it takes all the pain away because there's a magical thing in marijuana that takes away bad memories."

"Okay, let me try it," I said.

I took a puff, coughed, blew out smoke. I tried it again and handed it back.

Tammy took a huge drag and held in the smoke. She released a puff out the window and whispered, "Do you feel it?"

"No," I said. "What's it supposed to feel like?"

"Kinda like eating air," she giggled.

"Well, I don't feel like I'm eating air. In fact I don't feel any different."

"You've only had one toke." She grinned. "Tony says you have to smoke it a couple of times to get the full effect."

"Whatever," I said.

"Tony also says that people can get a *contact high* from just being in the same room with someone who's stoned."

"Good," I said, "I'll go for the contact high."

Sugar took another toke and snuffed the joint on the outer windowsill. She held the blackened end in her fingertips.

"This is a roach." She tilted her head back and smiled. "We reek."

"You mean *stink*?"

"Yeah, like stink, like smoke, like toke, like dope." She laughed.

"Shh," I said. "What are you going to do with the evidence?"

"Put it with these." She pulled out a handful of cigarette butts from her pocket.

"You're a walking ashtray. You're gonna get busted if you don't watch it."

"Well, what am I supposed to do with 'em?" she said.

"What do you usually do?"

"Throw 'em outside."

"I have a better idea."

Opening a blue gingham envelope that Gramma had sent, I felt a pang of guilt. Sugar put the roach and the butts in. I crawled over and shook some baby powder in, licked it, and sealed it with a kiss. I stuck it in the bottom of my waste basket and covered it up with wads of math problems.

Sugar giggled. "Nighty night!"

"I don't feel any different, but I'm glad you're having fun," I said.

She laughed again and slid down the ladder.

"Lights out!" Stella Mae bellowed. We hadn't even heard her come home.

chapter twenty-six

Sweet Sixteen

Although darkness covered Tammy like a coffin lid, I needed to be with her. In my naive teenage mind I believed I could help her—possibly save her from herself.

Many nights she was frightened, claiming it was after midnight when the demons came; when all the terror and sadness of the world was right there in her bedroom. From my room I heard her grind her teeth in her sleep and whimper when the nightmares took over. I often snuck down the ladder to lie beside her. If I massaged her temples or scratched the back of her neck, the grinding ceased. When she trembled fiercely, I pressed myself against her back and held her until the shaking stopped. It was during those black, cold nights I knew that bad people truly existed, and because she couldn't cry about it, I cried for her.

But somehow we always slept. Somehow daylight always came.

It was late afternoon when Sugar and I were lying on my bed looking at the ceiling. She had a ringlet curled around her thumb, chewing on it gently. The slanted walls creaked and moaned from the wind. "Hear that?" I said, "I hope there's a summer storm coming."

"I don't care about storms."

"Your fingers look so much better," I said. "They've healed up nicely."

She looked at her hands and frowned.

"What's the matter now?"

"Do you ever think about suicide?" she said.

"About what?"

"About killing yourself."

"No."

"Never? Come on, you must've thought about it."

"Well, not about killing myself. Maybe about how someone could actually go through with it."

"Do you know anybody who has?"

"Only my dad."

"I've been thinking about it since I was twelve," she said, "when I first started my period. I figure if bein' a kid's been this bad, then bein' an adult could only be worse."

"Well, I think suicide is selfish."

"You're wrong, Eve. It's a gift. The one thing that makes me happy is that the end is just sitting right there, waiting for me to grab it. Death is the only thing that's real."

"No, life is the only thing that's real."

"You're kiddin' me, right?" she scowled. "Life is torture. Think about it. We're all here just waiting to get out."

A branch hit the window and I flinched. "The wind's picking up," I said.

"My dad always told me if I didn't do what he said, he'd kill me, but *that's* the selfish act. I had the barrel in my mouth so many times, I begged him to pull the trigger and get it over with. Then one day I knew... I wanted it only for me, not him. He doesn't deserve the satisfaction."

I sat up and put my hand on her cheek. "Don't you know there's so much more out there? Sugar, we have a whole life ahead of us. We can become who we want and—"

"We're not gonna become anything else. This is it. We are what we are and we can't change it."

"Well, that's one way to look at it, but killing yourself sounds horrible to me."

"There's no difference between horrible and beautiful. My reward is waitin' for me whenever I'm ready. But it won't be with a gun."

"Well, do me a favor. I happen to love you, so if you plan on doing yourself in, please don't do it in my lifetime."

"Don't worry." She slid my hand to her lips and kissed it. "Can I smoke now?"

"No. I'm out of envelopes."

We heard a thump below. "Girls!" Stella screamed. "I told you not to be hangin' out in each another's room. Ya got yer own room fer a reason. If I let everbody in everbody's bedroom we'd have a bigger mess than we already got. Now git down here right now. Eve, yer in fer it."

Sugar covered her mouth. "Oh shit," she whispered. We heard Stella stomp away. Sugar went down first and jumped onto her bed. She grabbed a book and pulled an afghan over her shoulders. "Whatcha in trouble for now?"

"I haven't the slightest idea. Trouble just follows me around this house."

She opened her book. "Good luck."

"Thanks. Hey, do you tell your therapist this stuff?"

She stuck her face in the book and shook her head. I stifled the urge to kick her bed to get her to look at me.

"You should," I said.

She gazed at the page.

"Tomorrow. Do it tomorrow as soon as you get to your therapist's door." I walked out.

In the kitchen there stood a giant sheriff. Stella waved a blue gingham envelope in front of my face.

"Well looky here, Sheriff, we got us a smoker. I found this stuffed in the bottom of 'er trashcan a while back. She even put powder in it but that dint fool me none!"

How did she even get up my ladder, let alone fit through the hole? I looked past the sheriff's gun and handcuffs and saw Jim and Dennis watching from the front room. I should have taken Jim up on his offer. Just that morning he said he would teach me how to snap someone's neck, do a Ragdoll, and a Roman candle. He said you never know when you'll need to defend yourself.

"Stella Mae. Sheriff. I can explain," I said.

"No need, missy," the sheriff said. "I gotta take you in. For breaking probation."

"Yeah," said Stella. "Don't think yer so clever. You been goin' ta Bellinham ta see yer sisters. I got wind of it all. I heard it straight from yer mother."

I felt like I had inhaled a sock. I placed my hands on my neck and opened my mouth. "What are you talking about, Stella Mae?" I squeaked.

But I knew. It had taken exactly four months to get caught.

I spent that night in Juvenile Hall, alone in room number six, listening to the wind howl and wondering if the old janitor was still there. I gobbled up instant mashed potatoes with chipped beef gravy and canned corn. At five o'clock the next morning a probation officer took me into the interrogation room. He was a weak-looking man with penny-sized glasses and a sprig of orange hair under his nose. A year had passed since I had been there, but the chairs appeared to be in the same place and the light bulb had the same bleak glow. I sat in a metal chair and he stood over me holding a big black pen with a shiny gold tip. It was too large for his hand, in my opinion.

"Apparently, Miss Chanteau, you've forgotten your obligation to abide by the rules of the Carlyle House and the Court. I'm here to inform you that if you break probation again, you can kiss the Carlyles goodbye. You may think that's appealing but I promise you—" He leaned so close I could smell his coffee breath. How could anyone drink that stuff so early in the morning? "I promise you that Seattle Sites is no walk in the park and will, without a shadow of a doubt, be your next stop. Seattle Sites has zero tolerance for sneaks and liars and they've got a reputation for being the best at punishment and reform. Now do you agree to return to the Carlyle House and keep your nose clean? Yes or no." He shoved the pen in my face.

I nodded and signed away my sisters.

Along with the yellow copy of my release was the police report. It included a statement in my mother's beautiful handwriting.

Only six days earlier I had met Angie in the park. Bobb and Brucey had driven to Texas and I *had* to show up in the park that Saturday. I took the bus that went from Lynden to Bellingham. We had a joyous time as usual, until I had to leave. I explained that I needed to run to Fountain Avenue in time to make the bus back before Stella got home. I kissed Angie and Amber and patted Three Legs on the butt. I was almost out of the park when Angie yelled, "I'm running away from home too."

I stopped in my tracks and looked back at her. She had Amber by the arm, rushing the other way. They were at the park's edge, almost to Walnut Street. I cupped my hands around my mouth and screamed, "No! Don't!"

The police report stated that Amber told Mom, "Myeve said no don't, no don't, no don't! Myeve says no don't, Mommy."

September 2, 1976
Dear Gramma,

How are you? I'm fine. Stella wouldn't let me get a job this summer, so I've been pulling weeds and flattening soup cans. I have also been attending "Good News" on Thursday nights with the Mitzelfeldt family. They have 10 children and a big van that beeps when it backs up. They have bumper stickers all over the doors that say WWJD, which stands for What Would Jesus Do? Shamefully I admit I like to go to Good News because we get a candy bar if we memorize the Bible verse, but better yet, when they have a break I get to play the church piano.

Yes, all the same kids are still here but Jim's court date is coming soon and I'm scared for him. His stepdad teased him for years about not getting to have a piñata for his birthday. After 10 years of that Jim tied his stepdad up and turned him into a piñata. I'm sorry to sound so crude but it does explain why we probably won't get Jim back. He will most likely get sent up to McClaren, which is where the worst boys go, although he is anything but the worst. He is beautiful and misunderstood, Gramma, and all you have to do is look at him to see that he is one of God's greatest works.

I miss you more than Christmas.
Lotsa Love,
Eve

P.S. Tell Grampa the neighbor with the peacock farm got two baby goats!

In early October I came home from Good News to find a box sitting by my ladder. Sugar was nowhere to be found, but her things were all in order so I figured she was probably with her Aunt Linda. Inside the box were some old clothes I had outgrown. There was a journal from seventh grade, a comb with missing teeth, and the miniature vase Mom had given me years before that said "It's up to you."

Stella walked up behind me. "Yer mother came out this afternoon."

I inhaled sharply. "She did? She came *here*?"

"Yep. She's a perty woman, ain't she?"

"Did she come to see *me*?"

"Nope. She was jis in the neighborhood and had that box a stuff fer ya. Theys movin' to another house."

"Moving? Where are they moving to?"

She put her hands on her hips. "Theys goin' across town, over there in the Fairhaven part a Bellinham. I hear that's where the richies live."

"Did she say anything else? Like am I going to go back ho—back there? Ever?"

Stella clacked her teeth. "She dint say much else other'n she could see why ya'd be real happy here."

"She said that?"

"Yep. Said ya always done better in the country than in town and ya like yard work."

"Stella Mae, did she like, come in? Sit down? Talk about the family?"

"Na, none a that. She did say to watch out fer that Steve Henry feller. He's an arsonist from Oregon."

I stared right into her eyes. "What else did she say, Stella Mae?"

"Nuthin that matters," she said, and puttered away.

I hated Stella Mae. Not because she was so nasty, but because she didn't tell me what I wanted to hear. All those nights spent comforting Tammy had led me to believe that sadness could really wreck a person, but at that moment I knew it was anger that could do the most damage.

Jim stood by the front door, much taller than his probation officer. Dennis shook Jim's hand and said, "Hey, good luck, man. Maybe I'll see you on the outside."

I walked over to Jim, stood on my tippy toes, and gave him a long hug. "See you later Jim." He put his hand on the small of my back and held me there. "Remember what I taught you," he said.

"I will."

"And don't use it unless you need it."

They went out the front door and got into the probation officer's car. I watched him drive away, taking a piece of me with him. The next day he would be admitted to McClaren, stepping into a uniform he hated, while I stayed at the Carlyle House and turned sixteen.

Brucey brought pizza for my birthday. Bobb presented a giant bank in the shape of a pig that he had made in ceramics class. On its belly was etched *To Sis, Lovingly, Bobb.* He had fired the piggybank with no bottom access, only a slot on the top. He said if I filled it with money I would have enough to buy a new wardrobe and that I couldn't break it until it was full. The fine apparel could wait. I wanted braces. Brucey gave me a mood ring and Barbara gave me a dirty look because it wasn't her birthday.

Gramma sent a Sweet Sixteen nightgown. I admired it with tears in my eyes knowing the hours of work she had put into it. It was made of soft cream flannel with tiny blue flowers. Gramma had done perfect buttonhole stitching around the yoke and cuffs. Up in my room I slipped the nightgown on and felt the love wrapped around my body. I set the piggybank next to me in bed and turned my attention to the birthday cards Gramma and Louanne had sent.

Sugar came up, moved the pig over, and lay beside me.

"Happy birthday, sweet girl. I'm sorry I don't have a present for you."

"I'm just glad I have *you*," I said

"You're bummed about Jim, aren't you?"

"Yeah. I miss him," I said.

"Do you think you'll ever do any of those things he taught you?"

"Nah. I don't really have it in me to kill anyone."

"I do," she said.

"Did you know a Ragdoll's a mafia move? When you jab a knife into the back of their neck, they flop like a doll and their tongue hangs out the side of their mouth."

"That's cool," she said. "What about a Roman candle?"

"Jim said they do it in Ireland. You kidney-shock the person by kicking them right here, in the back. When they go down, they pass out and then you stick a gas-soaked rag down their throat and light it. He almost did it to his stepdad once."

"I bet he wishes he had now." She began rubbing her lower abdomen and looking at the ceiling.

"Does it hurt?" I said.

"No, it's not a big deal, just a little cramping below my belly button. I can't believe you still haven't started yet."

"Do you think there's something wrong with me?"

"No," she said, "everyone's different. Where did you get this?" She picked up a bottle of Love's Baby Soft Spray.

"Louanne sent me a package and Gramma sent a night gown. Isn't it beautiful?"

"Yep."

"I bet all the girls in our class have periods," I said.

"Yeah, you're probably right. I can't stand Sandy Ryder. She's so snotty because she's cute and rich and wears black pants from Nordstroms. She has pierced ears and wears birthstone studs."

"Sugar, please. Don't be jealous, it's not good for your complexion. Besides, maybe the rich girls wear black pants to cover up the blood that leaks out when they're having their cycle."

"Yeah, maybe. Do you think we're ever gonna wear black pants from Nordstroms?"

"We will if we want to."

"Do you think we'll ever have pierced ears?"

"You probably will, but I won't because my mom cursed my ear-lobes."

"What's that supposed to mean?" she said.

"Mom says piercing your ears is an unnatural act, disrespectable, and she will not allow it. She said if I ever did it, my earlobes would become deformed."

"Do you believe that?" she said.

"I did at the time, but I don't know now. Hey Sugar, do you think Stella would let me get a job?"

"Probably not. Why do you want a job anyway?" She sat up and set her huge brown eyes on me. "Are you planning to run away?" she asked.

"Please, it doesn't make sense that I would want a job if I was planning an escape. I want a job so I can make enough money to buy braces. I hate my teeth."

"How much do they cost?" she asked.

"I don't know for sure but it's probably somewhere around a thousand."

"A thousand dollars?" she screamed. I rolled over and covered her mouth with my hand. "Shh!" I held my hand there and she put her hands over mine. Our noses touched.

"I *am* going to get a job and get my teeth straightened, and if Stella Mae tries to stop me, I'm going to figure out another way." I uncovered her mouth.

"Geez, Eve, Okay. Good luck with that one."

"I love you." I shot her a buck-tooth smile.

"I love you too," she said and threw a pillow in my face.

No sooner had I set my sights on getting a job, when it was Career Day at school. Sugar and I sat next to each other in an auditorium full of juniors and seniors. We heard speeches from an agricultural expert, hair stylist, bank teller, and a police officer with a dye job like Stella Mae's. When the presentation was over we were handed a self-evaluation form. We were to list our most valued life experiences, our strengths, and career goals.

The possibilities seemed endless. After the time I had spent in Juvenile Hall, I could aspire to becoming a ping-pong champion. I could be a large animal veterinarian or a professional quilt-maker. Maybe I could become a teacher, or go into medical research and find the real cure for poison oak. Perhaps an inspector for the County Health Department would be satisfying, where I could tidy up places like Stella and Clyde's.

I wrote, "I would like to go to college, make a positive impact on the world, and be a nice person."

Sugar wrote, "If I'm still alive I wanna be rich."

Throughout that fall and winter we got three new kids. One was a fourteen-month-old baby who stayed with us for three weeks until her adoption was finalized. She was bald-headed and called baby B because no one had named her yet. We had to keep Barbara away from Baby B because there was something about her that set Barbara off. We put the baby in a crib at the bottom of my ladder and Stella Mae put me in charge of taking care of her. Although I had fun feeding and changing her, it made me lonely for Amber.

The relentless winds of January blew in a fifteen-year-old girl named Sally Jean who arrived on the doorstep like a leftover Christmas present. She was barely four feet tall and had huge, black eyes. Her face was pitted, but her features were doll-like. She had a little button nose and a dimple in her chin. Sally didn't smile.

Stella told me about Sally's drug problem. She said she had done the "big-time" drugs, like cocaine, speedballs, PCP, and heroin. Dennis called them the "high-roller poisons." Her juvenile record was a series of ER admissions, overdoses, and relapses. Sally's tracks were the first I had ever seen. Little purple-brown bumps lined her arms like ants. Sally had a family, Stella Mae said, but she was temporary placement with us until a county rehab facility had an opening for her. She was put in the green room in a twin bed across from Baby B's crib. I felt sorry for little Sally Jean. She stayed deep inside herself and didn't talk to any of us.

Sugar was unhappy about her new roommates so she spent most of her time in the cubby hole describing what she planned to do with what life she had left. After confessing her suicidal thoughts to her therapist, Sugar decided she was going to wait a while, live into her thirties, but no longer. She would have a brand new house with white carpet and a peach-colored love seat. I would have a lovely plot of land with a small cabin on it. She would drive a Mercedes Benz and have a long-haired white cat while I would drive a Toyota pick-up with a chocolate lab by my side.

"I'm gonna have a microwave in my new house," she said.

"Well, I'm going to have a wood stove and cut my own firewood," I countered.

"I'm gonna have that fake grass put in so it'll look perfect next to my sidewalk," she said.

"I'm going have a front yard filled with flowers and a cobblestone walkway leading to my front door."

"I'm gonna have my own post office box."

"I'm going to *make* my own mailbox that will be an *exact* replica of my little cabin."

We burst out laughing. Suddenly Stella was at the bottom of the ladder. "Eve and Tammy? You two come down here. We gotta new kid I want ya to meet."

We went down to the living room to meet our new foster boy. Dennis and Sally were sitting on the couch. Barbara was standing next to Stella, looking nervous, and Sugar and I stood side by side. The kid stood by the front door, as we all had done.

Stella said, "This here's Raminold Lakka. He's an Injun and he goes by Rami."

He had long, black hair and dark eyes. Native American dream catchers hung from his ears. He looked around the room as we all stared at him and mumbled, "Hello Rami." He reminded me of a small version of the big Indian from *One Flew over the Cuckoo's Nest.*

Rami was put in the boy's pad and spoke to no one for two weeks. Baby B got adopted by a couple from Mt. Vernon. I cried when they drove away because her new parents were too old and had four mangy cats sprawled across their dashboard.

Rami's dream catchers inspired me to pierce my ears.

Stella and Barbara had gone out to eat grease and Rami was sitting on the orange couch staring at nothing.

"Hey, Rami," I said. "I'm going to pierce my ears. Do you want to help?"

He nodded and stood up. We went into the kitchen and I pulled out the things I had gathered: frozen corn, a sewing needle, matches, potato, broom, and a chair. I sat down and held one package of corn on each side of my left earlobe until my head was frozen.

Rami stood there looking unimpressed.

"Do you want to sterilize the needle?" I said. He nodded, lit the match and passed the needle back and forth through the flame until it was red-hot. After it cooled down, he slid the blackened tip through the sleeve of his shirt to remove the soot.

I set the corn down and picked up the potato. Holding the potato behind my ear, I said, "Okay, push it through."

Rami touched my hand. I heard a crunch as he punched the needle through the earlobe and into the spud. He pulled the needle out and stuck a small piece of broom straw into the hole. We did the same thing on the right side, but this time I pushed the needle while he held the potato.

Tammy walked in and asked if we were smoking when she saw the pile of burned matches on the counter.

"Hey, Sugar. Do you want your ears pierced?"

"Does it hurt?"

"No, but it sounds funny."

"Okay, she said. "Why not? It couldn't hurt more than an eyebrow pluckin.'" I held the frozen corn on her ears while Rami burned the needle again. I poked the needle into Sugar's milky-white earlobes. After we were done she said, "Hey Rami, go get Dennis."

The corn was starting to thaw, so I traded it for a package of frozen hamburger and a can of grape juice. Dennis stepped in. "Cool," he said, "but only my left ear. I don't wanna get Bobbette and Brucey all excited. We froze Dennis' earlobe and watched his face, but he didn't flinch as the needle went through his lobe. Sally already had many holes in her ears so we left her alone. Rami said the straw had to stay in for three to five days, then could be replaced by real earrings. We all agreed to keep our ears covered with our hair so Stella Mae wouldn't see.

Rami burned the dull needle and handed it to me. He grabbed a dream catcher and pulled, stretching out his earlobe.

"Do you want another hole in this one?" I said.

He nodded.

"Don't you want to freeze it first?" Sugar said.

He shook his head slowly.

"Okay," I said, "but it might hurt and I don't want to hurt you, Rami."

I put the potato behind his ear and began to push the needle through. Piercing a piece of raw gristle felt much different than lancing a frozen one. The skin squished up into itself and the needle didn't feel like it could go through. Sugar covered her eyes and I pushed harder. Rami didn't budge as the needle finally popped through.

"I'm sorry, Rami, but I can't get the potato off." He reached up and pulled it off, yanked the needle through, and stuck a piece of straw in the bloody hole.

We cleaned up the mess and got to our rooms by the time Stella pulled in. I wrote to Louanne, telling her I finally had pierced ears.

The next morning I awoke to an aching head. My earlobes were puffed up like cherry tomatoes. I looked in the mirror and saw that the straw sticks had festered and were sitting in pockets of pus. I squeezed, and both straws popped out.

Within three days Sugar wore birthstone earrings from Aunt Linda, Dennis sported a diamond stud, Rami wore a new loop of colored thread, and my lobes were healed, and sealed completely shut.

chapter twenty-seven

Sugar

Just south of the Canadian border sat an oceanfront expanse called Birch Bay. In winter the northern winds and the pacific waters ransacked the shoreline, but during the summer months the bay was calm and the area buzzed with fair-weather residents and droves of tourists.

Barbara had to take a double dose of anti-anxiety meds the day we went to Birch Bay. Four of us were to be part of a study being conducted by a psychology student from Western Washington State University. Wendy Peal was working on her Masters in Adolescent Deviant Behavior. Stella had consented to letting me, Rami, Dennis, and Barbara go to Birch Bay in a van with Wendy and her driver. Sally was on house arrest and Sugar was laid up in bed with a fever and a broken heart.

The day was bright and warm when we all piled into the van. Wendy had introduced herself in the driveway. Her hair was back in a loose knot and she wore glasses with violet rims. A clipboard rested on her lap as we drove away.

I looked out the window and thought how great it would be if I ran into Louanne at Birch Bay. I still couldn't believe she'd had a baby. Then my thoughts went to Tammy. I hoped Stella Mae would leave her alone and let her rest. The closer it got to Sugar's court date, the more time she spent sick in bed.

We cruised past the peacock farm, and Dennis winked at me. Wendy turned to us from the front seat. I felt a bit sorry for her that collectively, we had little to offer the research project. There was a slight chance Barbara could explode, but really we were just trapped teenagers out for some fresh air.

I looked over at Rami, who sat quietly with a small leather knapsack under his arm.

"What's in the bag, Rami?" I said. He ignored me.

June 27
Dear Gramma,

How are you? I am fine. We got to go to Birch Bay to swim last Saturday. The water was lovely until I got hit in the head with a rock. Rami threw it, but I know it was an accident. Anyway, I was in shoulder-deep water when I fainted. Two Canadians pulled me out and a medic shot my head with Novocain and put in two stitches.

When the driver got us all back in the van, Rami was missing. He's been gone for 6 days now and they think he walked or swam over the border during all the commotion.

Brothers and sisters come and go like wild geese around here.

I'll write more later. Stella's yelling about something and I gotta go.

I love you and Grampa more than mashed potatoes,

Eve

I was sitting on my bed when Tammy popped her head into the cubby hole.

"Oh my God! You are so busted," she said. "I can't believe you did that."

I had written on my wall in pencil the song "Stairway to Heaven." Four hundred and one words began next to my pillow and traveled across the wall and up to the ceiling. Each verse was in the shape of a stair step.

"It's cool, but aren't you afraid Stella's gonna see it?" she said.

"No. She can barely fit up the ladder." We fell back on the bed and looked at the lyrics.

"Eve?" she said, "I've got something I have to tell you."

I looked into her eyes. "Okay, fess up," I said.

"I can't do it."

"Can't do what?"

"I can't press charges."

"Pardon me?" I sat up.

"I can't press charges against my dad."

"What? Did he contact you?"

"No." She put her hands to her temples.

"Then what do you mean, you can't press charges?" My palms began to sweat.

"I just can't."

"Sugar, this man almost destroyed your life."

"I know, but that doesn't matter now," she said quietly.

"What do you mean, it doesn't matter? It *does* too matter!"

"I just don't wanna do it anymore," she said.

"He would have killed you if he had to, Sugar. He's sick."

"I know, but…"

"He is really, really messed up, and you're the only person who can stop him."

"I'm scared," she said.

"Of course you're scared, but oh my God, I can't *believe* this."

"Please don't get so upset. Just listen to me." She put her hand on my knee. "My court date is next Thursday and the closer it gets, I feel like it's not the right thing to do."

"What he did to you was not the *right* thing to do!"

"I can't bust my own father," she said.

"He isn't a father, he's a whacko pervert."

"I know," she said, "but…"

"What if he just gets away with it and does it to some other girl, like a sweet little girl who's just tiny, like the ones on the milk cartons? It's so wrong, Sugar. You have to rethink this. This is crazy. You don't know what you're saying." I put both hands on her shoulders. "Please stop and listen to yourself. Come on, you've been through enough therapy to know that you can be free of him, and until he's behind bars he will stalk you and haunt you and maybe even kill you!"

We stared at one another and she didn't have to say anything because we both knew how sick and confusing it is when your darkest fear is your own parent.

"I met somebody," she said.

"Who?" I shot back.

"His name is Gary," she said, holding her gaze.

"So what about *Gary*?"

"Gary loves me, I know he does. He can help me get away from Dad and keep me safe."

"When did you meet him?" I said.

"Well, I met him a long time ago through Aunt Linda, but it was only recently that he left his wife."

"I see."

"Remember how we asked each other if we were ever gonna get married and you said only if your husband would love you, feed you, and keep you warm?"

"Yeah, that sounds familiar," I said.

"Well, then I said I would want to be married only if I could have a husband who would…"

"Never close the bedroom door," we said in unison.

"Yes I do remember that very well," I said.

"But you can't have any of that if you're dead, and that's exactly what you'll be if Elroy finds you. He even *told* you that!"

"He won't find me."

"How do you *know* that?" I put a pillow to my face. Her eyes brimmed with tears and she put her head down on my legs. I rubbed her soft hair.

"Oh, Sugar. I just don't want anything bad to ever happen to you again. I'll do anything I can to help you," I said.

She sat up and faced me. We pressed our foreheads together, held hands, and watched the tears fall onto our fingers.

"I'm gonna run away," she whispered.

My head shot up. "When?"

"Soon."

"You're sixteen. If you get busted, it'll mess up your entire life."

She explained that when you're in love anything is possible, Gary could fix everything, Aunt Linda supported the idea, and Tony would too. Gary was real smart, she said, and although they didn't know where they were going, he would figure it out because he was way older than Elroy. He was almost forty and knew a lot more about the world than anyone she had ever met.

I put my hand to her chin. "Well, what about Elroy?"

"He's gonna have to live his own hell without me in it," she said.

"Aren't you scared he'll find you?"

"I was, but I'm not anymore because I have Gary to protect me." She smiled and sniffed, leaned over, and kissed me on the lips. "I love you," she said and crawled down the ladder.

I fell back on my pillow and regarded the stairway on the wall. I followed the lyrics to the top. *...and she's buying a stairway to Heaven...* I slept for twelve hours.

The next morning Sugar came back up the ladder. We spent two more hours talking about her plan. Although I tried my hardest to convince her otherwise, she believed it would be best to skip her court appearance.

"I gotta tell you something else," she said.

"What?"

"I'm pregnant."

I passed through Sugar's bedroom and saw the list on her bed. *Overalls, Seventeen magazine, underwear, address book, contact solution.* Next to each item was a checkmark. I looked around at her unmade bed and the empty bedside table. I opened the drawer where she kept her dictionary and it was gone. Her dresser drawers were empty.

My stomach felt hot. I decided to go upstairs and lie down, let it pass, not think of killing her when I found out where she was. At the top of the ladder sat her dictionary and a note.

Dear Eve,

I will always love you. I'll find you after the baby comes.

Love, Your Sugar

I fell back on my bed and thought of mashed potatoes and better days to come. I prayed that Gary would be good to her and she would stop smoking long enough to have a healthy baby. I asked God to guide Sugar and help her to be a loving mother in spite of her past. I thought of Lori Mezo and Louanne, and wondered if I would ever grow up and fall in love and have a baby. And would I ever see my Sugar again?

chapter twenty-eight

Hilltop Cafe

It was not my intention to incite trouble at Stella Mae's, but the overcrowded house, the squalid conditions, and Clyde's escalating drunkenness was leading me to the edge. Even Flash was fainthearted. By midsummer we had thirteen kids in the house. Bobb moved out and Dennis was sent to Toutle River, a boy's reform camp at the base of Mt. St. Helen. The day they took him away, he held my hand and pressed my Swiss army knife into my palm. As my fingers curled around it, he winked, and then walked out to the patrol car. My brother-love and beloved thief.

After Dennis left, we got a sexual deviant named Cindy. She said she "did bikers". A spaced-out girl named Liz arrived, who claimed she was a singer/songwriter on her way to Hollywood when she got busted for possession. Rayanne was a thirteen-year-old cutter who had crashed through an upper story window. After being sewn up in the Emergency Room, she ripped out her stitches with a safety pin. Diane was a bulimic with swollen neck glands from pressing on the back of her throat, the enamel on her teeth melted away from stomach acid. Kevin Suanders, who had been in eight boy's homes, was a sad replacement for Dennis. He had long, greasy hair and pustules of acne up his neck and into his scalp. He refused to brush his teeth. The place was packed-out with kids who could never look happy, like Clyde could never look clean.

The day I came home and saw Cindy leaning on Clyde's back with her hand in his pants, I knew something had to give. She was wearing a black dress hiked up over her thighs, the straps hanging off her shoulders. Clyde was slumped over, moaning like an old dog. The TV was humming out a Pepsi commercial. I backed up and ran outside. Where was everyone?

When Stella finally came home with a carload of kids, I went in the house. Cindy was sitting at the table, wearing jeans and a T-shirt. Clyde was asleep in his chair.

I glared at her. "How are you today?" I said.

She gave me a twitchy smile. "I have a sore throat," she said.

I approached each kid but Barbara. Four wanted out. Liz planned on hitchhiking to California, Kevin was going to deal pot with his friend, Will. Cindy wanted to find a gang she knew, and Sally was going to live with her sister in Seattle. That night I took my Swiss army knife and slit the window screen in the green room. I sliced it along the frame, down one side and across the bottom.

It was after midnight. Stella and Clyde were snoring as I crept past their bedroom door. Kevin was standing by a couch with his backpack. He stepped toward me and we tiptoed back through the kitchen and past Barbara's room. Liz and Cindy were awake and ready. In silence I held the screen back, and one by one they slipped out.

The moon was high and bright. We gathered the things we had stashed in the bushes earlier that day, including Liz's guitar. We ran down Bartlett, across Pole road, and to the Guide. We stayed in a ditch until Will pulled up in an El Dorado. The kids jumped in, and they took off.

I made it back through the screen and into bed by four. I dreamed that Mom was driving a big car. I was beside her in the front seat and she offered me a sip of her coffee.

August 21

Dear Gramma,

Stella Mae finally let me get a job! I am working at the Hilltop Café out on the Guide Meridian. My shift is Friday and Saturday nights, but don't worry. Fatso, the cook, has been there nine years and he watches out for the employees. The owner, Beverly, could pass for Stella Mae's sister.

Soon I will send a picture of me with braces!!

Love, Eve

At work I wore an orange apron with my name written on an iron-on patch. Every other Sunday, Beverly Clemmons would remove the five aprons from the hooks and take them home to launder. Out of the four other employees, Brenda was the meanest. She stole ten dollar bills from the till and used them to snort coke in the bathroom. She called me "Skinny Bitch" behind my back.

There were three things I liked about the Hilltop Café; Fatso gave me free French fries, I got a cupful of quarters after the bar rush, and at two in the morning David Hovander came in to order ham and eggs. He was a musician. He played in a rock band at a bar in Bellingham, wore tight white pants, and was catch-me-I-may-faint handsome.

"I'll have ham and eggs, sunny-side up with white toast and chocolate milk," he'd smile.

"Chocolate milk's not good for you," I'd say. Then we would just stare at each other. He always left a good tip and wrote poetry on paper napkins.

Stella called an orthodontist when my piggybank was full. We all gathered around on the living room floor, the bank on a towel and a hammer in my hand. Barbara screamed that it was cruel to hit a pig. I drew back and struck hard enough to crack it cleanly down the middle. After stacking and counting all the coins, I had $334.

I glued the pig back together with superglue and worked through the winter to fill it up again. Dr. Lakey was a general dentist and an orthodontist. His office manager said it would be a $300 deposit and I could make twelve monthly payments of $58. Dr. Lakey said we could skip putting in spacers because I already had adequate spacing.

"Come on in," Beverly said. It was a Sunday and the Hilltop was empty. Fatso was out back, smoking. Stella grunted as she stuffed herself into the booth next to Beverly, and I slid in across from them.

"Well, what do you have to say for yourself?" said Beverly.

I looked at her and then at Stella.

"Well?" said Stella.

"Me?" I said. "What do you mean?"

"Someone's been stealing money from the till, not ringing up certain sales, and now my gold bracelet is missing," said Beverly.

"Not me," I said with my hand on my mouth. "I have never stolen anything, Mrs. Clemmons." I turned to Stella Mae. She was shaking her head.

"Well, I know it ain't Brenda who's stealing and I'm damn sure it wouldn't be Debbie or Karla, so that leaves *you*," Beverly said.

I put my face down and tried not to cry. Through the blur I saw something shiny, like a coin, in the crack of the seat. I looked up while trying to dislodge it with my finger.

"Stella Mae, tell her I wouldn't do that. I value this job and work hard for every penny. I even pay for all the food I eat, except for the French fries Fatso gives me sometimes." Without looking down, I pulled it out. It felt like a chain.

"Well, I can't afford to have no thief working here. You're fired. Stella, we been friends a long time and I told you I was willing to try a foster kid just this once, but I ain't doin' it again. They're all ruined."

Stella began pushing herself out of the booth.

"I'm going to say goodbye to Fatso," I said. I got up and walked through the kitchen. I dropped Beverly's bracelet in Brenda's apron pocket and walked out the back door and got in the car.

chapter twenty-nine

Eighteenth Birthday

Three days before my eighteenth birthday Aunt Linda sent word that Sugar had gotten married in Las Vegas and had had a baby girl. Her name was Stephanie, but Tammy called her Baby Sugar.

That evening I asked, "Stella Mae, do you think it would be all right if I went to Seattle with Louanne? She wants to have a birthday party for me."

"No," she said.

"Why not?"

"Because I said so, that's why."

"Well, you know I'm going to be eighteen, so…"

"So *what*?" she said. "You ain't eighteen yet."

"But Stella Mae, I'll be eighteen in like sixty-eight hours."

"I said no and I mean it," she said and slapped the countertop. "There's mail fer ya."

I got birthday cards from Gramma and Tim.

Happy Bday Ruby Jane,

Jill and I are getting married and we're going to have a baby in February. I hope you can break out and meet the little guy. (I'm hoping for a boy!)

Heads up! Steve Henry's coming to see you. I'll keep you posted,

Love, Bro Tim

The next day I stuck a clean pair of underwear and my best blouse in my backpack and went to school. At 3:00 sharp, there sat Louanne in front of the school in her brand new blue Toyota Celica.

"Nice car! Matches your eyes," I said.

"Oh my God! Look at you!" she squealed.

I reached through the window and hugged her.

"Get in," she said. I jumped in and we sped out.

"Where's the baby?"

"I left her with my parents. Well, you know Dad. He freaked out when he found out I was pregnant, but now he's just crazy about Erika."

"I can't believe you have a baby. Where have I been all these years?"

"Trapped in the twilight zone," she said. "So, how's it being a senior? And how many credits did you say you need to graduate?" We turned onto the Guide.

"Not too many, actually. I have about a semester's worth to go, but I'm going to schedule it so I can graduate with my class in the spring. I'm also going to take a correspondence course through North Carolina State University to become an RDA."

"What's an RDA?"

"A Registered Dental Assistant. Dr. Lakey is going to give me a job as a rover. That's a person who helps the dental assistants."

Louanne rolled her eyes. "I can't believe you actually made it all these years in that crazy place. And look at you—a virgin with braces! Are you really going to be *eighteen*?"

"Yes I am."

We drove to the onramp and headed south down I-5. We chatted and laughed, and told stories all the way to Seattle. I told her of my plan to move out of Stella's. I was going to get my braces off soon and I could make enough money if I worked every day to buy a new bicycle.

"Why not a car?" she said.

"Because after I have enough money saved up, I'm going to see some of the world I've missed out on. I'm going to fly to Hawaii, crew a boat down to Bora Bora and Australia, then ride my bike around New Zealand. Then I'm going to come back and go to college."

She shook her head. "You're still crazy, aren't you?"

Sunday morning was frosty when Louanne and I drove back to

Stella Mae's. We listened to the new Bad Company tape and cruised along, exhausted from staying up so late.

As we pulled into Stella Mae's driveway, the tires crunched on the icy edges of the mud puddles. Louanne put her car in park and I leaned over to give her a long hug goodbye.

"Thank you so much for the fun time. I'll let you know what the future brings. I guess I'll try to find somewhere else to live and start my new job next week," I said.

"Totally! Good luck. We'll be in touch."

She stared at the house, "Oh shit," she said.

I looked up to see that all my belongings had been thrown on the front step. There sat my clothes, my toiletries, books, and my stationery box. There was a paper sack with letters sticking out. The mess was topped off with my pillowcase, my cookbook from Bobb, and the pig.

"Oh my God!" said Louanne. "You've been kicked out! Didn't Stella know you were with me?"

"Well, she told me I couldn't go. She's probably just mad and overreacting. Could you just wait here a minute while I go talk to her?" I said.

"Sure, no problem," she said, and turned off the motor.

I ran up to the door and tried to open it, but it was locked. Stella's car was there and I could see through the window that light bulbs were burning brightly. I knocked loudly, but no one came to the door. I knocked again and again and then ran around to the backdoor. Clyde's car was parked in its usual crooked manner. I tried the doorknob, but the backdoor was locked as well. I rapped on the glass loudly.

I kicked the door hard and yelled, "Hello? Stella Mae? Clyde? Barbara? Anybody? Hello?"

I loaded my stuff from Stella's porch into Louanne's trunk. I held the sack of letters on my lap.

"Well," said Louanne. "Where to?"

"I don't know. I wasn't prepared for this."

"Since when were you ever prepared for anything? Your life is just one surprise after another. What kind of a nut case would do that?" she said.

"Okay, let me think. I still have five months before graduation."

"Drop out."

"Not an option." I opened the bag and saw an unopened letter addressed to me in beautiful handwriting. It had been mailed from Sumas, a border town ten miles away.

"Who's that from?" Louanne asked.

I opened it and read it out loud. It was a poem from David, to "The girl with the wheat field hair." He said he missed me at the Hilltop and wanted to see me again. He signed it with a heart and his phone number.

"Who's David?" she asked.

"He's this really nice guy I met at work, before I got fired. He used to come in at two in the morning. He plays in a band and every time he ordered ham and eggs sunny-side up and chocolate milk, I brought him plain milk and he always drank it. He asked me to go on a picnic in Stanley Park, but I told him I wasn't allowed to do anything until I was eighteen."

"Well, you're eighteen now. Why don't you call him?"

"Because he's so handsome and kind and he's twenty-one and has a really nice family with four sisters and two brothers and probably a wonderful mother and father."

"Sounds perfect," she said.

"But he's so …well, normal. I wouldn't know how to behave around a normal person."

"Well, I'm normal," she giggled. "Besides, you'll never know until you try."

"Maybe we should go to Bellingham and drive by my parent's house. They still live in Fairhaven. Or should I call David?"

"You decide," she said.

chapter thirty

Eruptions

We were asleep on Louanne's floor when we heard the explosion.

It was a Sunday morning in May and five of us were strewn about the front room in the wake of Louanne's twenty-third birthday bash. The boys were gone, and so was the entire keg and the handle of Cuervo Gold. Cigarette butts and lime slices floated in half-full plastic party cups. I had opened all the windows around 4:00 a.m. and now the house was freezing.

"What the hell was that?" moaned Louanne. I rolled over and crawled to the window. The street looked sleepy. No smoke in sight, no sirens. Seattle was quiet. I suddenly remembered I had a plane to catch.

"I don't know," I said, "but it sounded like dynamite."

"Jesus, my head hurts. What time is it?" said Louanne's roommate, Bonnie.

"God only knows," said Louanne. "My alarm clock's blinking. Eve, turn on the tube and find out the time." I switched on the TV and we stared at a haze.

Mount Saint Helens had just blown up.

More than a year had passed since Louanne and I had sat in Stella Mae's driveway trying to decide what to do. I chose David Hovander.

Shortly after I met his parents, David took me to Stanley Park where he read me his poetry; we drank a bottle of Boones Farm Strawberry wine and rolled on a soft bed of leaves. Then he proposed and promised that Rod Stewart knew the truth: *The first cut is the deepest.*

David and I lived in a tiny house on Front Street in Sumas, and I was still a senior at Meridian High. Each morning he drove me to school in his brown Buick and then went to work at Copeland Lumber. He had saved enough money, he said, for matching wedding bands and a honeymoon in California.

I took David to meet Mom and tell her of our engagement. She said "That's the stupidest thing I've ever heard."

Mrs. Hovander arranged the wedding.

Stanley Park was thickly wooded and bordered Canada. We selected a grove of Douglas fir as the ceremony site. David's mother ordered platters of cold cuts and cheese trays. Louanne's mom offered to make the wedding cake. There were to be twenty guests, including Mom, Larry, Max, and Angie. When the big day arrived on the fifth of May, I wore a white summer dress. Louanne picked me up in her Celica with a carrot cake swaying in the back seat.

I looked at the cake as we drove up the Guide toward Stanley Park.

"Don't stick your finger in the frosting, *Mrs. Hovander.*"

"Lou, let's just hit the border."

"Are you crazy? Do you have cold feet or what?"

"I don't feel right about this. I mean, do you seriously think I'm ready to get married?"

"Sure, I mean you love the guy, right?"

I looked at the plastic bride and groom shaking on top of the cake. I should have bought a veil and some better shoes.

"Right?" she said, louder.

"Who are you to talk? *You're* not even married. We're getting close to the park. Will you please just drive over the border?"

"Eve, you can't just leave those people standing out there waiting for you."

"Border."

"No," she said, and pulled the car into the gravel parking lot. She turned off the engine and leaned toward me. "Are you afraid of seeing your mom?"

"Yes. That and the fact that I know she disapproves of me marrying a musician. Also, Gramma is concerned I'm too young and I'm just looking for a nice family. I think she might be right. I wish she could be here today. I don't know, I just feel like I'm not following my guiding light—"

Louanne gently touched my arm. "I had a miscarriage this morning," she said. "You'll be alright."

The marriage lasted twenty-two days. Being that David was a music man, he said, he was required to stay out all night on the weekends because his fans expected it. And, he added, it was not his fault that so many girls loved him—blame it on his stage presence. On graduation night I stood at the podium giving a speech of how we were destined for success because of the love and support of our parents. I was senior vice president, at the top of my class, and the only divorced student.

I moved to Bellingham, rented a room in a large yellow Victorian, and went to work for Dr. Lakey. Three months later I moved to the "Hobbit Hole," a 300-square-foot duplex in Bellingham and the cheapest rent I could find with my dental assistant paycheck. On the other side of the kitchen wall lived a guy named Brad who constantly knocked on my door for something: salt, toilet paper, a bobby pin to pick his earwax.

My parents now owned the largest antique business in the Pacific Northwest. They lived in an 8,000 square-foot mansion that sat high on a hill overlooking Bellingham Bay. The house had been built by a sea captain in 1865 and they had converted it into a bed and breakfast called "The Castle." Tim and Toby were both married, and Max had just started high school. Angie, Amber, and I still met secretly whenever we could.

I tried to worm my way back into the family, but blew it big time when I found Amber alone in the Castle and took her to Dr. Lakey for a check-up. She had six cavities in her baby teeth, so we filled them. Mom got madder than I had ever seen. My need to run had surpassed all else. I moved out of the Hobbit Hole, leaving everything to Brad, including the Hobbit mail boxes I had made. I bought a twelve-speed bike and a one-way ticket to Hawaii.

Rawlin Claude introduced himself to me on Makapuu Beach on the island of Oahu. He was a L.A. businessman who came to Hawaii five times a year. He stood at the lifeguard tower, wearing only a red Speedo, talking to his lifeguard friend. I was walking along the beach on my way to my bike when he approached. He was about five foot ten and had bulging muscles and green eyes. He blocked my path.

"What's your name?" he said.

I stopped and squinted at him. "Eve Chanteau."

"Well, well," he said.

"Well, well, *what*?"

"There are two things we won't have to change."

"What's *that* supposed to mean?"

"We keep the blue bikini— it matches your eyes beautifully. And… you won't have to change your initials when we get married."

Rawlin was forty-one. I was nineteen.

September 12, 1982

Dear Gramma,

I now live in Los Angeles. After a year on the island, I decided to come here and go to school. I worked in oral surgery in Hawaii, and now I know I want to be a nurse, and there are more opportunities here. Although I told you I have given up on men forever, I did meet someone. His name is Rawlin. I'm sorry, because I know you want me to come back to Oregon and marry a farmer. Rawlin owns a copy product company in L.A. and paper mills in Columbia and Peru. Rawlin's brother Scott is married to Page Forsythe, who has the same birthday as I do. (Her dad is on a show called Dynasty and she gets $1,000 per month for answering his fan mail.)

Thank you again for the Crazy Quilt and the Jane Eyre novel. Give my love to Grampa and Buddy and tell them I'm so sad about Choppy. (We all have to pass to the next realm eventually.)

Please write soon.

Love, Eve

After presenting me with a two-karat diamond ring, Rawlin planned our entire wedding. He also took the liberty of inviting my family, which I hadn't seen in more than three years.

I made my second wedding dress out of a lace tablecloth from a vintage fabric store in Santa Monica. There were hundreds of beads around the cuffs and up the bodice. I worked on it for two months and wearing it now, standing in front of a lake and an Ashram, I felt nauseated.

Standing beside me, Louanne, Angie, and Sugar wore the lavender waterfall dresses Rawlin had chosen. Looking around the lake, into the distance I watched a mass of 300 guests I didn't know. Directly overhead a crow screeched. I panicked.

I covered my ears. "Oh my God. This is an omen!"

"You and your crows," said Angie. "Why do you hate crows so much? Sheez, that diamond's so big, it's almost ugly."

I pointed behind us. "Lou, see that Jack in the Box?"

"No."

"Yeah, look. It's over there on Sunset."

"God, don't tell me you're hungry *again*?" Louanne said. "And don't get any crazy ideas."

"Yes I'm hungry. Come on, let's go."

"Eve, don't cha be freakin' on us now," said Sugar. "Rawlin's totally gorgeous *and* rich. I'll take him if you don't want him. Can I smoke now?"

"No you can't smoke," I said. "And please Sugar, put that beer down. I want to go to Jack in the Box, Louanne, you know I mean it too."

"You mean like skip out on the wedding?" said Angie. "What about all the presents?"

"Seriously, Eve," said Louanne, "we've been through this before. What's going on with you?"

"I'm not feeling right about marrying Rawlin. First of all, he reminds me of Mom. He's got very erratic behavior and, in all honesty, I'm afraid of him. Last night after the rehearsal dinner this guy named Joe came to our house."

"Oh, I get it," said Angie. "Did Joe hit on you?"

"Shut up. Joe is horrible. He's Rawlin's dealer. He told me everything Rawlin's into and then told me to pretend I know nothing."

"Score!" said Sugar. "Can you get free weed?"

"You guys, this isn't funny. Rawlin has lied to me for three months. He doesn't even own a paper mill. He runs cocaine out of South America. I don't know what to do. Joe put a pile of coke on a mirror and lined out my name and told me to snort it with his hundred dollar bill. He spelled EVELYN."

"Oh shit," said Louanne "Where was Rawlin when all this was happening?"

"I don't know. That's what so creepy. Rawlin disappears for days at a time, and when I told him I wanted to go to South America with him, he said he had applied for my passport and it would take a few weeks to get it. I finally went and checked for myself and there's no record of an application."

The wedding march music started and Sugar tossed her beer can into a bush and began walking, just as Rawlin had instructed the previous evening. Angie followed, then Louanne. A surge of fear shot through me. I looked over at the Jack in the Box, then at Louanne. She pointed a finger at me. "Remember, count to five, then start walking. Stay right behind me."

After the ceremony, I stood next to Rawlin in the greeting line. We were Mr. and Mrs. Rawlin Claude of West L.A. When Mom and Larry came by, she stared at my dress. She had gained weight, her jaw line was drooping as if she were sad, and her hands looked older. "Where'd you get that dress?" she said.

"I made it."

"Look at that, Larry. She says she made it. That's 1920s Brussels lace. Hey Eve, if you ever want to sell it, let me know."

A girl in tears, wearing an ultra-mini skirt, hung on Rawlin's neck and locked her mouth onto his lips. I turned away.

"Thanks, Mom. I will. And thanks for coming."

"Hell," she said, "Rawlin paid for everything. I like that guy. We have an understanding, him and me. Hah! He's gonna keep you right in line."

Living in my twenty-fourth house with Rawlin had a few good points. I was much closer to Sugar, who had left Gary, found her mom in Visalia, California, and she and little Stephanie had moved in with her. I could ride my bike to school and work, and we had a backyard where I could garden and keep a jar of eggshell water hidden because it disgusted Rawlin and he refused to have it in the house. Rawlin bought an upright piano, which sat by the big front window. He said I had one year to pay him back the three hundred dollars it cost and I could never play it when he was around—he hated the piano. He said that once the piano loan was paid off, he would loan me enough for a car.

Rawlin was controlling to the point of destruction. We dined in the finest restaurants, but I was allowed to eat only what he ordered. He insisted I eat bleu cheese, raw meat, and drink old scotch. He dressed me in designer clothes and four-inch heels. We frequented the theatre, the opera, the Russian ballet, and too many social galas. Every time sleazy Joe came around, I dreamed of planning an escape.

Rawlin believed I could make him a lot of money by modeling and becoming a commercial actress. He took me to the Playboy mansion, where I met Hugh Hefner (in his robe); he also introduced me to Alex, the head of a modeling agency. He enrolled me in John Robert Powers modeling school in Beverly Hills. He insisted he make all the appointments with Hollywood agents and he attend every interview.

The first agent I met was Franque Flowers, a plump version of Elton John. Rawlin and I sat across from him on a plush couch while Franque fondled a sleek platinum pen as he read my stats.

"Mmm, five-nine, one-seventeen." He tapped the pen on his lip. "You could stand to lose about fifteen el bees. Nice contrast, dark brows with blonde hair, but it's blatantly clear your nose is too close to your upper lip." He tossed the paper and pen on his desk and leaned back in his lime green chair. "I strongly suggest you sprinkle cayenne pepper on your food so you won't be so tempted to eat."

I stood up. "Well," I said, "you could try arsenic on yours." I walked out.

When Rawlin found me waiting in the parking garage by his

Porsche, he was livid.

"What the hell was that?" he sneered.

"The guy's a jerk," I said.

Rawlin slapped me across the face. I cowered behind the car.

"You, young lady, better change your attitude right now or I'll have to change it for you."

I stood up straight. "If you ever hit me again, I'll be gone. I'm not here to beat, or belittle. And, *no one* is going to tell me what I can and can't eat."

"Not so," he said. "You're a goddamn spitfire! You will do exactly what I say. I won't take any more shit from you. You are *my* wife. I can see what the problem is here. We have to get the goddamn county girl out of you."

"Yeah, right. You can't take the country out of someone any more than you can carve out their soul and fill it with concrete! I hate this, Rawlin! I hate this city and this stinking smog! I hate being paraded around and hauled around and shown off …for what? Money? I don't care about money!"

"Get your ass in the car and keep your mouth shut on the next interview."

"And I *hate* bleu cheese."

By the time we squealed down three levels of polished slate and reached the street, I had begun to seriously formulate my getaway plan.

A week later I was hired as a sportswear ramp model at Bullocks Wilshire and signed on with the Herb Tannon Agency for TV commercials. I was sent on cattle calls, where they needed a blonde, blue eyed female for Pizza Hut or Carefree. When I arrived at the call there were 300 girls who fit the description. The day I got the callback for Southwest Bell, Rawlin went on a three-day binge. Joe was over every night and I was failing algebra.

April 27, 1983
Dear Gramma,
How are you? I'm fine. The weather here is beautiful most of the

time. I am half way through the fourth quarter and hopefully will transfer to University soon.

The plants love the eggshell protein water and we have tomatoes growing in the backyard like crazy. I am teaching Rawlin how to make real gravy and have almost learned Moonlight Sonata on the piano. Rawlin was so sweet to get the piano!

Tell Grampa he's a crackup for watching Dynasty and calling John Forsythe "Uncle John."

I'm going to try and come up this summer.

I miss you too much.

Love, Eve

Sugar often called, crying and slurring her words. She said she hated having a selfish drunk for a mom.

"I gotta come and see you Eve. I hate it here."

"Sug, what about Stephanie?"

"She can stay here. I just need to get away. I'll drive. Are you still at that same house?"

"Yes, 224 Barry Avenue."

"Did you make a matching mailbox?"

"Yep."

Rawlin was gone when Sugar arrived at 9:30 one Friday night. She had a case of beer, and we parked a few blocks away and talked in the car until three in the morning. By the time we rolled in the driveway Rawlin was on us like a charging bull. He reached through the open car window and pulled me out, threw me across the driveway, then began kicking in the side of Tammy's car. She had her window rolled up and the door locked. I managed to get up and run to the house to call the police. I stopped on the front step, took off my boot, and hurled it, hitting Rawlin in the side of the head. He staggered toward me. I ran through the front door, out the back, around the side of the garage, and jumped in the car. As Sugar screeched out, we heard the crash, then the sirens.

Rawlin had shoved the piano through the plate-glass window.

chapter thirty-one

Thunder and Stillness

The huge engines of the transport plane fired up with a thunder-ous roar. I was sitting in the cockpit with an eight-year-old Chilean boy strapped onto my lap. He was one of the cleft lip and palate patients who, along with a U.S. surgical team, Chilean diplomats, and two dogs, were bound for La Serena. We were lifting off from the Santiago airport, where we had just transferred a ton of medical supplies onto the colossal ves-sel piloted by two Chilean Air Force pilots. In the rear of the giant cargo plane they had cabled down a car, which had its own passengers belted in. We all wore earmuffs against the howl of the engines.

When I was asked to sit in the vast cockpit, my heart flipped. Hug-ging the little boy closely, I looked back at our surgical team strapped into the side seats. There were two plastic surgeons from San Francisco, two anesthesiologists, three surgical nurses including myself, two translators, a pediatric nurse, and a recovery room nurse.

As we leveled off, the towering Andes came into view. My lap child pressed back against my chest. I squeezed him with delight until he turned with a questioning look on his crooked little face. "*Sucre!*" I yelled in his ear. Sweet . . . because he smelled like *Sugar Babies*. I held the skinny little guy more closely as we began to battle through the increasing turbulence. As I placed my chin on his head and sniffed him, I thought of my own son, Cole, who was now five years old. Of the many things that had transpired over the last few years, Cole was my greatest gift of all. I had left him at home in the hands of our neighbor, caretaker, and friend, Linda, for two weeks. I need not worry. Linda was my angel, another gift from God.

Within minutes the boy was slouched over, sound asleep. Even after the seventeen-hour travel day I was too excited to sleep. I closed my eyes and began counting houses, which usually made me drowsy, but my thoughts turned to Sugar. She had come to LAX to say goodbye, convinced I would never return. There she stood, waving with a beer in her hand and Stephanie's baby on her hip. How often my fury for her was inevitably overcome with pity. She would never be able to rise above the darkness. She was slowly killing herself by swimming in a sea of alcohol and drifting on a cloud of smoke.

Seven years had passed since Sugar witnessed my escape from Rawlin. She was there when he bashed in our mailbox. When he cracked my tailbone with an iron poker and sped out of the driveway, I questioned who I really was. What would Jesus do? Forgive him. What would Joe do? Take his passport and blow up his car. What would Louanne do? Send me a book called *Smart Women-Foolish Choices.* What would Gramma do? Pray.

I resorted to revenge.

After mailing the Brussels lace wedding dress to Mom and leaving the diamond ring on the kitchen counter with a note that said I no longer wished to be married to him, I poured putrid eggshell water down his heating vents and dropped in a hunk of rancid bleu cheese, turned the thermostat to eighty-eight, and left.

By the time Rawlin tracked me down and offered me $500 to sign the divorce papers, we had been married for a total of eleven months. I burned the check.

During nursing school I redecorated an old lady's house in trade for room and board. It was the scholarship from the Moose Ladies and my bartending job at Marie Calendars in Marina Del Rey that got me through the program. When I graduated I called Mom to tell her I had passed the boards and was a registered nurse. She said she didn't think you would have to go to school for *that.* She also said that leaving Rawlin was the biggest mistake of my life.

Then I met Milan, a good-looking Serbian who knew how to have fun. We dated for a few months, then within two years, moved out of Los

Angeles, and got married without telling anyone. Milan never met Mom. When I got pregnant with Cole I was happier than I had ever been. Our marriage made it to Cole's first birthday.

January 30, 1992
Dear Gramma,

Milan has moved back to L.A. He thinks Monterey is "Hicksville" and says he isn't cut out for the whole marriage and kid thing. He says I need professional help because I have a problem with commitment. I'm sure it's true to some extent, but when I look into my baby's sweet face I know I would do anything in the world for him. I've never been more committed to anything in my life. I know how you must have felt with Dad hanging on your apron, singing like a songbird.

I am never going to get married again. I am going to raise this child to be a positive contribution to the world and I'm going to buy a house, even if it takes me five years to save a down payment. Cole has got a beautiful spirit. Being a mother really wants me to be closer to Mom. She just showed up here on her birthday! I took them out to dinner. I can't believe she's sixty. She told me David Hovander passed away from alcoholism, which makes me a triple divorcee and a widow. She said I was messed up in the head for not taking money from any of these men and I'm stubborn for always having to do everything myself. I'm ashamed to say I'm glad she only stayed at my house for one hour.

Please note the new address. I am renting a place in Pacific Grove. It's brown with orange trim, so I call it the A&W House. I will bring Cole up to see you and Grampa again soon.

Love,
Eve

A soft rain fell the night Steve Henry was killed. Brother Tim called and said Steve was driving down I-5, bound for California when he swerved and hit a tree head-on. I pictured the deer standing frozen before the speeding Mach I. The truth was, Tim said, it was a dog.

I lay on my bed without moving, and watching the rain and a sky as pale as milk, and thinking I had never seen rain quite like this one, so gentle it seemed barely to fall, yet slowly laying a gleam on the world outside. I hoped he went without pain. As I drifted off, I thought of Cole sleeping safely in his bed in the little room next to mine, and how there were no crows or cars in Heaven and surely the dogs had wings.

On my thirty-fifth birthday I closed escrow on a house in Carmel Valley. It was the thirty-fifth house I'd lived in. Ivy was growing through the windows and we had no furniture, but Cole and I made the best of it by placing pillows in the corners of the living room and running bases for fun. I worked at the hospital to pay the mortgage and we camped and fished and ate on the roof whenever we wanted.

When Cole was seven and I was about to go on another surgical mission to Argentina, I met Pierre at a party. He was a tall, blue-eyed Frenchmen with a smile like sunshine.

"Where are you traveling this year, Pierre?" someone asked him.

"India," he said.

"You're going to India?" I said.

"Yeah, me and my friend Marc are going next month. You wanna go with us?"

"Well, I was going to Argentina, but India sounds interesting."

I could hear Louanne's voice telling me if I went to India with someone I had just met, I was crazy. Sugar would say "Go for it!" Gramma would say, "Oh, Honey, it sounds so dangerous." I said yes to India and yes to Pierre.

The dawn sky was a multitude of blue and pink hues, a magically common occurrence for a Carmel Valley November morning. I was three weeks from my due date, in active labor. As we drove toward the hospital Pierre put his hand on my leg and said, "If it's a girl I think we should name her Kahli after the Kahli Gandaki River in India."

"But what if it's a boy?"

"It won't be," he said.

We checked into Labor and Delivery, and soon I was in a patient gown as an I.V. infused and a blood pressure cuff squeezed my arm every few minutes. Mary, our Labor and Delivery nurse, came and hooked me up to the bedside monitor. She squirted KY jelly on my tummy and slid the gooey paddle around my bulge from left to right. "The little bugger is hiding from me," she smiled. "Do you know yet if it's a boy or a girl?" she asked as she studied the screen. A contraction tore through me.

"We know it's one or the other," Pierre said.

She placed the paddle back on the monitor and said, "I'm going to call Dr. Bradley now," and left the room. Within moments Dr. Bradley came quickly through the door.

"Hello," he said with a fleeting smile. I had chosen Dr. Bradley as my obstetrician because he had small hands.

"Hello, Dr. Bradley, how are you?" I said.

"Fine, thank you."

He sat down and placed the paddle on my belly, and immediately located the black dot he was looking for. I exhaled an enormous sigh of relief followed by a gasp with the next contraction, which was the strongest one yet. I squeezed Pierre's hand too hard. Dr. Bradley waited for the pain to pass and met my eyes.

Something was missing. The room was too quiet.

After Dr. Bradley told us there was no heart beat, everything real disappeared. Before Mary and Dr. Bradley left the room they said we had decisions to make: autopsy, burial, cremation? Pierre went to make a phone call or pass out in the bathroom. I was left alone in the spinning room with no air. With a final searing stab between my legs I delivered Kahli right there on the bed. I reached between my thighs and picked up the bloody bundle, still attached to my insides by the umbilical cord. I hugged her sticky, limp body to my chest and hid under the blankets. I could have licked her clean and never let go. She had a beautiful cherub face, a tuft of strawberry blonde hair, ten perfect fingers and toes, and a sweet heart-shaped mouth the size of a Cheerio. I tried to blow my breath into her mouth.

Eventually they pried her away and cleaned her up, then Pierre held her until she went cold. She was perfect. Perfect, but dead.

I would take a truckload of postpartum blues over a drop of the catatonic state that follows a stillborn delivery. I slipped into a dark, gray haze of postmortem depression. My inner light was reduced to a minute smoldering ember. Our happy world had been picked up, unjustly shaken, and dumped out into an ugly heap. I lay around the house, feeling like I was inside a silent sandstorm, numb and robbed, and unable to establish clarity from the dull blur that enveloped me.

Three days after the delivery, the cruelty of nature ripped me out of my stupor when my milk came in. My breasts were swollen rock-hard, with tributaries of blue veins and ripened nipples. I had enough breast milk to feed a village, but no baby to suck it. My arms literally ached, which is a natural phenomenon when a new mother doesn't have a baby to hold. The visiting nurse was gentle as she placed hot compresses on my swollen breasts. She pushed the warm milk onto a washcloth, truly the epitome of waste. Once the pressure was off, the nurse instructed me on how to pump my breast milk when I became too uncomfortable. She said it would be best to try and endure the discomfort so that the milk would dry up.

Endure discomfort? Oh, I can do that.

The following week the man from the mortuary notified us that our "remains" were ready for pick up. We drove to Paul's Mortuary and parked in front of the place. Pierre and I looked at each other and took a deep breath. We entered the small, brown room where a man in a suit sat behind a mahogany desk. He had a retail display of urns sitting on a shelf behind him.

We told him our name and he left the room and returned with a little cardboard box. Inside the box was a small plastic bag containing tiny bones and ashes. We both stared at the miniature femur fragment and dusty ashes, and then put the lid back on the box. I crossed over the line from depression to madness, when the mortician said, "I am sorry for your loss. Will you be using Visa or MasterCard today?"

I looked at Pierre and covered my mouth. I inhaled sharply, started laughing, then began coughing. I backed up and hit the exit door with my hip and it opened. When Pierre reached for his wallet, I let out the high–pitched laughter of a psychotic vagrant. I backed out of the mortuary door, ran to the car, and closed myself into the passenger seat.

Hunching down, I continued to cough and laugh hysterically and cried, "Visa or MasterCard? What about American Express? What about the holiday cremation special at a ten percent discount?" I crawled down on the floorboards and my hysterical laughter turned into uncontrollable sobs, then silence.

Three weeks later we drove to Oregon to spend Thanksgiving with Brother Tim.

Tim and I were in his kitchen and I stood at the sink, peeling potatoes. The house was filled with the aroma of the roasting turkey. Pierre was in the living room reading *National Geographic* Magazine and Cole was outside looking for banana slugs.

"Yeah, Ruby Jane, I'm sure sorry to hear about you guys losing your baby. That was a real bummer."

I smiled at his choice of words. I supposed it could be classified as a "bummer" as well as a tragedy, depending on your perspective.

"Was there anything you could have done about it?" he said.

"No. At first they thought maybe the cord was wrapped around her neck, but that wasn't the case. The doctor said the hardest thing about it is that we will never know the reason."

"Well, you know it's not true what Mom said."

"What's not true? What did she say?"

"Oh, she told us all that you killed the baby by doing drugs and alcohol." He shook his head. "But I never believed any of it."

There I stood, although my knees wanted to buckle. I dropped the potato and the peeler. I turned on the water to rinse my hands, bent down, and stuck my cheek in the running tap water. I thought maybe I was hearing things, so I took a moment to regain my senses before putting my head up and drying my face with a dishtowel.

"I can't believe that," I said in a far away voice. "The woman is unbelievable."

"I know. I also know the things she has done to you are *unforgivable!*" he said.

My hands began to shake. A black sky was crawling right over my favorite holiday.

"Well, I know that forgiveness is the only way to freedom," I said.

"That's a bunch of bullshit. Where'd you hear that anyway? I suppose some therapist in California said you need to forgive your bitch of a mother in order to be *free.*" He shook his head.

"Well, yes, essentially that *is* what I have come to accept as my truth. If I hate her then it simply puts me down to her level and that's a place I will never go. Through love and compassion I am breaking the vicious cycle."

"Well, I don't know how you do it. You are way too nice in my opinion, and she still treats you like shit. She's jealous of you and has been since the day you were born," he scowled.

"That may be true," I said, "but I plan on the ultimate revenge, which is to have a relationship with my own child that will be a normal one, based on love, not hatred. Mom has obviously had a horrid past and sees me as a rivalry on some level. The higher my achievements, the more she hates me. I've learned and accepted all this by now. It's really pretty pathetic. Yes, our baby died, but the doctor said it was no fault of mine or anyone else, and that there's no reason we can't have another baby one day."

"Well, that's good to hear. So did you really spend a bunch of time and money going through all that pscho shit?"

"Therapy? Yes. I had to in order to save myself. Did you know it takes far less effort to despise someone than it does to forgive them? It's exhausting. What I realized was that I was feeling sorrier for Mom than I was for myself and it was crippling me."

"Well, you've never seemed crippled to me. I think you're one hell of a woman and I suppose I'm just surprised you didn't blow her head off after all you went through."

"The truth is, years ago I actually had her exorcised from my body and then put her into perspective. She isn't a witch with super powers that can control my life. She is a woman who's had a rough tow and never worked through her issues, but that is none of my business, because it's *me* I need to heal. We can only be responsible for ourselves, brother."

"Amen to that."

When we got back home I wrote Mom a letter. I explained that the death of Kahli was very painful and that I didn't understand why she would say or think that I did drugs. I explained that I had a good life, free from negativity and that I was surrounded by love and support and beauty.

She wrote back, saying I was born with bad karma and that people have miscarriages every day.

chapter thirty-two

Go In Peace

Pierre and I were gifted with two more children, Logan and Anna-belle, each of them healthy and happy. We bought a little house that was falling apart and recycled it. When we built house number thirty-seven, I made a mailbox replica. I was gluing on the last shingle when the phone rang. It was Sugar's husband, Jim.

"Hello?"

"Hello, is this Eve?"

"Yes."

"This is Jim Vandergriff."

"Oh, hi, Jim. How are you?"

"Well, not too good. I'm sorry to have to tell you this but, Tammy passed away this morning." There was a long silence.

"What happened?"

"Well, you know she drank an awful lot and she was pretty sick. Her dad came to visit in June. I was surprised because she never told me anything about her dad, and I just assumed he was dead. I don't know if you ever knew him, but anyway, after that she just got real sad and stopped eating,"

"Did she stop drinking?"

"No, and she got really sick. She was down to ninety-two pounds and I finally made her a doctor's appointment for Thursday morning at 10:00."

"Did she go?"

"Well, I went to work at 6:30, like I do every morning and I called her at 9:00 to make sure she was up. She didn't answer so I figured she was in the shower. I called again at 9:30 and then at 9:45 I decided to go home just to make sure she had gone to her appointment."

"Yeah?"

"When I came home I found her lying across the bed. Apparently she had woke up and got a beer. She drank some and threw up. She fell on the bed and inhaled some of the vomit." His voice began to shake. "I called 911 and tried to give her CPR until they got there. I mean, she was alive but unconscious. I rode with her in the ambulance." He began to cry.

"I'm so sorry, Jim."

"They put her in ICU with a buncha tubes in her. They said if her lungs could make it through the night, she had a good chance of surviving." He was silent for a long time.

"Where are the kids?"

"They went with the neighbors. Now I've got our daughter Sarah and Stephanie's little girl to raise."

"Oh, Jim, I'm so sorry. You didn't see it coming? I mean, when did you see she wasn't eating?"

"It's funny. When you live with someone and see them every day, you just don't notice those things," he said. "Her lungs made it through the night, but her heart stopped at 7:25 this morning."

"Again, I am so sorry. If there is anything I can do, please let me know. Thank you so much for calling, otherwise I may never have known. I talked to her about six months ago."

"She didn't want to have any kind of a memorial service. She told me that when we first met. She had a little note in her dresser with your phone number on it that said, *If anything happens to me call Eve. She's the only woman who ever understood me, and the only woman I'll ever love.*

"Thank you for that," I said.

"Yeah, well, take care."

"Jim, I know this is an odd question, but did you guys have white carpet in your house?"

"Yes we did," he said, "Tammy insisted on it."

When I got the news from Brother Tim that Mom had cancer, I wasn't surprised to hear that after receiving her diagnosis she promptly told the doctors they had shit for brains and could all go to hell.

She had begun coughing and feeling uncomfortable, and Larry finally convinced her to get a chest X-ray. One small nodule was located on her right lung and it was recommended that she get a biopsy and possibly an excision of the nodule. She said, "Hell no."

In late April Larry called to say the cancer had spread from Mom's lungs into her esophagus, leaving her without a voice. She continued to speak, but with a hoarseness that was barely audible.

He also said Mom wanted to see me.

"Me?"

"Yes," he said. "You."

I got nervous and excited and scared. I started to revert back to the child within and imagined I was being summoned to finally reconcile our differences face to face. I fabricated conversations and played them over and over in my mind of how she had loved me all along, but was too stubborn to admit it and that she was so sorry for all that had happened between us and regretted all that didn't happen. I decided it be best if I went to visit her, for it could very well be the last time I would ever get the chance to hear what I secretly had hoped to hear all my life. I called Tim to ask him to join me but he said he couldn't.

"Well, don't you want to see her? What if she dies before you visit her?" I said.

"Well, I just can't handle it, Ruby Jane. I would rather remember her as the powerhouse she was rather than see her sick," he said. "I hope you aren't going up there expecting some great apology from her just because she's dying. Every time you set yourself up, you get your butt kicked."

"No, I'm not expecting anything," I said.

"You are too."

"Am not."

"Then why are you going?"

"Because Larry said she wants to see me," I said.

"Well, you'd better take Pierre with you. *Don't go it alone,* as they say."

"Pierre is going to watch the boys and I'm going to take Annabelle with me. Having a sweet, five-year-old girl could only disarm her, right?"

"Yeah, whatever. Keep me posted."

Pierre went online and got Annabelle and I an e-ticket and took us to the airport. We flew over California and above the cloud cover of the Oregon sky. When we landed in Washington, I rented a car and drove over to Amber's house. We hugged and loved each other up as if we had never been apart.

"Aren't you scared?" said Amber.

"Yes and no. I mean I'm prepared for anything and nothing all at the same time. I packed lightly, but I brought an extra bag of the emotional tools I need to deal with whatever happens."

"Do you want me to go with you?" she said.

"No, thank you. I'll just take Annabelle and hope for the best. How does Mom look anyway?"

"Well, you'll probably be shocked because you never see her, but I see her enough to know she has lost about fifty pounds and she's hunched over."

"Oh how awful!" My heart was pounding, as it had been for the past week. I was in such a strange, barely manageable place. One moment I would feel some weird sense of elation and then the next I caved into a bout of tears.

"Well, when you're done visiting, just come back here. How long are you staying in Bellingham anyway?" she asked.

"Two days."

"That's not very long."

"I have a feeling it'll be long enough."

"I like your outfit," said Amber. I was wearing a sweat suit.

"Oh, thanks. It's just simple and comfortable for traveling."

"No offense, but do you want to brush your hair or anything before you go out there?"

" Okay. I just don't want to make it look like I'm making a big effort to show off or anything."

"Hey, we know who you are," she said.

We went to her bathroom and looked in the mirror together. Sisters can do that for hours. Annabelle stood next to me, her arms around my leg. "You're both extremely beautiful," she said. I giggled. Annabelle had begun using big words.

"The other day she said something like 'elective' or 'persuasive.'"

"No, Mama, I said 'perceptive.'"

"Wow," Amber arched her eyebrows.

"I know, right?" I sighed. "Look, my jaw line is starting to drop." I said. "And my hands are looking old."

"Hey, do you want a pair of plain silver hoops? They would look perfect with the casual wear." Amber held up a pair of earrings.

"I'd love that, but I don't have pierced ears, remember?"

"For real? I keep forgetting. Didn't you ever get them re-pierced?" she frowned.

"No, but here, let me see if there's still a hole in here." I took the big silver hoop in my hand.

"No! Don't hurt yourself!" she said.

I placed it to my ear. I set the wire into the hole and gave it a push. The earring slid through, pushing a tiny white core ahead of it.

"Oh my God! I can't believe my ears are still pierced after, like, thirty years!"

"Amazing. And, totally cute!" said Amber.

I bid Amber goodbye and Annabelle and I drove out to the shore-front to see Mom and Larry. They had sold the Bed and Breakfast and moved to a small house on the bay. My stomach was upset.

I was shocked to see Mom, who was obviously sickly but still able to walk slowly in her very baggy pants. She mouthed a muffled hello to me and acknowledged Annabelle, who was busy looking around at the foreign terrain. I offered to make Mom a cup of tea but she refused. She walked outside and I followed her to the deck. She sat down on a blanket and I sat across from her with my legs folded.

It was a beautiful spring day and the flowers were in full bloom all around us. Annabelle wandered around the yard, followed a butterfly and sang "Edelweiss" softly to herself. I sat and looked around with sunglasses on and tried to calm my pounding heart.

"Do you have something to say to me?" Mom said in her hoarse voice.

"Do you have something to say to me?" was all I could come up with.

"Well, you know why I had to send you away when you were young, don't you?" she whispered in a raspy growl.

I shook my head.

"You were just born bad. I tried everything I could with you but you always hated me. I used to dress you up in a cute dress and you would just shit all over it and rub the crap all over the crib as if to say, *I hate you!*" she glared.

I could feel the tears welling up, but held my composure. She continued in her ghostly voice. "I had no other choice. You were always out of control and I had to get rid of you to save the other children."

"Mom, I don't get why you have to be so mean to me," I said.

She pointed her finger at me and said, "You know what the problem with you is, Eve? I was never *mean enough* to you."

Just then Annabelle came over and said, "Mama, I'm thirsty."

"O.K. sweetheart, just one minute and I'll get you something to drink," I said.

"You know where the faucet is!" Mom growled at her. Annabelle took a step backward, not sure what to do.

"But I can't reach the sink," she said.

"Here, I'll go get you something right now," I said and I started to get up.

"Could I please have milk, Mama?"

"Of course you can, I'll be right back." I ran to the house to find some milk.

When I came back with the glass of milk, my heart sank. Annabelle was sobbing.

"What happened?" I asked. Mom sat there, shaking her head.

"Gwamma says there are good little girls and there are bad little girls and I'm a bad one."

It has been said that a mother can lift a car if her child is in danger, and at that moment I could have easily pulled a fifty-year-old apple tree out by its roots. I glared at Mom, took Annabelle's hand and left. I drove back to Bellingham and checked into the nicest hotel I could find. I called Amber.

"Well, how'd it go?" she said.

"Not great, but I'm not done yet. I am determined to do the right thing. I want my last words to be true, so that I can live with myself the rest of my life, knowing I said the right thing."

"Yeah? That's good," she said.

"I'm going to pray, then write down four different farewell statements and let you choose which one is the best," I said.

"That sounds healthy. Do you have any on the list so far?"

"Well, that's the problem, the only thing I can come up with is, *I hope you rot in hell.*"

Amber laughed, "Well now, we're going to have to improve on that one."

That night in the hotel room I drank four glasses of wine and did push-ups while Annabelle slept. The anger, once released like a genie from a bottle could not be curtailed. Hatred was its own creature; it rose, burned out, and reappeared on its own accord. I had protected myself all along by protecting Mom. All the experiences I had denied came back to me right there on the hotel carpet: so many times my head had been flushed in the toilet, my wet legs bloodied from being hit with a board while swinging from the shower curtain rod, being yanked by the hair off the piano bench, and pounded with a rake for out-running the state champion. She was a wolf, the way other people are lambs, or saints, or sparrows.

Tomorrow I would open her door without knocking and tell her, You hate me for big reasons that have nothing to do with me. You have never been fair, yet you have never bothered to look beyond yourself and see that the world is not out to get you, that I'm not out to get you. You are my mother, and like your own mother did to you, you have shaped my life. I made a choice a long time ago that although you are in my bones, I will avoid following in your footsteps at all cost. I pity you and pray that the next place you go will be gentle on you and give you the happiness you deserve because we all deserve to be happy, embraced, and loved. I love you Mom. Go in peace.

When Amber and I got there the next day, we left Annabelle in the car with an etch-a-sketch and I knocked on the door. Amber opened it and we walked in. Mom was sitting on the couch.

I stood there speechless. All my grand plans eroded and fell at my feet. I saw a bottle of ativan sitting on the coffee table and felt like eating a whole handful. Amber said something about how nice the flowers looked.

"Well Mom, I'm going to go now. I have a flight in an hour," I said.

She said nothing. I went to her and gave her a hug. "You're in good hands. I love you."

I went out the door as Amber was saying she would see her tomorrow, and I got in the car. I smiled at Annabelle and said, "Grandma says she's sorry she hurt your feelings and to tell you goodbye."

"Oh that's nice," said Annabelle. "I love Gwamma."

chapter thirty-three

Light and Love

The cancer grew and crept through her body like a serpent, down her throat, deep into both lungs, and into her bones and spine. She died a few days before my birthday with the sound of gurgling water seeping out her mouth. She was in her bedroom with Angie and Larry at her side.

The day of the funeral was cold, wet, and miserable. As I sat between Tim and Amber it occurred to me that I had gone my entire life without attending a funeral other than Dad's.

I learned that Mom's people were from Minnesota and that she really was a little girl once. She shared the same birthday with Elvis Presley. I learned that she had traveled a lot and was a strong figure in the local business world. There was not much mention of her kids except to say that she had six children and what she had given them was "independence."

In the reception area Leta Felleck came to me holding an old gray photo. "I want to share this with you, Eve," she said. The picture was of a little boy, in a highchair with a bowl of spaghetti on his head. "This is your brother Tim," she said.

"I was with your mother the night this happened. She called and asked me to come over. I found her under the table screaming that she was going to kill the baby inside her with a coat hanger. She asked me to take a picture of Timmy first, and then get her a hanger. I took the photo, but of course I didn't get the hanger."

"Was I that baby inside her?"

"Yes, I'm sorry to say. She just wasn't herself that night. She had had a fight, first with your dad, then her parents. They had told her an awful family secret. She didn't tell a soul, except me, and when she knew she was dying she asked that I tell you this story, in hopes that you may understand her and forgive her for the way she treated you."

So, we sat down and Leta told me about my beautiful, resilient mother.

In the early 1900s, Ellen and Francis Sisk were third-generation farmers in the southern region of Minnesota. They had sixteen children who were bred for working the crops; their fourteen boys were followed by two girls, Erna and Martha.

By the spring of 1933, all the Sisk boys had married and moved on to their own farms, leaving Ellen and Francis with Erna, fifteen, and Martha, sixteen. Knowing he was shorthanded for planting season, Francis went to St. Paul to find farmhands. Swedish immigration had grown to over a million and everyone knew Swedes were excellent help when it came to working the land.

Francis brought back four burly Swedish brothers ranging from seventeen to twenty-six years old. He bunked them down in the barn and Ellen, Martha, and Erna saw to it they were fed three hearty meals a day. All through the summer the brothers worked, planting and maintaining the crops, nurturing them to harvest. When the last sheaves had been hauled in, the farmhands joined one fifth of their fellow immigrants and sailed back to their homeland in Southern Sweden. The Sisks never learned their names, nor did they ever hear from them again.

It was a riveting day when both Erna and Martha discovered they were pregnant. It was even more shocking when they realized they had both lain in the barn with the same nineteen-year-old Swede.

The Sisks decided to hide Erna in the house and keep her swollen belly a secret. Francis called upon Albert Koff, a classmate of Martha's, to marry her. Albert married her quickly and pursued his lifetime dream of moving to Oregon to be an onion farmer. In January the baby girl was born. They named her Gloria. After Gloria, they had five more kids.

As time went by it was clear that Gloria was very different from her siblings. The pretty girl was willful and defiant. Albert beat her with sticks and strapped her back with a leather belt. But for every cruel thing he did, she sprouted another spike in her armor.

By the time Gloria was a teenager, she rolled with a rage that blew most people out of her way. The only one she tolerated was her best friend, Leta. She and Leta did everything together.

One night Gloria snuck out and met Leta for a dance at the local grange hall. The parking lot was jammed, the line to the front door extremely long. Gloria grabbed Leta by the sweater sleeve and hauled her through the crowd to the entrance.

"Hey, you can't cut!" protested a girl at the front of the line.

Gloria said, "Watch me," and yanked Leta straight through the doors and into the hazy, low-lit dance hall. The rhythm of the music wound Gloria up to an edgy pitch. The girls bobbed their way through the dancers and began doing some moves they had made up in Leta's living room, something like a single-footed jitterbug.

Gloria pulled Leta closer to the stage and that's when Gloria saw the man who got her attention more than anyone ever had. When she laid eyes on Ted, the band's piano player, she knew she had to have him. She didn't much care for the piano, but she could get rid of that later. Leta winced when Gloria clutched her hand and squeezed much too hard. They stood in front of the stage.

When Ted looked up from the keys, his calm blue eyes caught her gaze. The music ended and he stood and stepped off the stage. Gloria stepped in his way.

Standing so close, she realized how tall he was, at least six foot two and pass-out handsome at that. Looking at his long fingers, she couldn't wait to prove to him his fingertips would meet around her waist.

"I haven't seen you here before," he said.

"Well, you haven't been looking very hard," she said.

"My name is Ted."

Leta hung back at a distance, knowing Gloria didn't appreciate distractions. The room was loud with the din of dancers, but Gloria and Ted didn't notice.

"And I'm Gloria," she smiled. "We could dance together."

"Well, I can't. I have to play with the band."

"You don't *have* to do anything," she said.

"I suppose not, but I would like to keep my job," he said.

"You could always just take me for a ride. You got a car, don't you?"

"Ah—yes. I have a—I have a Chevrolet. A Chevrolet station wagon."

"Ted! Let's kick it!" the drummer yelled from the stage. The three band members were clearly eager to start the next set.

And so it went like that. A strike. A flame. An inferno. Gloria and Ted. Two people from opposite planets, pulled together by a power bigger than the both of them, trapped in a swirling magnetic field that held them close for a while, and then ripped them apart.

When they gazed into each others eyes, hers vibrant, and Nordic cool, and his, deep, and soulful, the two colors blended together, creating an unmistakable shade of forever blue.

"He's a goddamned Catholic! You better stay away from Ted Chanteau!" her father threatened.

"I will not!" screamed Gloria.

"You're a goddamn spitfire! If you defy me, you'll never set foot in this house again!" Albert yelled.

"Fine!" she sneered. He raised his arm and knocked her over with an irreparable slap across the face. Gloria hit the floor. She bounced up, hissed at her parents, and ran out of the room.

Gloria was gone before the sun came up the next morning. Within hours she had found Ted, grabbed Leta for a witness, and set off for the Justice of the Peace.

Four years later, Gloria was twenty-three and pregnant with her third child. She and Ted lived in a small house in Gervais, six miles from her family's onion farm. The few times she had seen her parents and siblings something always went awry because of her *way* and their unwillingness to forgive. One evening, she was feeling more distraught then usual after another fight with Ted. They fought mostly about his love of music. She had made a nice dinner of noodles with ketchup and little round oyster crackers. For special, she served the main course in her Grandma Sisk's Haviland china bowls, even for the boys (who were both in high chairs). Ted had ended the scrap by walking out. He always closed the door gently, even when he was upset; she followed behind him, opened the door and slammed it hard. She decided to call home for a change and see if her mother could help her sort things out.

The conversation heated up as Gloria grew more defensive. It then quickly escalated into an exchange of hysteria. The roof rumbled when her angry parents finally spilled the entire bag of beans. By the time the family truth was out, all Gloria remembered was Albert's slashing words, "The problem with you, Gloria, is you just ain't my kid! You ain't nothin' but *shit*."

She was so sickened by the betrayal, she felt vomit roil in the back of her mouth. She clutched the phone in one hand and her throat in the other to hold the eruption at bay.

Her brothers and sisters were *half*-brothers and sisters? Why hadn't someone told her before now? No wonder that bastard she called Dad was so mean to her but didn't lay a hand on the other kids. And oh, Lord Jesus, her cousin Velma in Minnesota was really her half-sister too?

Driven by blue-hot fury, she called Leta to come over right away, then hurled the phone across the room and smashed the only lamp they had. She knocked all the dirty dishes off the table with a single sweep of her arm. Her ears rang with the crash of shattered glass and crying babies as she fell to the floor, slumped amid the broken spaghetti bowls. Her heart smashed in her chest. She stared blankly at the ketchup on the walls, the cracked glasses of spilled Tang.

"Looka my sketti!" cried two-year-old Timmy. His bowl sat on his head like a crooked china hat. Noodles and ketchup dangled from his forehead and hung over his ears. A single-tooth grin pressed into his saucy cheeks.

Gloria lunged forward, clenched both fists, and punched her stomach repeatedly as hard as she could. As she lay in a fetal curl, panting and spent, she vowed this miserable thing inside her was going to be a *bad* baby.

———

If a general consensus were taken, it would undoubtedly be determined that when we lose our mother we are essentially an amputee or a living organ donor because our loss is a vital part of who we are. We only have one mother and she is regarded as the pillar of our strength and the honorable Saint of Light and Love. It is our mom who has guided us and coveted us, protected us, and beamed with pride because of us.

We rarely, if ever, take our mother off her glowing pedestal, because above all others, we have adored her the most. Our deeply seeded admirations prevail because we came from her very heart and are made of her tissue, her genetic coding, and her soul.

Her breast was our sustenance as she nurtured our pure innocence and provided us with security and life-sustaining immunities. There is no other way to arrive than through the womb of our mother. It is this miracle of life for which we are forever in awe and immensely grateful.

When a mean mommy dies, it is a truly different situation, one that illuminates an entire spectrum of emotional colors. It is a deepened monumental pain that is shared with guilt and disappointment.

The finality of death brings this truth to light and with the truth comes acceptance.

When we are orphaned, our place on the planet is elevated to a higher one. I have been elevated to that place. I am the mother who comforts the child within.

As I dwell blissfully in the sandwich generation, I find great peace and joy in taking soup to my elderly mother-in-law while caring for my own children. I instill in them the unmovable truth that they are of the greatest value and are cherished not only by me, but by their own inner light. My boys believe they are a contributing factor to the power and light of the universe itself.

I tell my precious baby girl Annabelle that she is like a Christmas present every day. Although she is only five, she has a warm wisdom that would take most people several lifetimes to achieve. Her Lightbug shines a bright sunshine yellow.

When I told her that Mom had passed away, she was standing on a chair at the kitchen sink with soap bubbles up to her tiny elbows. She stopped washing the plastic bowl and stared out the window into the far away sky.

"Well," she said, "Gwamma is sure going to be happy up there in heaven with Kahli."

"That's right," I said and kissed her softly on her cheek.

When she saw my tears she said, "Why are you sad, Mama?"

"Well, I'm just sorry that your Grandma didn't get to experience how beautiful the love can be between a mother and daughter. She missed out on *so* much, but I know it couldn't be helped. We're all different and we all have our own special way of showing our love."

"That's right," Annabelle said. "Your mommy really did love you because how could a mom not love her own daughter? Besides," she added, "it was just love of a *different dimension*."

Every heart finds a home

Made in the USA
San Bernardino, CA
16 December 2013